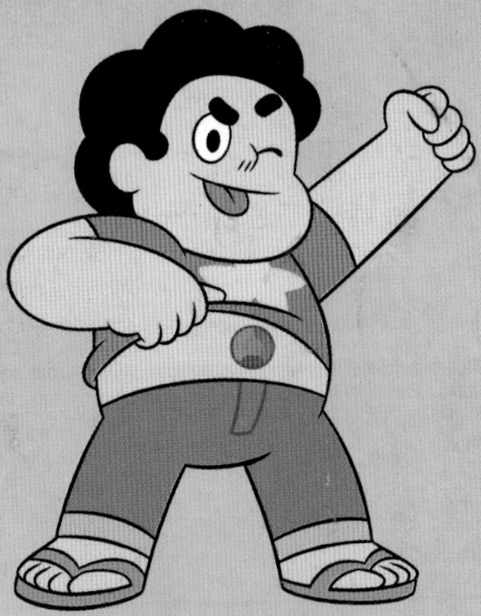

# STEVEN UNIVERSE™

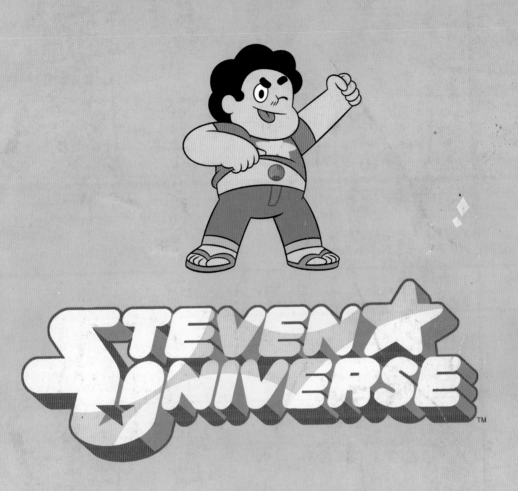

STEVEN UNIVERSE Volume Two, March 2016. Published by KaBOOM!,
a division of Boom Entertainment, Inc. STEVEN UNIVERSE, CARTOON
NETWORK, the logos, and all related characters and elements are
trademarks of and © Cartoon Network. (S16) Originally published in single
magazine form as STEVEN UNIVERSE 5-8 © Cartoon Network. (S14) All
rights reserved. KaBOOM!™ and the KaBOOM! logo are trademarks of
Boom Entertainment, Inc., registered in various countries and categories.
All characters, events, and institutions depicted herein are fictional. Any
similarity between any of the names, characters, persons, events, and/or
institutions in this publication to actual names, characters, and persons,
whether living or dead, events, and/or institutions is unintended and purely
coincidental. KaBOOM! does not read or accept unsolicited submissions
of ideas, stories, or artwork.

A catalog record of this book is available from OCLC and from the
KaBOOM! website, www.kaboom-studios.com, on the Librarians Page.

BOOM! Studios, 5670 Wilshire Boulevard, Suite 450, Los Angeles, CA
90036-5679. Printed in China. First Printing.

ISBN: 978-1-60886-796-7, eISBN: 978-1-61398-467-3

33614059689868

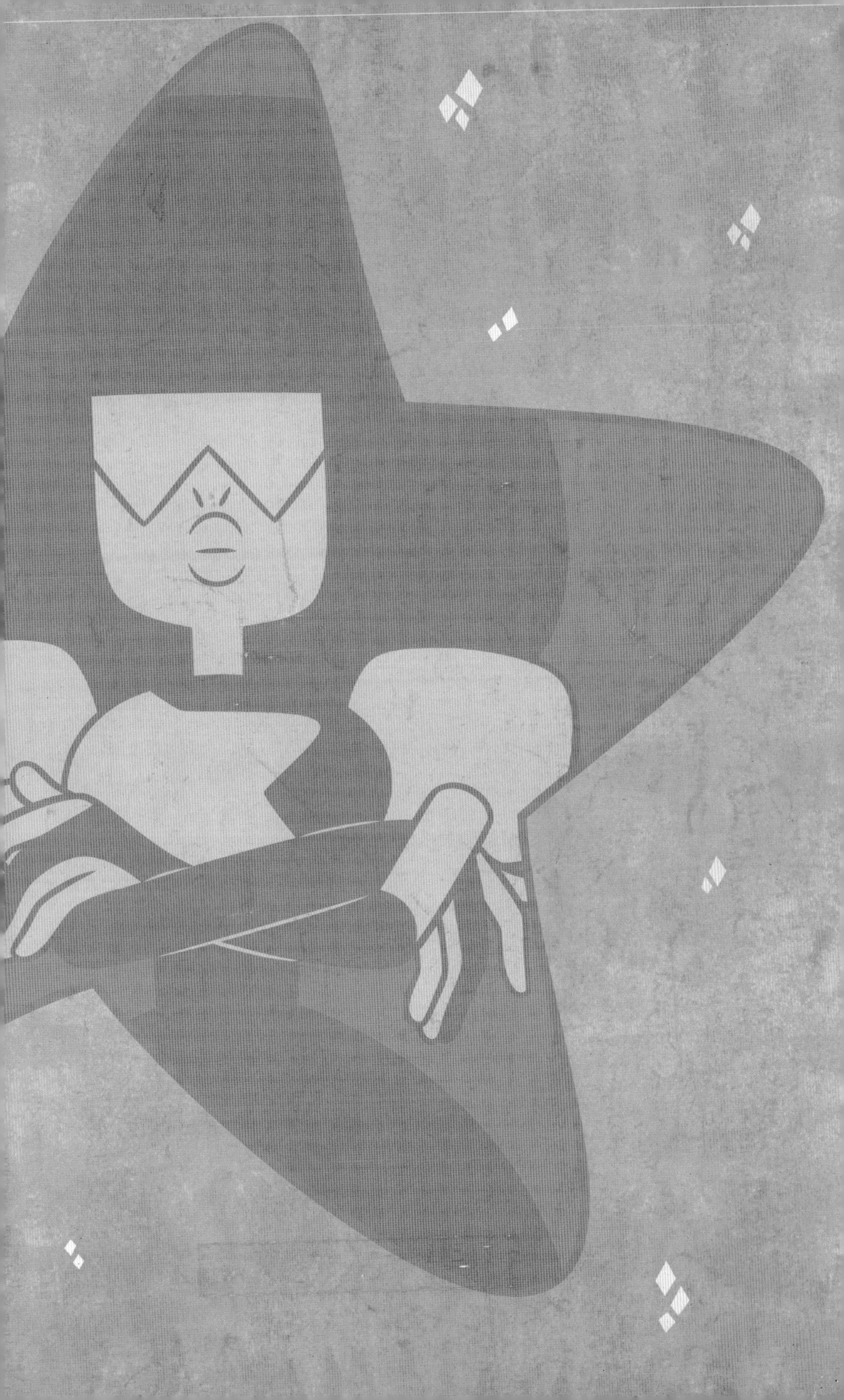

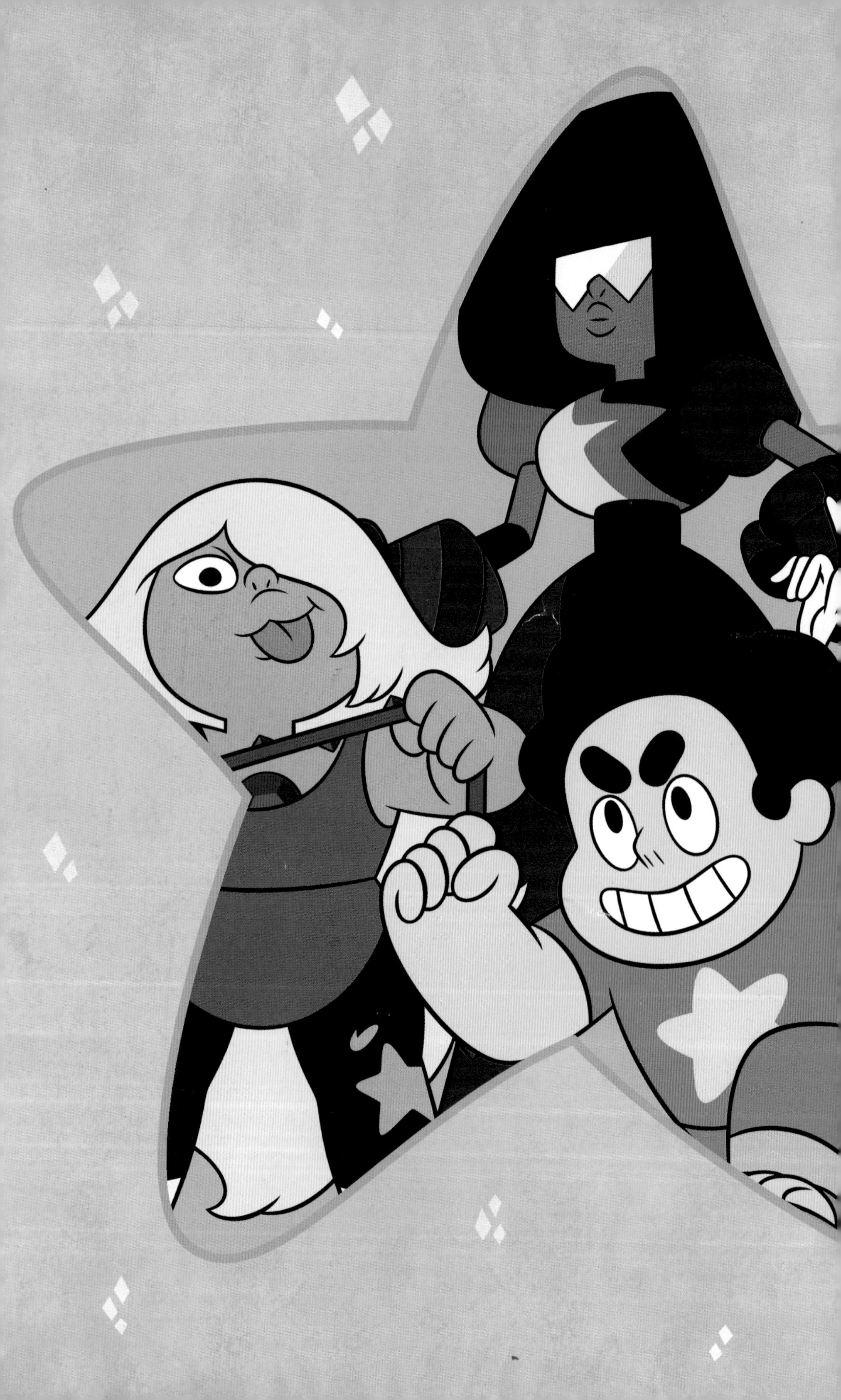

# STEVEN UNIVERSE

created by
**REBECCA SUGAR**

written by
**JEREMY SORESE**

illustrated by
**COLEMAN ENGLE**

also featuring
**MEGAN BRENNAN
REBEKKA DUNLAP
JOSCELINE FENTON
GRACE KRAFT
KRIS MUKAI
EVAN PALMER
MAD RUPERT
BRIDGET UNDERWOOD
T. ZYSK**

cover by
**AMBER ROGERS**

designer
**JILLIAN CRAB**

associate editor
**WHITNEY LEOPARD**

editor
**SHANNON WATTERS**

With Special Thanks to
Marisa Marionakis, Rick Blanco, Nicole Rivera, Conrad Montgomery,
Meghan Bradley, Curtis Lelash and the wonderful folks at Cartoon Network.

# "LIBRARY"
## PART ONE

also
featuring:

**"BUBBLE TROUBLE"**
written & illustrated by
**GRACE KRAFT**

**"SELFIE"**
illustrated by
**KRIS MUKAI**

**"SIDE TRACKS"**
written & illustrated by
**MEGAN BRENNAN**

**"A DAY
WITH ONION"**
written & illustrated by
**EVAN PALMER**

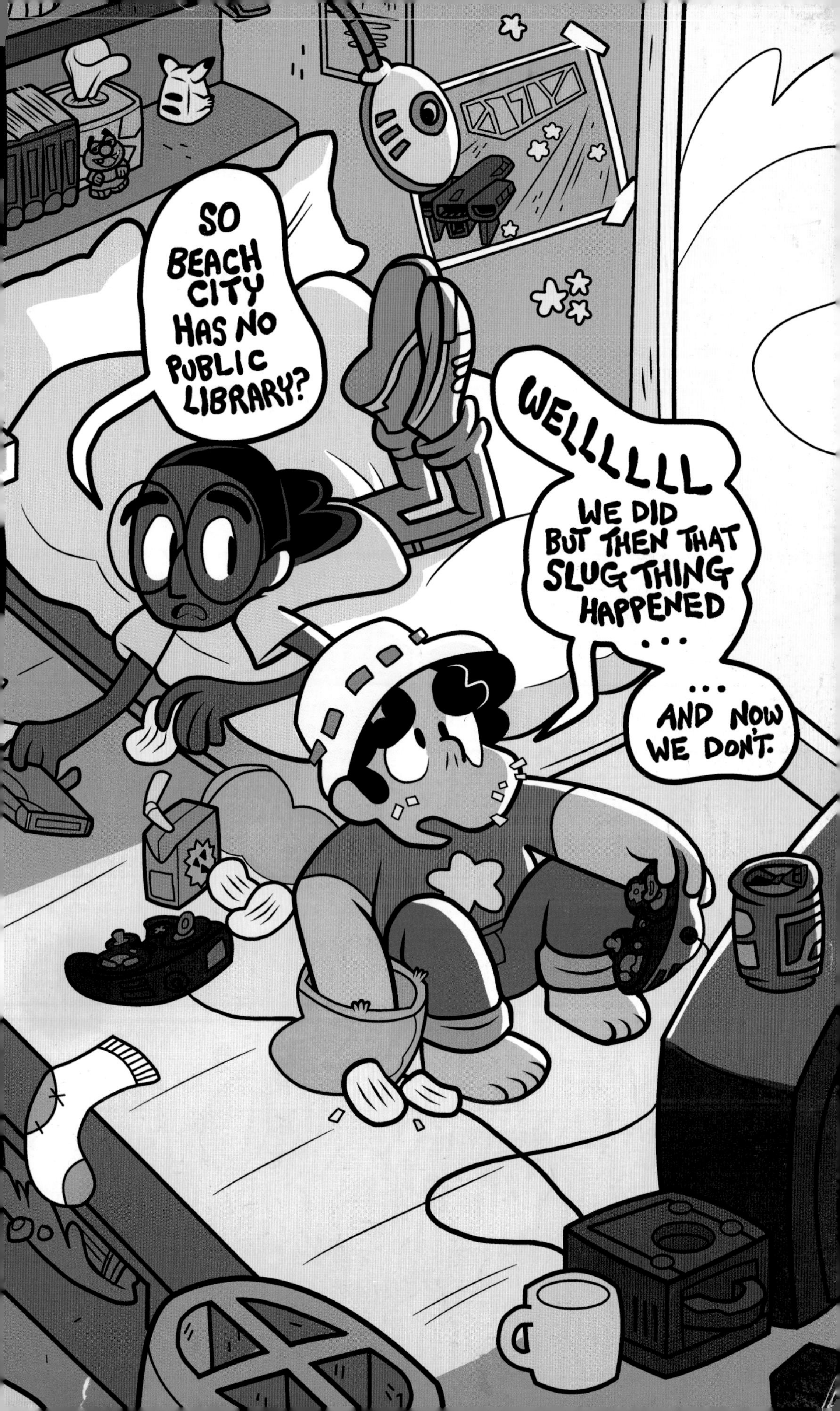
SO BEACH CITY HAS NO PUBLIC LIBRARY?
WELLLLLLL
WE DID BUT THEN THAT SLUG THING HAPPENED . . .
. . . AND NOW WE DON'T.

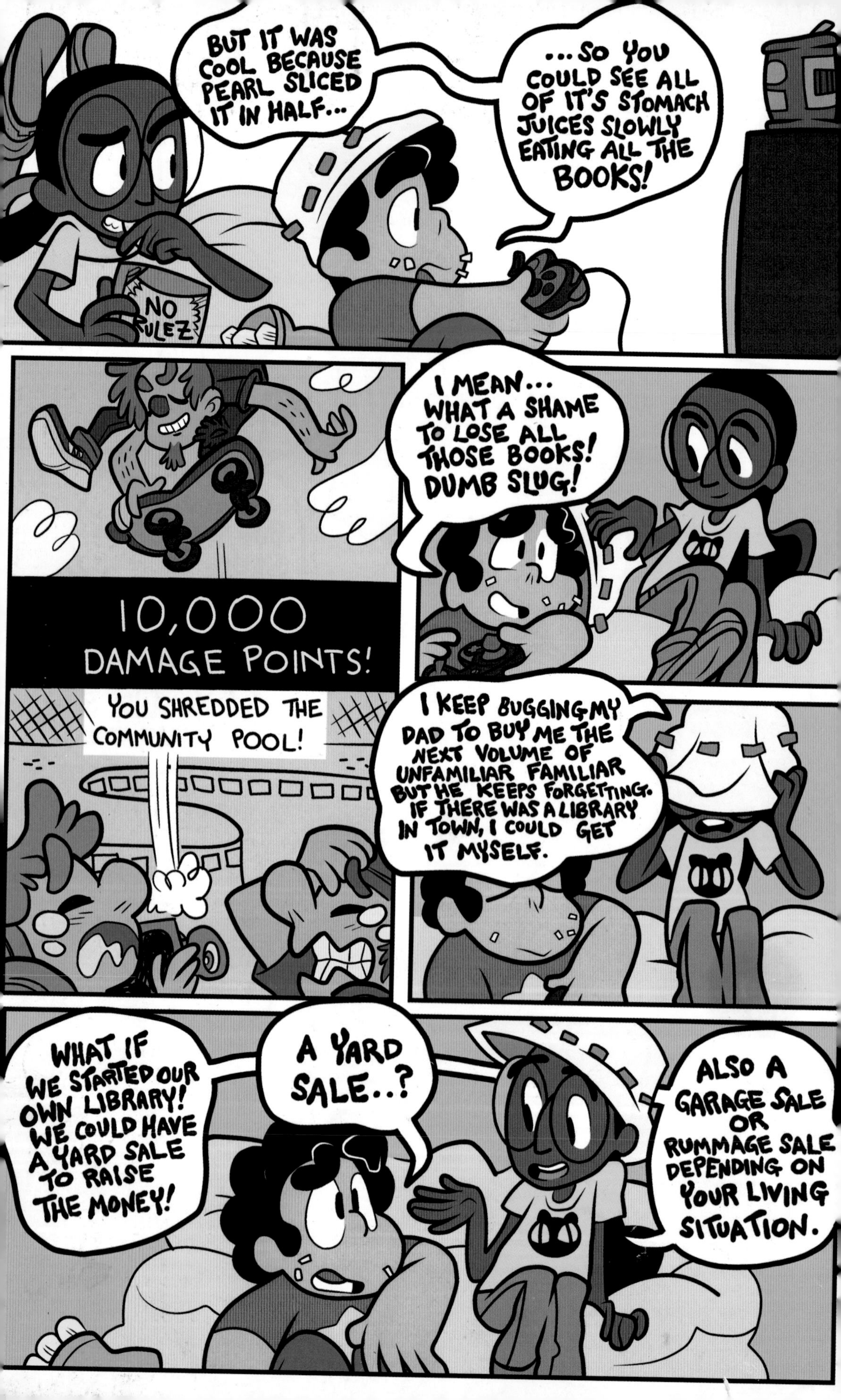
BUT IT WAS COOL BECAUSE PEARL SLICED IT IN HALF...
...SO YOU COULD SEE ALL OF IT'S STOMACH JUICES SLOWLY EATING ALL THE BOOKS!
NO RULEZ
I MEAN... WHAT A SHAME TO LOSE ALL THOSE BOOKS! DUMB SLUG!
10,000 DAMAGE POINTS!
YOU SHREDDED THE COMMUNITY POOL!
I KEEP BUGGING MY DAD TO BUY ME THE NEXT VOLUME OF UNFAMILIAR FAMILIAR BUT HE KEEPS FORGETTING. IF THERE WAS A LIBRARY IN TOWN, I COULD GET IT MYSELF.
WHAT IF WE STARTED OUR OWN LIBRARY! WE COULD HAVE A YARD SALE TO RAISE THE MONEY!
A YARD SALE..?
ALSO A GARAGE SALE OR RUMMAGE SALE DEPENDING ON YOUR LIVING SITUATION.

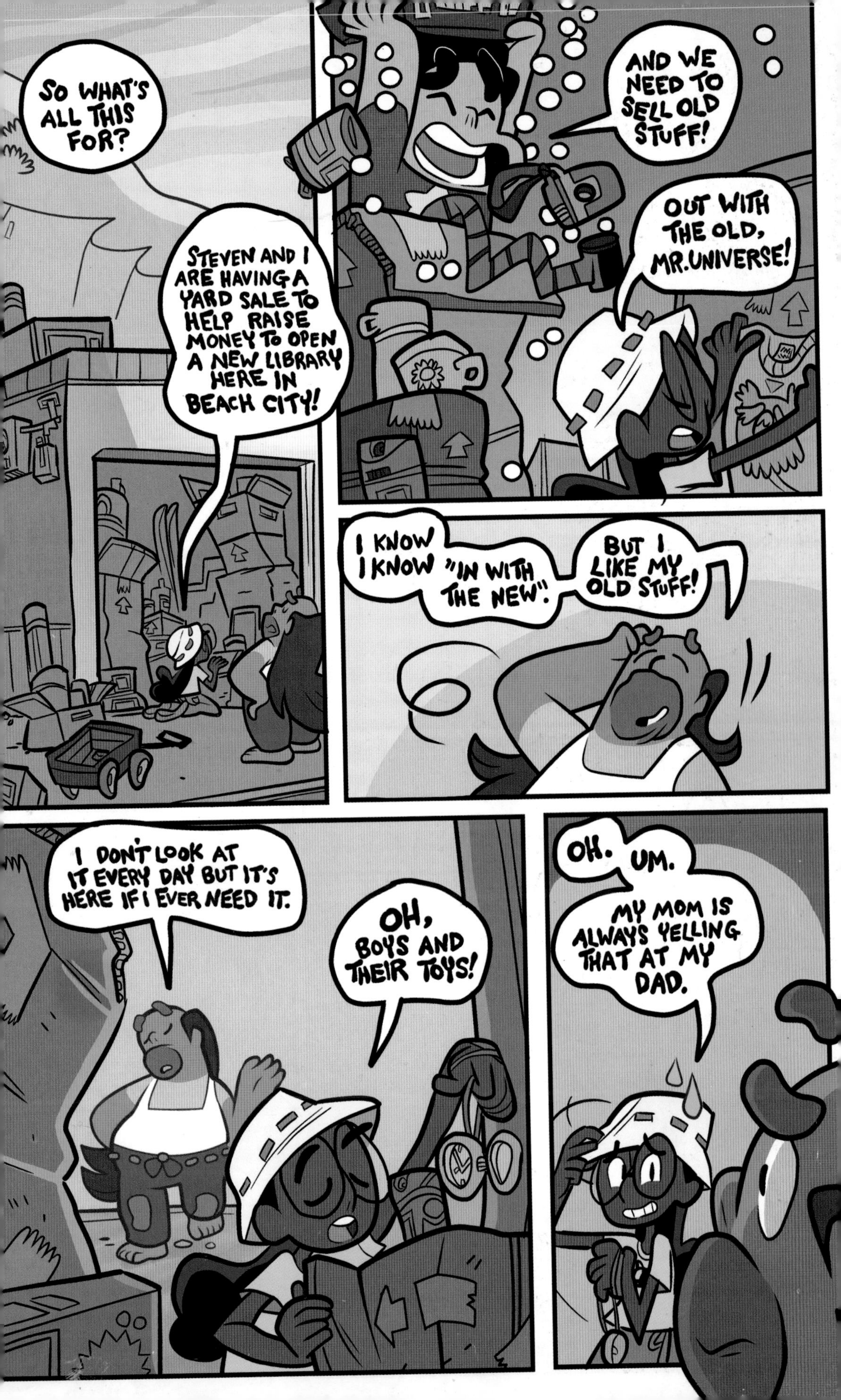
SO WHAT'S ALL THIS FOR?
STEVEN AND I ARE HAVING A YARD SALE TO HELP RAISE MONEY TO OPEN A NEW LIBRARY HERE IN BEACH CITY!
AND WE NEED TO SELL OLD STUFF!
OUT WITH THE OLD, MR. UNIVERSE!
I KNOW I KNOW "IN WITH THE NEW".
BUT I LIKE MY OLD STUFF!
I DON'T LOOK AT IT EVERY DAY BUT IT'S HERE IF I EVER NEED IT.
OH, BOYS AND THEIR TOYS!
OH.
UM.
MY MOM IS ALWAYS YELLING THAT AT MY DAD.

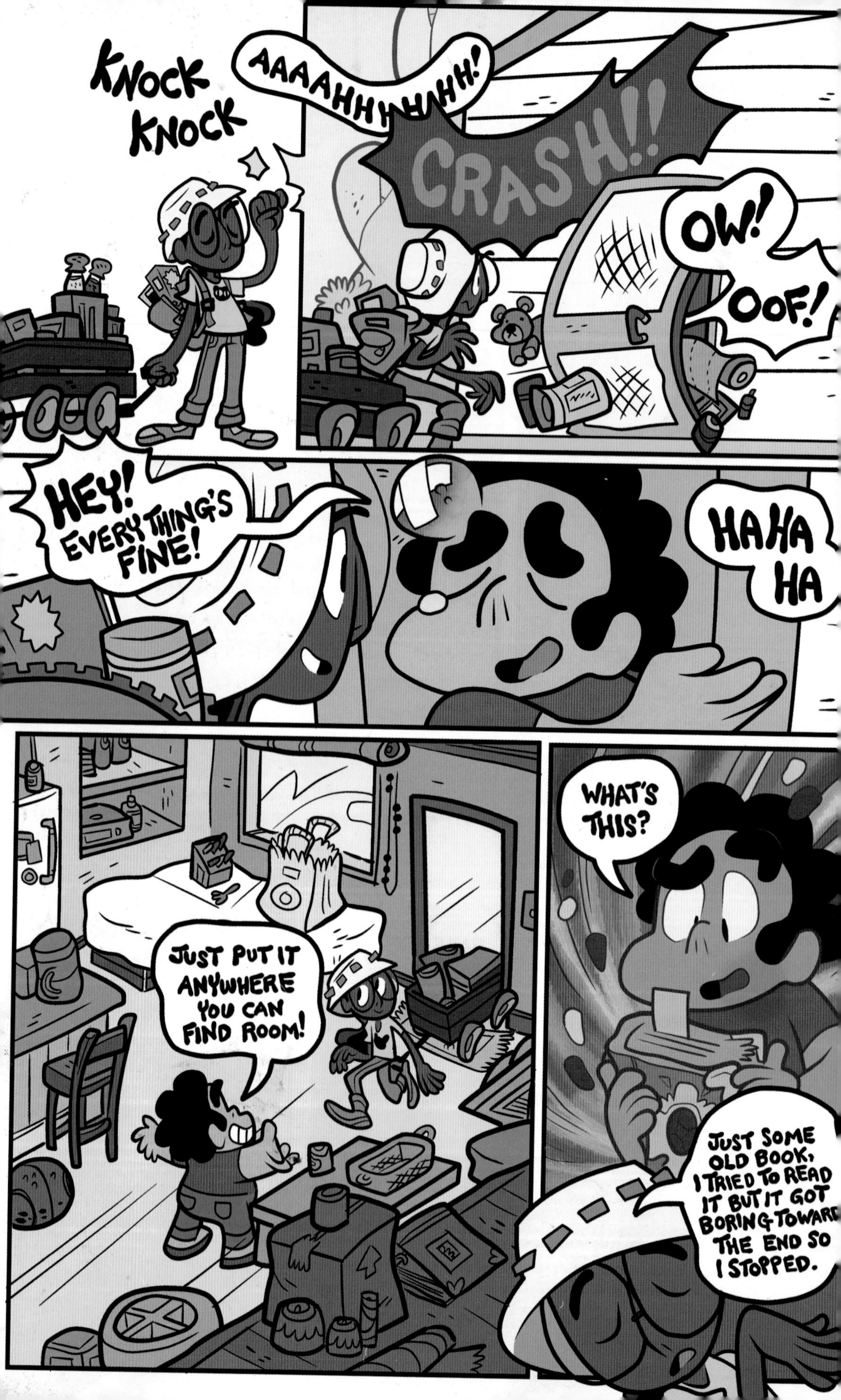
KNOCK KNOCK
AAAAHHHHHH!
CRASH!!
OW!
OOF!
HEY! EVERYTHING'S FINE!
HAHA HA
JUST PUT IT ANYWHERE YOU CAN FIND ROOM!
WHAT'S THIS?
JUST SOME OLD BOOK, I TRIED TO READ IT BUT IT GOT BORING TOWARD THE END SO I STOPPED.

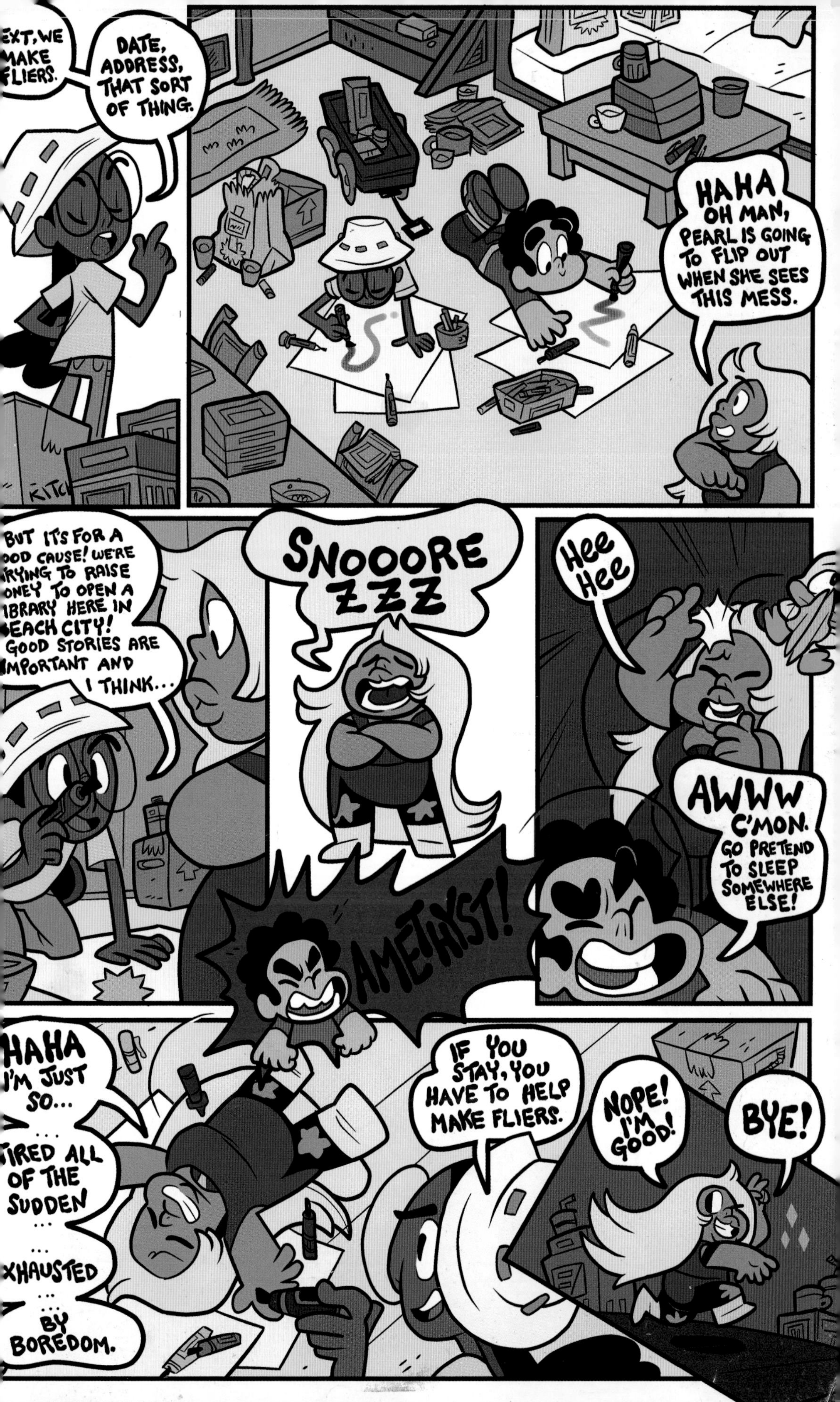

EXT, WE MAKE FLIERS.
DATE, ADDRESS, THAT SORT OF THING.
HAHA OH MAN, PEARL IS GOING TO FLIP OUT WHEN SHE SEES THIS MESS.
BUT IT'S FOR A OOD CAUSE! WE'RE RYING TO RAISE ONEY TO OPEN A IBRARY HERE IN EACH CITY! GOOD STORIES ARE MPORTANT AND I THINK...
SNOOORE ZZZ
Hee Hee
AWWW C'MON. GO PRETEND TO SLEEP SOMEWHERE ELSE!
AMETHYST!
HAHA I'M JUST SO... ... TIRED ALL OF THE SUDDEN ... ... XHAUSTED ... ... BY BOREDOM.
IF YOU STAY, YOU HAVE TO HELP MAKE FLIERS.
NOPE! I'M GOOD!
BYE!

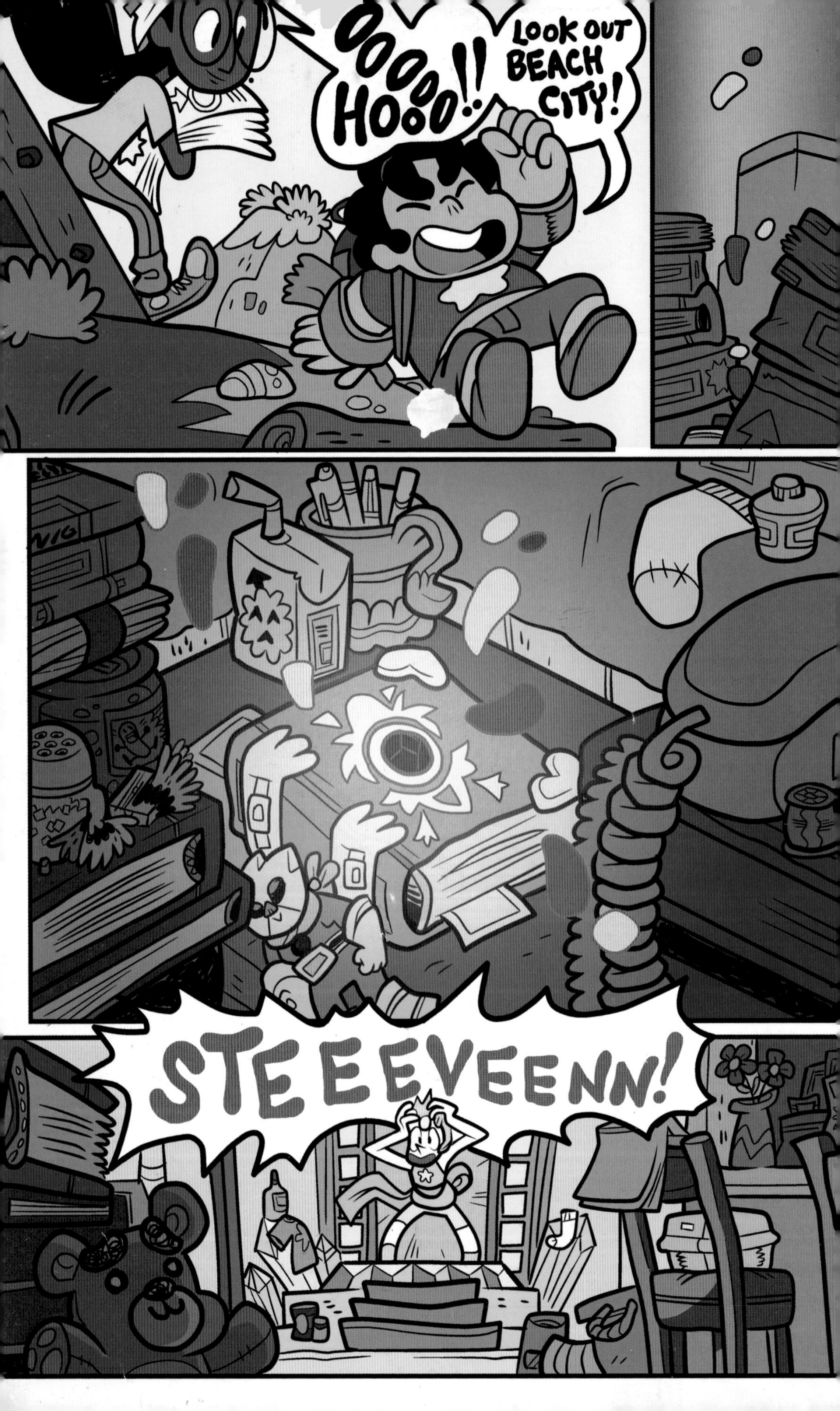

OOOOOO HOOOO!!
LOOK OUT BEACH CITY!
STEEEVEENN!

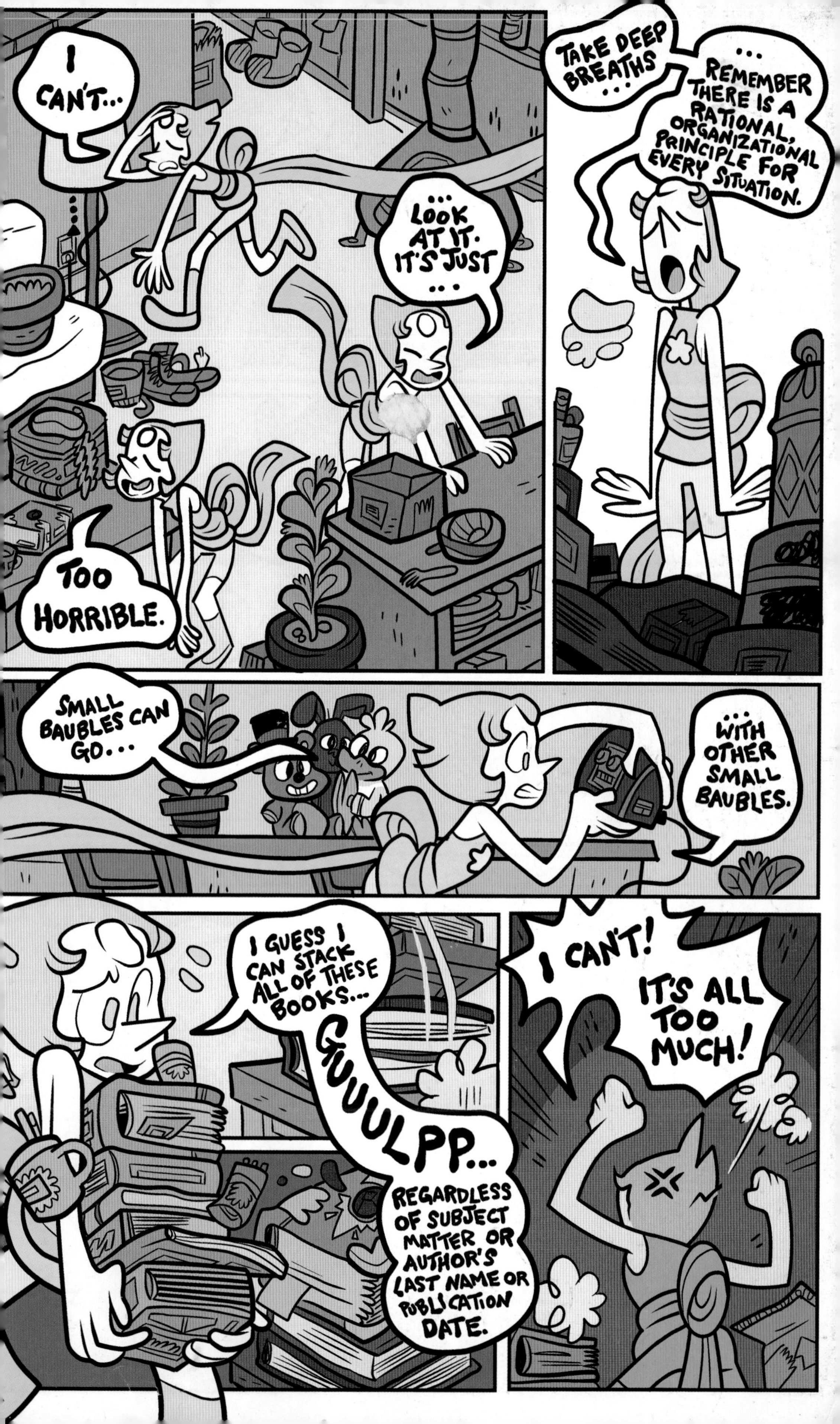
I CAN'T...
...LOOK AT IT. IT'S JUST ...
TOO HORRIBLE.
TAKE DEEP BREATHS ...
... REMEMBER THERE IS A RATIONAL, ORGANIZATIONAL PRINCIPLE FOR EVERY SITUATION.
SMALL BAUBLES CAN GO...
...WITH OTHER SMALL BAUBLES.
I GUESS I CAN STACK ALL OF THESE BOOKS...
GUUUULPP...
REGARDLESS OF SUBJECT MATTER OR AUTHOR'S LAST NAME OR PUBLICATION DATE.
I CAN'T!
IT'S ALL TOO MUCH!

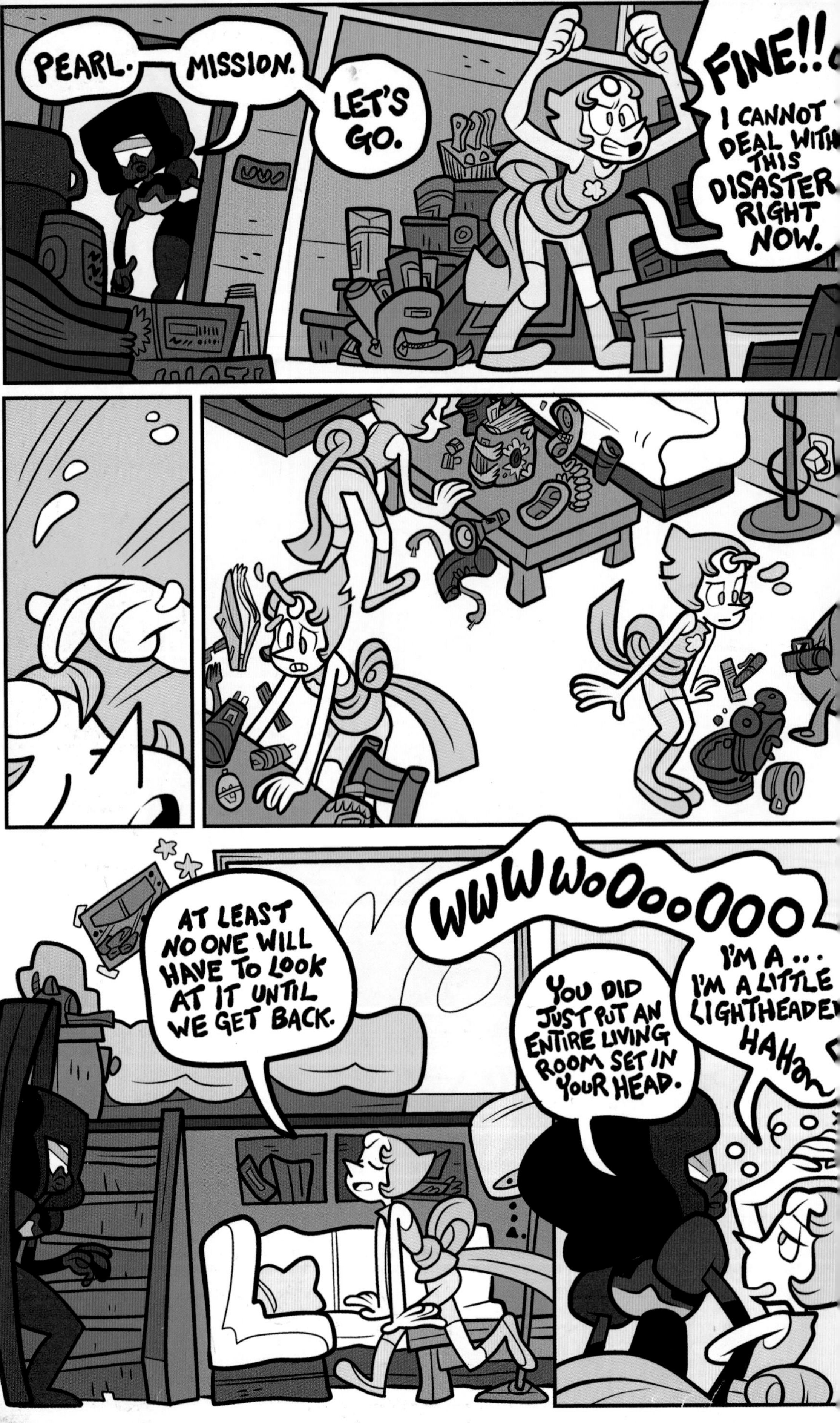
PEARL.
MISSION.
LET'S GO.
FINE!!
I CANNOT DEAL WITH THIS DISASTER RIGHT NOW.
AT LEAST NO ONE WILL HAVE TO LOOK AT IT UNTIL WE GET BACK.
WWWWoOooOOO
YOU DID JUST PUT AN ENTIRE LIVING ROOM SET IN YOUR HEAD.
I'M A... I'M A LITTLE LIGHTHEADE
HAHa

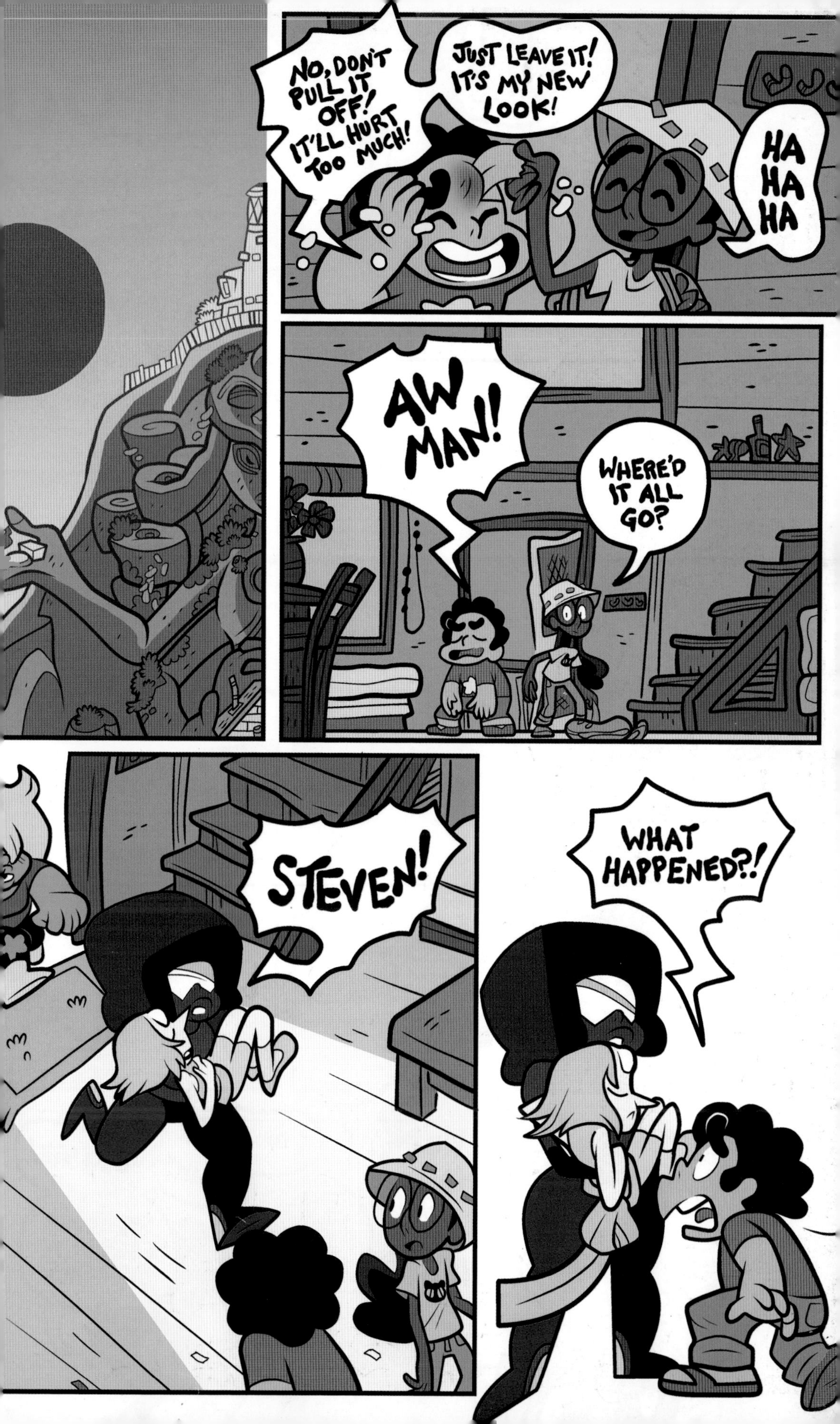
NO, DON'T PULL IT OFF! IT'LL HURT TOO MUCH!
JUST LEAVE IT! IT'S MY NEW LOOK!
HA HA HA
AW MAN!
WHERE'D IT ALL GO?
STEVEN!
WHAT HAPPENED?!

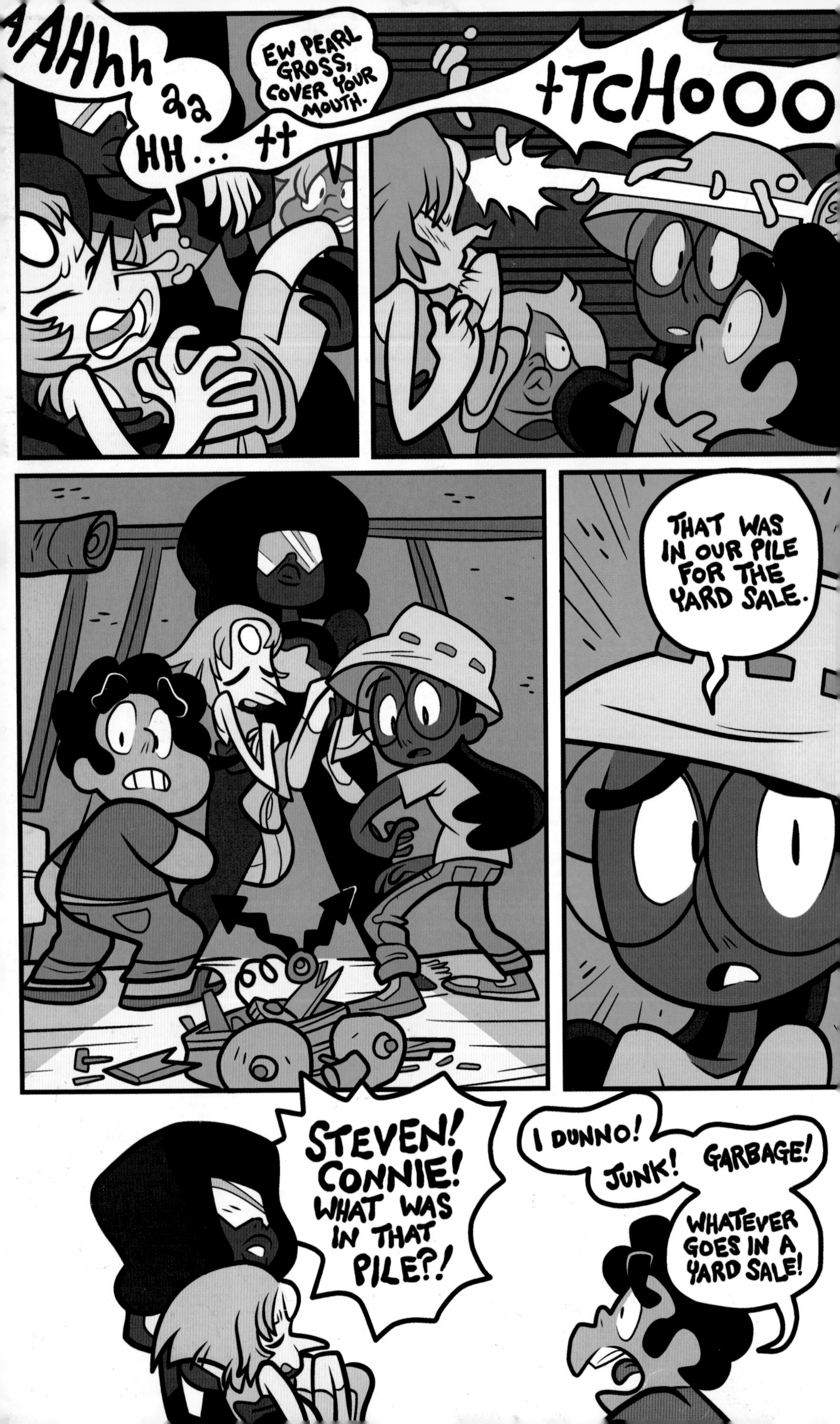
AAHhh aa HH... tt
EW PEARL GROSS, COVER YOUR MOUTH.
tTCHOOO
THAT WAS IN OUR PILE FOR THE YARD SALE.
STEVEN! CONNIE! WHAT WAS IN THAT PILE?!
I DUNNO!
JUNK! GARBAGE!
WHATEVER GOES IN A YARD SALE!

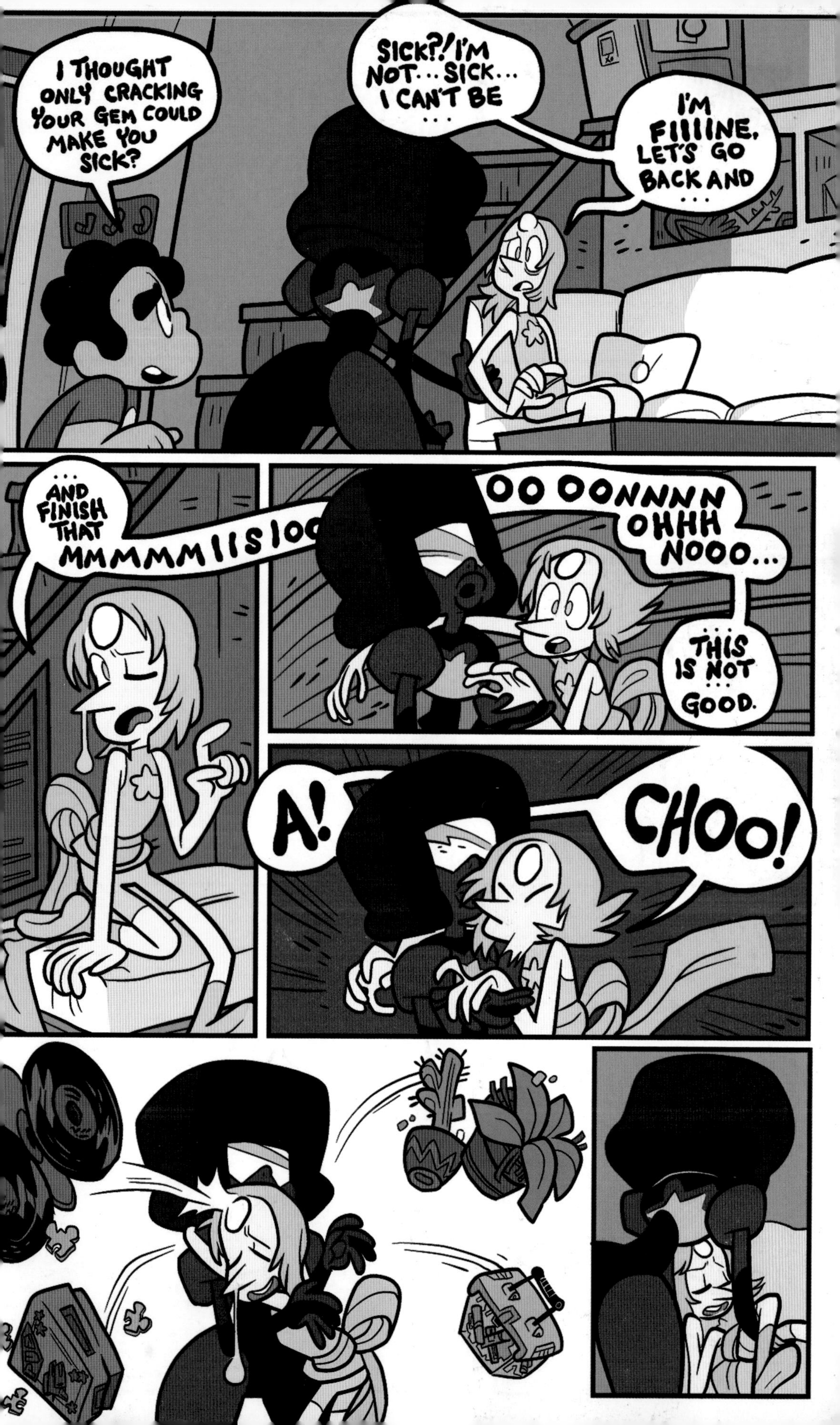
I THOUGHT ONLY CRACKING YOUR GEM COULD MAKE YOU SICK?
SICK?! I'M NOT... SICK... I CAN'T BE ...
I'M FIIIINE. LET'S GO BACK AND ...
... AND FINISH THAT MMMMMIISIOO
OO OONNNNN OHHH NOOO...
... THIS IS NOT ... GOOD.
A!
CHOO!

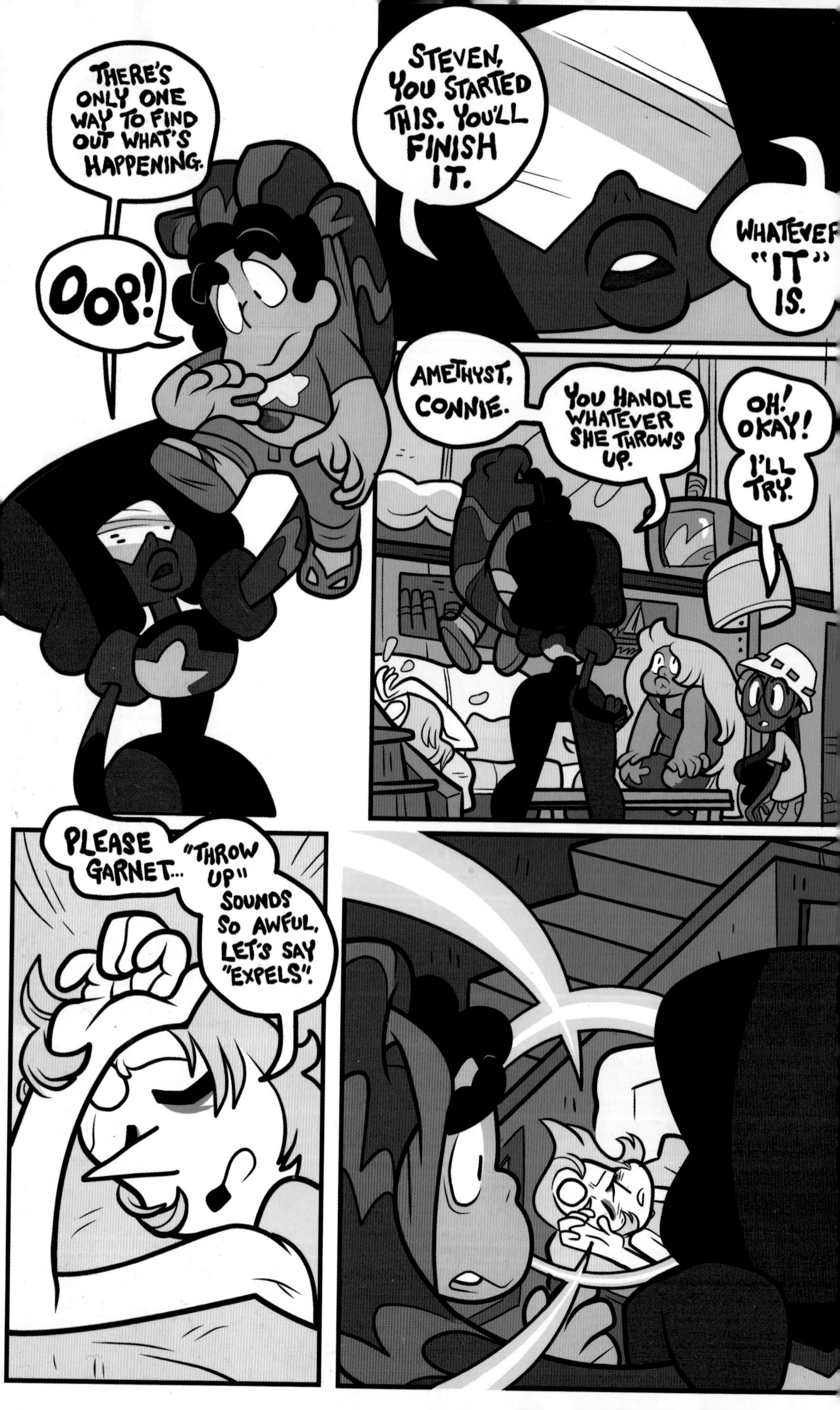
THERE'S ONLY ONE WAY TO FIND OUT WHAT'S HAPPENING.
OOP!
STEVEN, YOU STARTED THIS. YOU'LL FINISH IT.
WHATEVER "IT" IS.
AMETHYST, CONNIE.
YOU HANDLE WHATEVER SHE THROWS UP.
OH! OKAY!
I'LL TRY.
PLEASE GARNET...
"THROW UP" SOUNDS SO AWFUL, LET'S SAY "EXPELS".

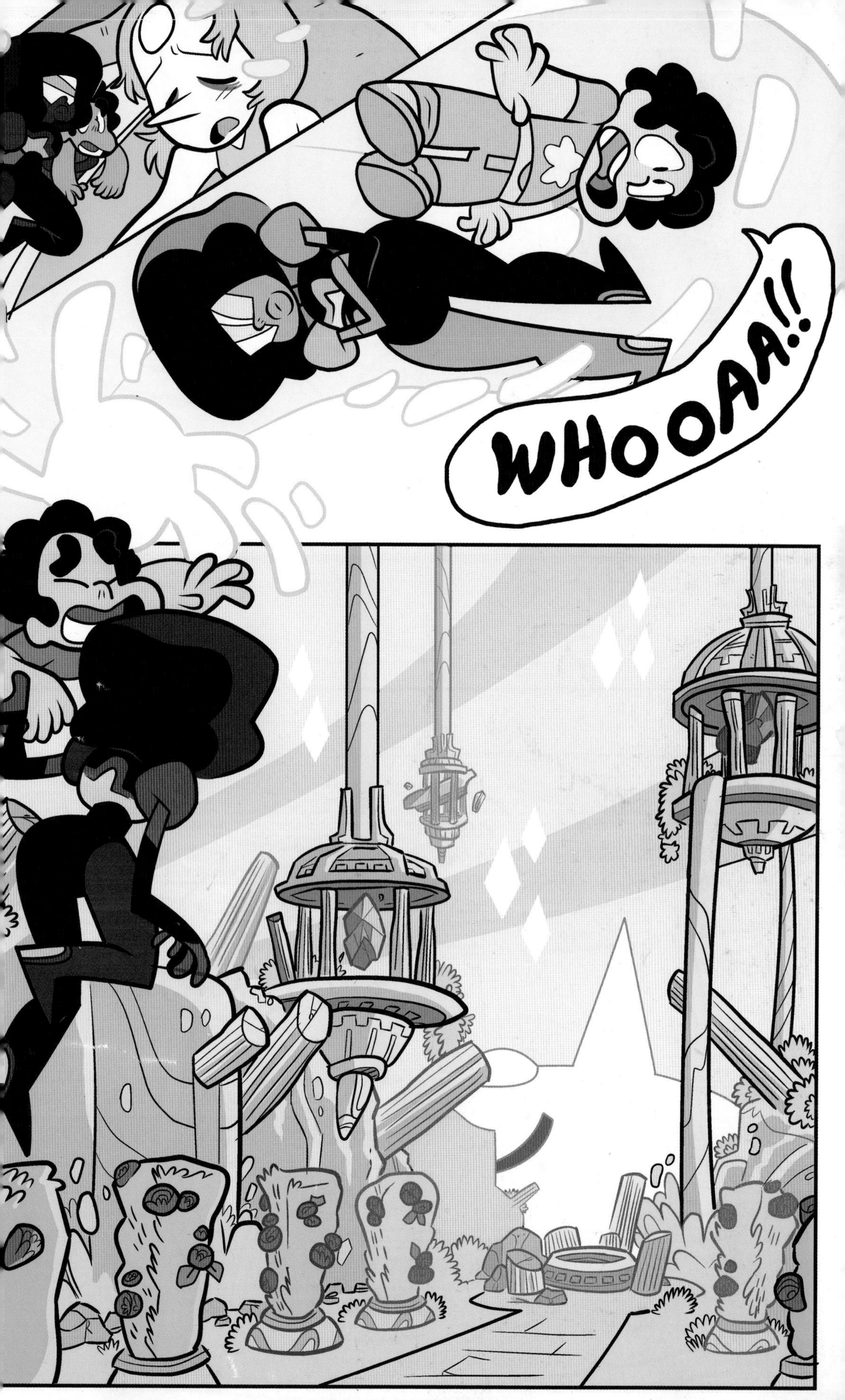
WHOOAA!!

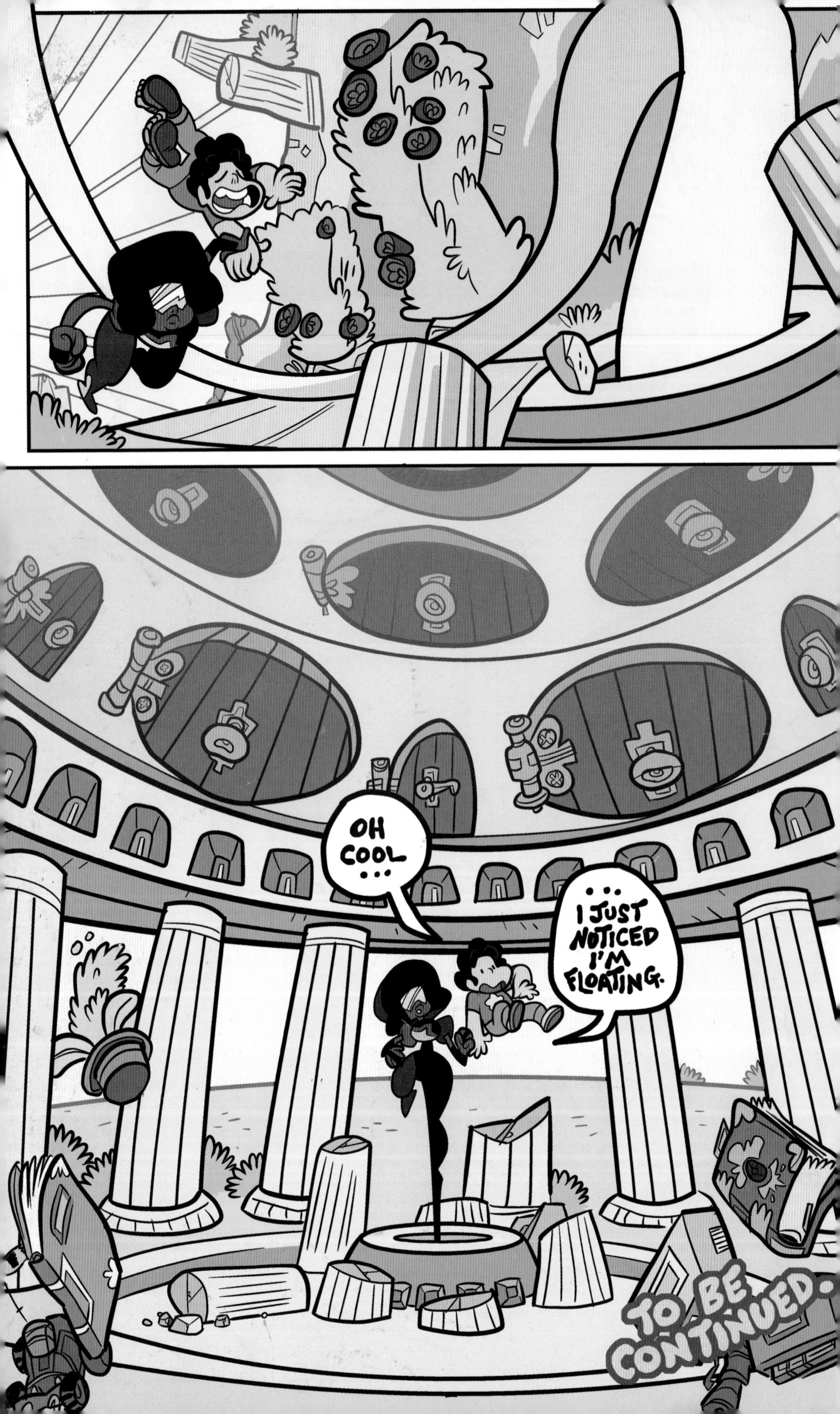
OH COOL...
...I JUST NOTICED I'M FLOATING.
TO BE CONTINUED.

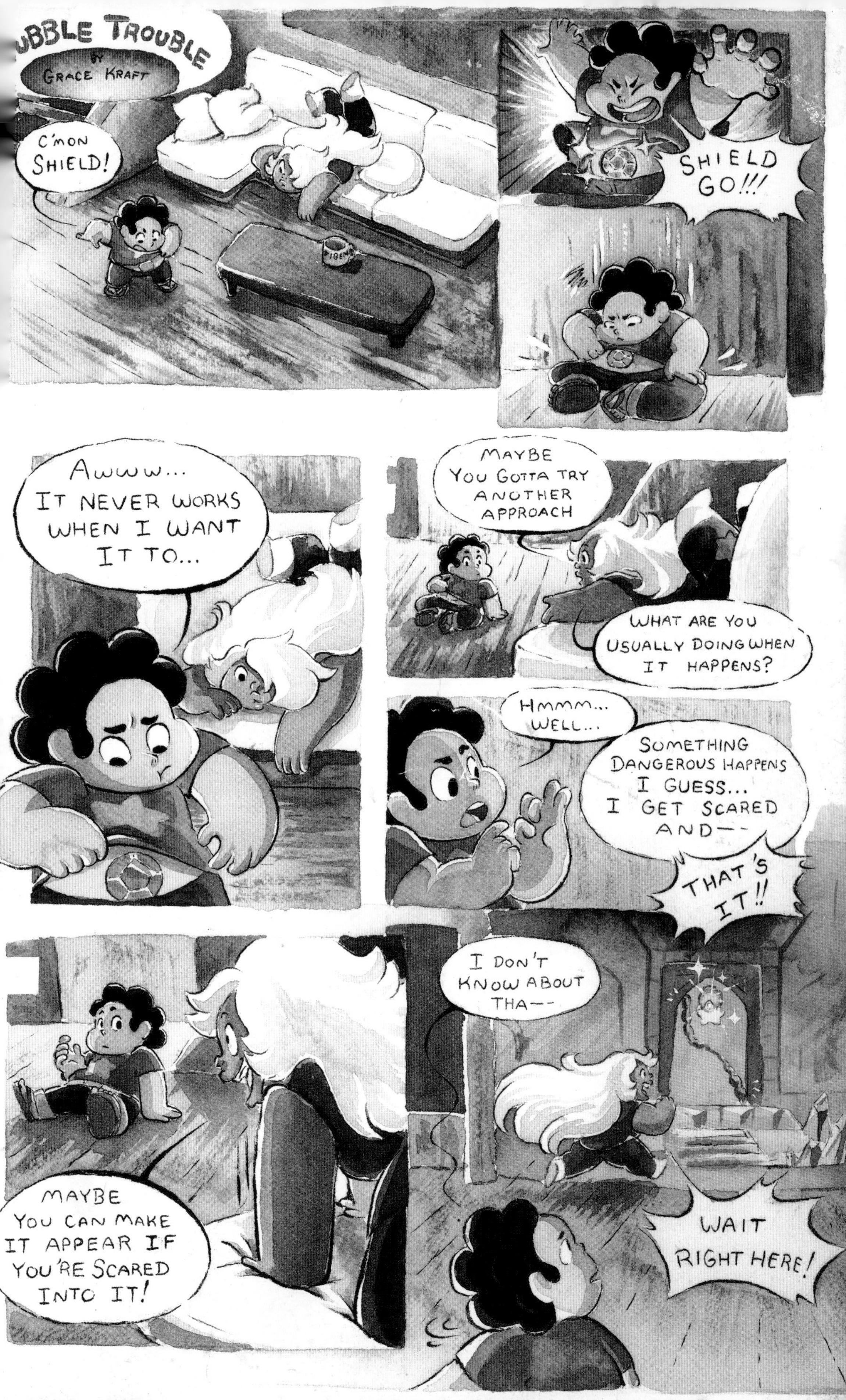
UBBLE TROUBLE
BY GRACE KRAFT
C'MON SHIELD!
SHIELD GO!!!
AWWW... IT NEVER WORKS WHEN I WANT IT TO...
MAYBE YOU GOTTA TRY ANOTHER APPROACH
WHAT ARE YOU USUALLY DOING WHEN IT HAPPENS?
HMMM... WELL...
SOMETHING DANGEROUS HAPPENS I GUESS... I GET SCARED AND--
THAT'S IT!!
MAYBE YOU CAN MAKE IT APPEAR IF YOU'RE SCARED INTO IT!
I DON'T KNOW ABOUT THA--
WAIT RIGHT HERE!

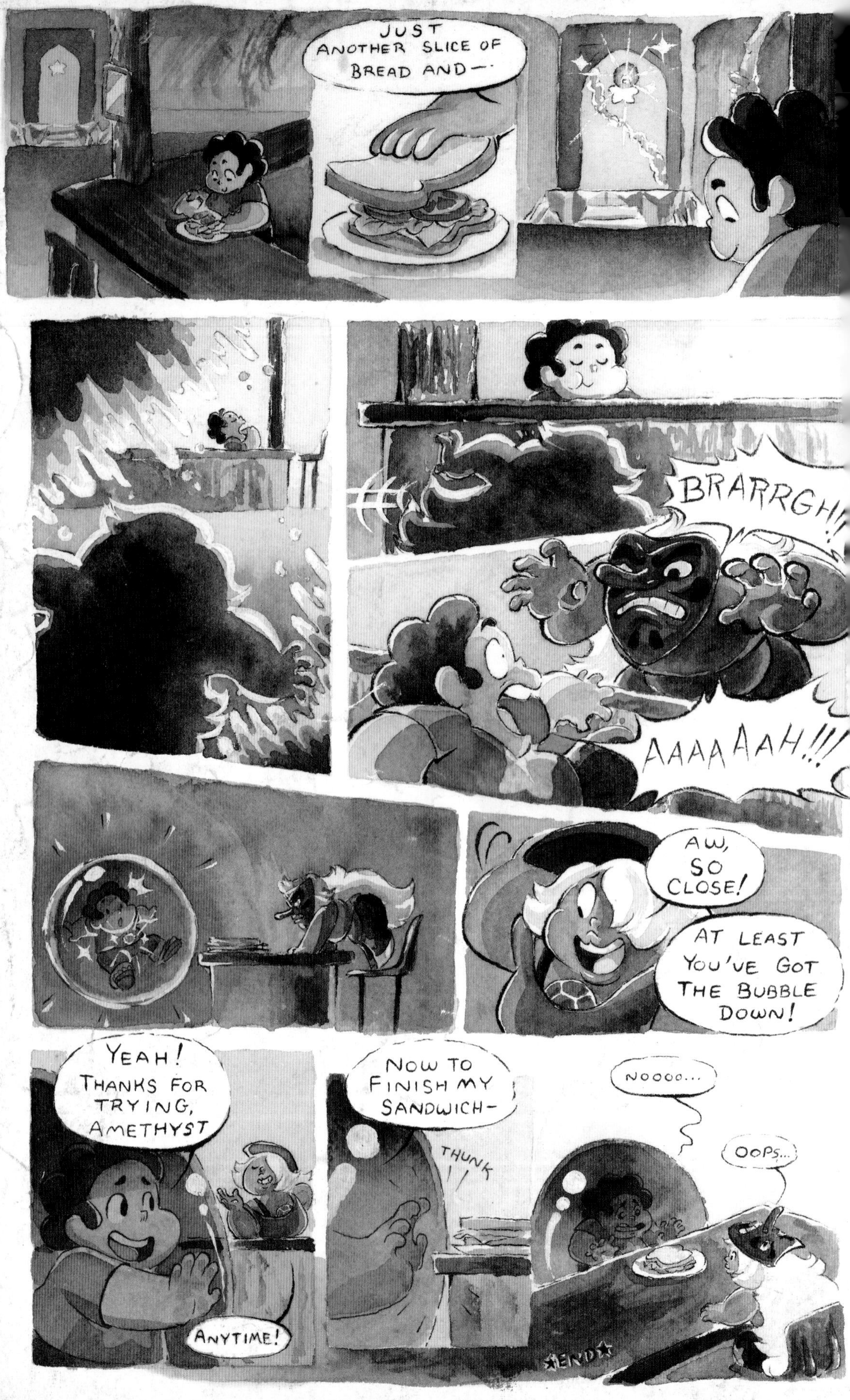
JUST ANOTHER SLICE OF BREAD AND—
BRARRGH!!
AAAAAAH!!!
AW, SO CLOSE!
AT LEAST YOU'VE GOT THE BUBBLE DOWN!
YEAH! THANKS FOR TRYING, AMETHYST
ANYTIME!
NOW TO FINISH MY SANDWICH-
THUNK
NOOOO...
OOPS...
END

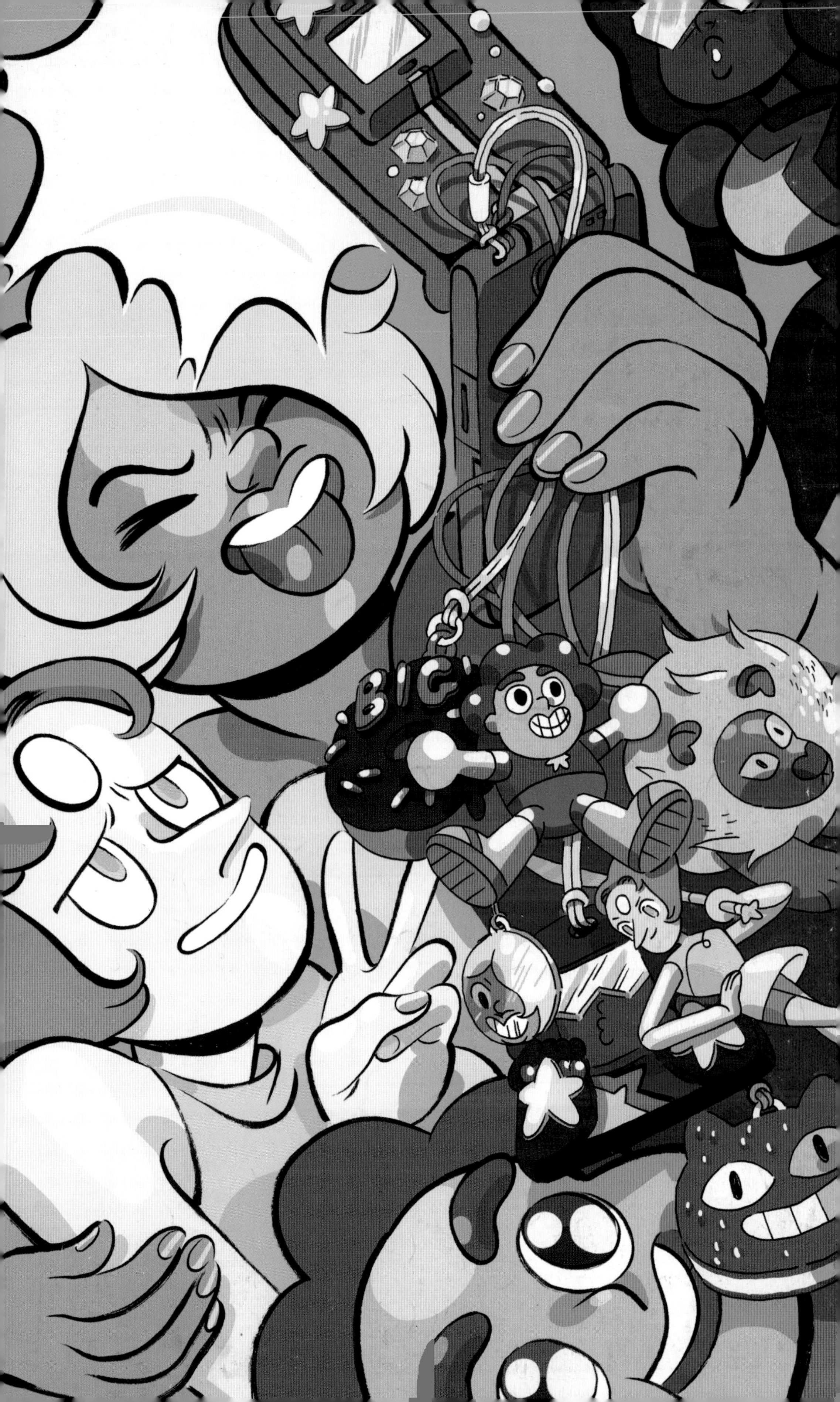
BIG

# Steven-less!

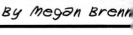

Steven?

KNOCK!

Uh!

Is Steven home? We're supposed to read the DogCopter novelization together today.

Oh he'll be back any minute, please come in, make yourself at home ha ha would you like some apple slices-

N-no thank you, Steven said he was gonna get donuts. I guess that's where he is. . .

He better save one for ME!

Is... is that AMETHYST?

DOG COPTER

She's stuck as a cat until we return the eternity chalice she dropped at the altar of learning.

oh. ok.

It's fine! she's fine! Just don't touch the space slime-

I'm sure Steven will be back soon!

SILENCE

Oh hey guys!

steven!

Phew!

En...

Winter in July

By Megan Brennan

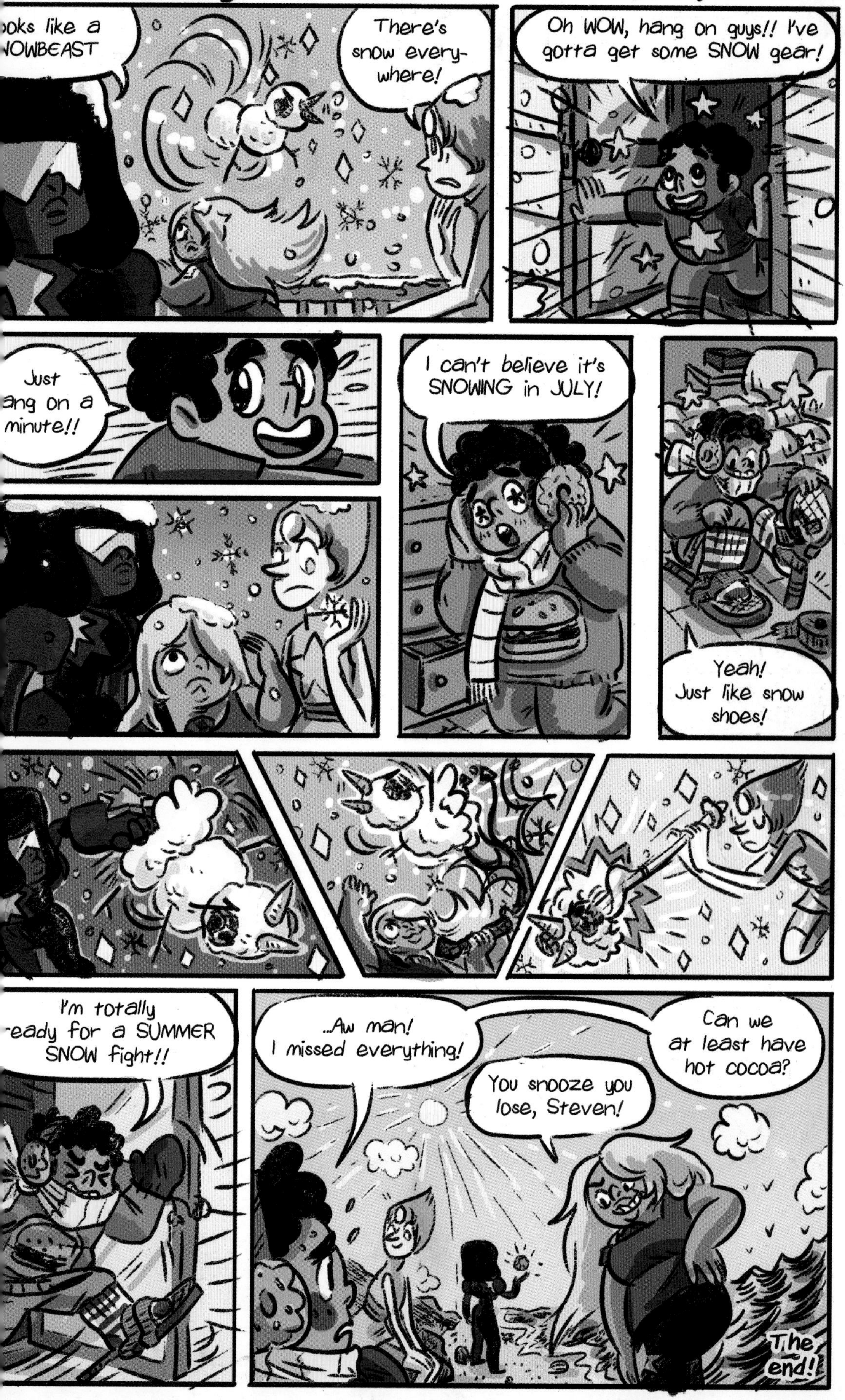
ooks like a
NOWBEAST
There's snow every-where!
Oh WOW, hang on guys!! I've gotta get some SNOW gear!
Just
ang on a minute!!
I can't believe it's SNOWING in JULY!
Yeah! Just like snow shoes!
I'm totally
ready for a SUMMER SNOW fight!!
...Aw man! I missed everything!
Can we at least have hot cocoa?
You snooze you lose, Steven!
The end!

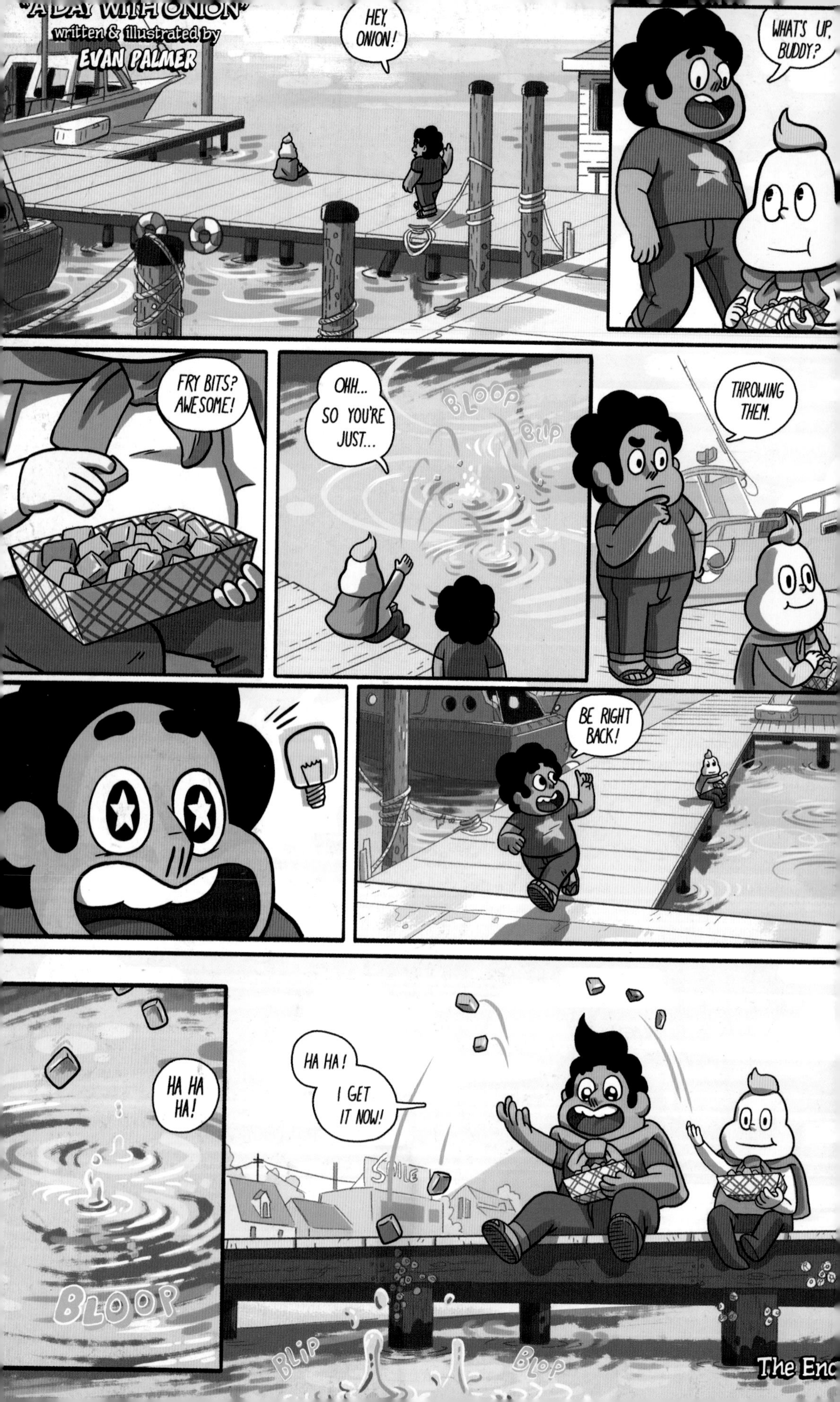
"A DAY WITH ONION"
written & illustrated by
EVAN PALMER
HEY, ONION!
WHAT'S UP, BUDDY?
FRY BITS? AWESOME!
OHH... SO YOU'RE JUST...
BLOOP
BLIP
THROWING THEM.
BE RIGHT BACK!
HA HA HA!
HA HA! I GET IT NOW!
BLOOP
BLIP
BLOP
The End

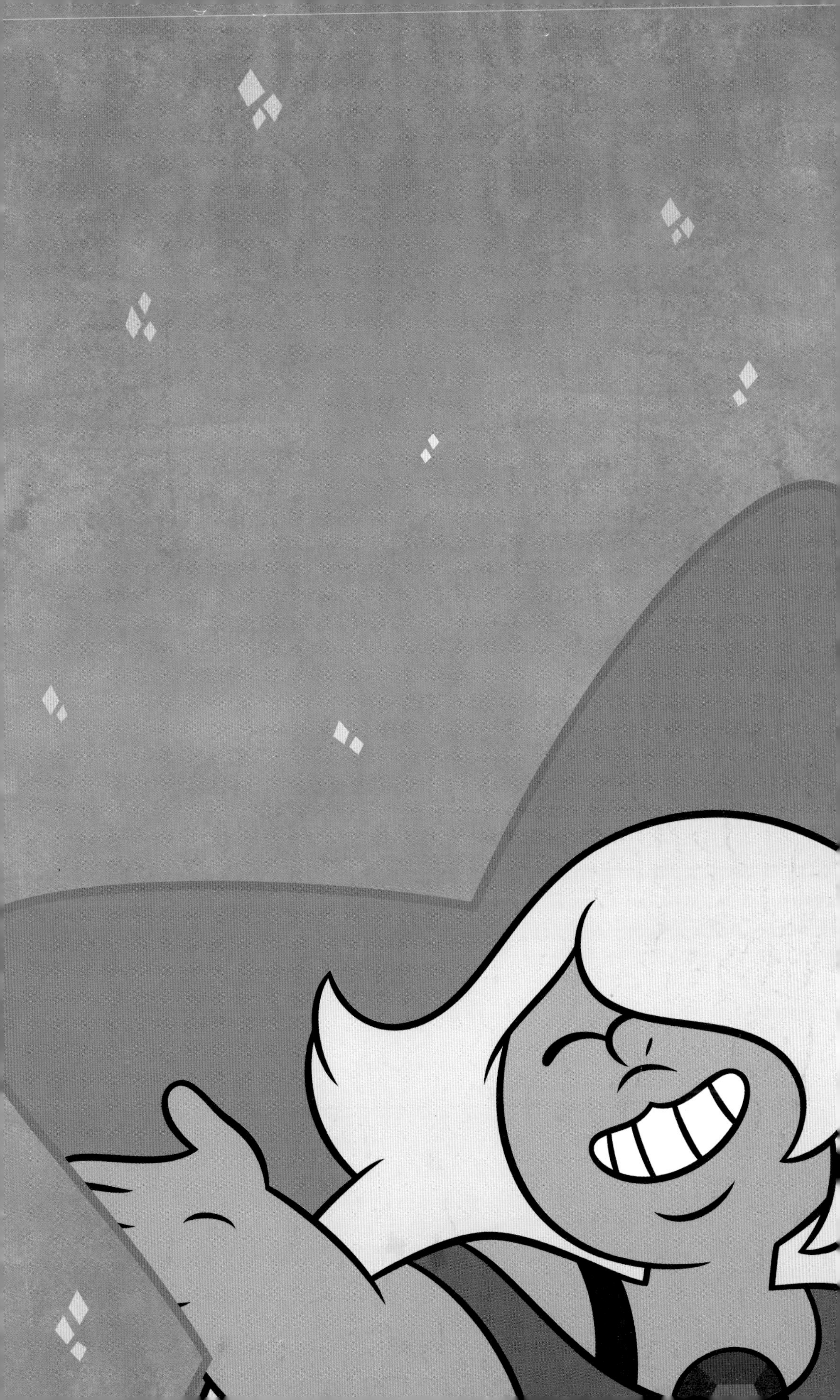

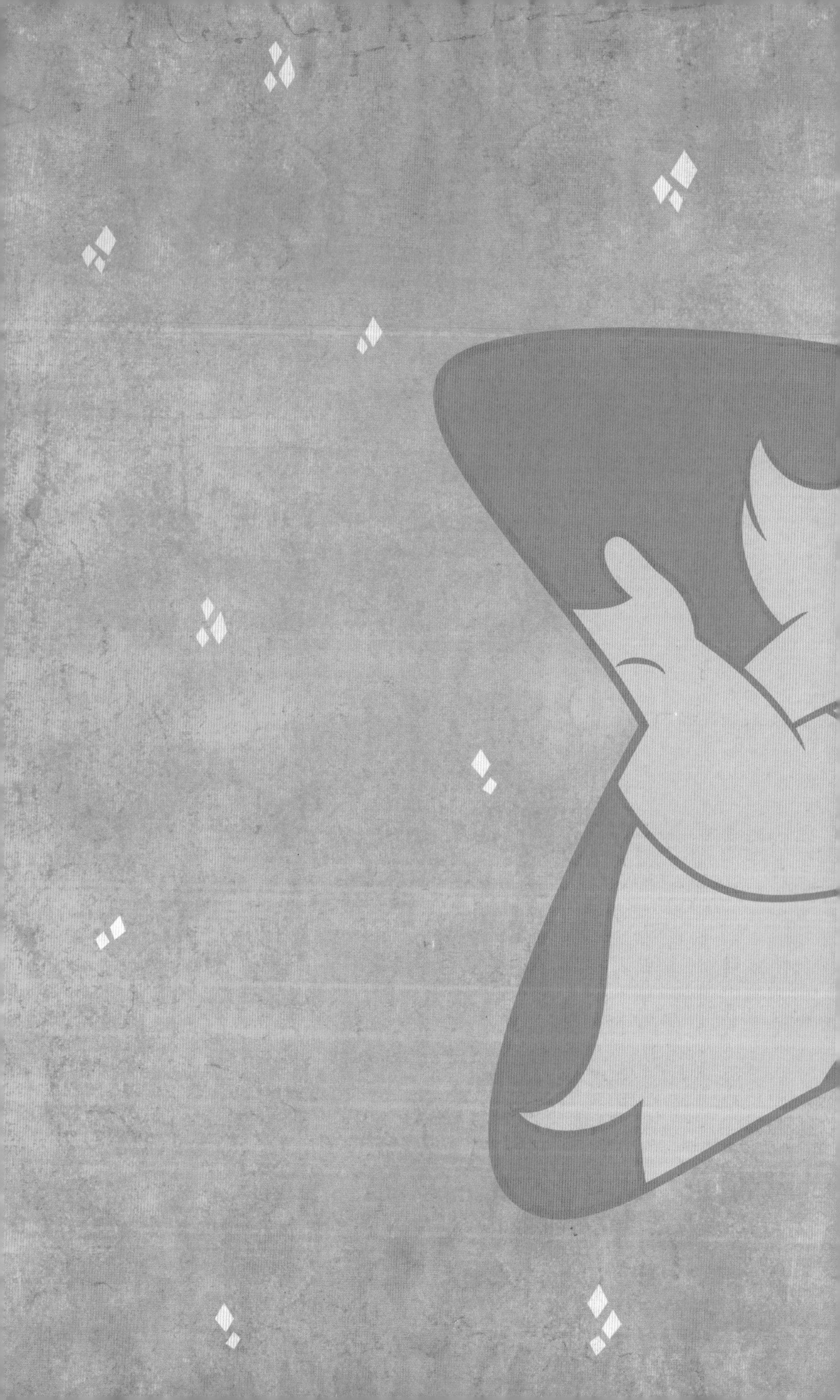

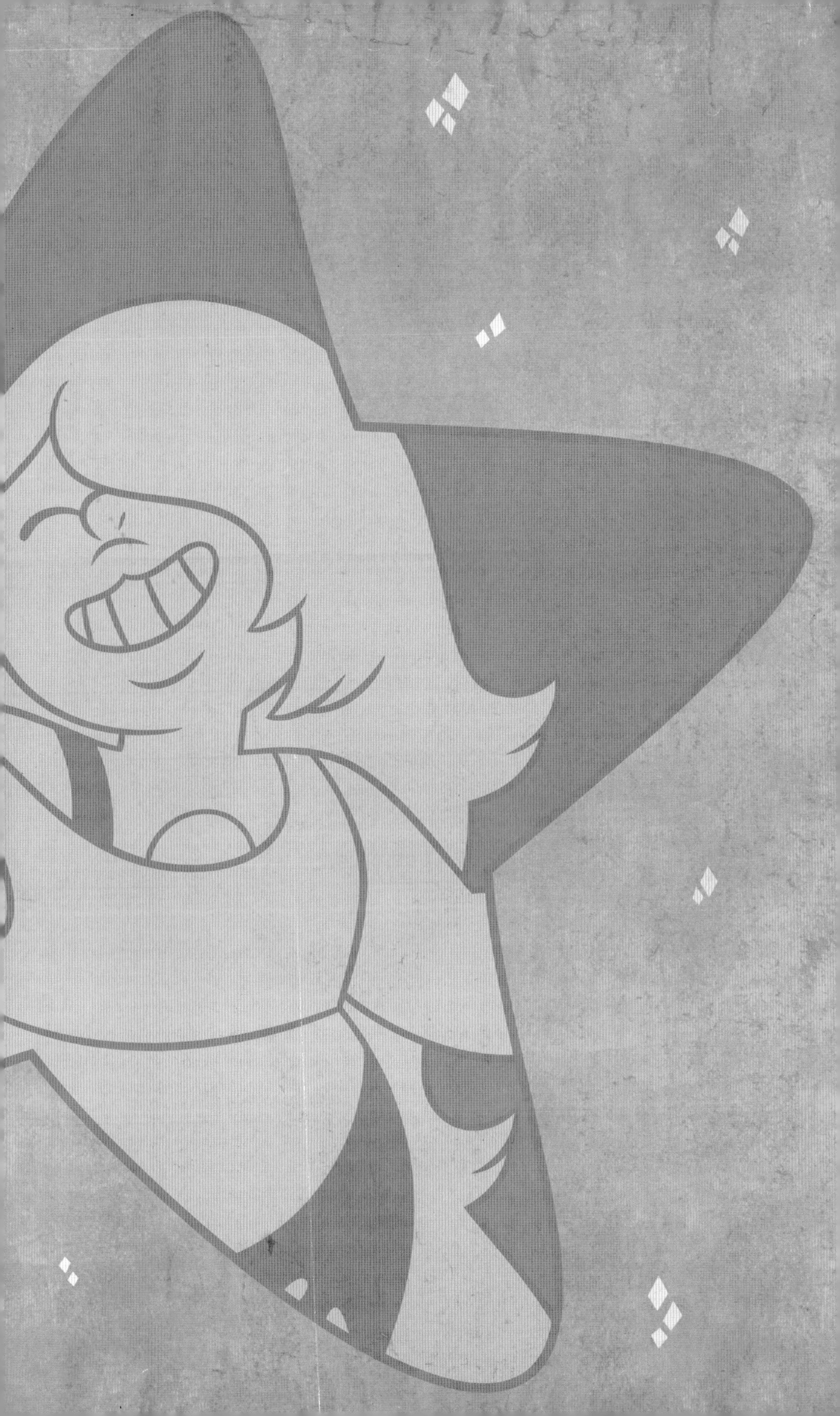

# "LIBRARY"
## PART TWO

also featuring:

**"LION'S SHARE"**
written & illustrated by
**GRACE KRAFT**

**"AIR CONTROL"**
illustrated by
**BRIDGET UNDERWOOD**

**"HOT DOG KING"**
written & illustrated by
**MEGAN BRENNAN**

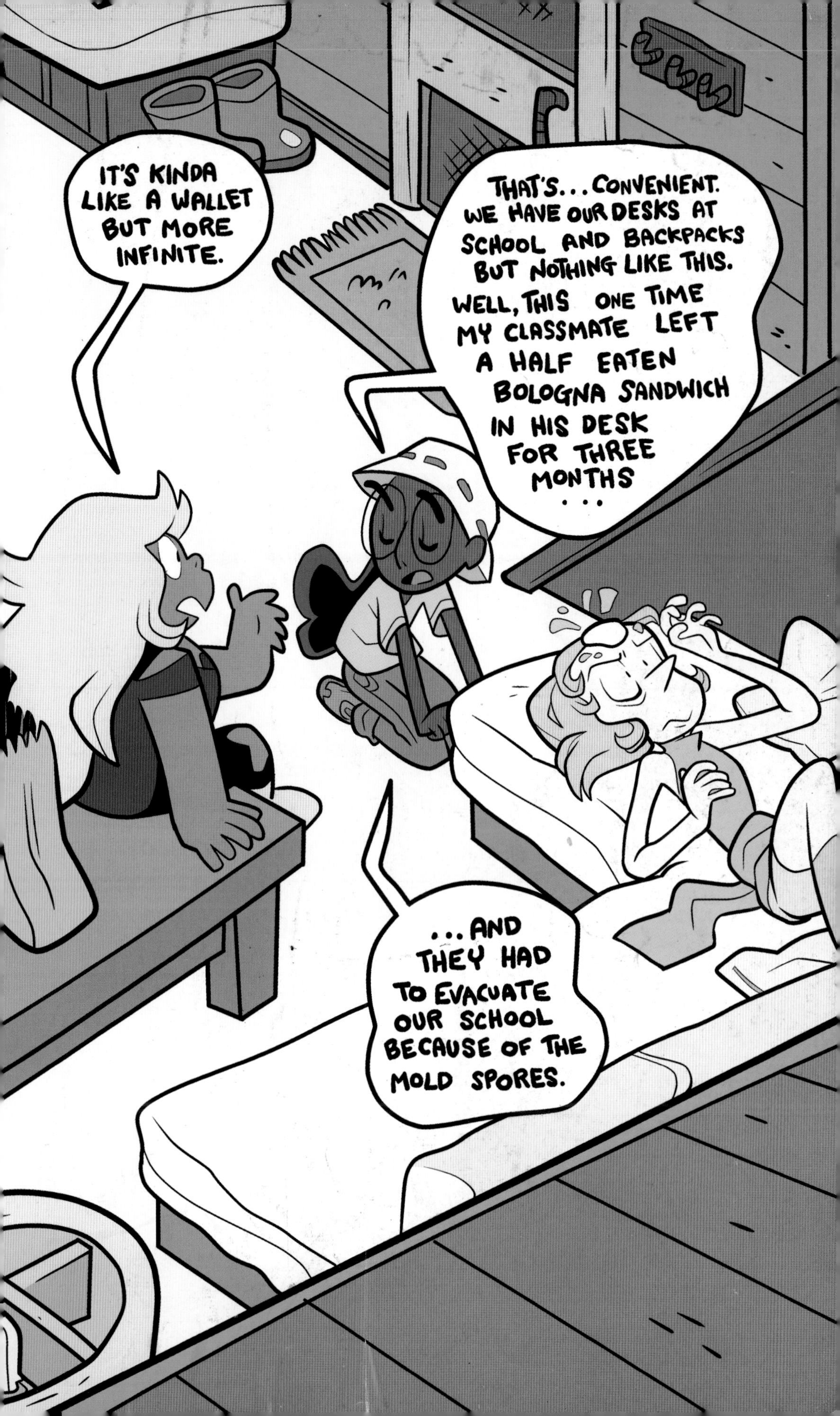
IT'S KINDA LIKE A WALLET BUT MORE INFINITE.
THAT'S... CONVENIENT. WE HAVE OUR DESKS AT SCHOOL AND BACKPACKS BUT NOTHING LIKE THIS. WELL, THIS ONE TIME MY CLASSMATE LEFT A HALF EATEN BOLOGNA SANDWICH IN HIS DESK FOR THREE MONTHS ...
...AND THEY HAD TO EVACUATE OUR SCHOOL BECAUSE OF THE MOLD SPORES.

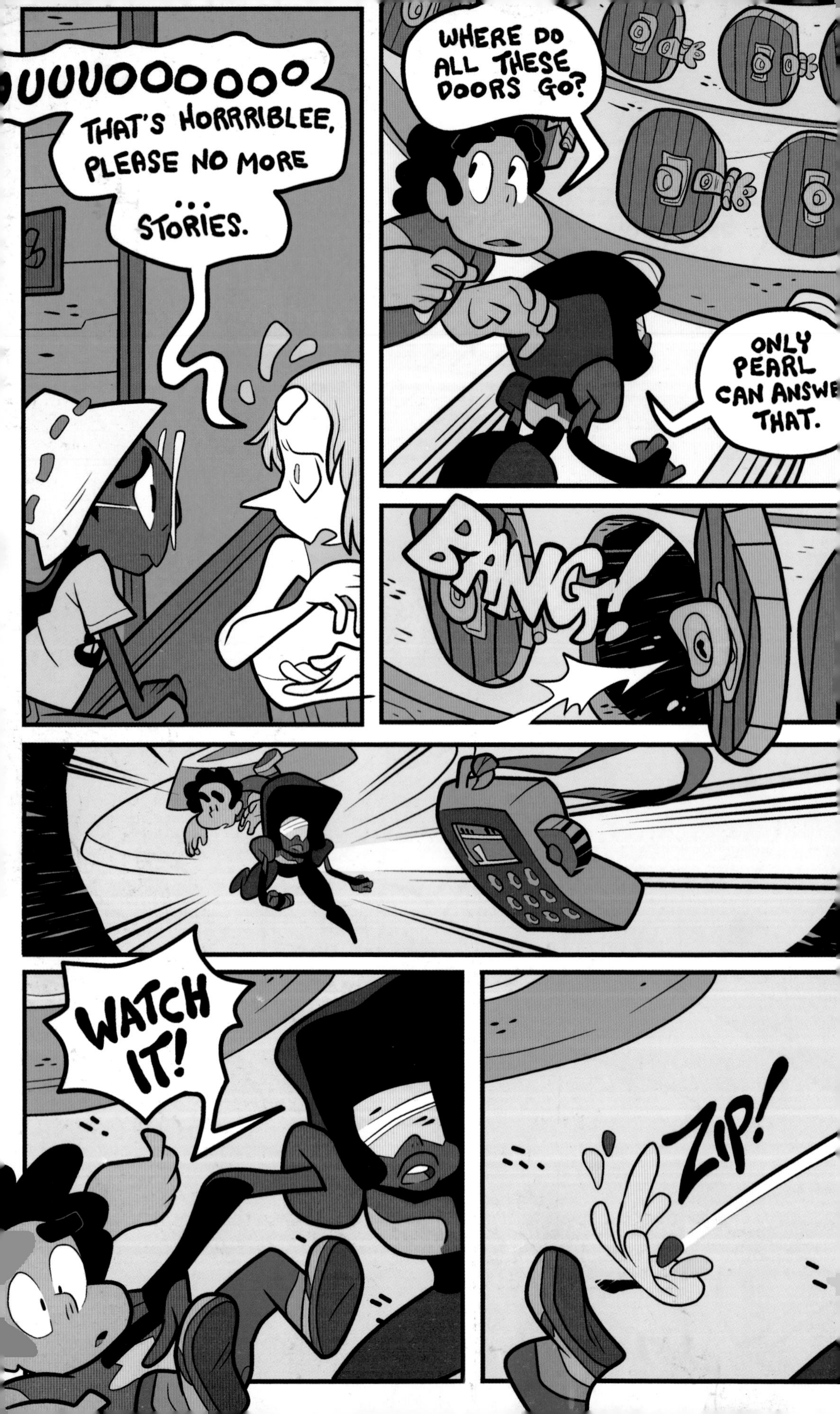
UUUVOOOOOOO
THAT'S HORRRIBLEE, PLEASE NO MORE ... STORIES.
WHERE DO ALL THESE DOORS GO?
ONLY PEARL CAN ANSWE THAT.
BANG!
WATCH IT!
ZIP!

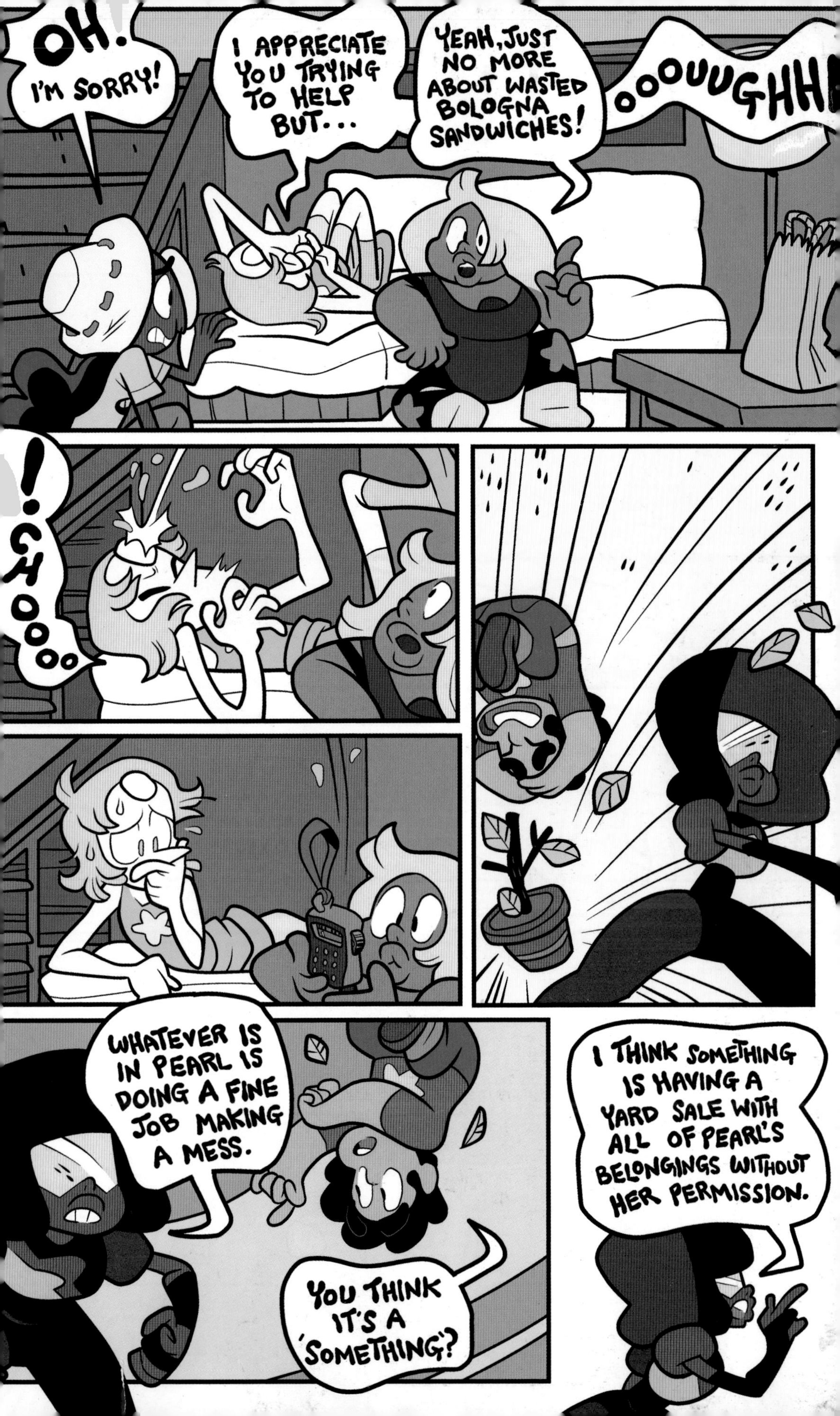
OH! I'M SORRY!
I APPRECIATE YOU TRYING TO HELP BUT...
YEAH, JUST NO MORE ABOUT WASTED BOLOGNA SANDWICHES!
OOOUUUGHHH
!CHOOOOO
WHATEVER IS IN PEARL IS DOING A FINE JOB MAKING A MESS.
YOU THINK IT'S A 'SOMETHING'?
I THINK SOMETHING IS HAVING A YARD SALE WITH ALL OF PEARL'S BELONGINGS WITHOUT HER PERMISSION.

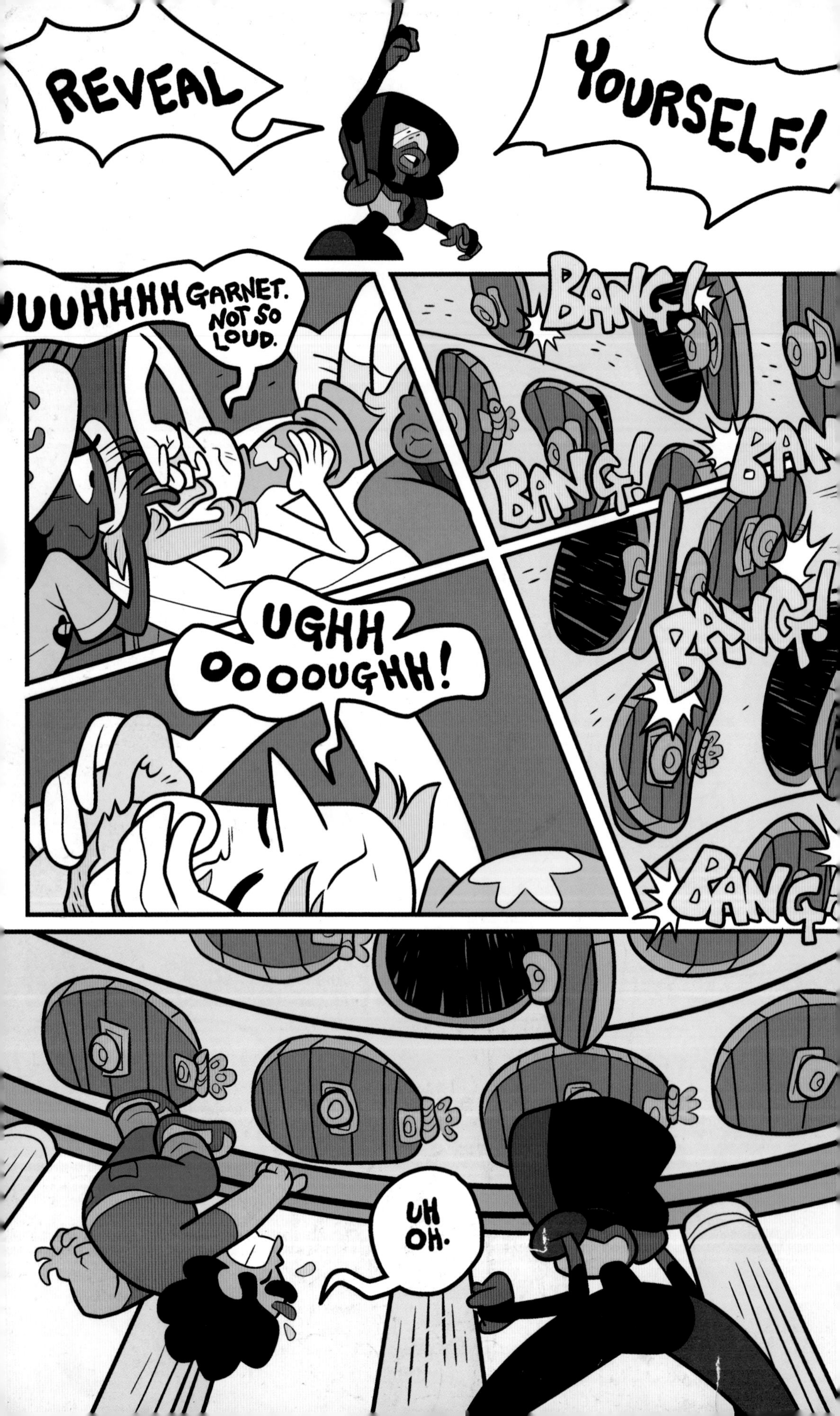
REVEAL
YOURSELF!
UUUHHHH GARNET. NOT SO LOUD.
BANG!
BANG!
UGHH OOOOUGHH!
BANG!
UH OH.

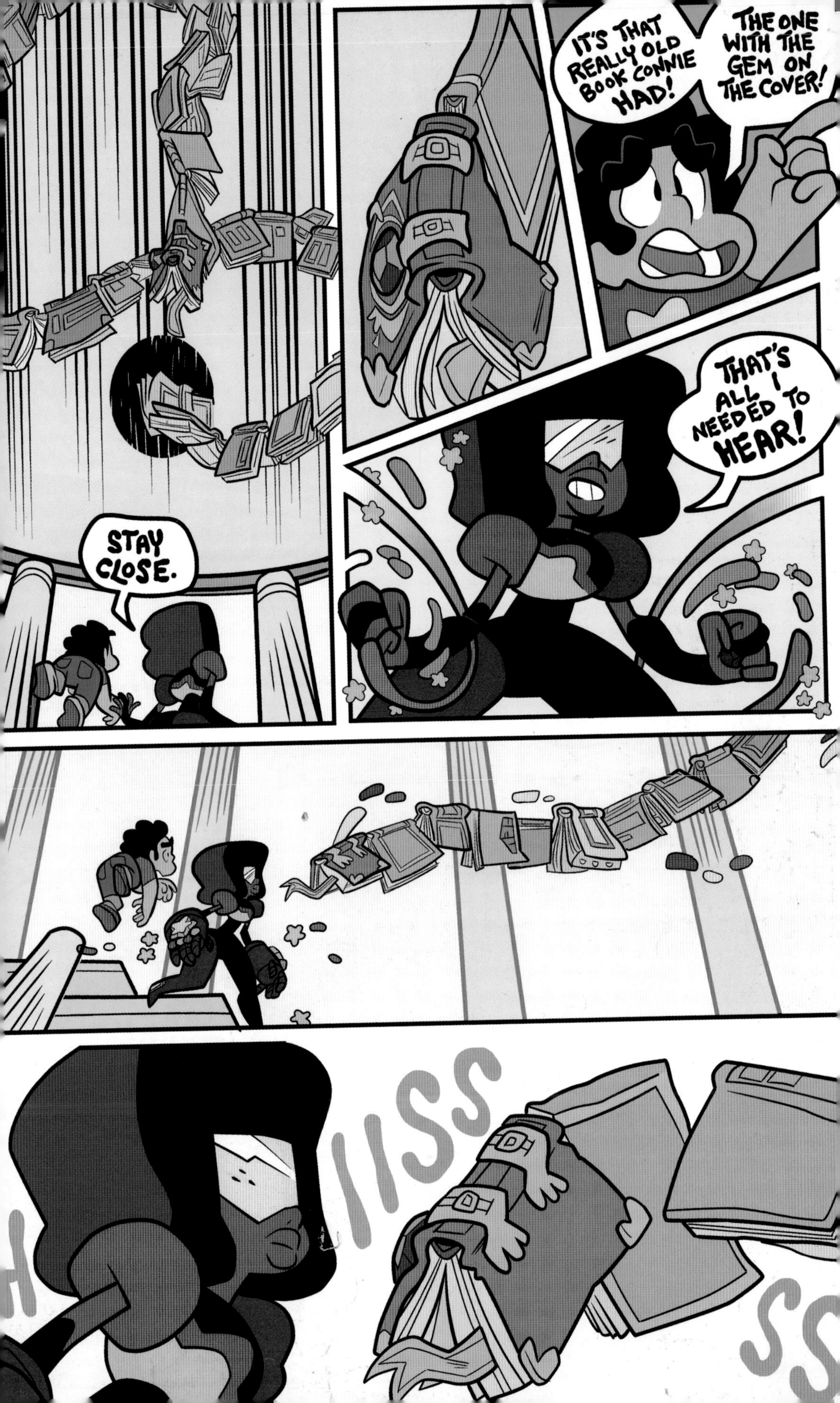
STAY CLOSE.
IT'S THAT REALLY OLD BOOK CONNIE HAD!
THE ONE WITH THE GEM ON THE COVER!
THAT'S ALL I NEEDED TO HEAR!
HISS
SS

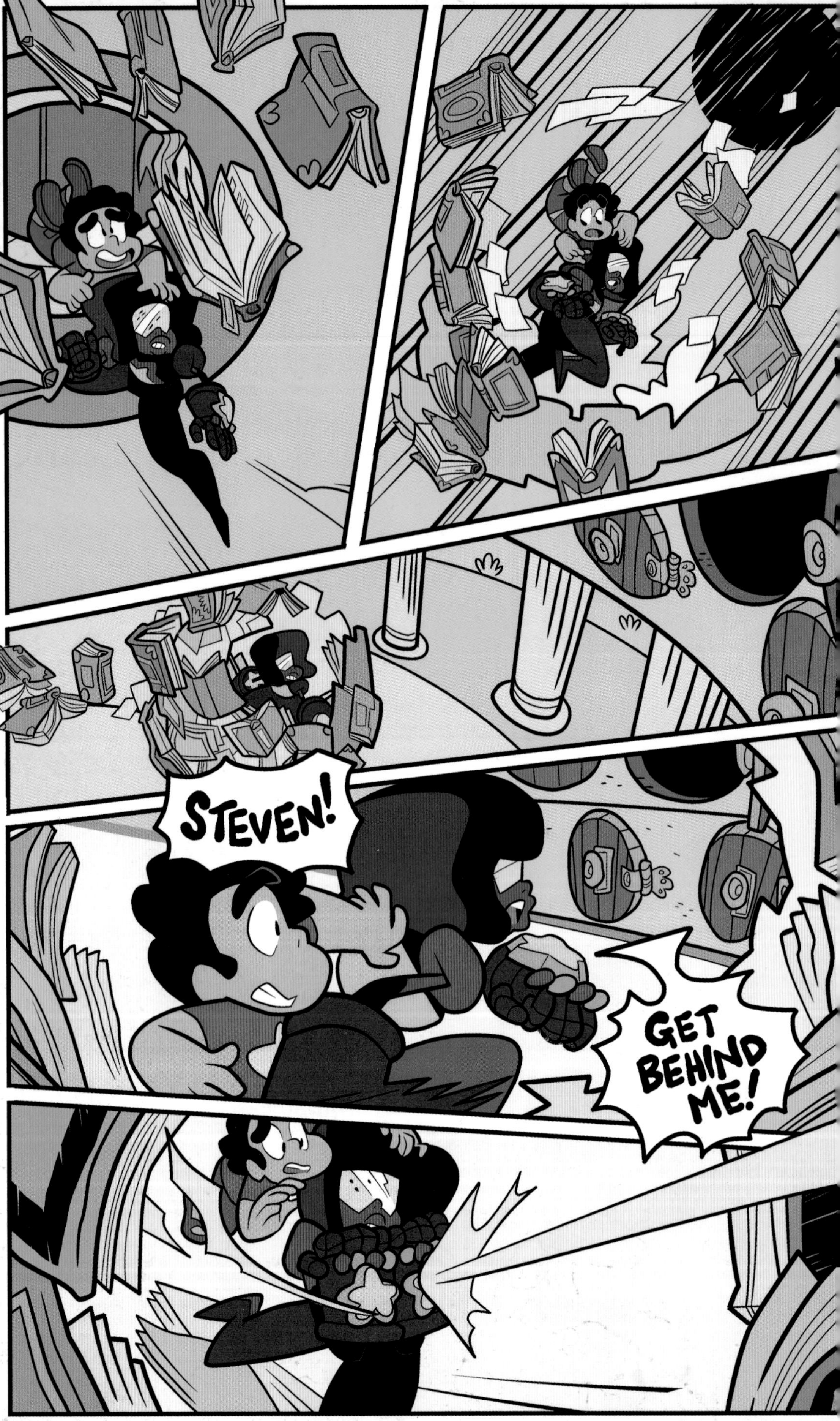
STEVEN!
GET BEHIND ME!

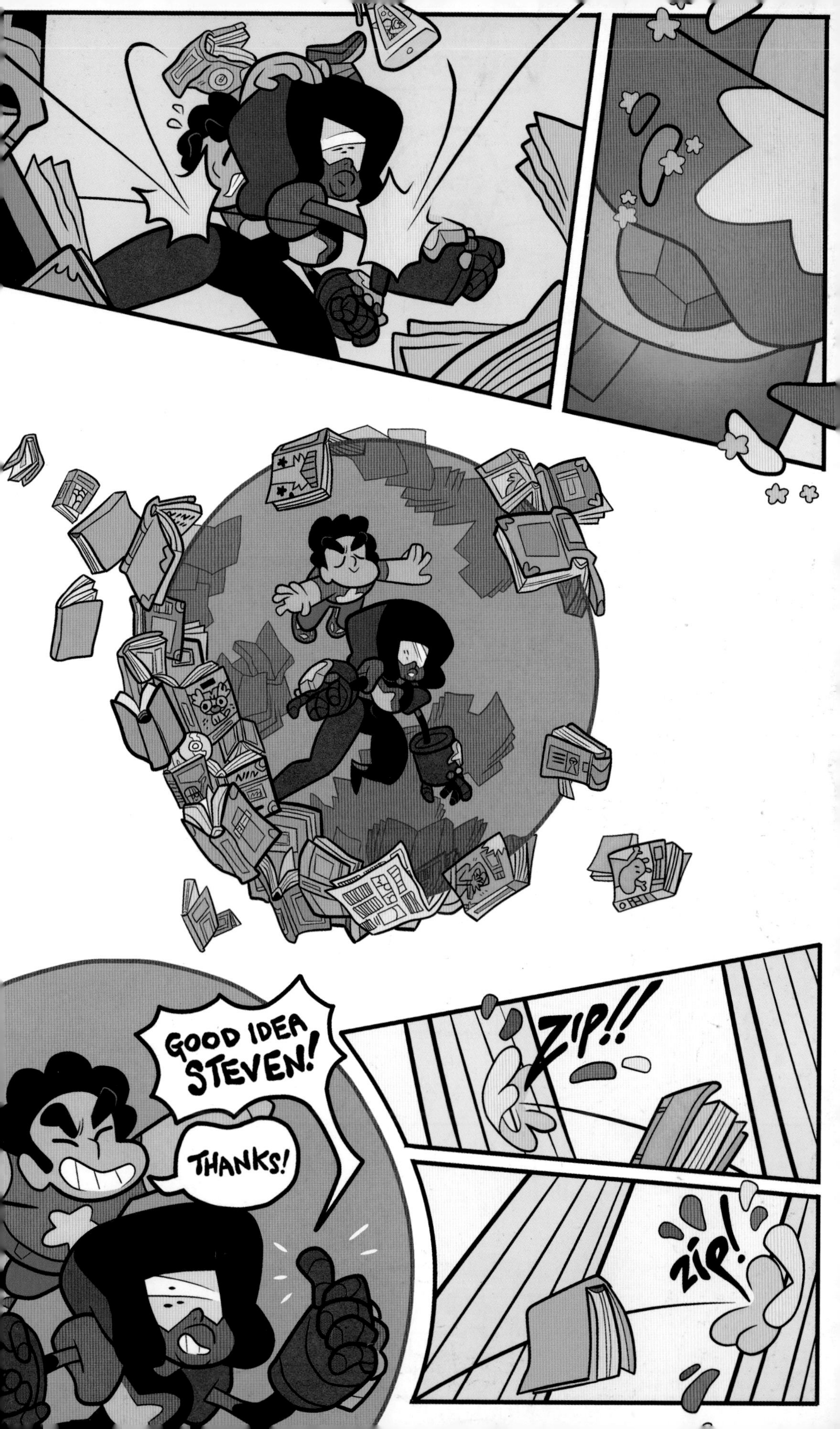
GOOD IDEA STEVEN!
THANKS!
ZIP!!
ZIP!

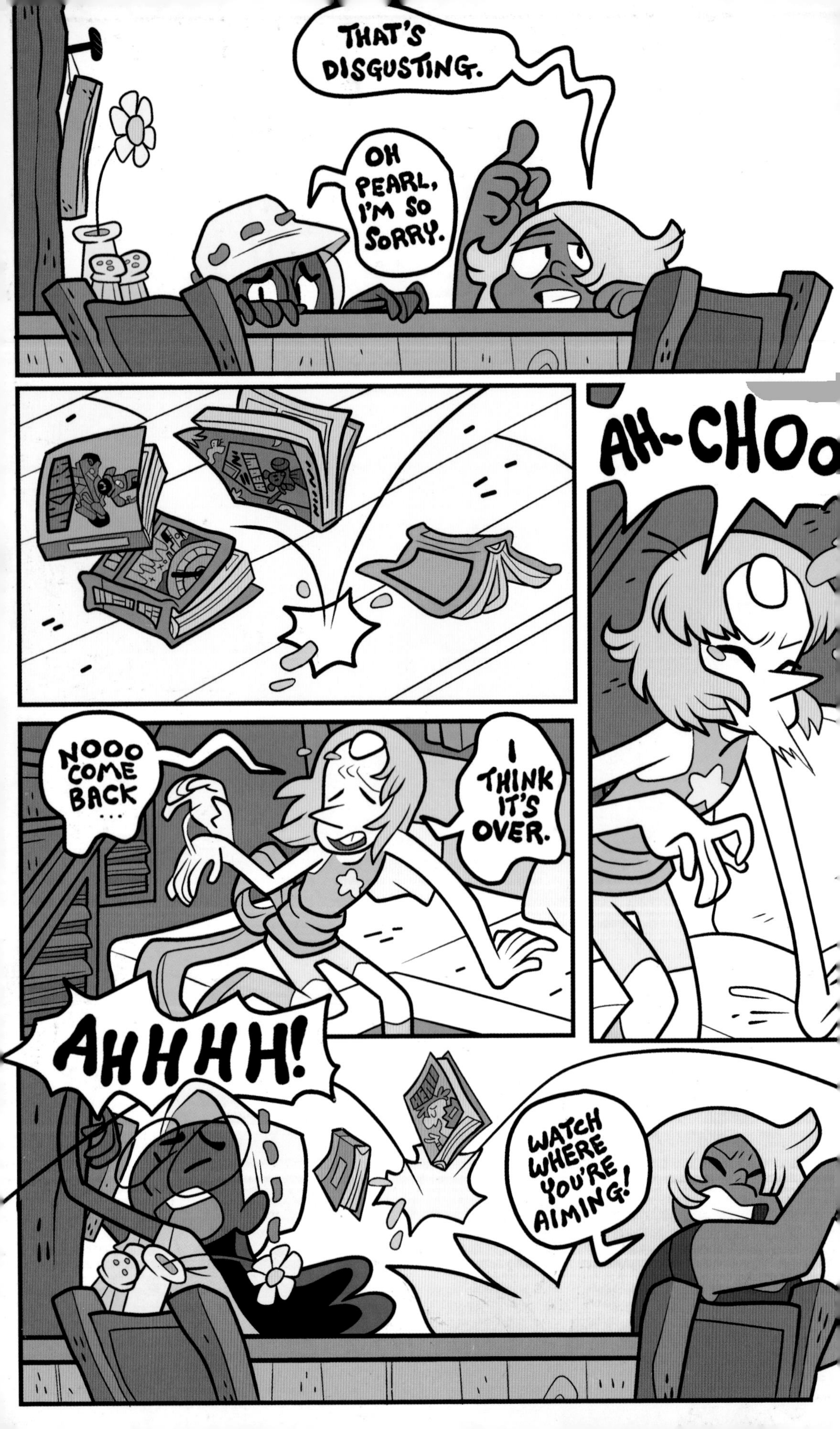
THAT'S DISGUSTING.
OH PEARL, I'M SO SORRY.
AH-CHOO
NOOO COME BACK...
I THINK IT'S OVER.
AHHHH!
WATCH WHERE YOU'RE AIMING!

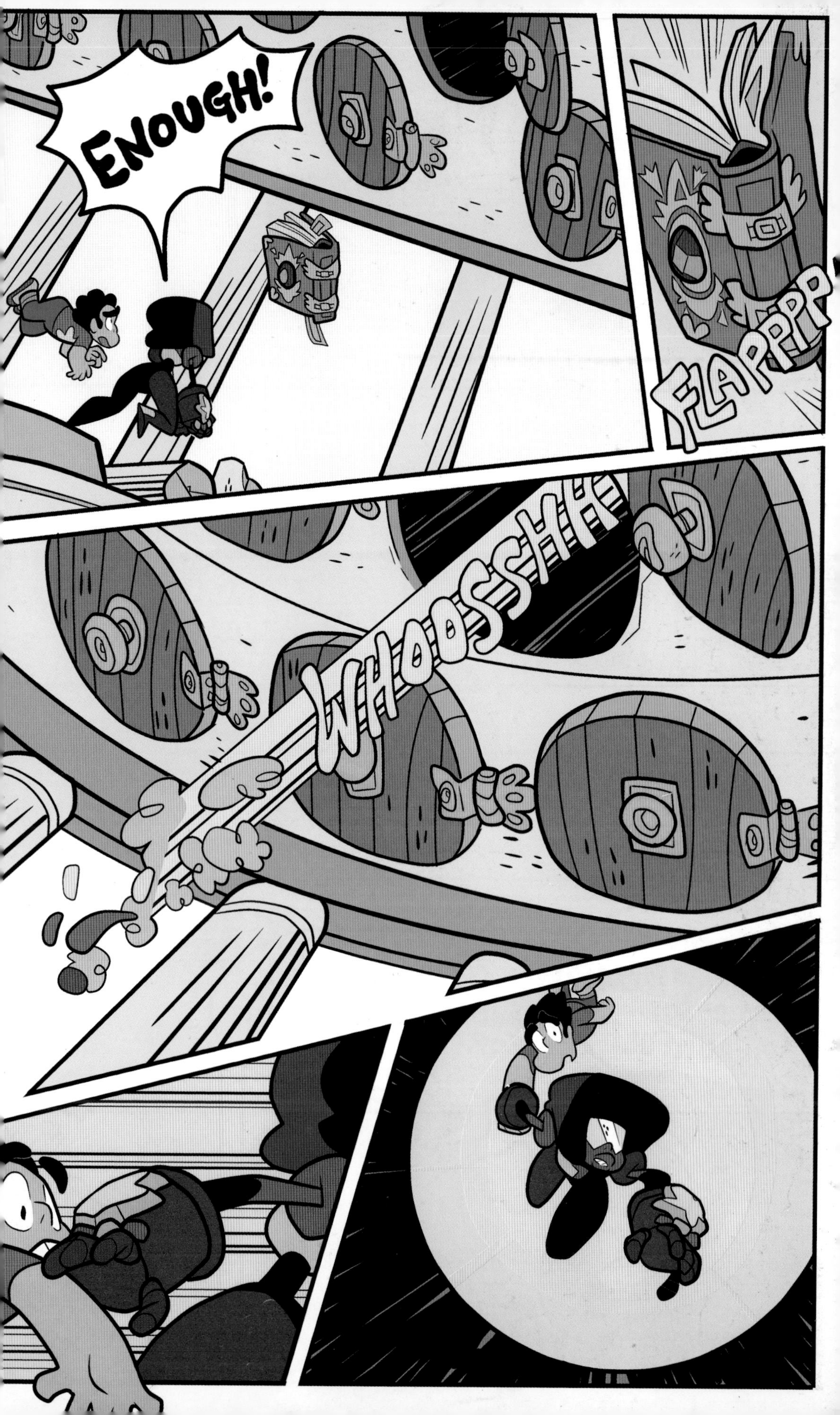
ENOUGH!
FLAPPPP
WHOOSSHH

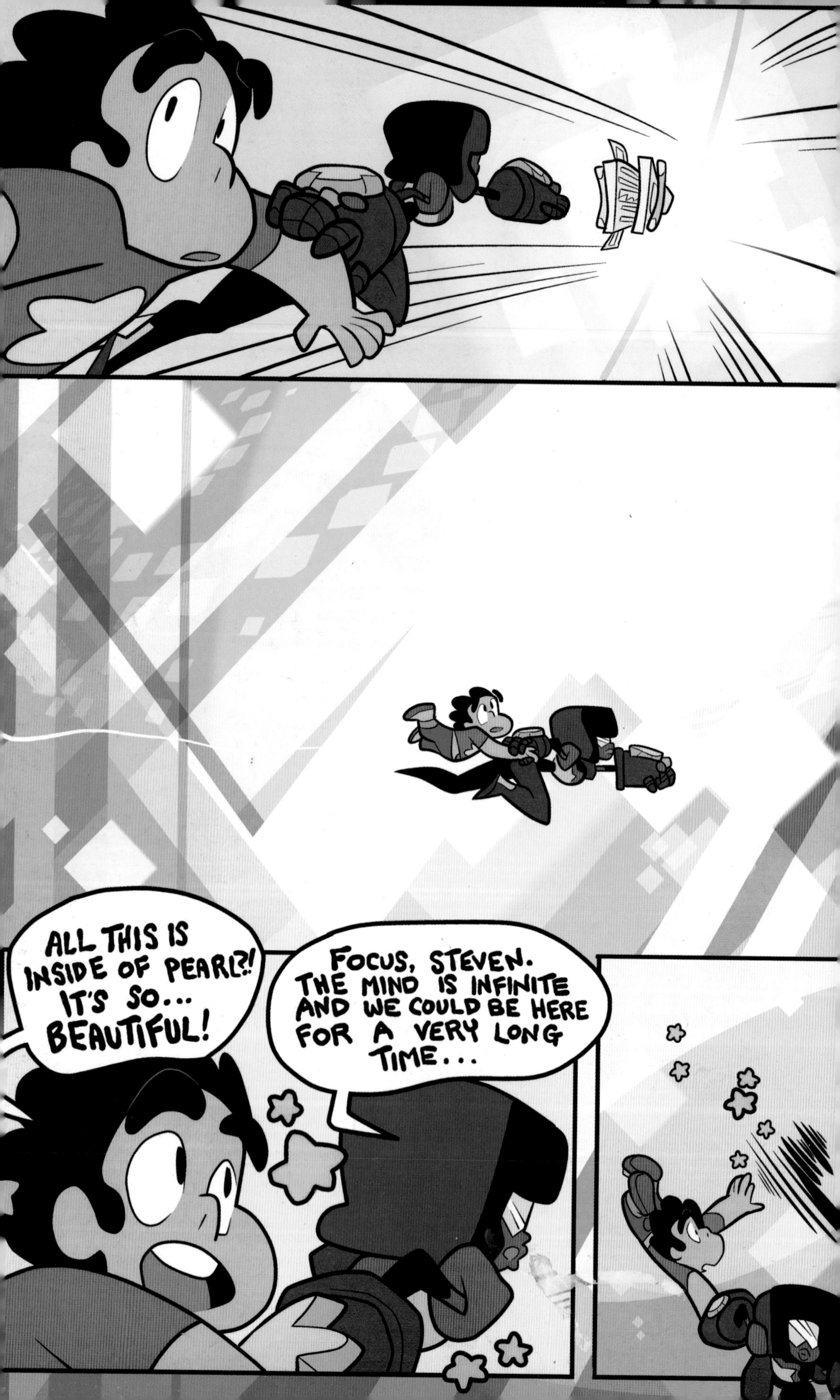
ALL THIS IS INSIDE OF PEARL?! IT'S SO... BEAUTIFUL!
FOCUS, STEVEN. THE MIND IS INFINITE AND WE COULD BE HERE FOR A VERY LONG TIME...

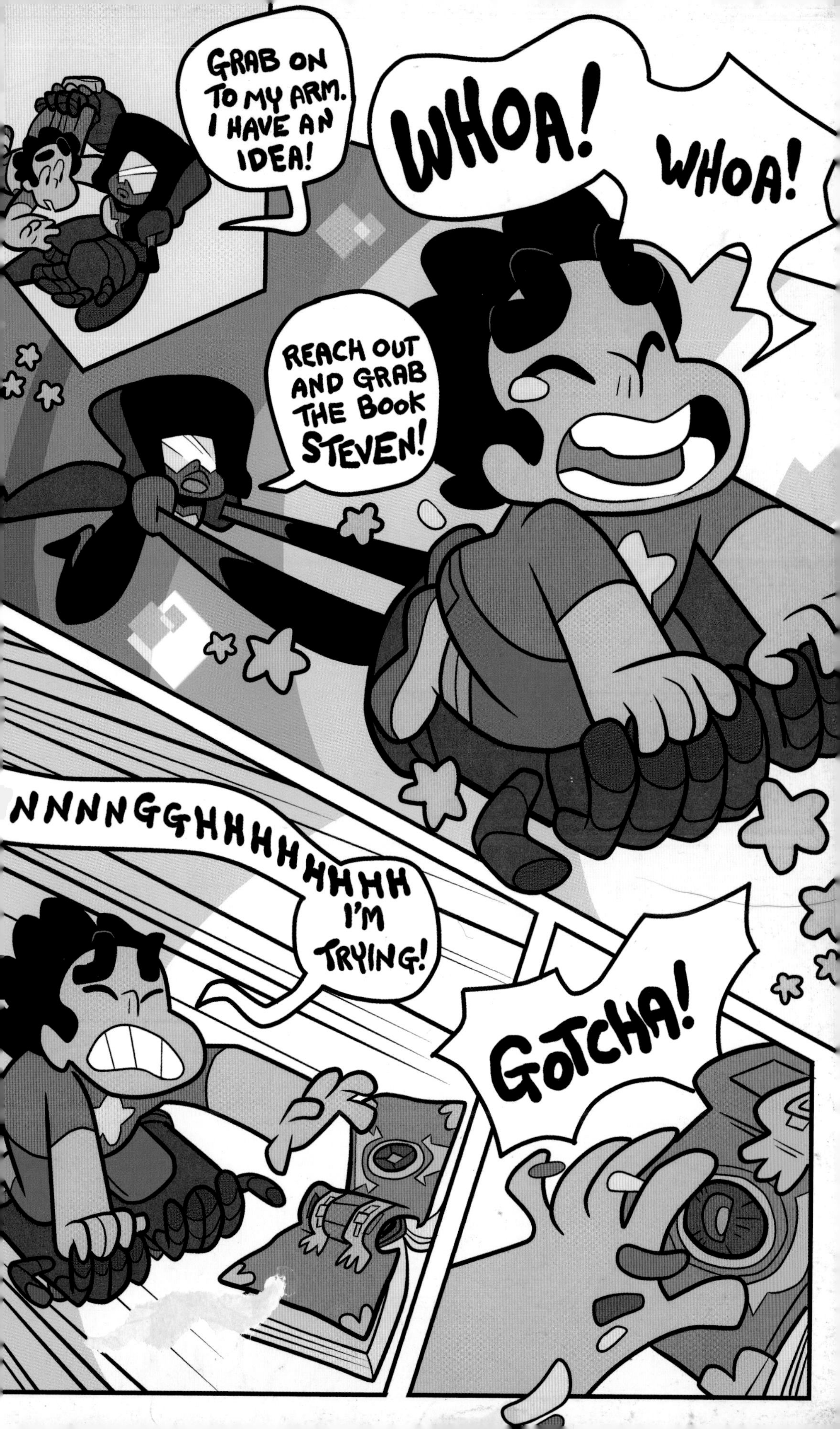
GRAB ON TO MY ARM. I HAVE AN IDEA!
WHOA!
WHOA!
REACH OUT AND GRAB THE BOOK STEVEN!
NNNNGGHHHHHHHHHH I'M TRYING!
GOTCHA!

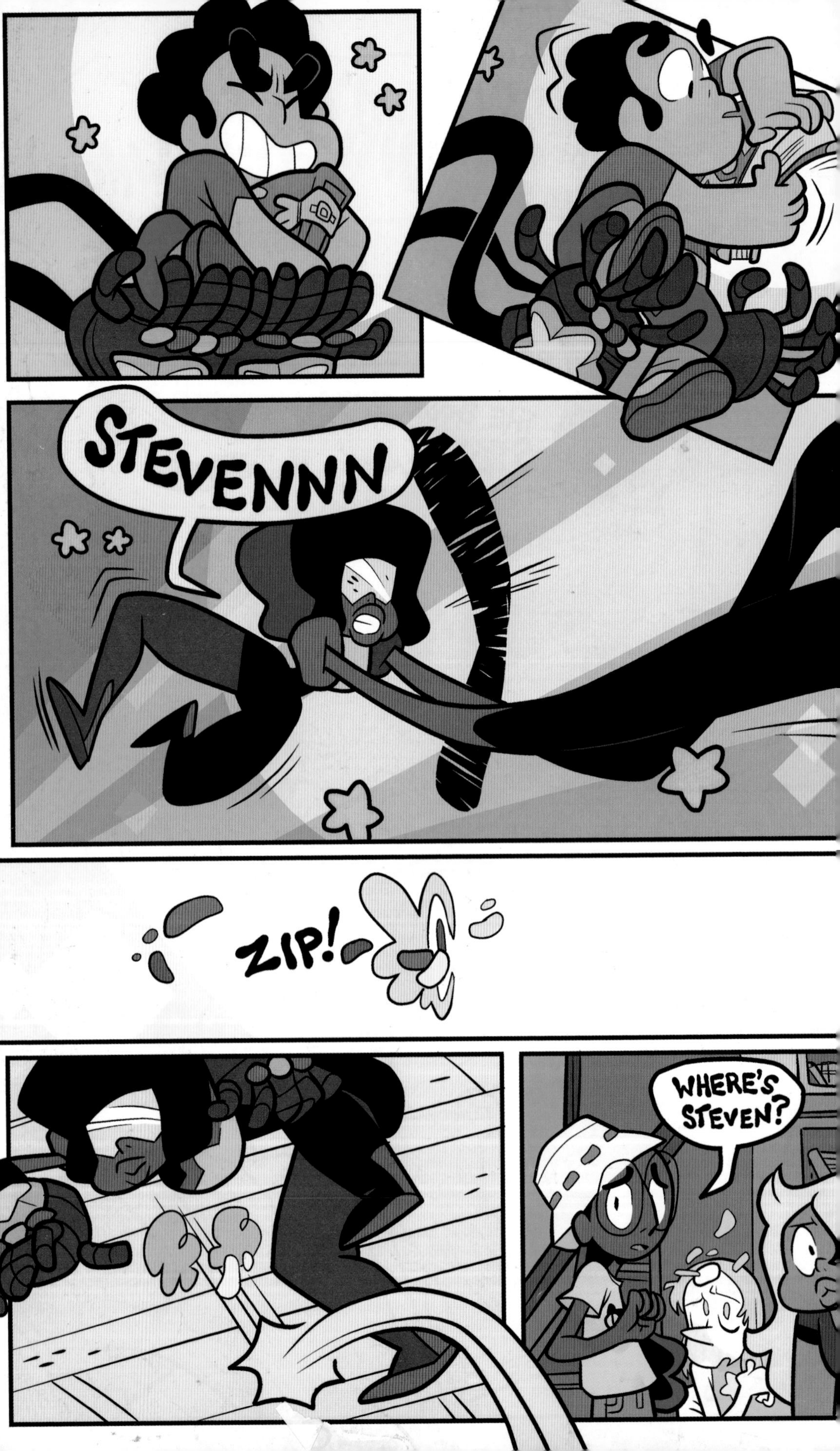
STEVENNN
ZIP!
WHERE'S STEVEN?

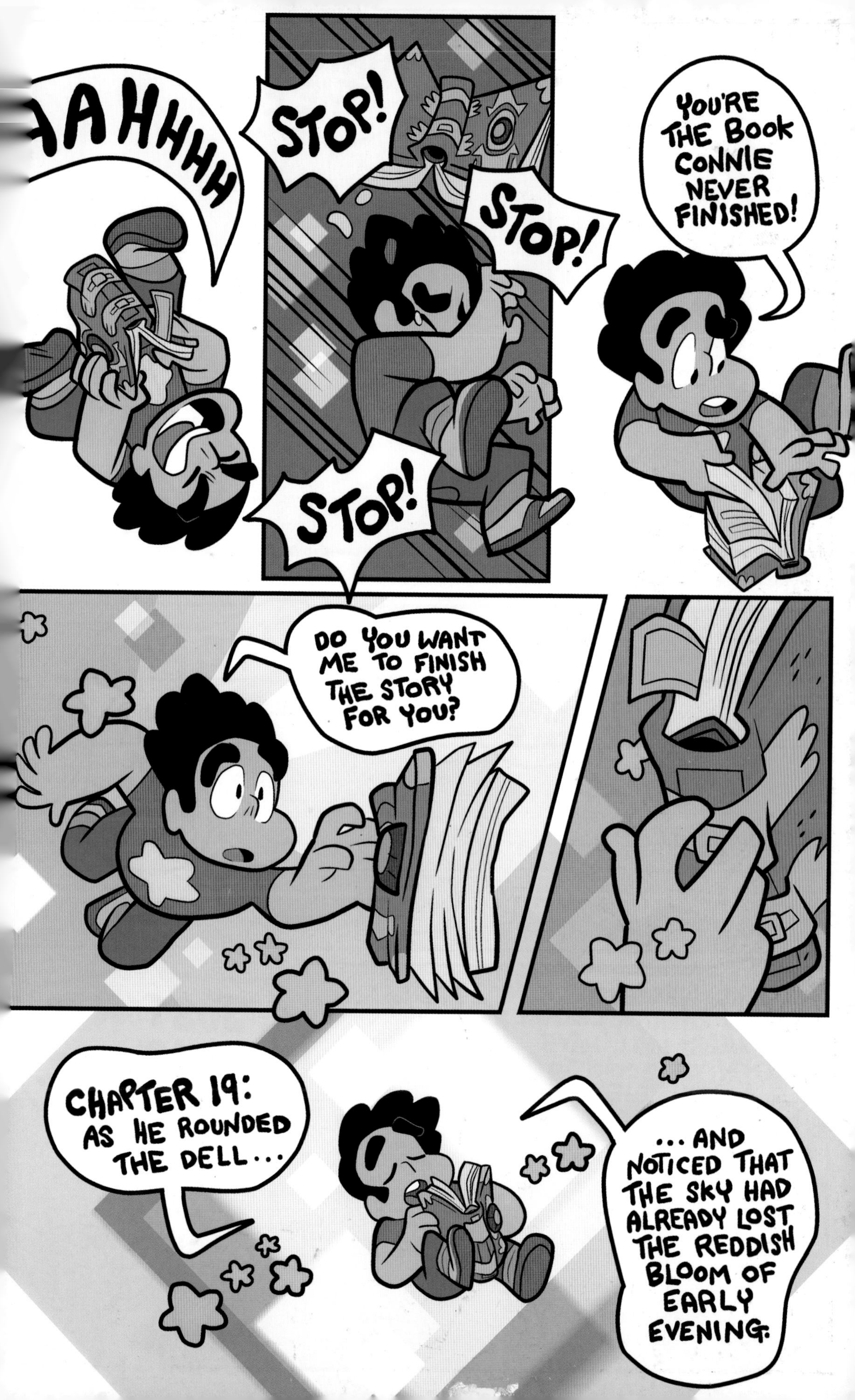
AAHHHHH
STOP!
STOP!
STOP!
YOU'RE THE BOOK CONNIE NEVER FINISHED!
DO YOU WANT ME TO FINISH THE STORY FOR YOU?
CHAPTER 19: AS HE ROUNDED THE DELL...
...AND NOTICED THAT THE SKY HAD ALREADY LOST THE REDDISH BLOOM OF EARLY EVENING.

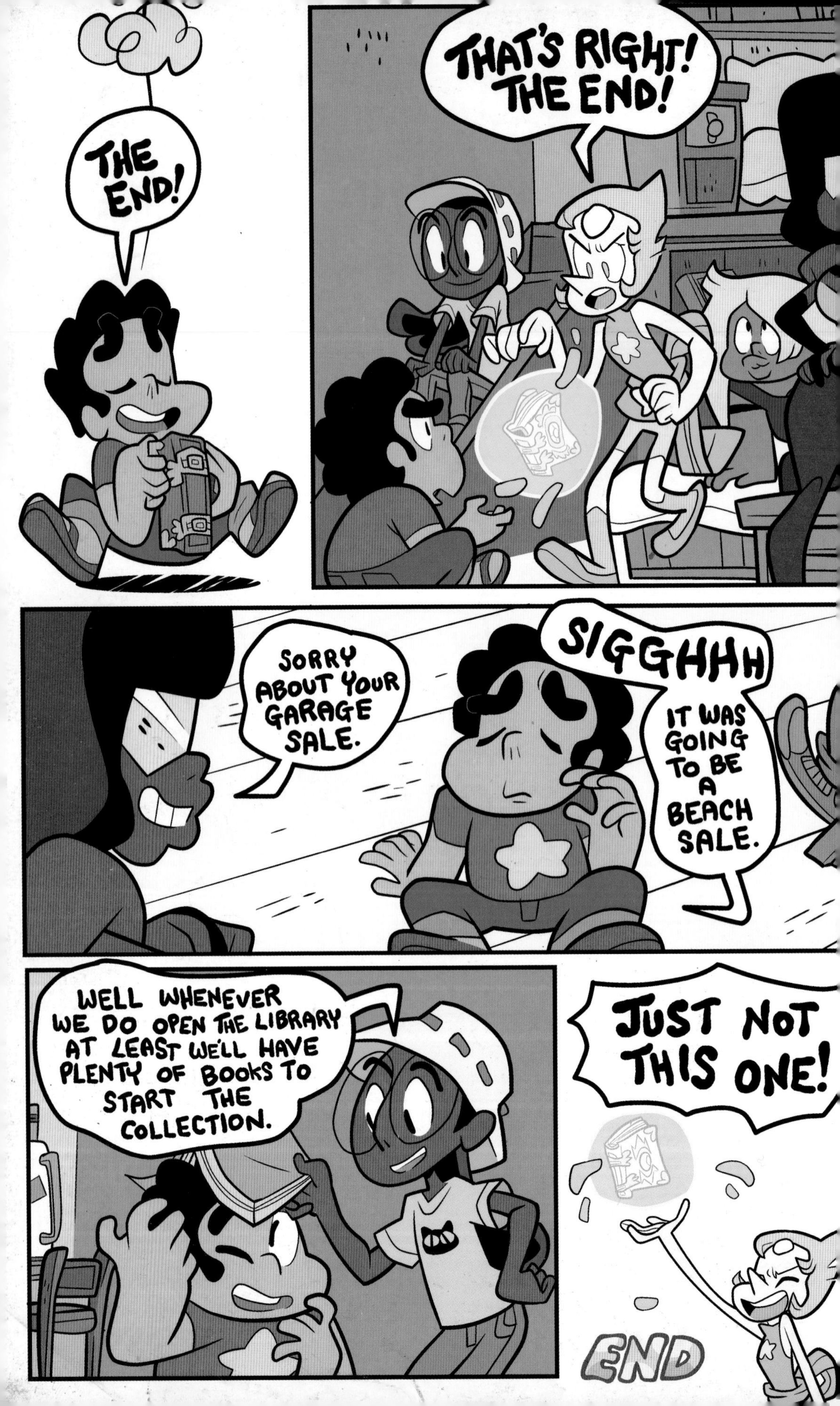
THE END!
THAT'S RIGHT! THE END!
SORRY ABOUT YOUR GARAGE SALE.
SIGGHHH
IT WAS GOING TO BE A BEACH SALE.
WELL WHENEVER WE DO OPEN THE LIBRARY AT LEAST WE'LL HAVE PLENTY OF BOOKS TO START THE COLLECTION.
JUST NOT THIS ONE!
END

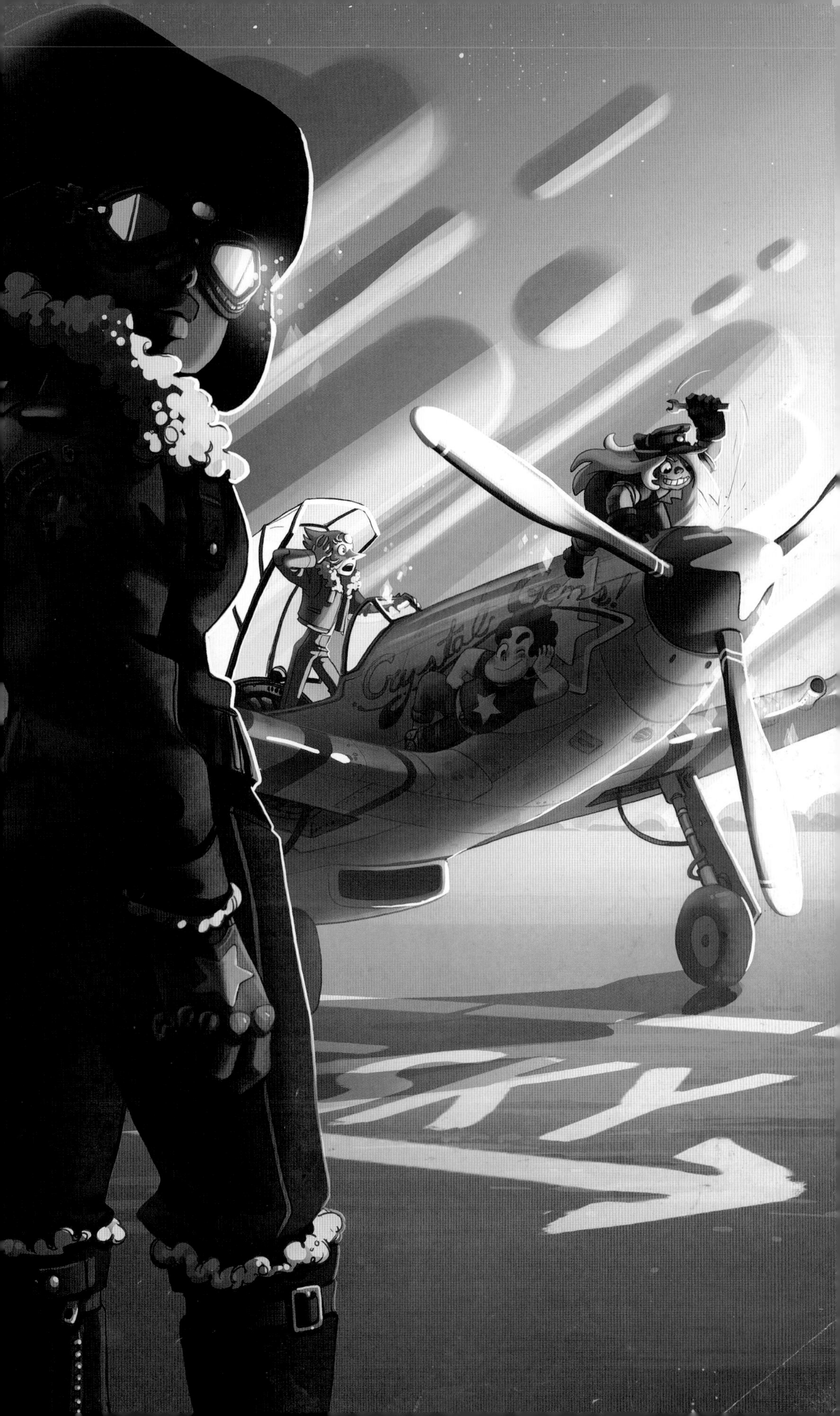
Crystal Gems!

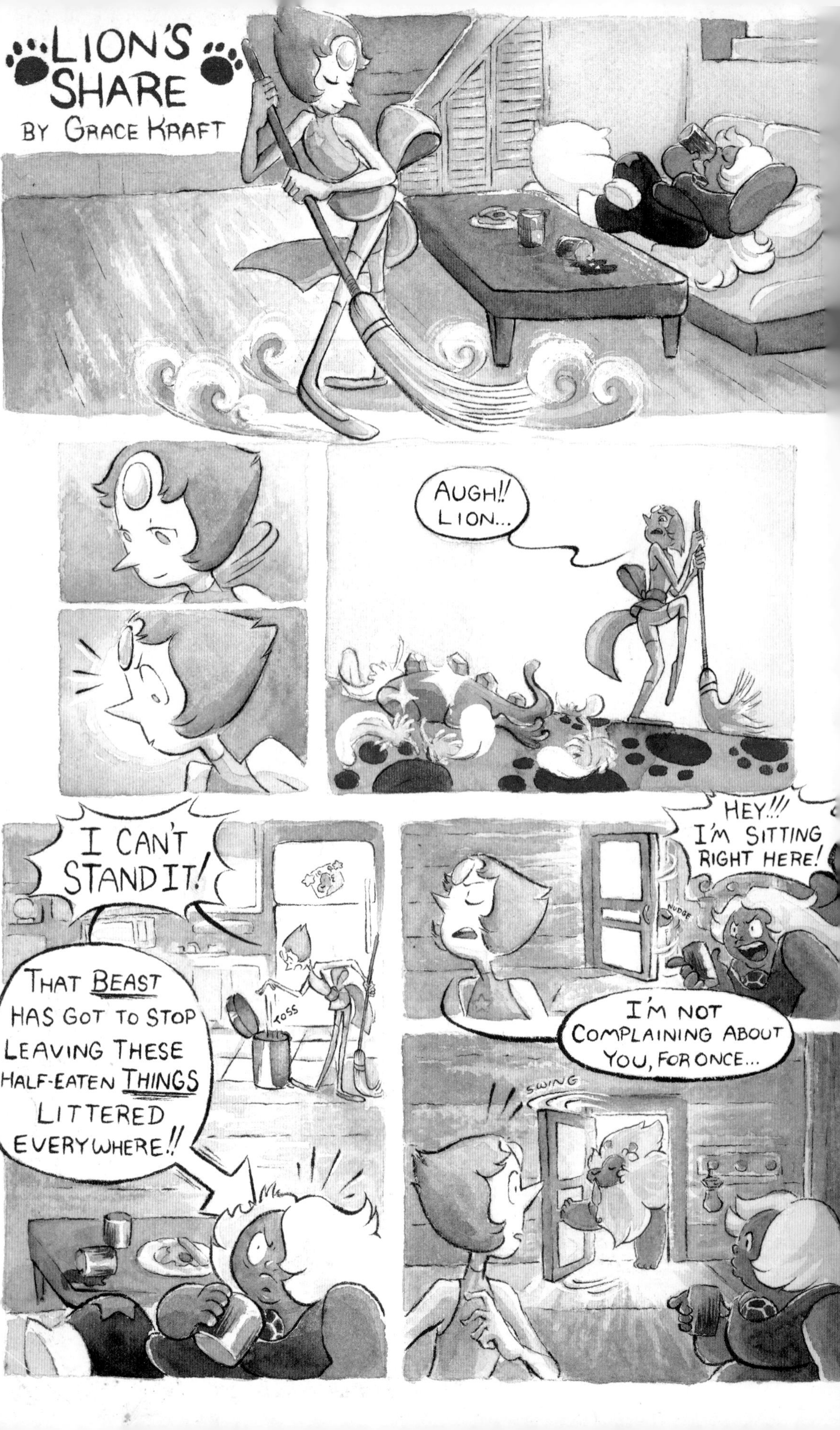
LION'S SHARE
BY GRACE KRAFT
AUGH!! LION...
I CAN'T STAND IT!
TOSS
THAT BEAST HAS GOT TO STOP LEAVING THESE HALF-EATEN THINGS LITTERED EVERYWHERE!!
HEY!!! I'M SITTING RIGHT HERE!
NUDGE
I'M NOT COMPLAINING ABOUT YOU, FOR ONCE...
SWING

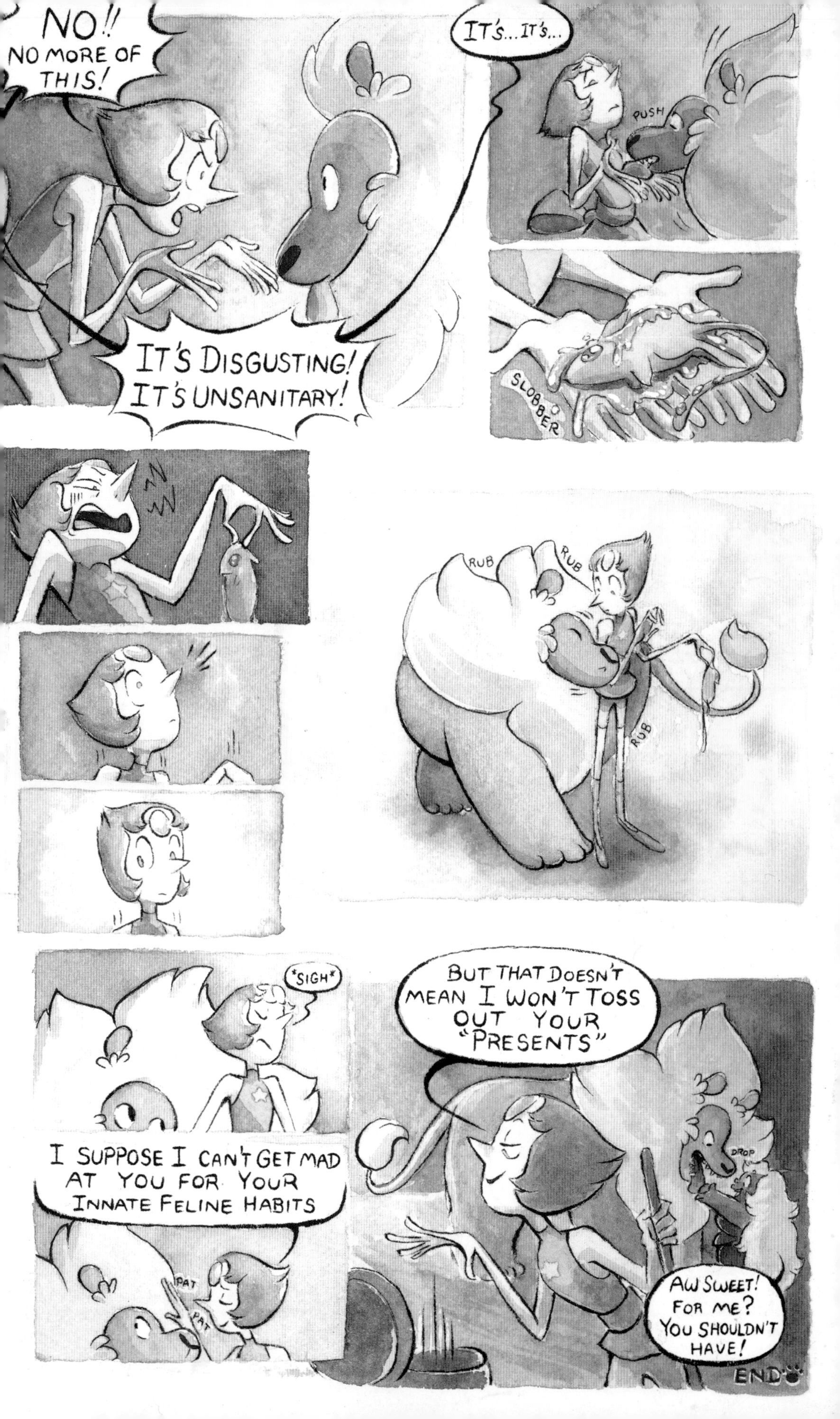
NO!! NO MORE OF THIS!
IT'S DISGUSTING! IT'S UNSANITARY!
IT'S... IT'S...
PUSH
SLOBBER
RUB
RUB
RUB
*SIGH*
I SUPPOSE I CAN'T GET MAD AT YOU FOR YOUR INNATE FELINE HABITS
PAT
PAT
BUT THAT DOESN'T MEAN I WON'T TOSS OUT YOUR "PRESENTS"
DROP
AW SWEET! FOR ME? YOU SHOULDN'T HAVE!
END

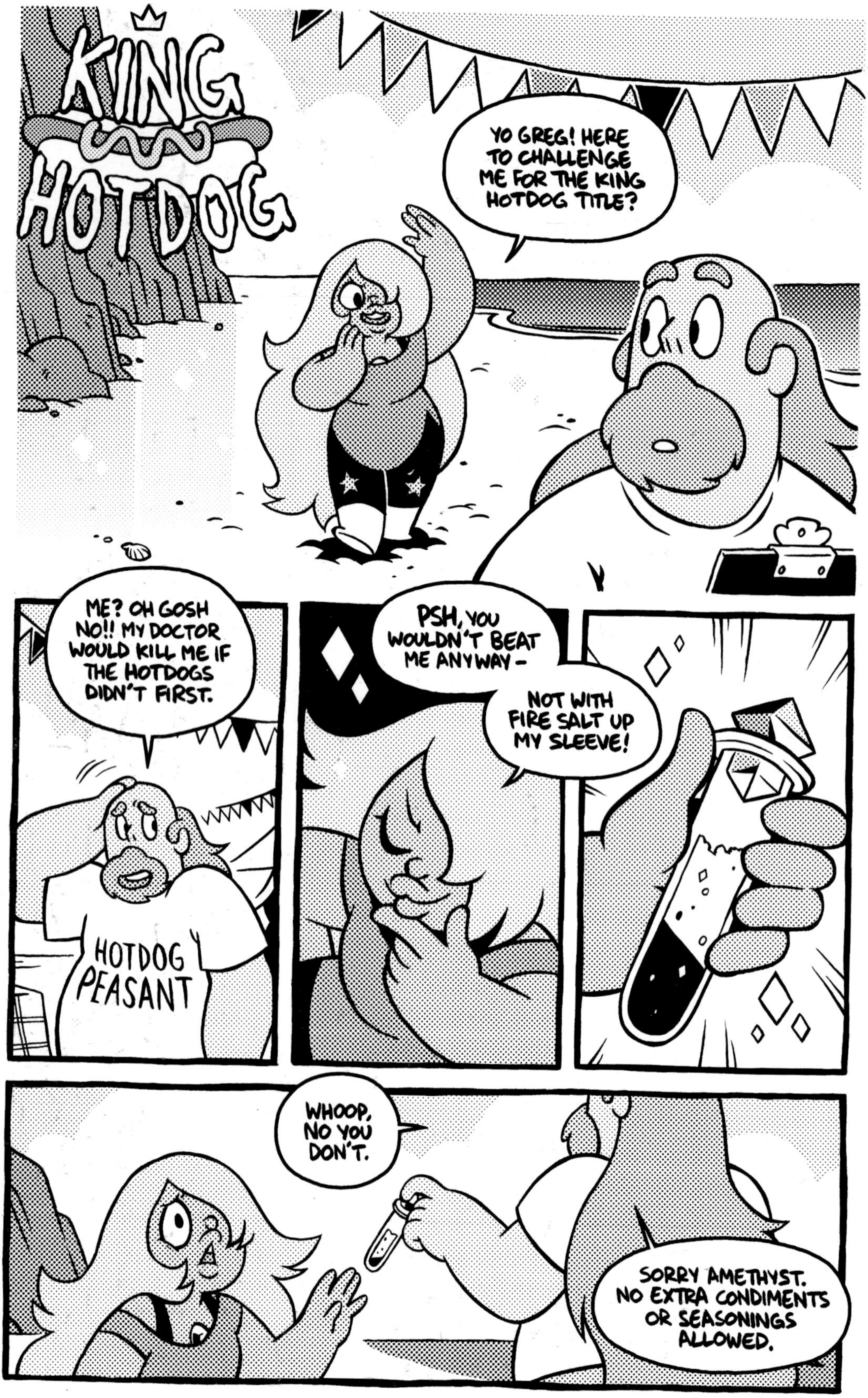
KING HOTDOG
YO GREG! HERE TO CHALLENGE ME FOR THE KING HOTDOG TITLE?
ME? OH GOSH NO!! MY DOCTOR WOULD KILL ME IF THE HOTDOGS DIDN'T FIRST.
HOTDOG PEASANT
PSH, YOU WOULDN'T BEAT ME ANYWAY-
NOT WITH FIRE SALT UP MY SLEEVE!
WHOOP, NO YOU DON'T.
SORRY AMETHYST. NO EXTRA CONDIMENTS OR SEASONINGS ALLOWED.

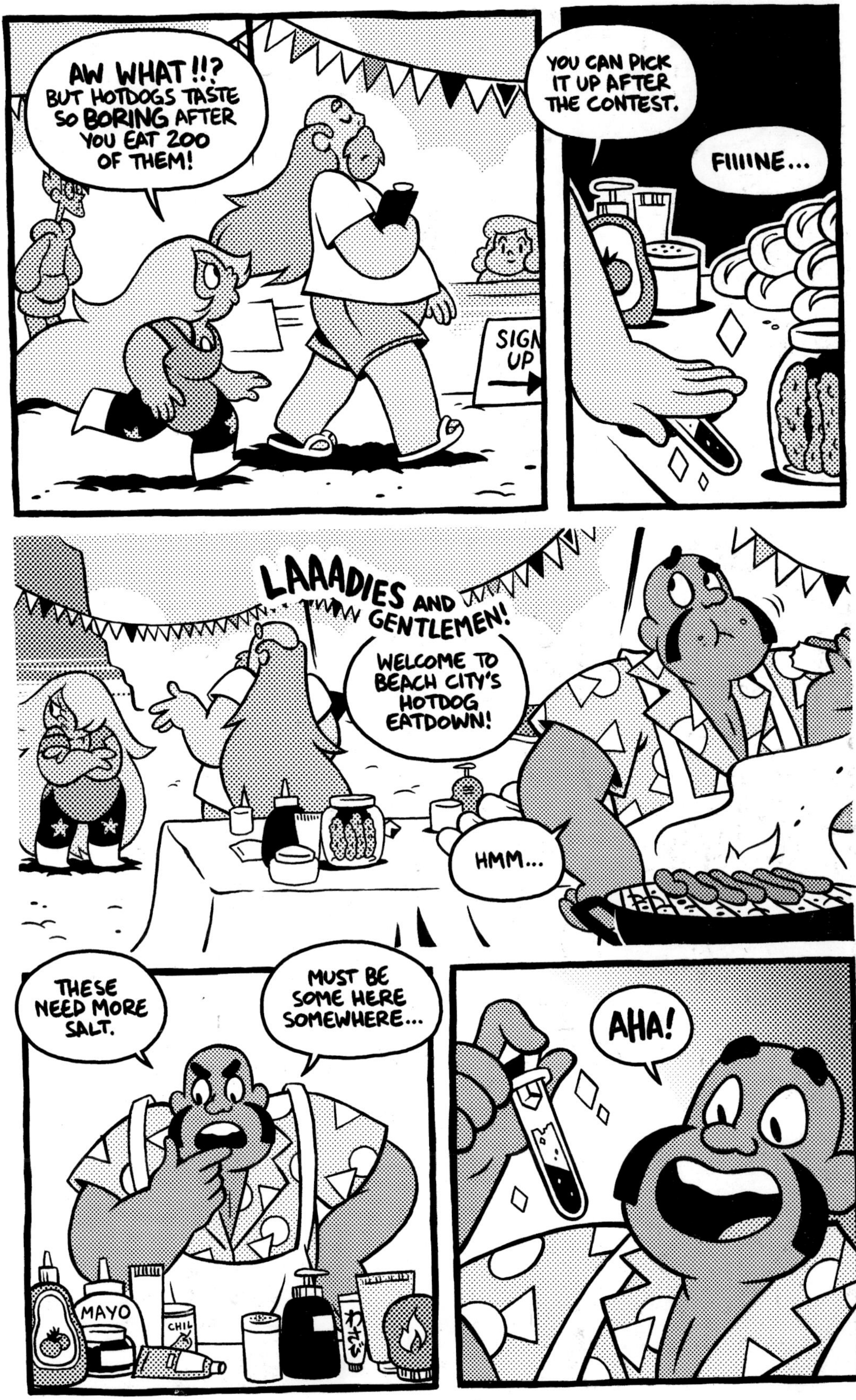
AW WHAT!!? BUT HOTDOGS TASTE SO BORING AFTER YOU EAT 200 OF THEM!
SIGN UP
YOU CAN PICK IT UP AFTER THE CONTEST.
FIIIINE...
LAAADIES AND GENTLEMEN!
WELCOME TO BEACH CITY'S HOTDOG EATDOWN!
HMM...
THESE NEED MORE SALT.
MUST BE SOME HERE SOMEWHERE...
MAYO
AHA!

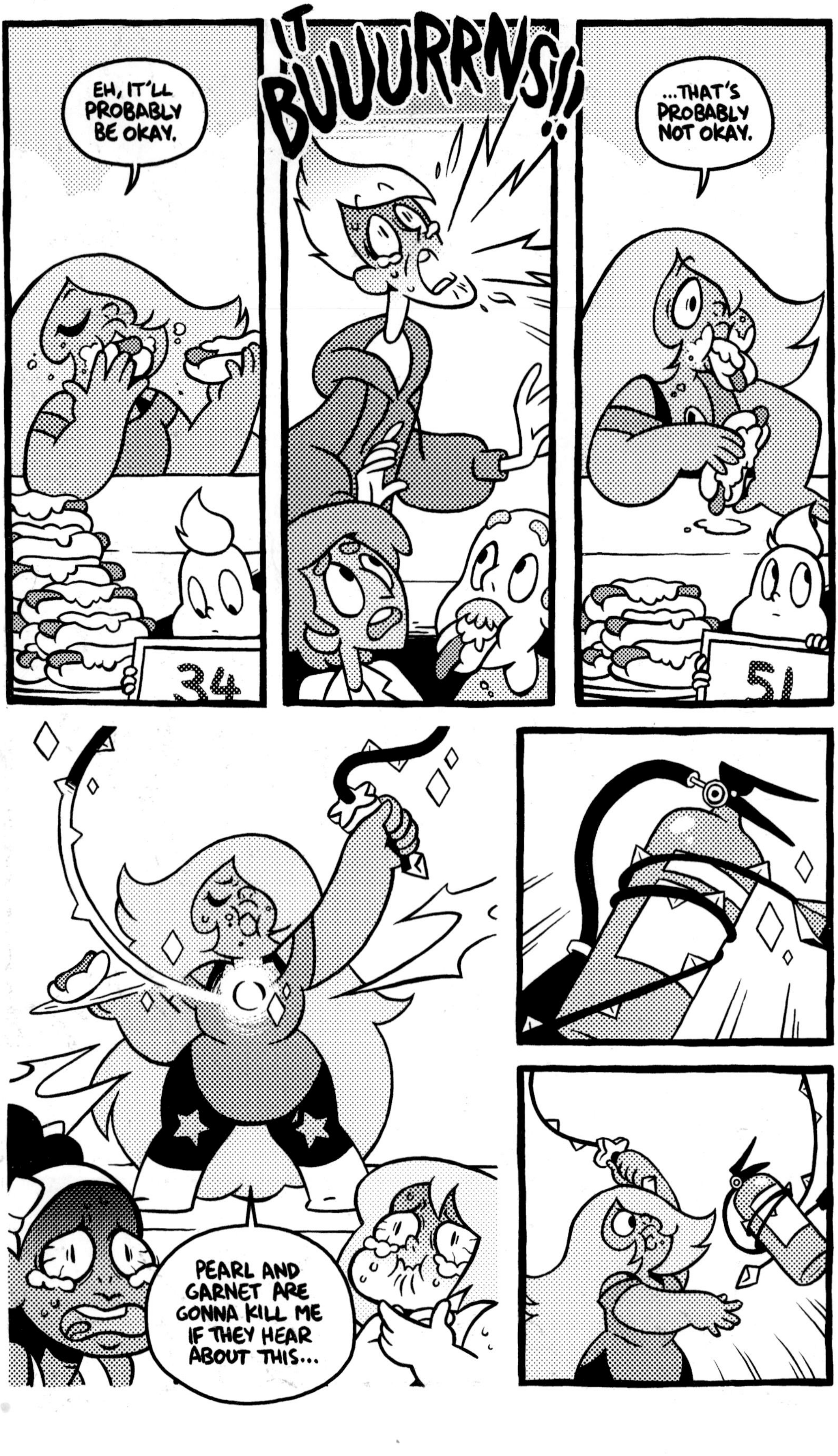
EH, IT'LL PROBABLY BE OKAY.
34
IT BUUURRNS!!
...THAT'S PROBABLY NOT OKAY.
51
PEARL AND GARNET ARE GONNA KILL ME IF THEY HEAR ABOUT THIS...

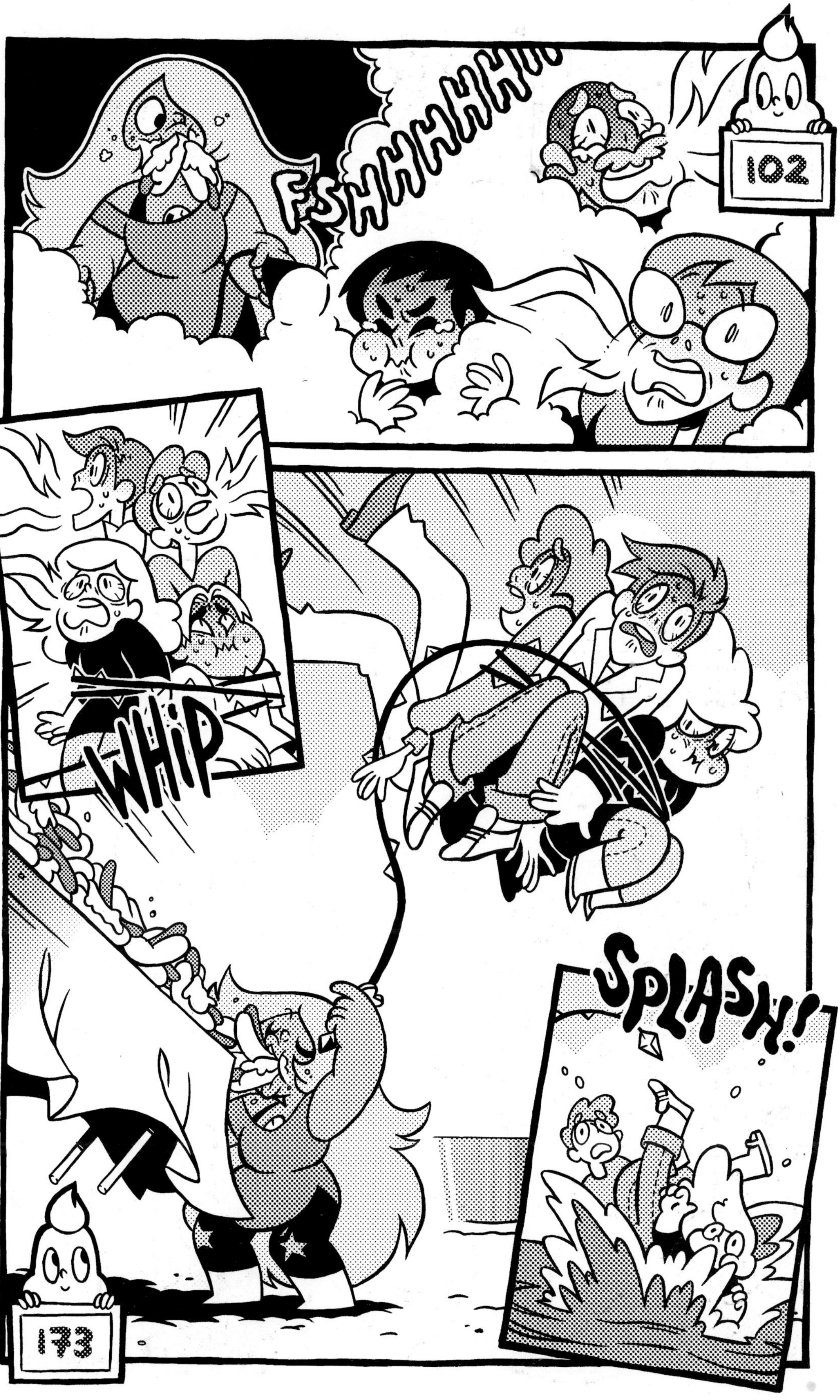
FSHHHHHH
102
WHIP
SPLASH!
173

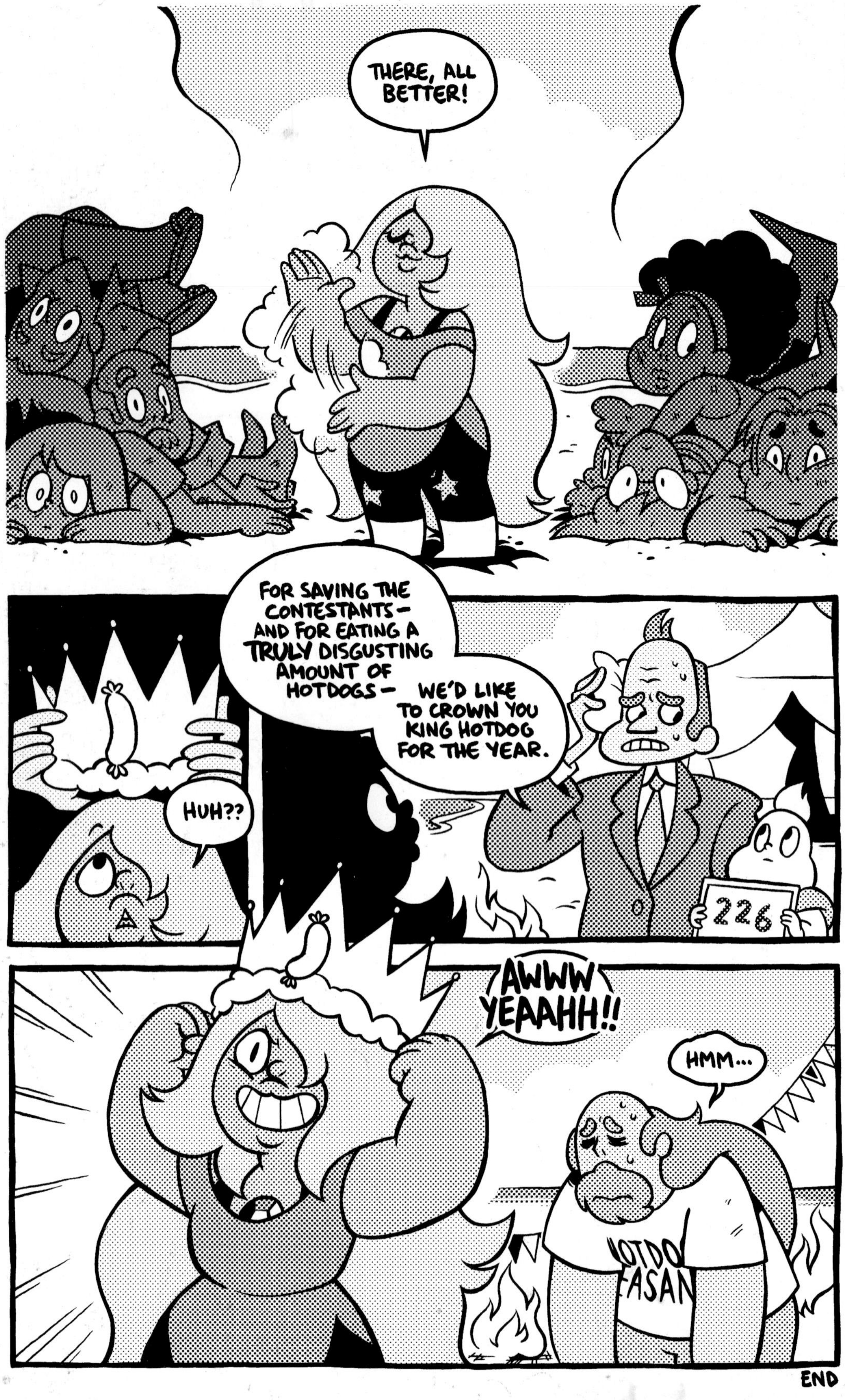
THERE, ALL BETTER!
FOR SAVING THE CONTESTANTS— AND FOR EATING A TRULY DISGUSTING AMOUNT OF HOTDOGS—
WE'D LIKE TO CROWN YOU KING HOTDOG FOR THE YEAR.
HUH??
226
AWWW YEAAHH!!
HMM...
END

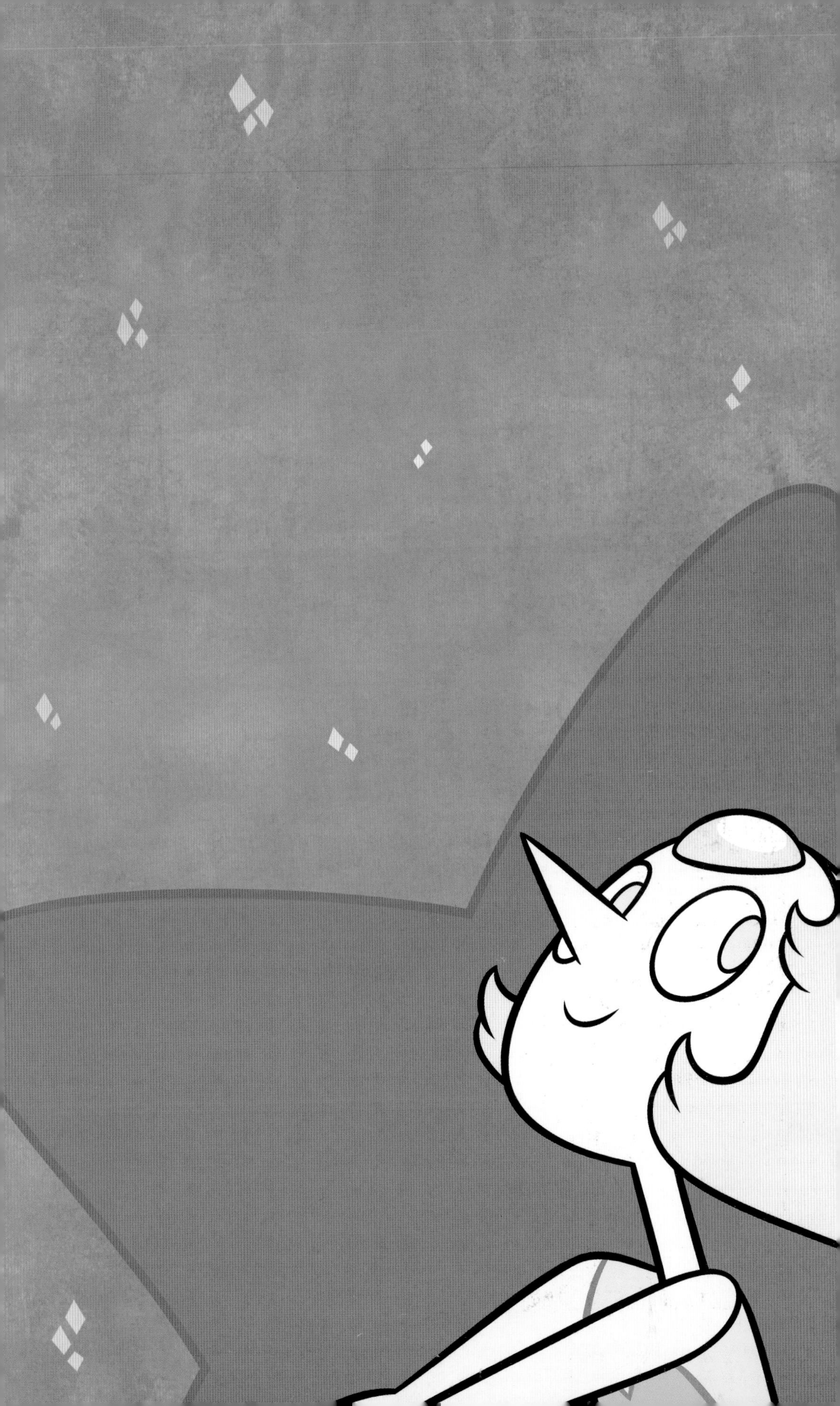

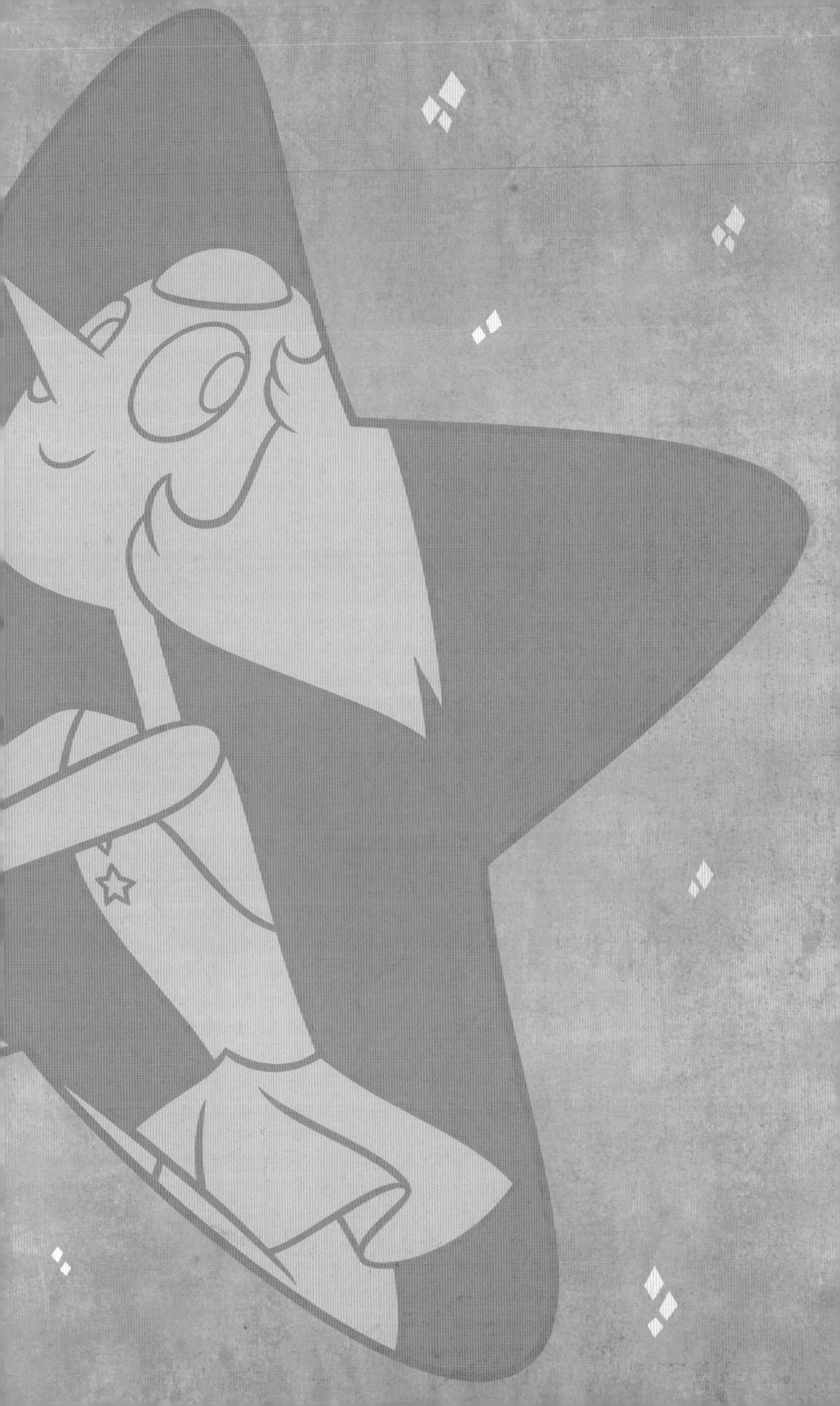

# "STORYTIME"

also featuring:

"CAR TROUBLE"
written & illustrated by
**GRACE KRAFT**

"GARDEN"
illustrated by
**REBEKKA DUNLAP**

"MEAN LOOK"
written by
**JOSCELINE FENTON**
illustrated by
**MAD RUPERT**

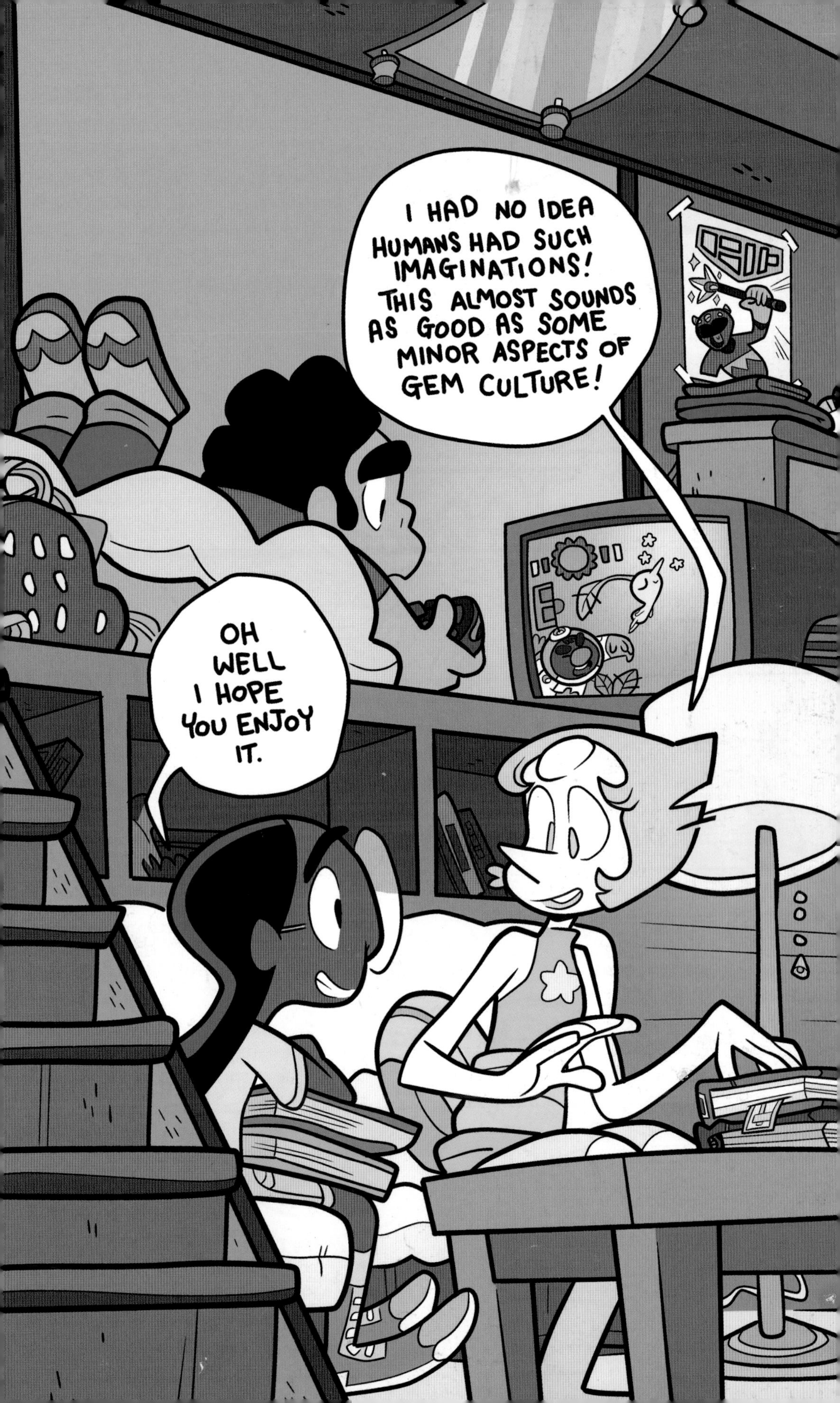
I HAD NO IDEA HUMANS HAD SUCH IMAGINATIONS! THIS ALMOST SOUNDS AS GOOD AS SOME MINOR ASPECTS OF GEM CULTURE!
OH WELL I HOPE YOU ENJOY IT.

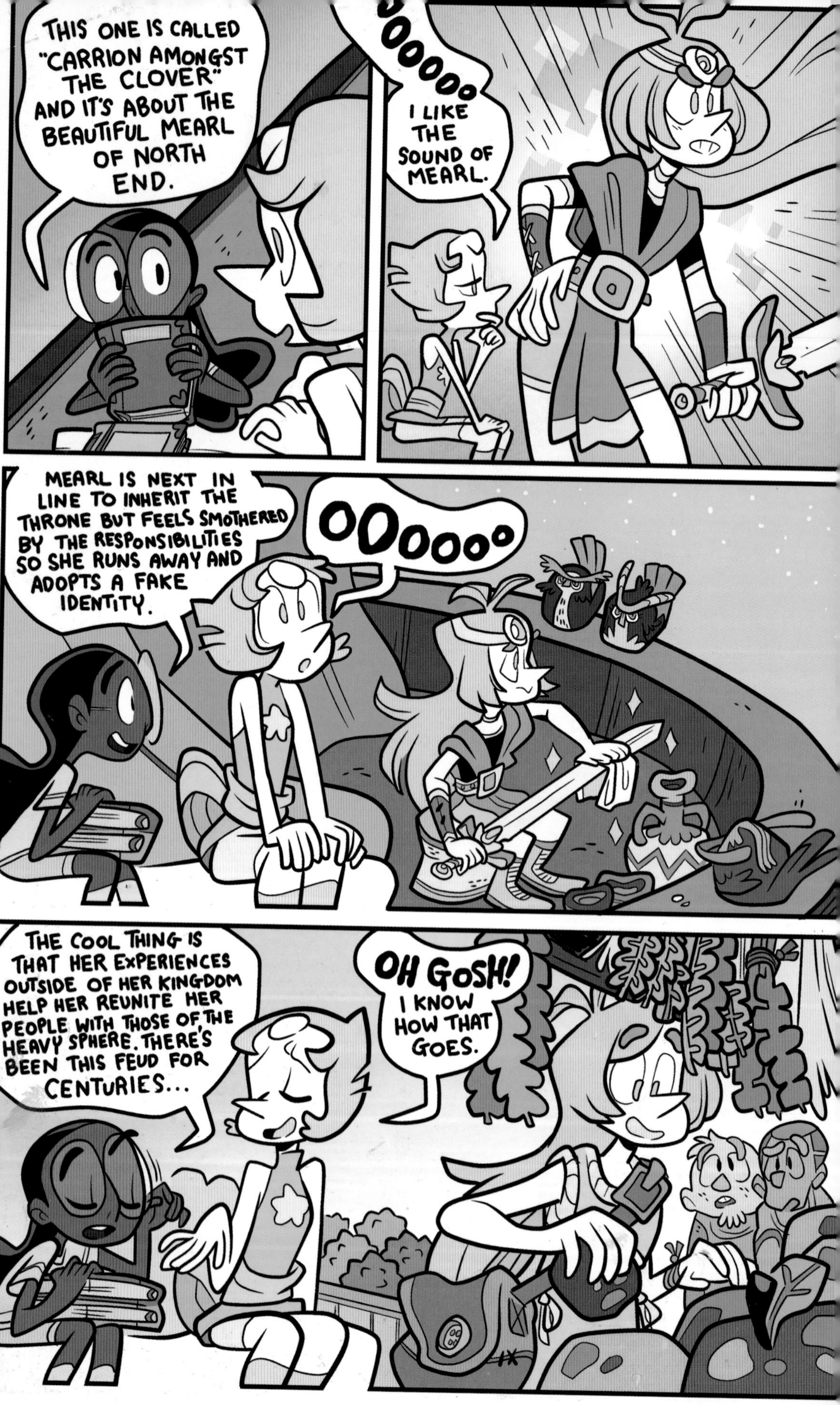
THIS ONE IS CALLED "CARRION AMONGST THE CLOVER" AND IT'S ABOUT THE BEAUTIFUL MEARL OF NORTH END.
OOOOOO
I LIKE THE SOUND OF MEARL.
MEARL IS NEXT IN LINE TO INHERIT THE THRONE BUT FEELS SMOTHERED BY THE RESPONSIBILITIES SO SHE RUNS AWAY AND ADOPTS A FAKE IDENTITY.
OOOOOO
THE COOL THING IS THAT HER EXPERIENCES OUTSIDE OF HER KINGDOM HELP HER REUNITE HER PEOPLE WITH THOSE OF THE HEAVY SPHERE. THERE'S BEEN THIS FEUD FOR CENTURIES...
OH GOSH! I KNOW HOW THAT GOES.

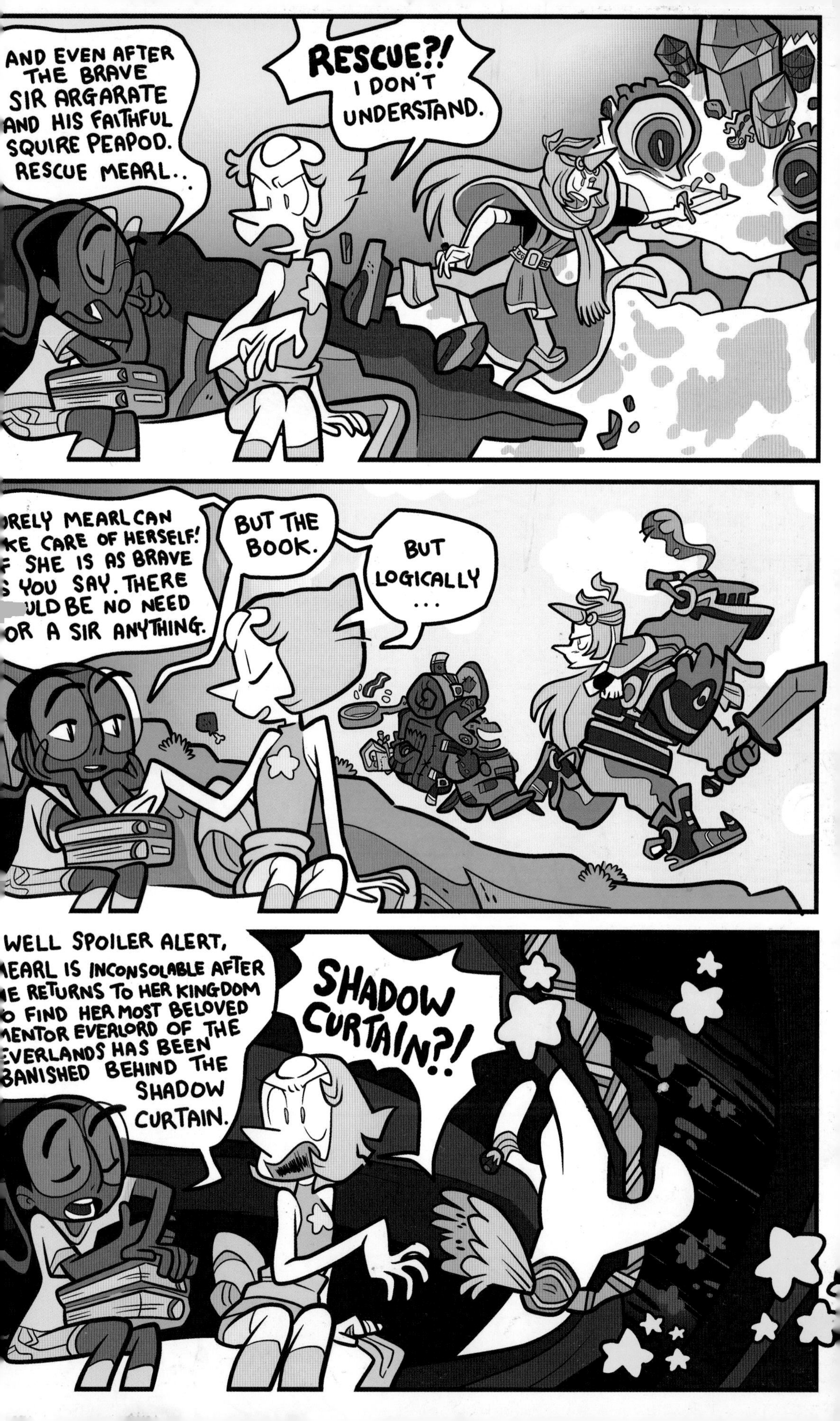
AND EVEN AFTER THE BRAVE SIR ARGARATE AND HIS FAITHFUL SQUIRE PEAPOD. RESCUE MEARL..
RESCUE?! I DON'T UNDERSTAND.
RELY MEARL CAN
KE CARE OF HERSELF!
F SHE IS AS BRAVE
S YOU SAY. THERE
ULD BE NO NEED
OR A SIR ANYTHING.
BUT THE BOOK.
BUT LOGICALLY ...
WELL SPOILER ALERT,
EARL IS INCONSOLABLE AFTER
E RETURNS TO HER KINGDOM
O FIND HER MOST BELOVED
ENTOR EVERLORD OF THE
VERLANDS HAS BEEN
BANISHED BEHIND THE
SHADOW CURTAIN.
SHADOW CURTAIN?!

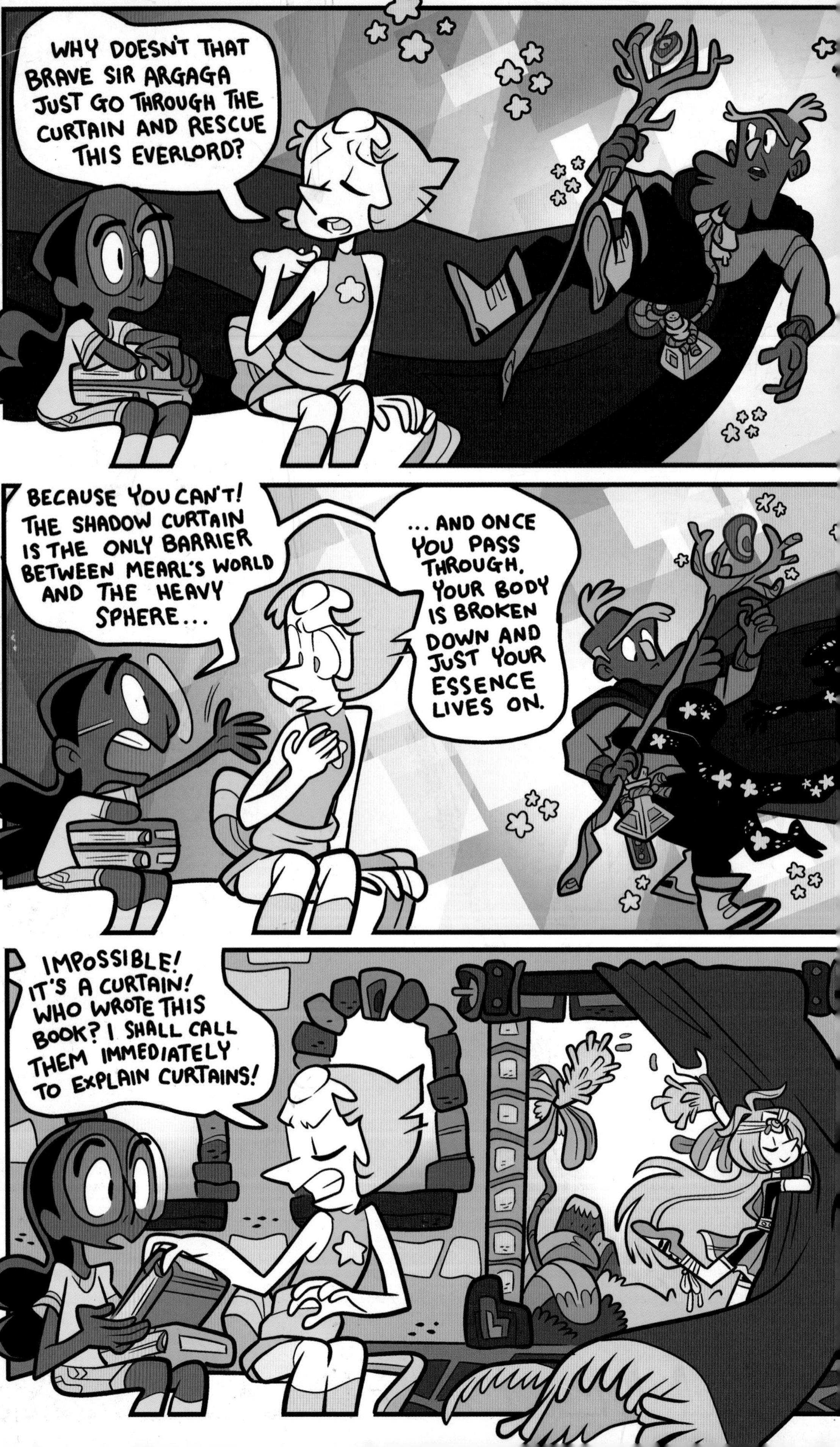
WHY DOESN'T THAT BRAVE SIR ARGAGA JUST GO THROUGH THE CURTAIN AND RESCUE THIS EVERLORD?
BECAUSE YOU CAN'T! THE SHADOW CURTAIN IS THE ONLY BARRIER BETWEEN MEARL'S WORLD AND THE HEAVY SPHERE...
...AND ONCE YOU PASS THROUGH, YOUR BODY IS BROKEN DOWN AND JUST YOUR ESSENCE LIVES ON.
IMPOSSIBLE! IT'S A CURTAIN! WHO WROTE THIS BOOK? I SHALL CALL THEM IMMEDIATELY TO EXPLAIN CURTAINS!

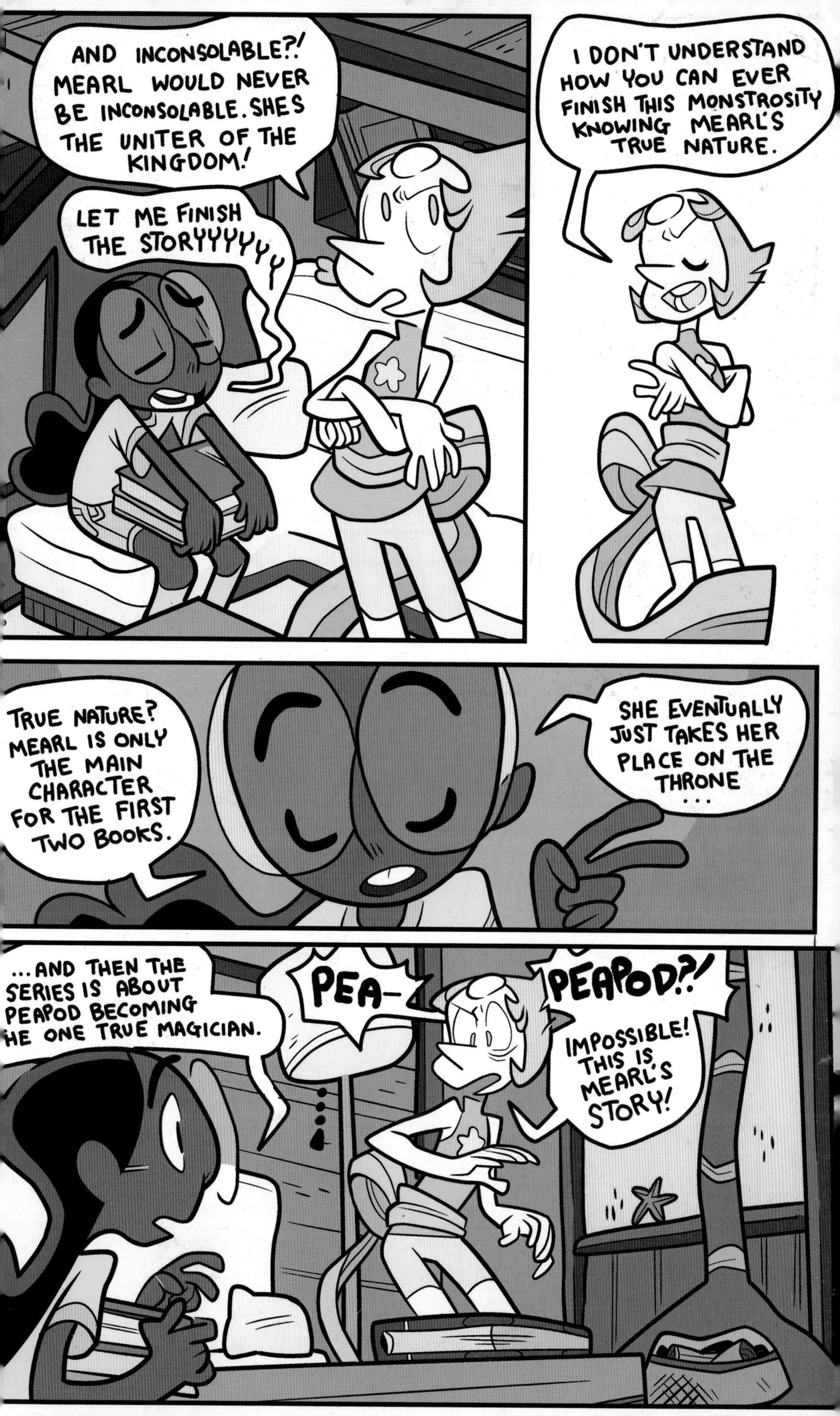
AND INCONSOLABLE?! MEARL WOULD NEVER BE INCONSOLABLE. SHES THE UNITER OF THE KINGDOM!
LET ME FINISH THE STORYYYYYYY
I DON'T UNDERSTAND HOW YOU CAN EVER FINISH THIS MONSTROSITY KNOWING MEARL'S TRUE NATURE.
TRUE NATURE? MEARL IS ONLY THE MAIN CHARACTER FOR THE FIRST TWO BOOKS.
SHE EVENTUALLY JUST TAKES HER PLACE ON THE THRONE ...
...AND THEN THE SERIES IS ABOUT PEAPOD BECOMING HE ONE TRUE MAGICIAN.
PEA-
PEAPOD?!
IMPOSSIBLE! THIS IS MEARL'S STORY!

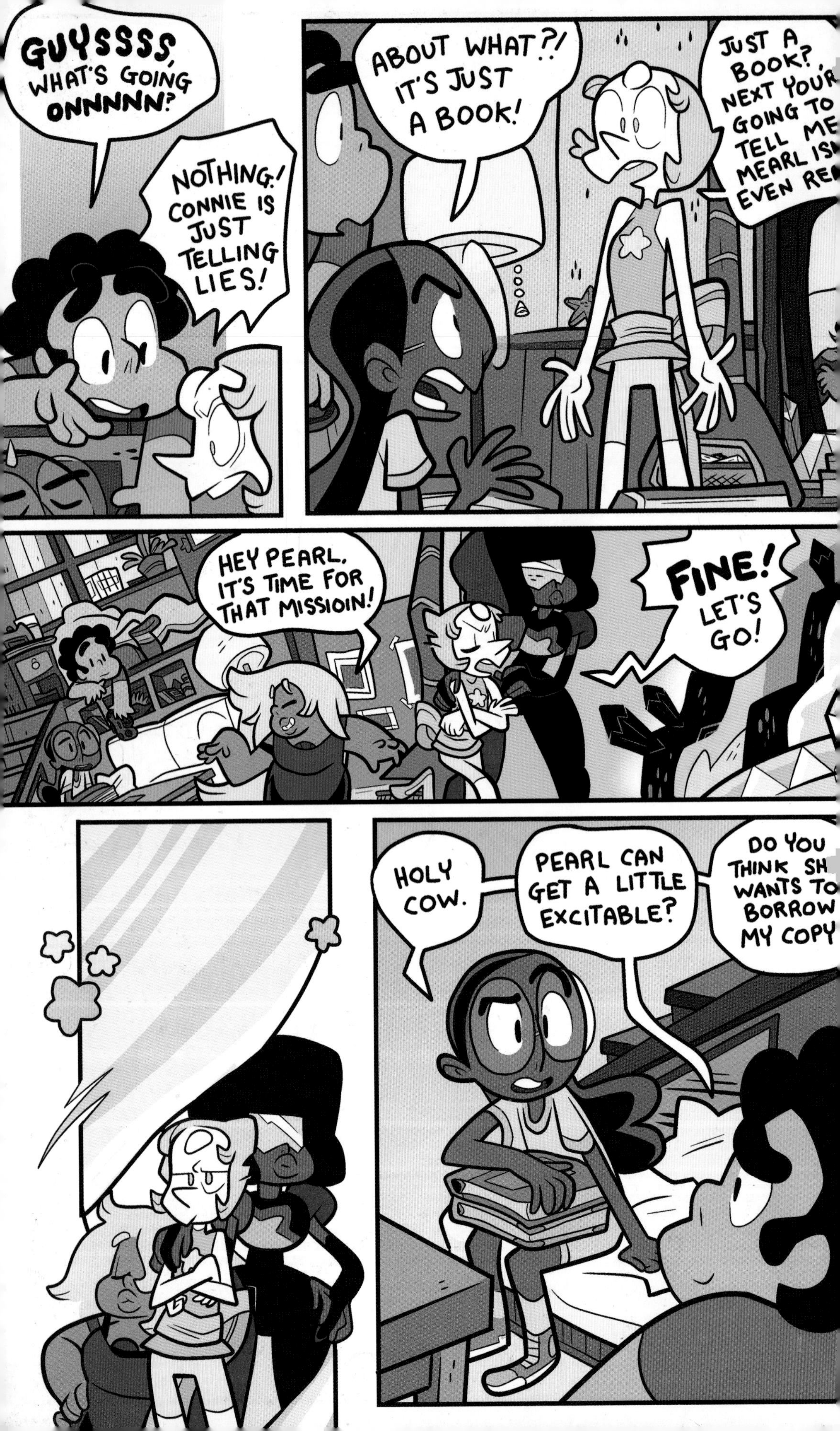
GUYSSSS, WHAT'S GOING ONNNNN?
NOTHING! CONNIE IS JUST TELLING LIES!
ABOUT WHAT?!! IT'S JUST A BOOK!
JUST A BOOK?, NEXT YOUR GOING TO TELL ME MEARL IS
EVEN RE
HEY PEARL, IT'S TIME FOR THAT MISSIOIN!
FINE! LET'S GO!
HOLY COW.
PEARL CAN GET A LITTLE EXCITABLE?
DO YOU THINK SH WANTS TO BORROW MY COPY

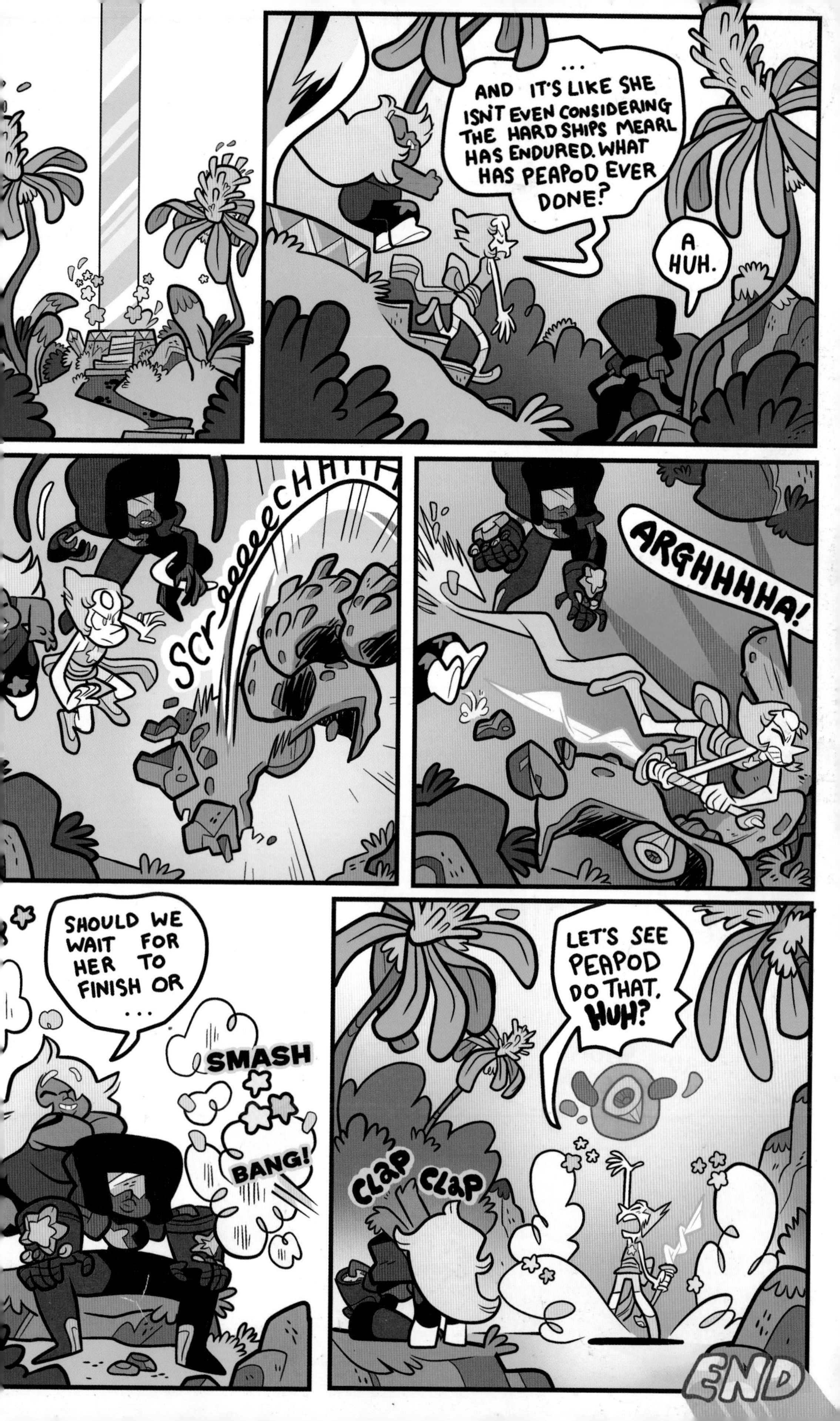

... AND IT'S LIKE SHE ISN'T EVEN CONSIDERING THE HARDSHIPS MEARL HAS ENDURED. WHAT HAS PEAPOD EVER DONE?
A HUH.
SCREEEEEECHHH
ARGHHHHHA!
SHOULD WE WAIT FOR HER TO FINISH OR ...
SMASH
BANG!
LET'S SEE PEAPOD DO THAT, HUH?
CLAP CLAP
END

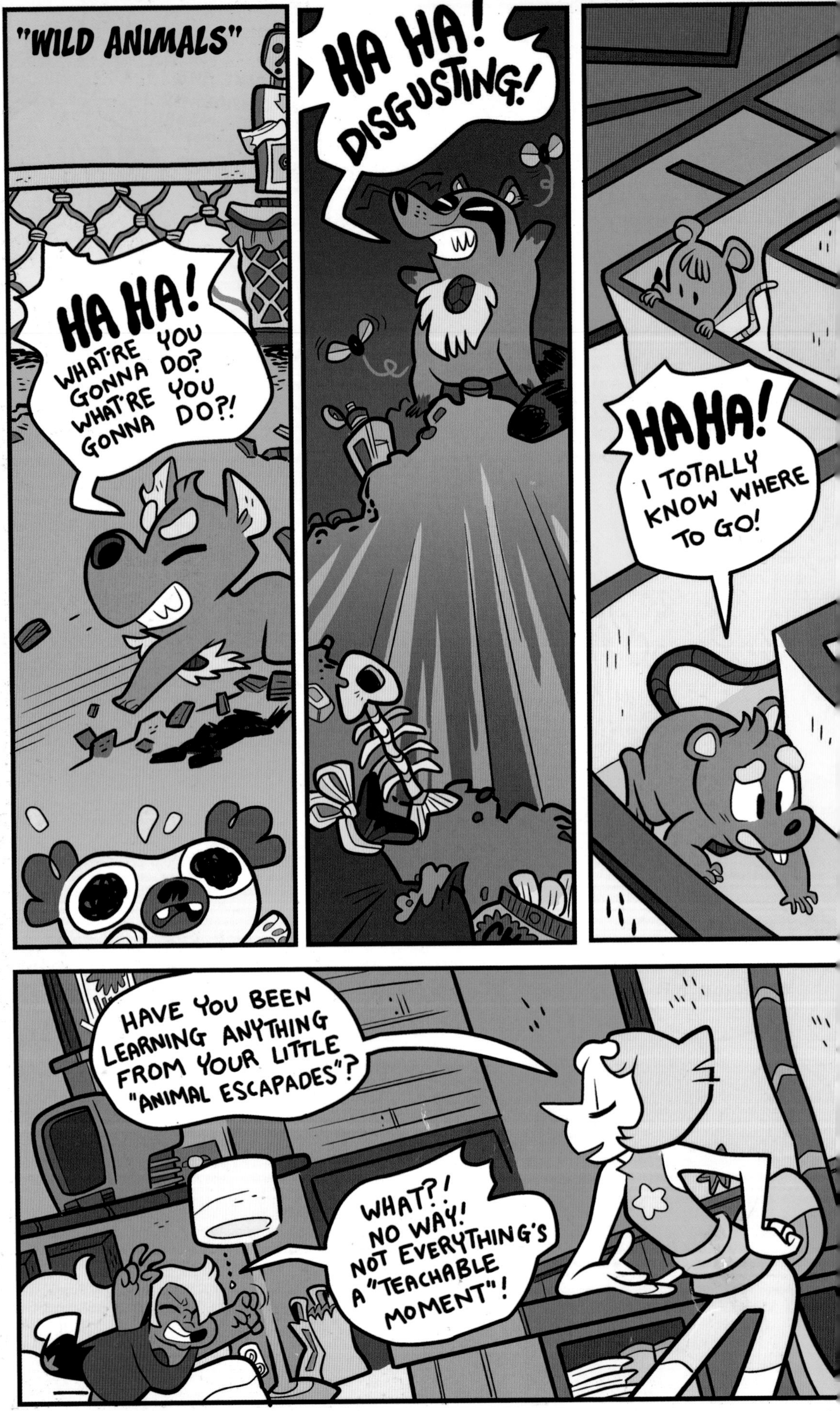

"WILD ANIMALS"
HA HA! WHAT'RE YOU GONNA DO? WHAT'RE YOU GONNA DO?!
HA HA! DISGUSTING!
HA HA! I TOTALLY KNOW WHERE TO GO!
HAVE YOU BEEN LEARNING ANYTHING FROM YOUR LITTLE "ANIMAL ESCAPADES"?
WHAT?! NO WAY! NOT EVERYTHING'S A "TEACHABLE MOMENT"!

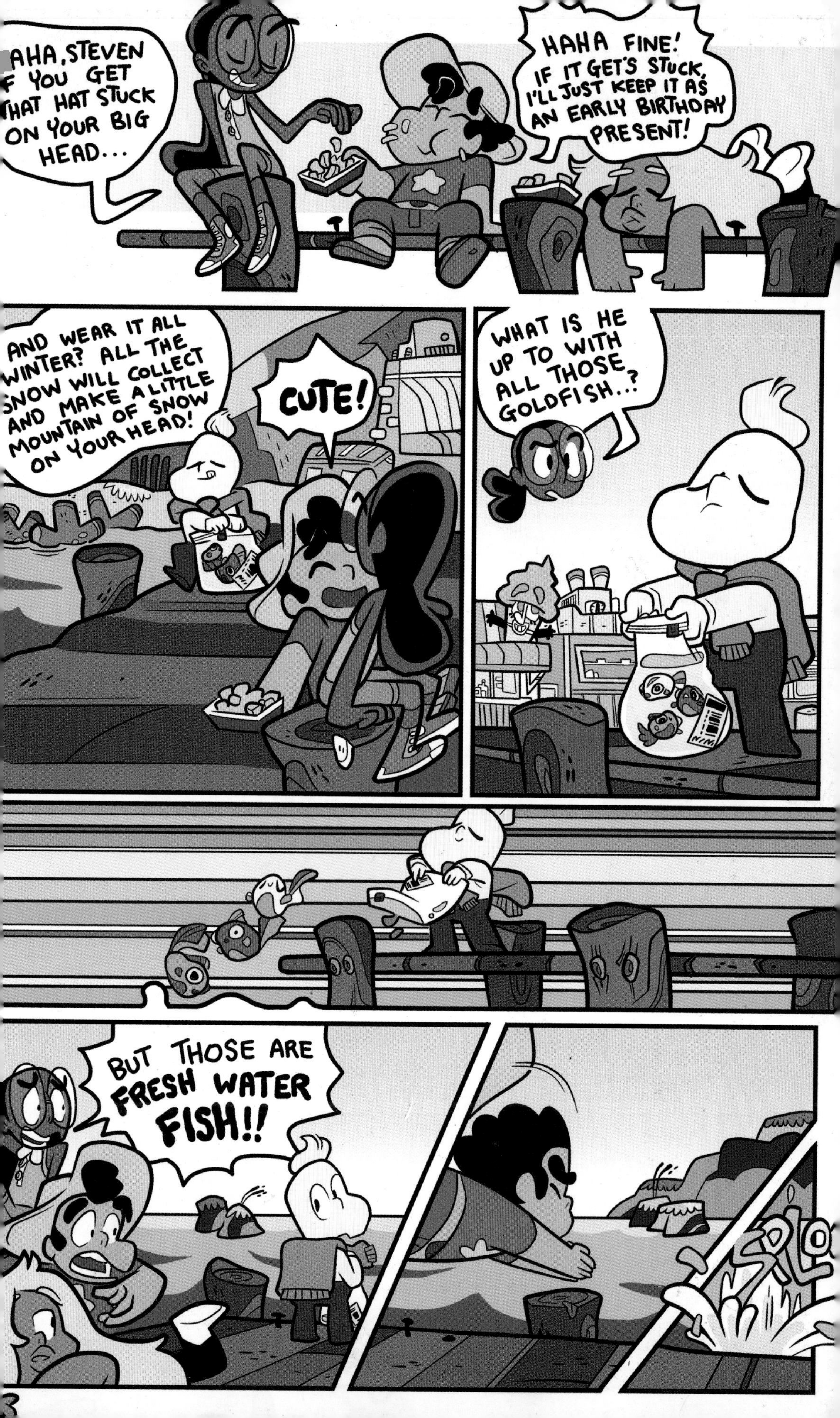
AHA, STEVEN
F YOU GET
THAT HAT STUCK
ON YOUR BIG
HEAD...
HAHA FINE!
IF IT GET'S STUCK,
I'LL JUST KEEP IT AS
AN EARLY BIRTHDAY
PRESENT!
AND WEAR IT ALL
WINTER? ALL THE
SNOW WILL COLLECT
AND MAKE A LITTLE
MOUNTAIN OF SNOW
ON YOUR HEAD!
CUTE!
WHAT IS HE
UP TO WITH
ALL THOSE
GOLDFISH..?
BUT THOSE ARE
FRESH WATER
FISH!!

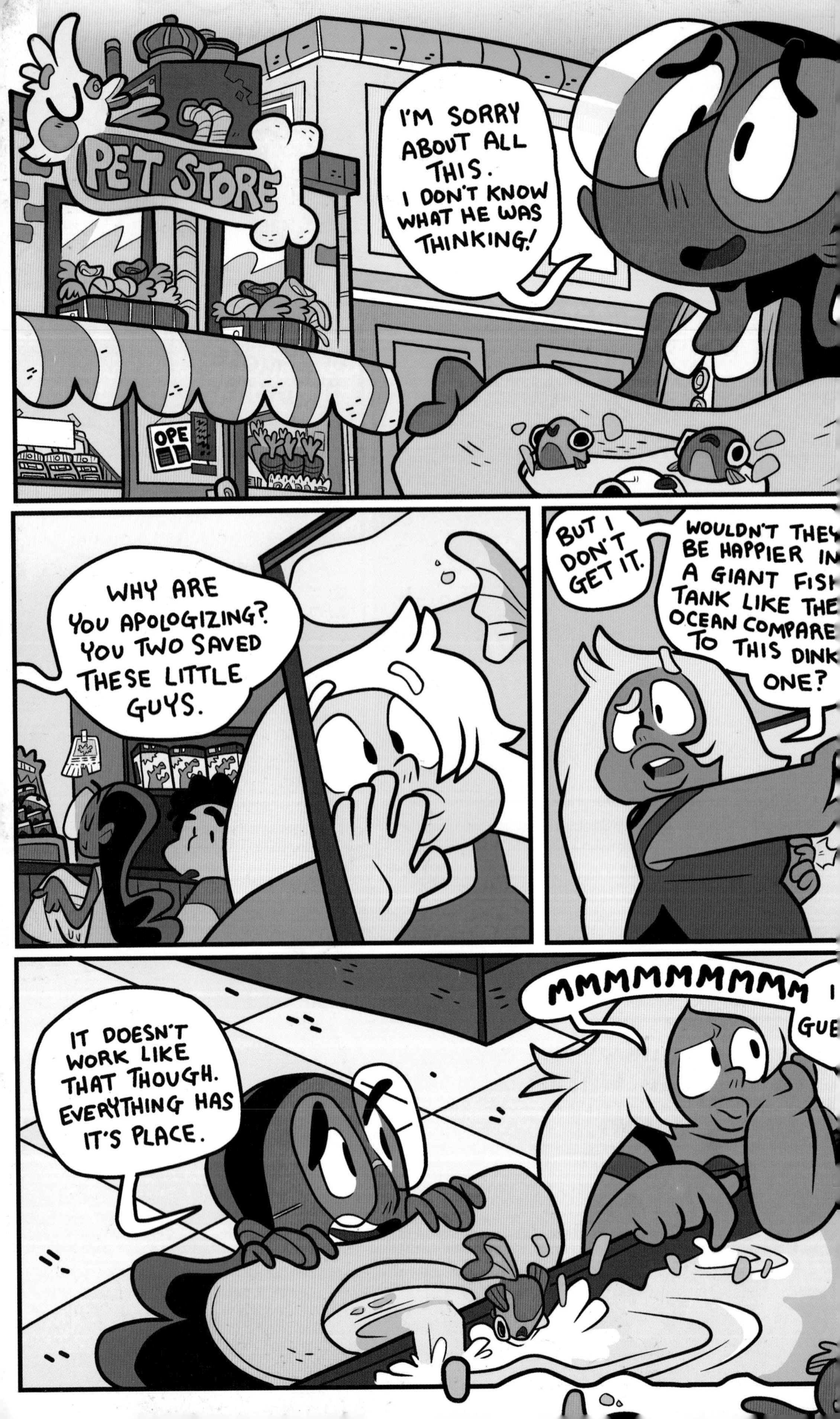
PET STORE
OPE
I'M SORRY ABOUT ALL THIS. I DON'T KNOW WHAT HE WAS THINKING!
WHY ARE YOU APOLOGIZING? YOU TWO SAVED THESE LITTLE GUYS.
BUT I DON'T GET IT.
IT DOESN'T WORK LIKE THAT THOUGH. EVERYTHING HAS IT'S PLACE.
MMMMMMMMM

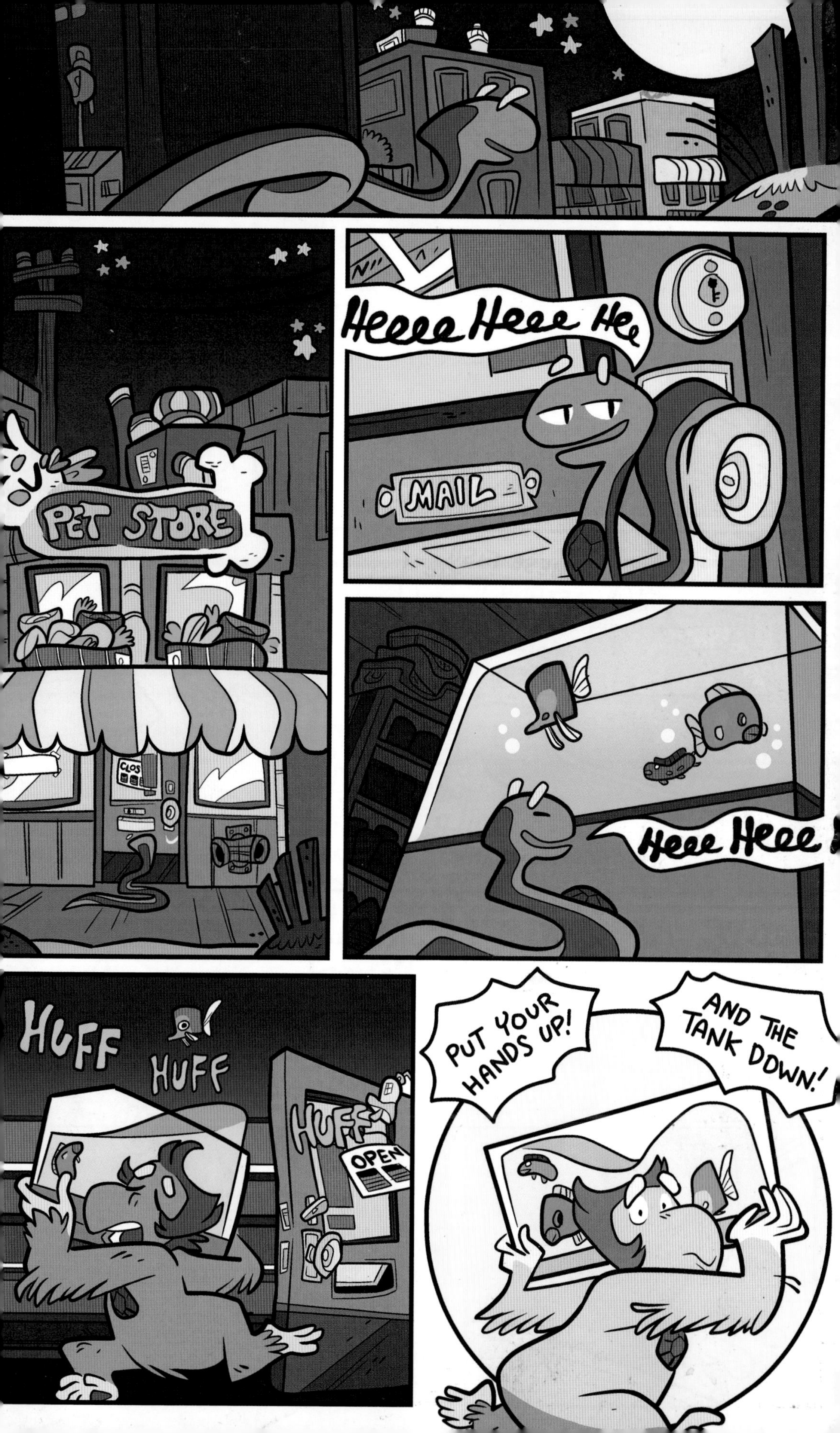
PET STORE
CLOS
MAIL
Heeee Heee Hee
Heee Heee!
HUFF
HUFF
HUFF
OPEN
PUT YOUR HANDS UP!
AND THE TANK DOWN!

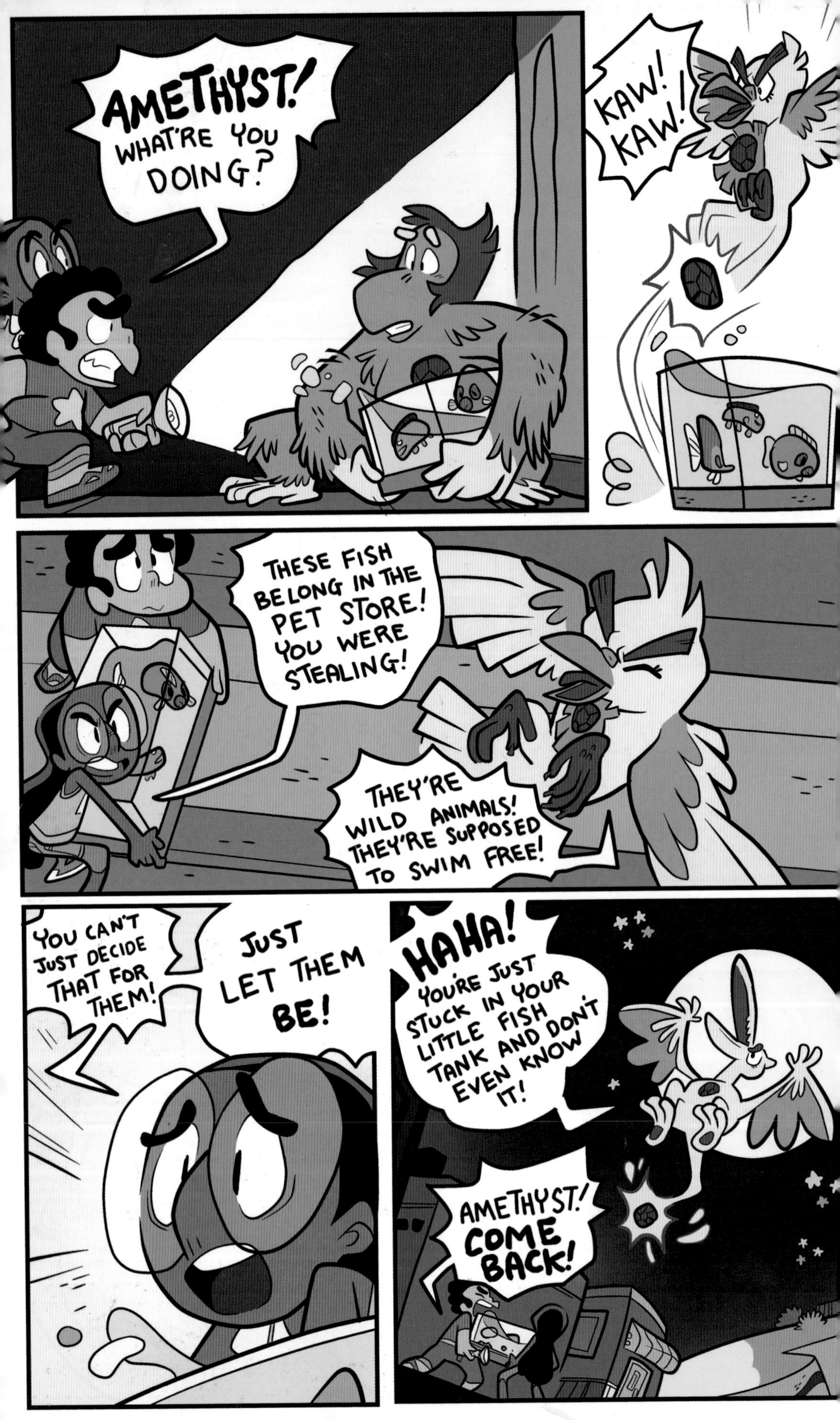
AMETHYST! WHAT'RE YOU DOING?
KAW! KAW!
THESE FISH BELONG IN THE PET STORE! YOU WERE STEALING!
THEY'RE WILD ANIMALS! THEY'RE SUPPOSED TO SWIM FREE!
YOU CAN'T JUST DECIDE THAT FOR THEM!
JUST LET THEM BE!
HAHA! YOU'RE JUST STUCK IN YOUR LITTLE FISH TANK AND DON'T EVEN KNOW IT!
AMETHYST! COME BACK!

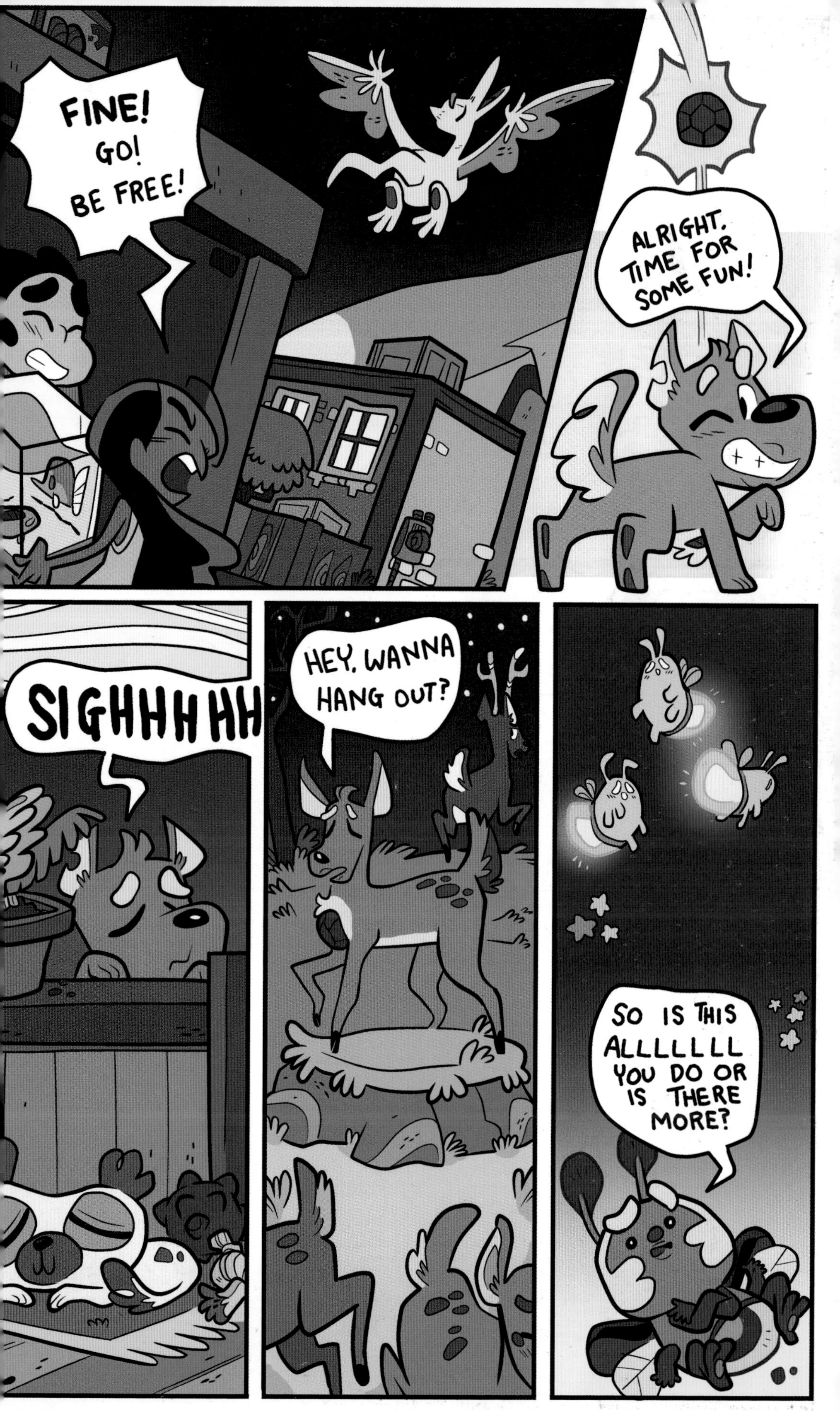
FINE! GO! BE FREE!
ALRIGHT, TIME FOR SOME FUN!
SIGHHHHHH
HEY, WANNA HANG OUT?
SO IS THIS ALLLLLLL YOU DO OR IS THERE MORE?

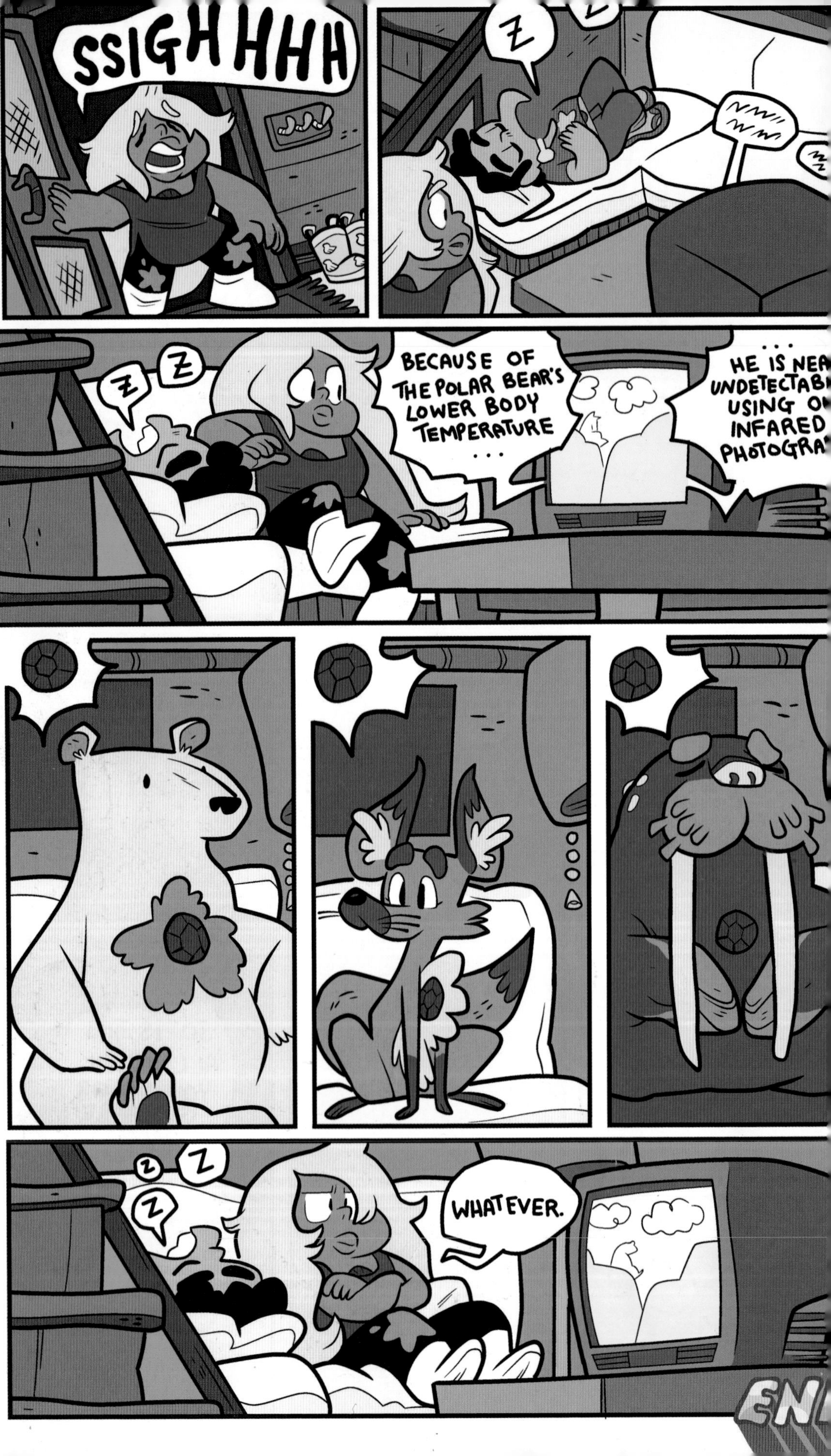
SSIGHHHH
Z
Z
Z
BECAUSE OF THE POLAR BEAR'S LOWER BODY TEMPERATURE . . .
. . .
HE IS NEA
UNDETECTAB
USING O
INFARED
PHOTOGRA
Z
Z
Z
WHATEVER.

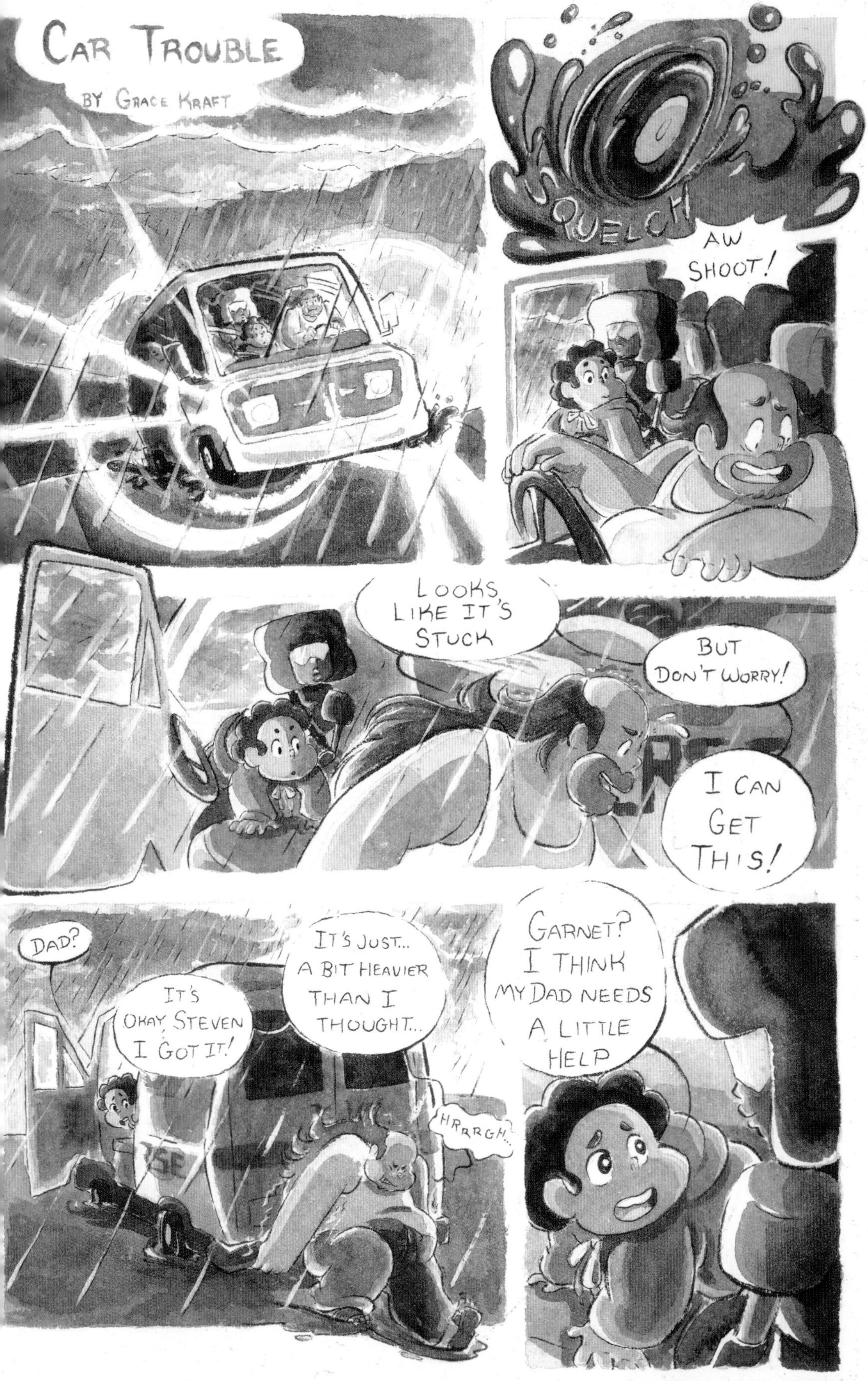
Car Trouble
by Grace Kraft
SQUELCH
AW SHOOT!
LOOKS LIKE IT'S STUCK
BUT DON'T WORRY!
I CAN GET THIS!
DAD?
IT'S OKAY, STEVEN I GOT IT!
IT'S JUST... A BIT HEAVIER THAN I THOUGHT...
HRRRGH...
GARNET? I THINK MY DAD NEEDS A LITTLE HELP

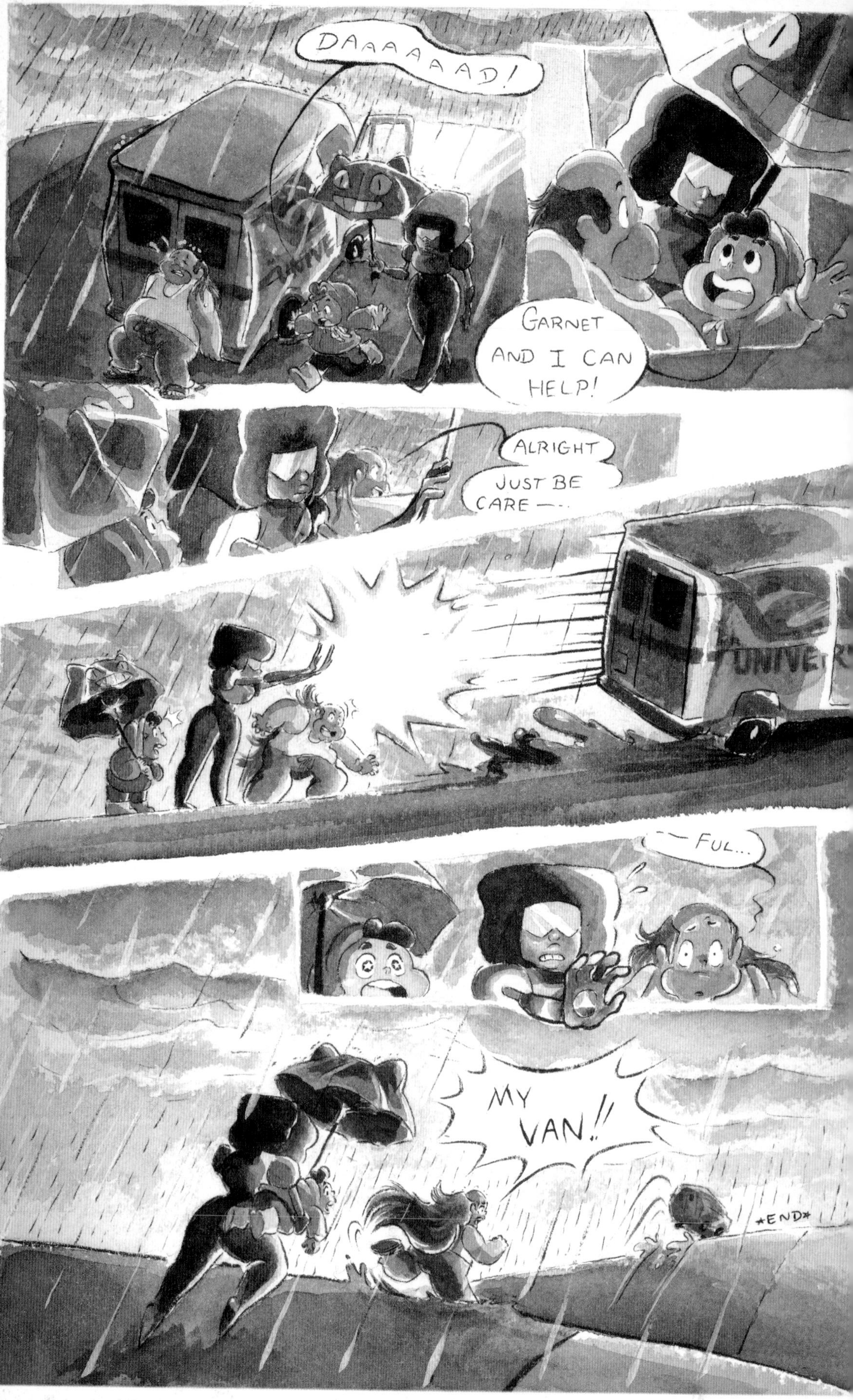
DAAAAAAAD!
GARNET AND I CAN HELP!
ALRIGHT
JUST BE CARE—
—FUL...
MY VAN!!
*END*

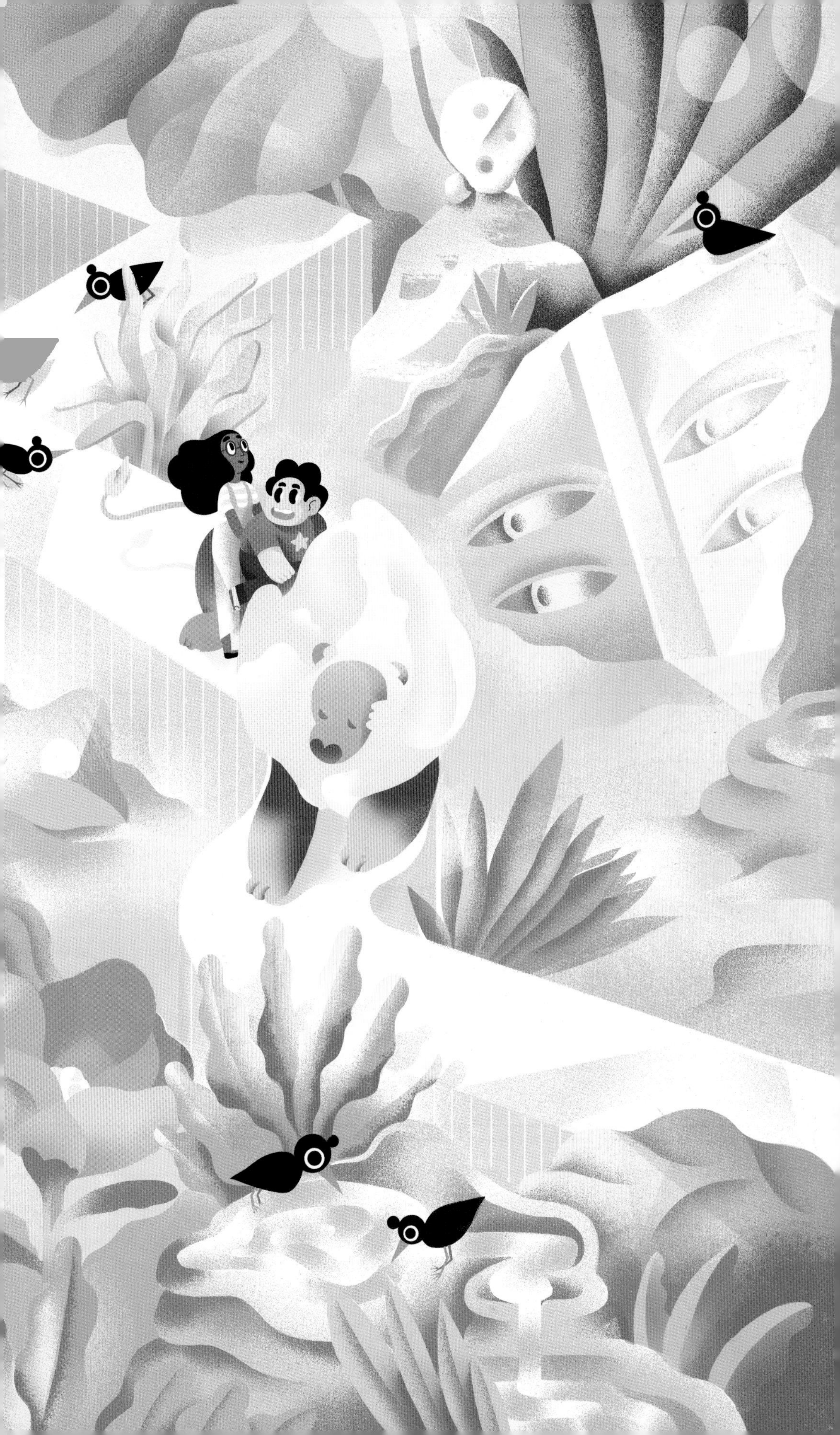

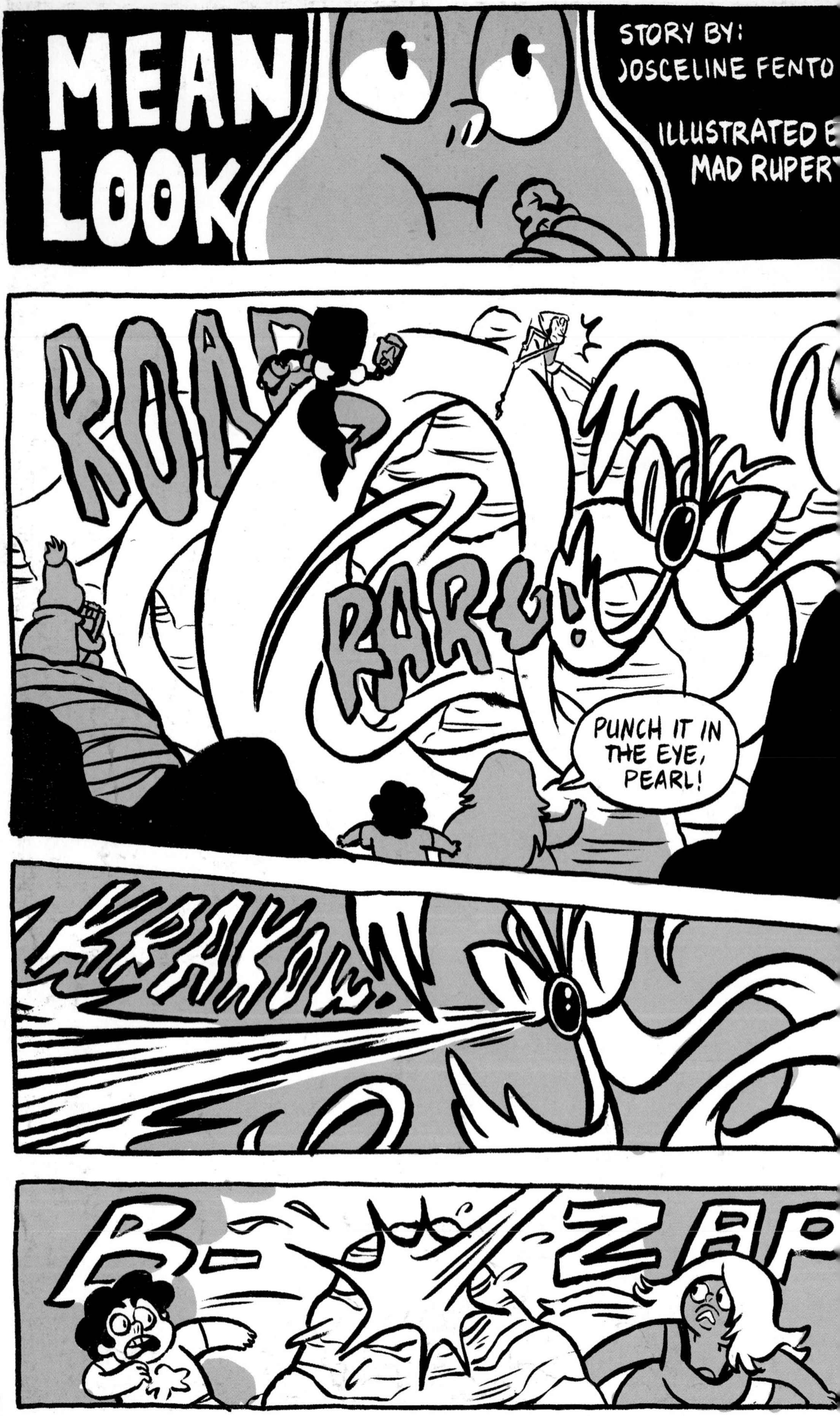
MEAN LOOK
STORY BY:
JOSCELINE FENTO
ILLUSTRATED B
MAD RUPERT
RARG!
PUNCH IT IN THE EYE, PEARL!

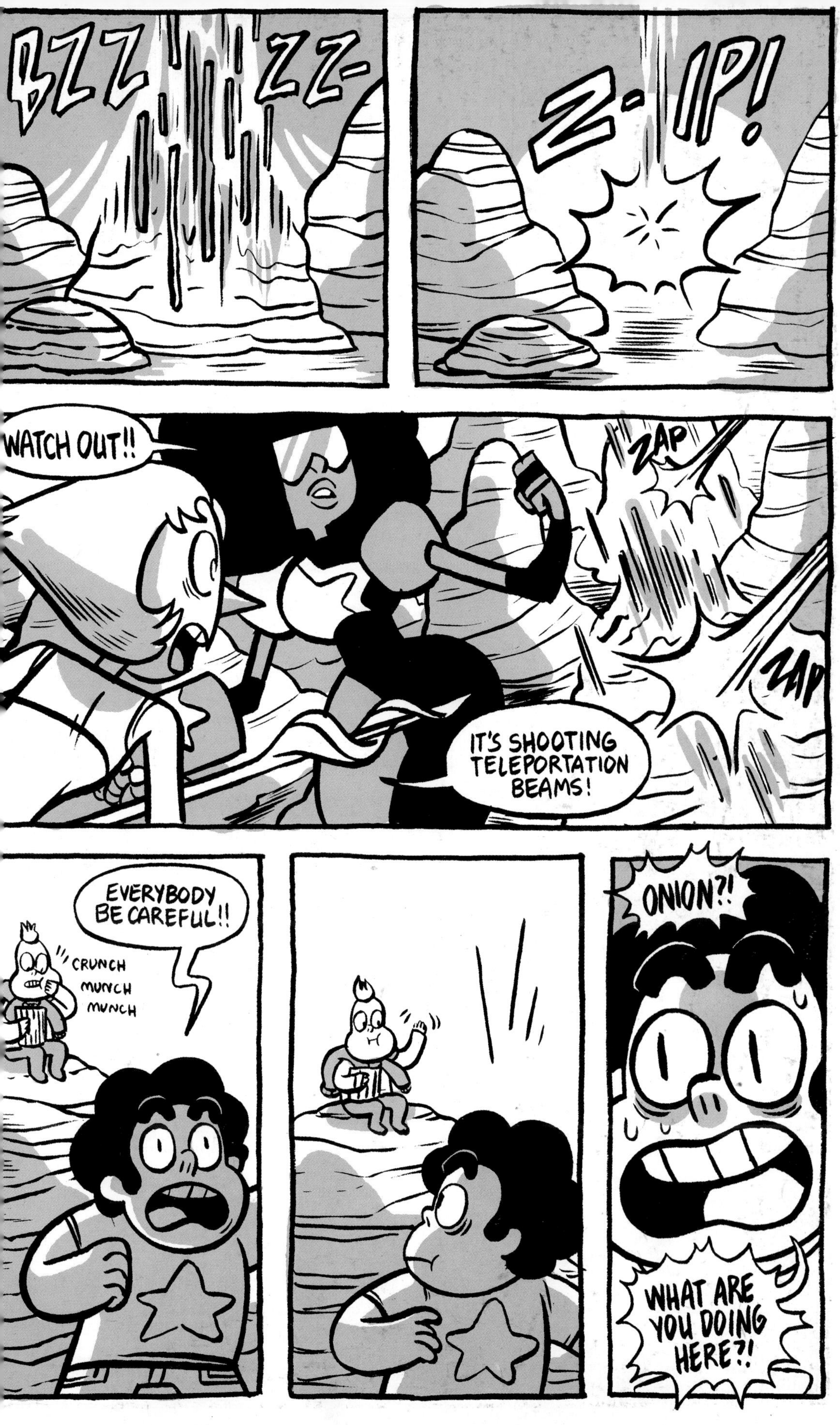
BZZ ZZ-
Z-IP!
WATCH OUT!!
ZAP
ZAP
IT'S SHOOTING TELEPORTATION BEAMS!
EVERYBODY BE CAREFUL!!
CRUNCH
MUNCH
MUNCH
ONION?!
WHAT ARE YOU DOING HERE?!

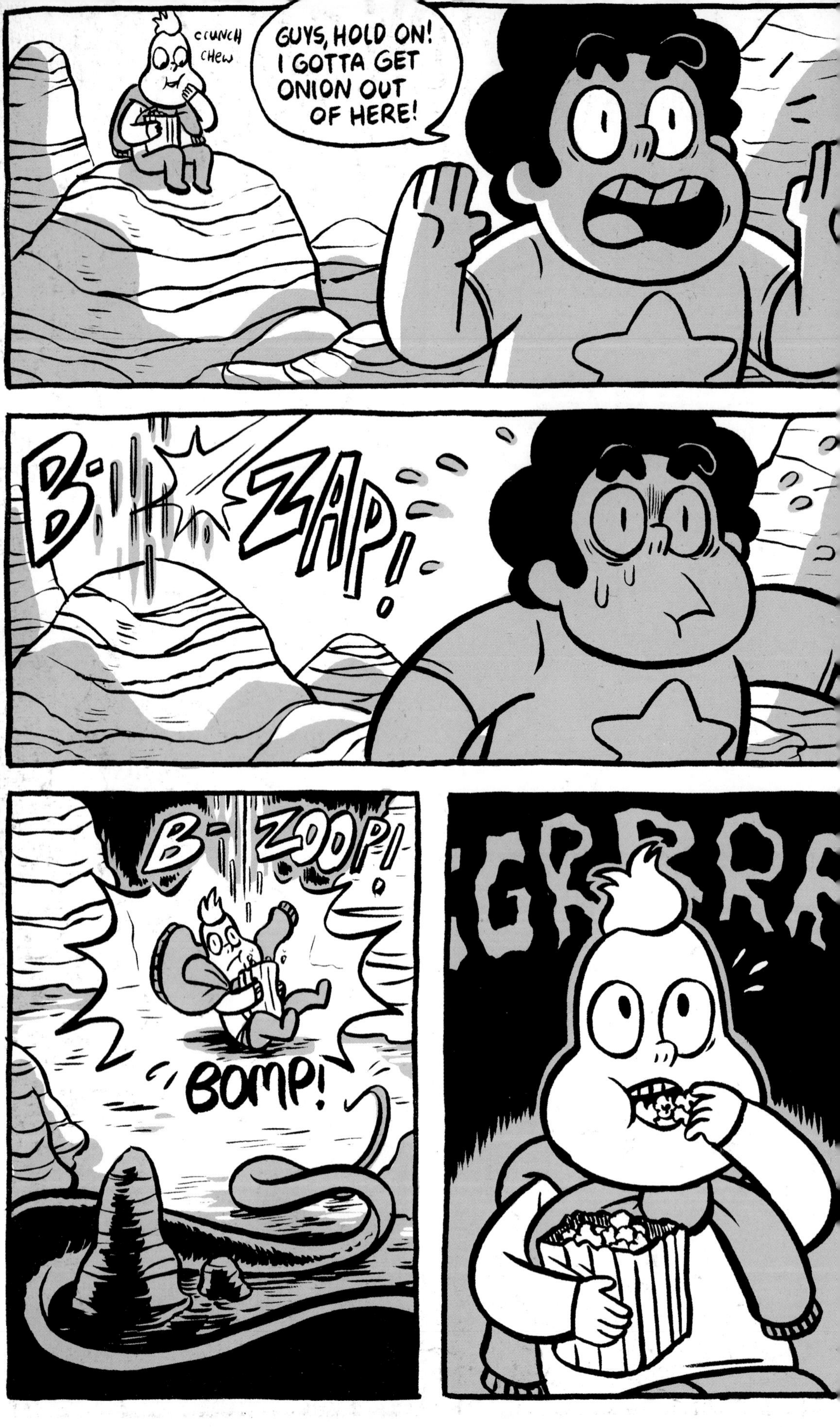
CRUNCH
CHEW
GUYS, HOLD ON! I GOTTA GET ONION OUT OF HERE!
B-ZAP!
B-ZOOP!
BOMP!
GRRRR

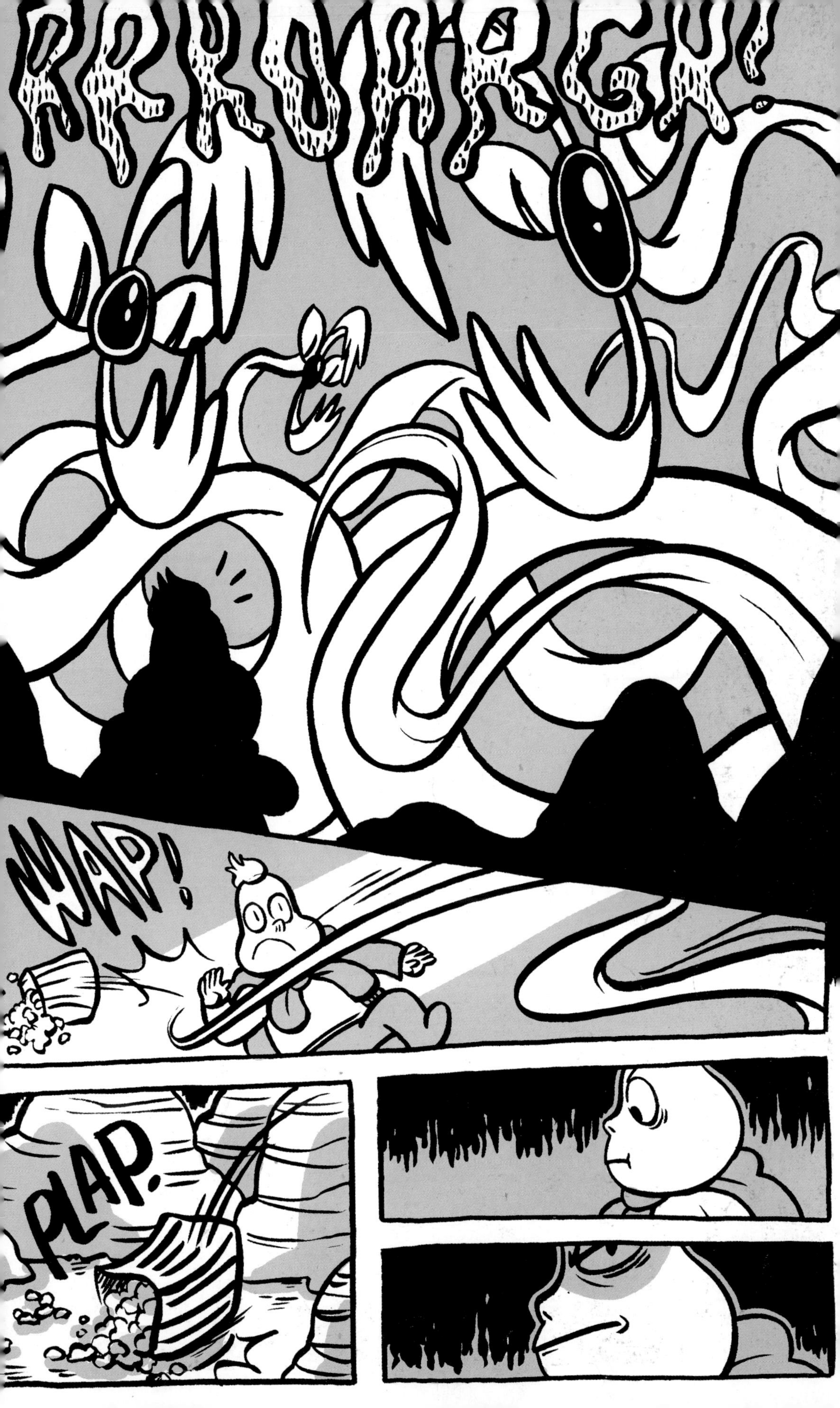
RRRWARGH!
WAP!
PLAP.

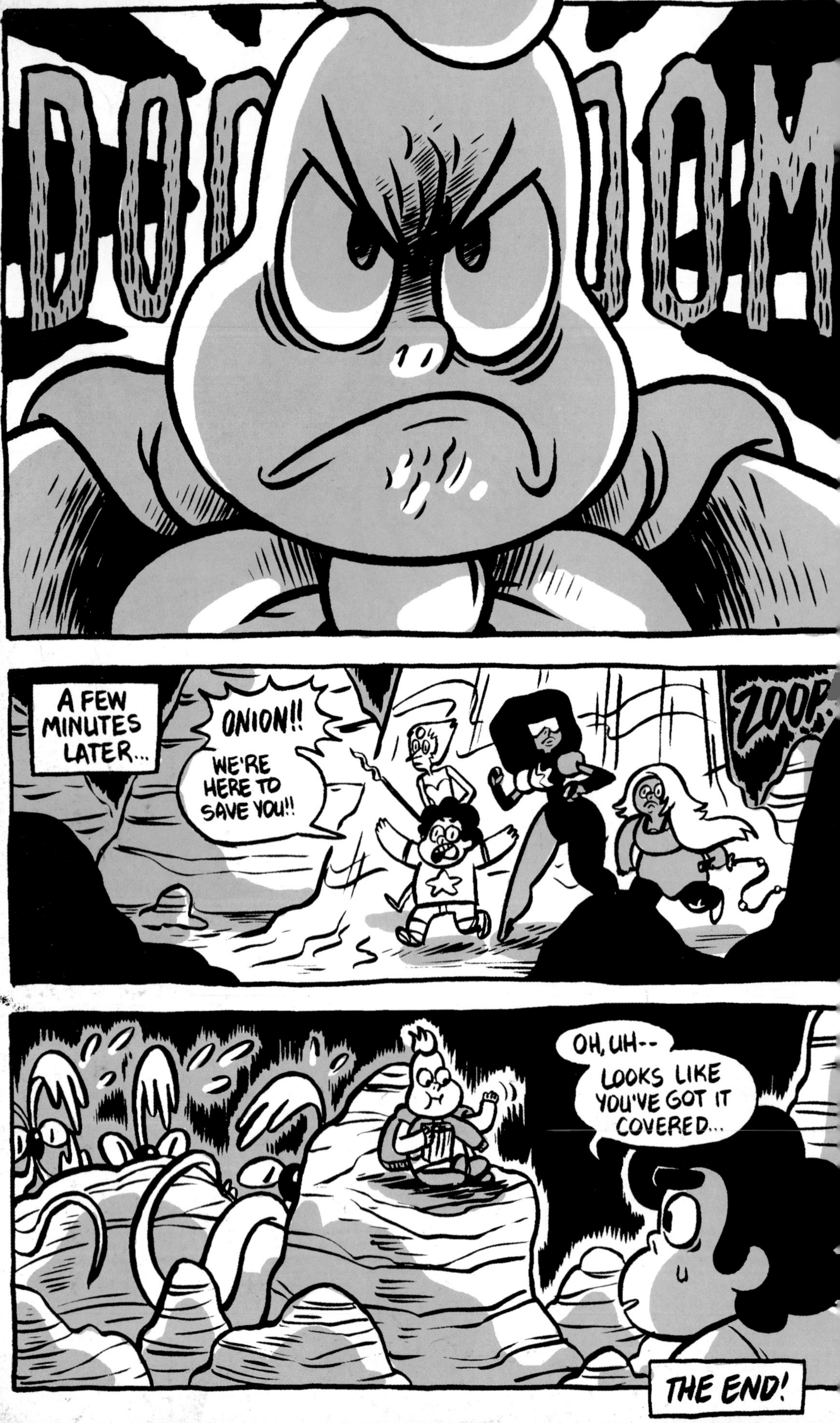
DOOOOM
A FEW MINUTES LATER...
ONION!!
WE'RE HERE TO SAVE YOU!!
ZOOP
OH, UH--
LOOKS LIKE YOU'VE GOT IT COVERED...
THE END!

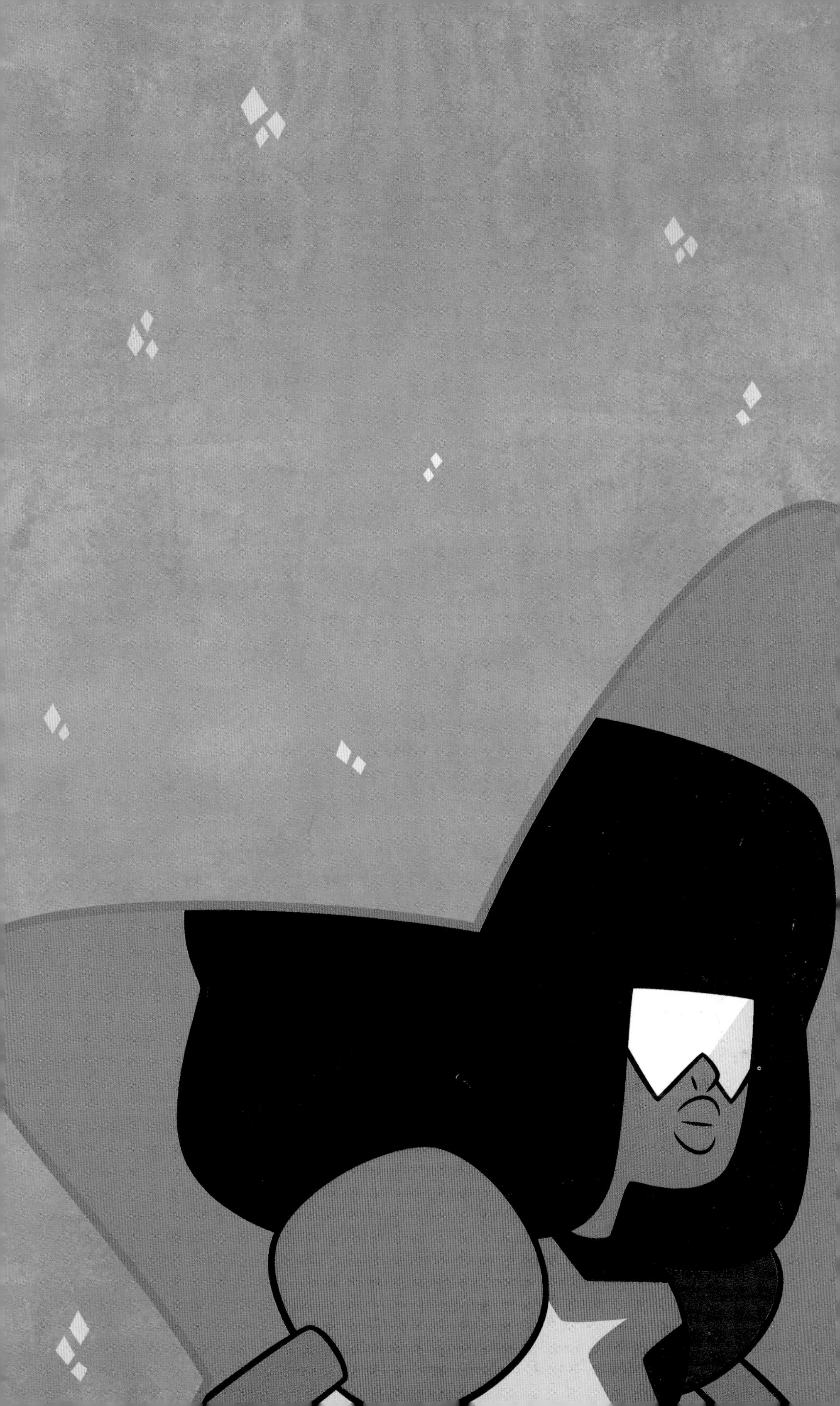

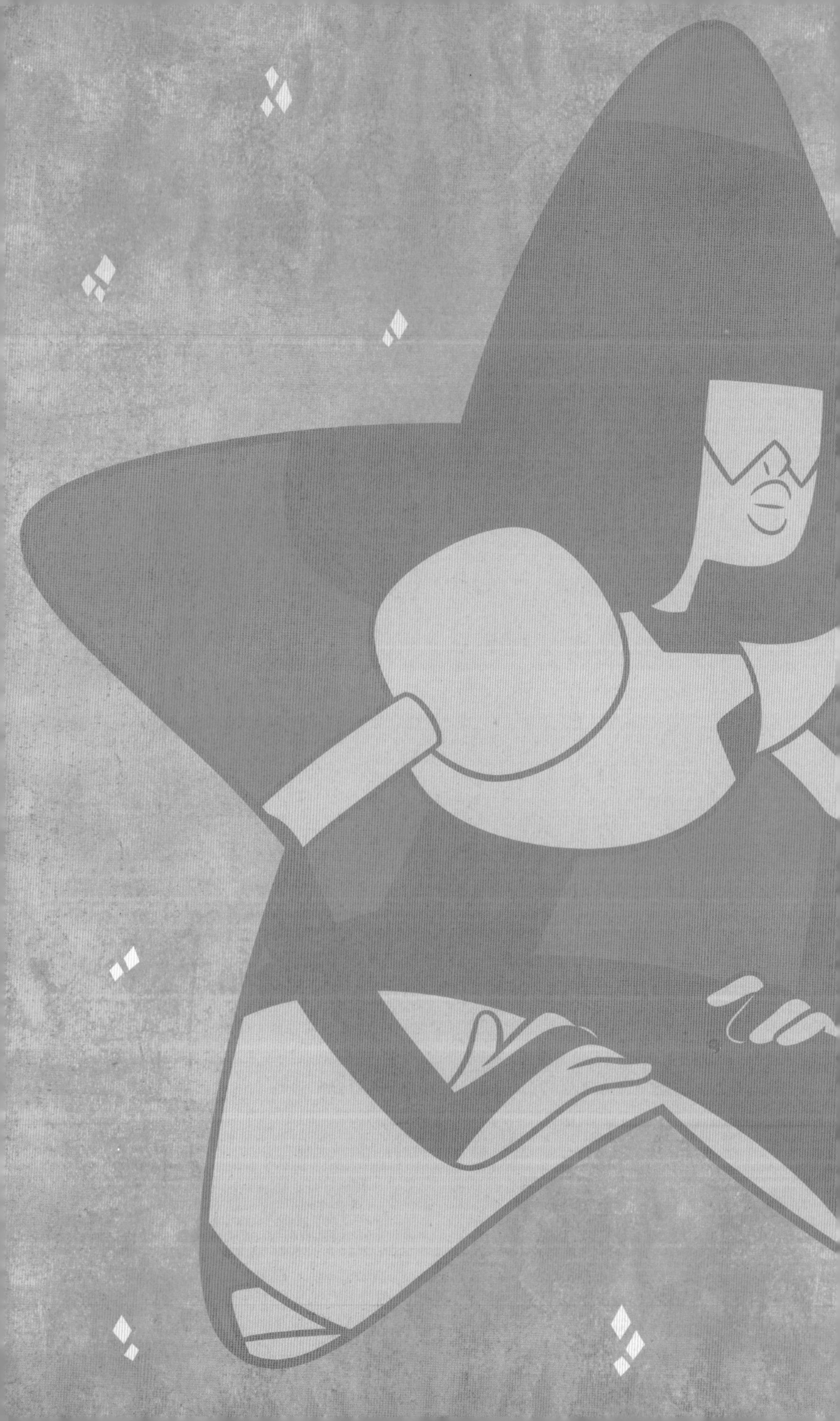

# "CLOCK WORK"

also featuring:

**"ENJOYING THE SUN"**
written & illustrated by
**T. ZYSK**

**"OPAL'S DAY OFF"**
illustrated by
**GRACE KRAFT**

**"DOG SHOW"**
written & illustrated by
**MAD RUPERT**

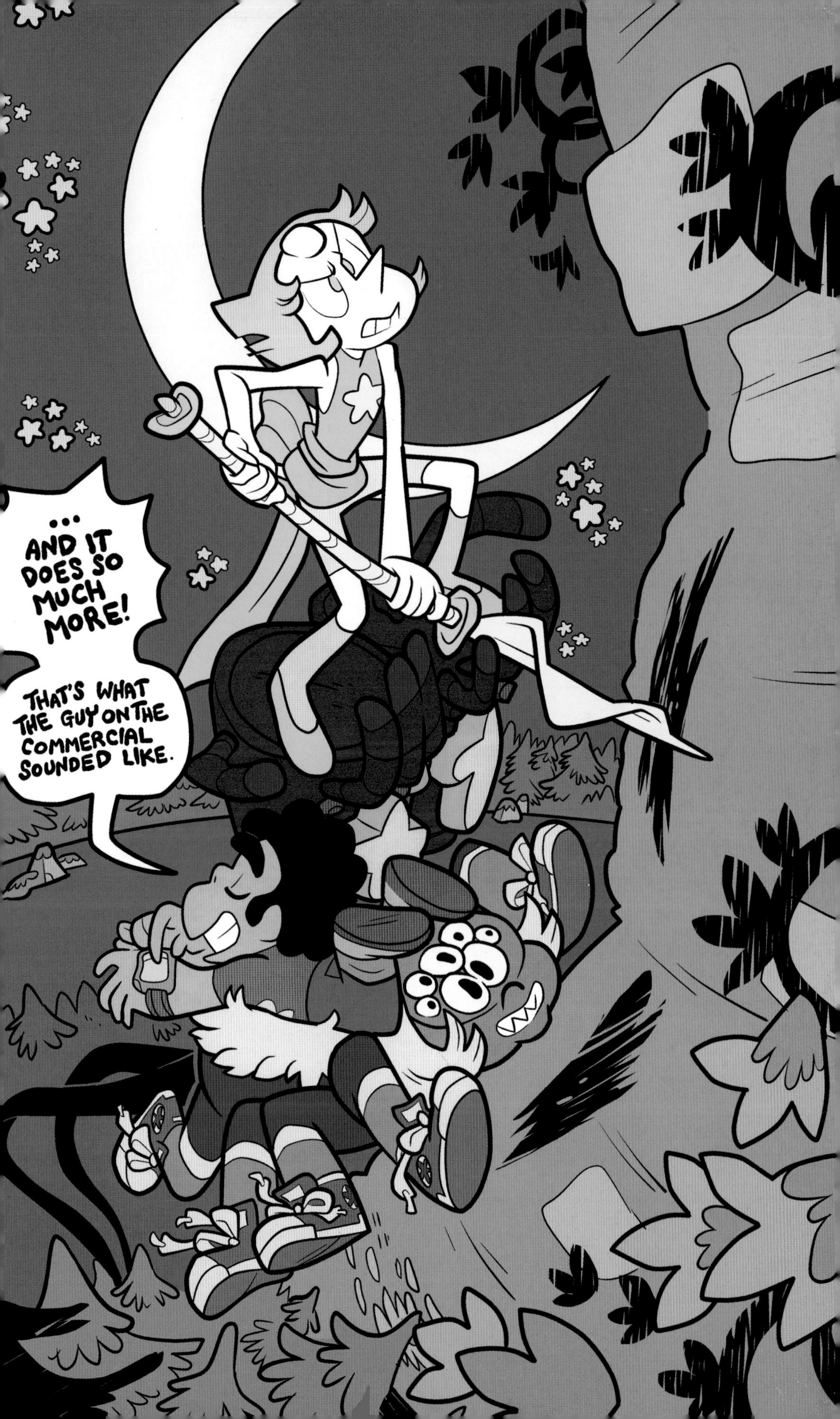
... AND IT DOES SO MUCH MORE!
THAT'S WHAT THE GUY ON THE COMMERCIAL SOUNDED LIKE.

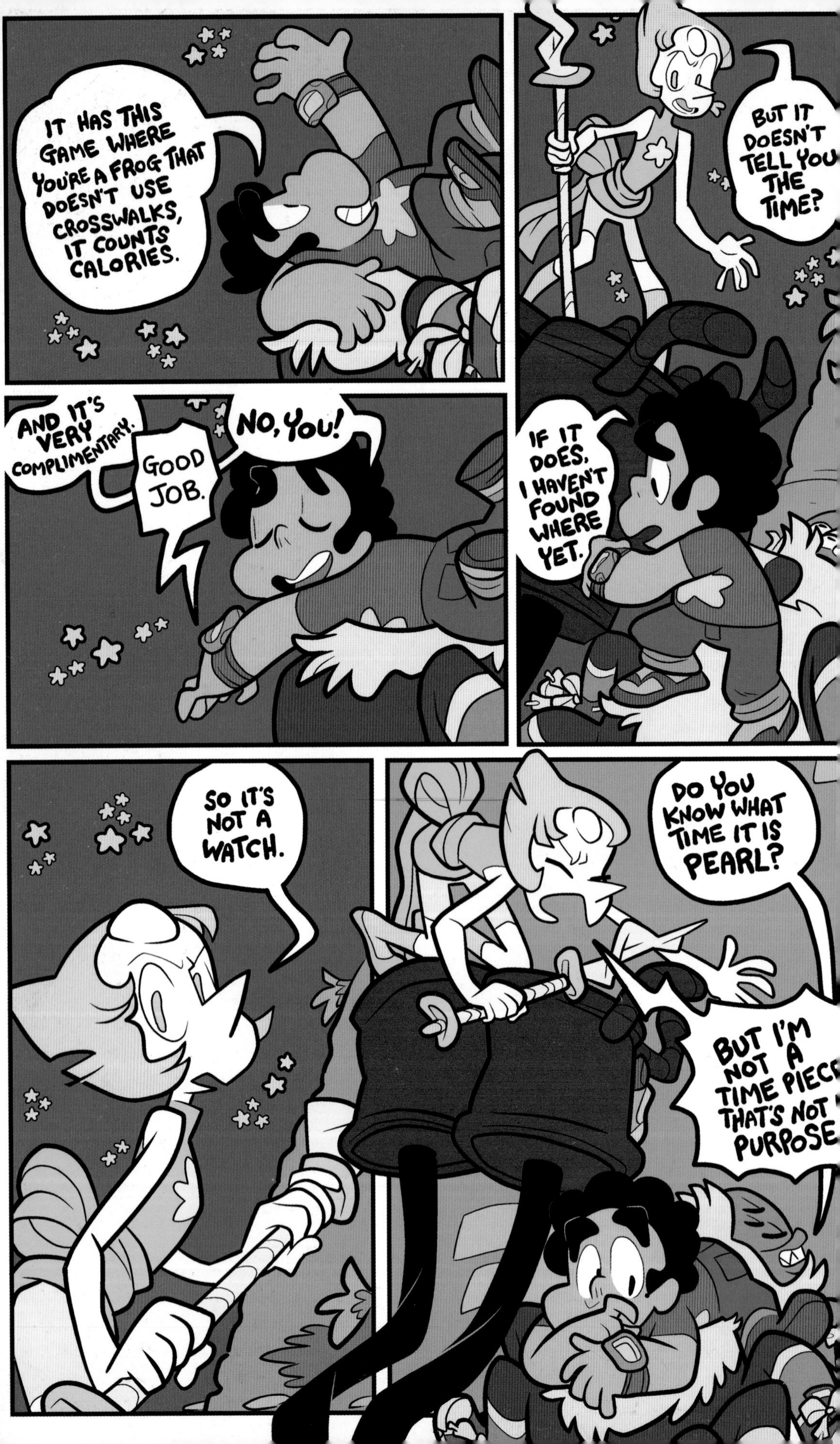
IT HAS THIS GAME WHERE YOU'RE A FROG THAT DOESN'T USE CROSSWALKS, IT COUNTS CALORIES.
BUT IT DOESN'T TELL YOU THE TIME?
AND IT'S VERY COMPLIMENTARY.
GOOD JOB.
NO, YOU!
IF IT DOES, I HAVEN'T FOUND WHERE YET.
SO IT'S NOT A WATCH.
DO YOU KNOW WHAT TIME IT IS PEARL?
BUT I'M NOT A TIME PIECE
THAT'S NOT
PURPOSE

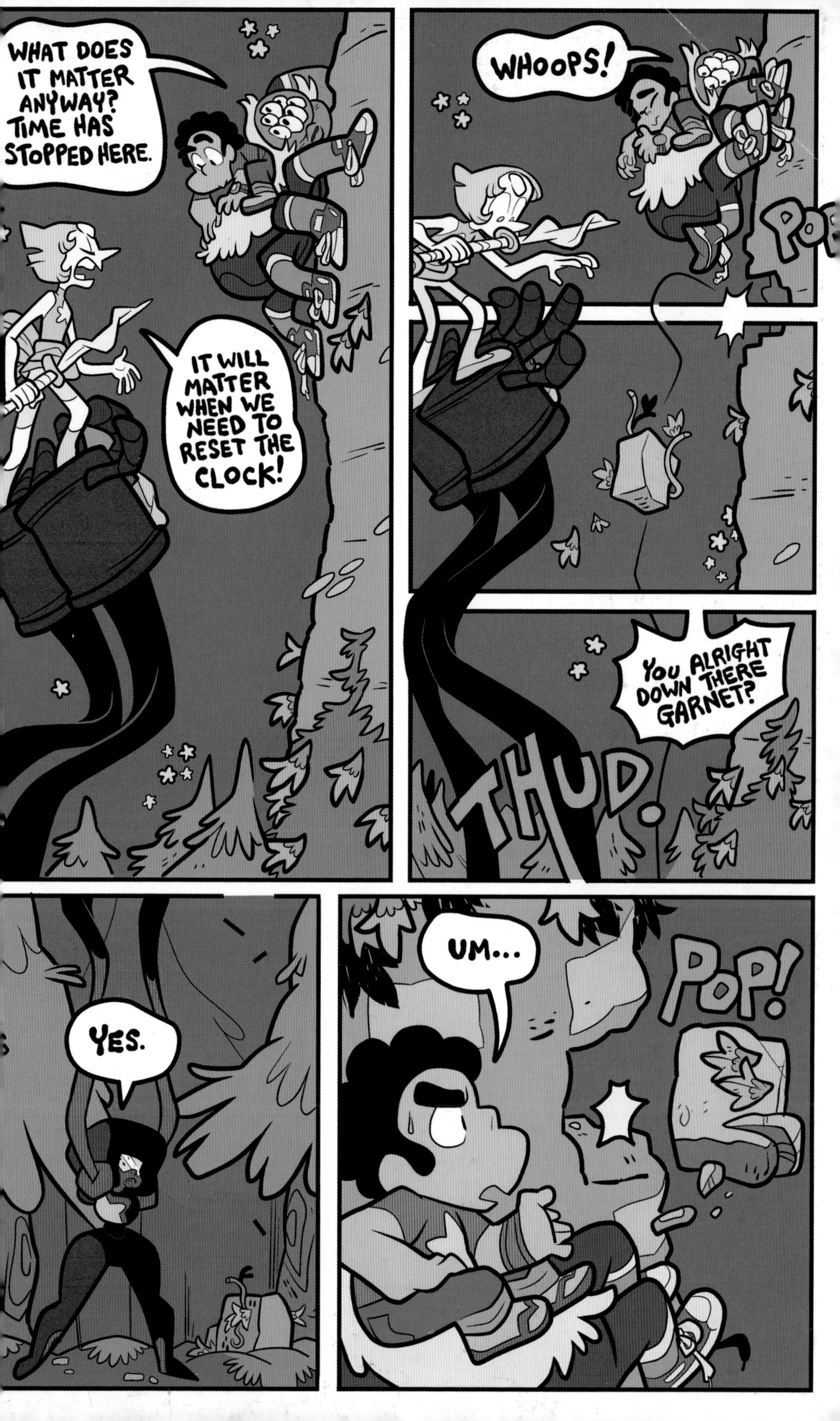
WHAT DOES IT MATTER ANYWAY? TIME HAS STOPPED HERE.
IT WILL MATTER WHEN WE NEED TO RESET THE CLOCK!
WHOOPS!
POP
YOU ALRIGHT DOWN THERE GARNET?
THUD.
YES.
UM...
POP!

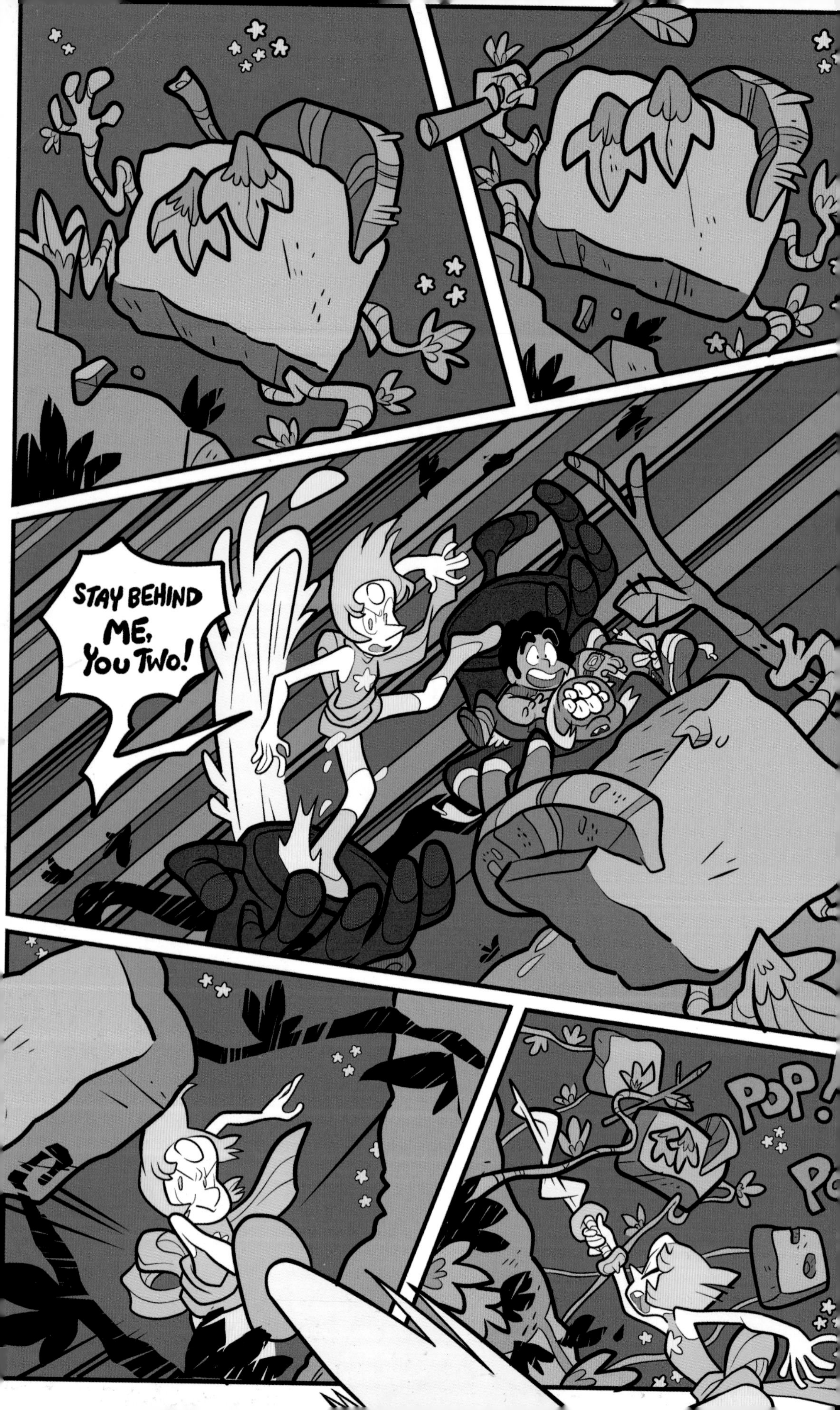
STAY BEHIND ME, YOU TWO!
POP!

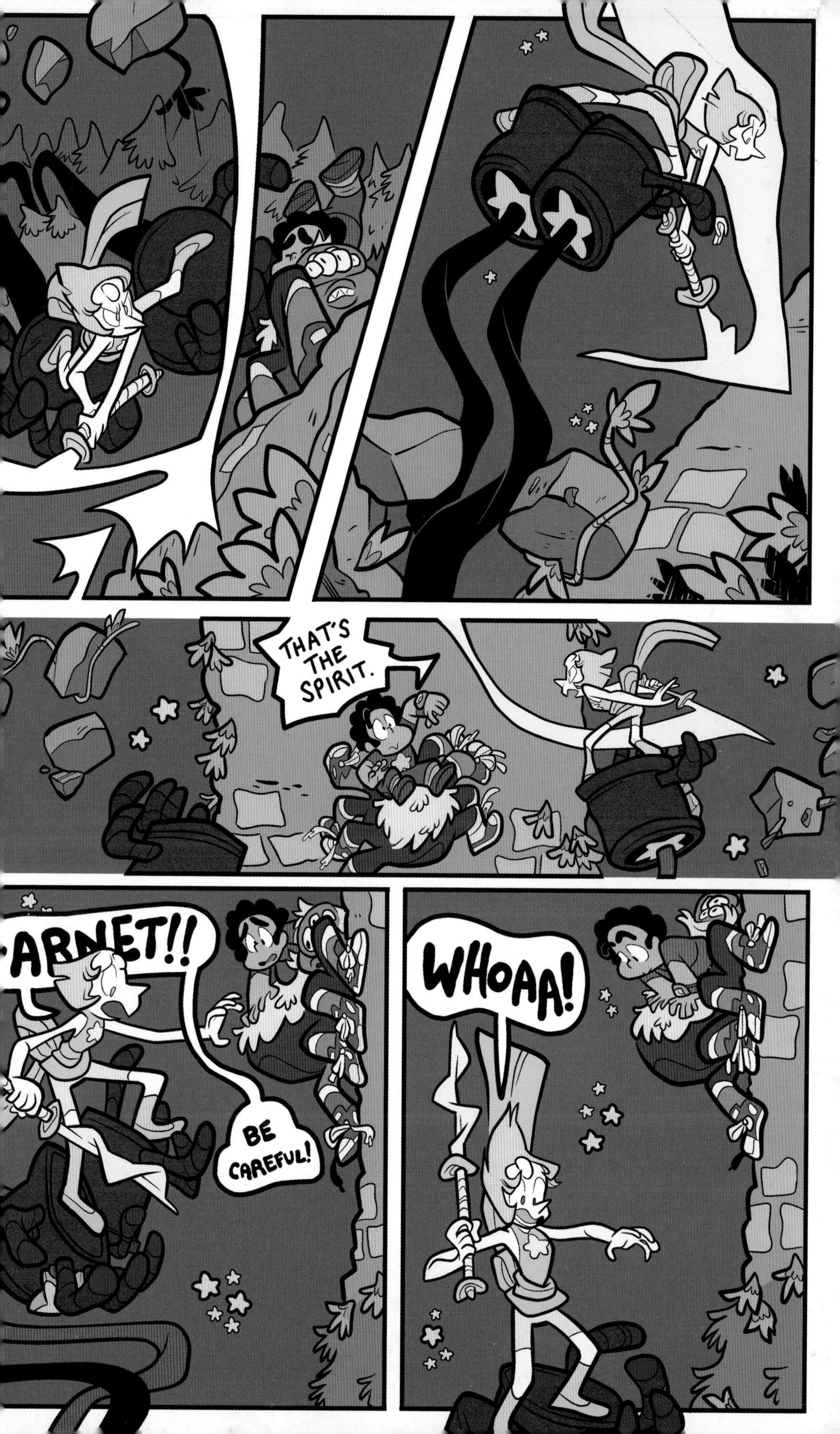
THAT'S THE SPIRIT.
ARNET!!
BE CAREFUL!
WHOAA!

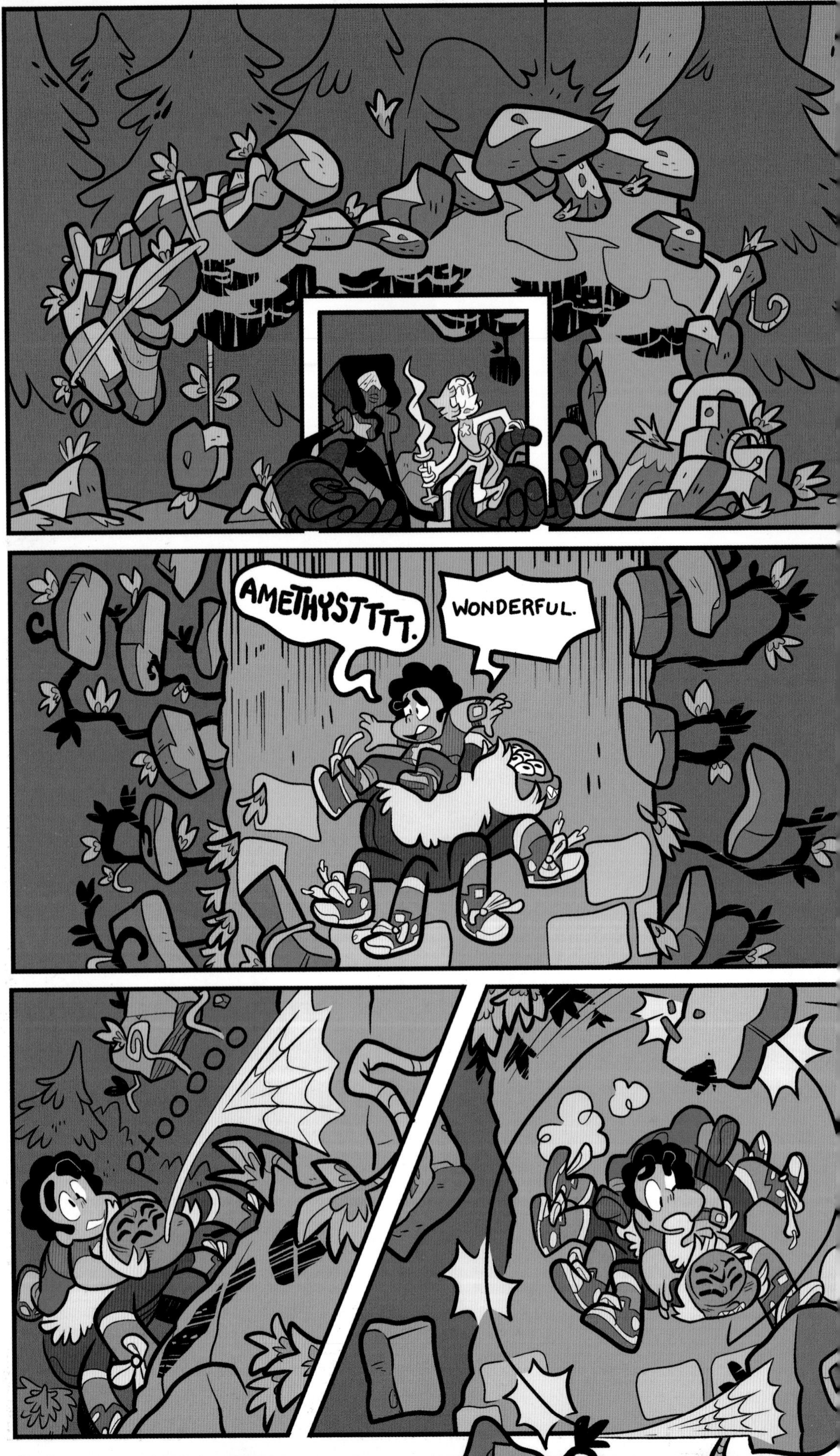
AMETHYSTTTTT.
WONDERFUL.

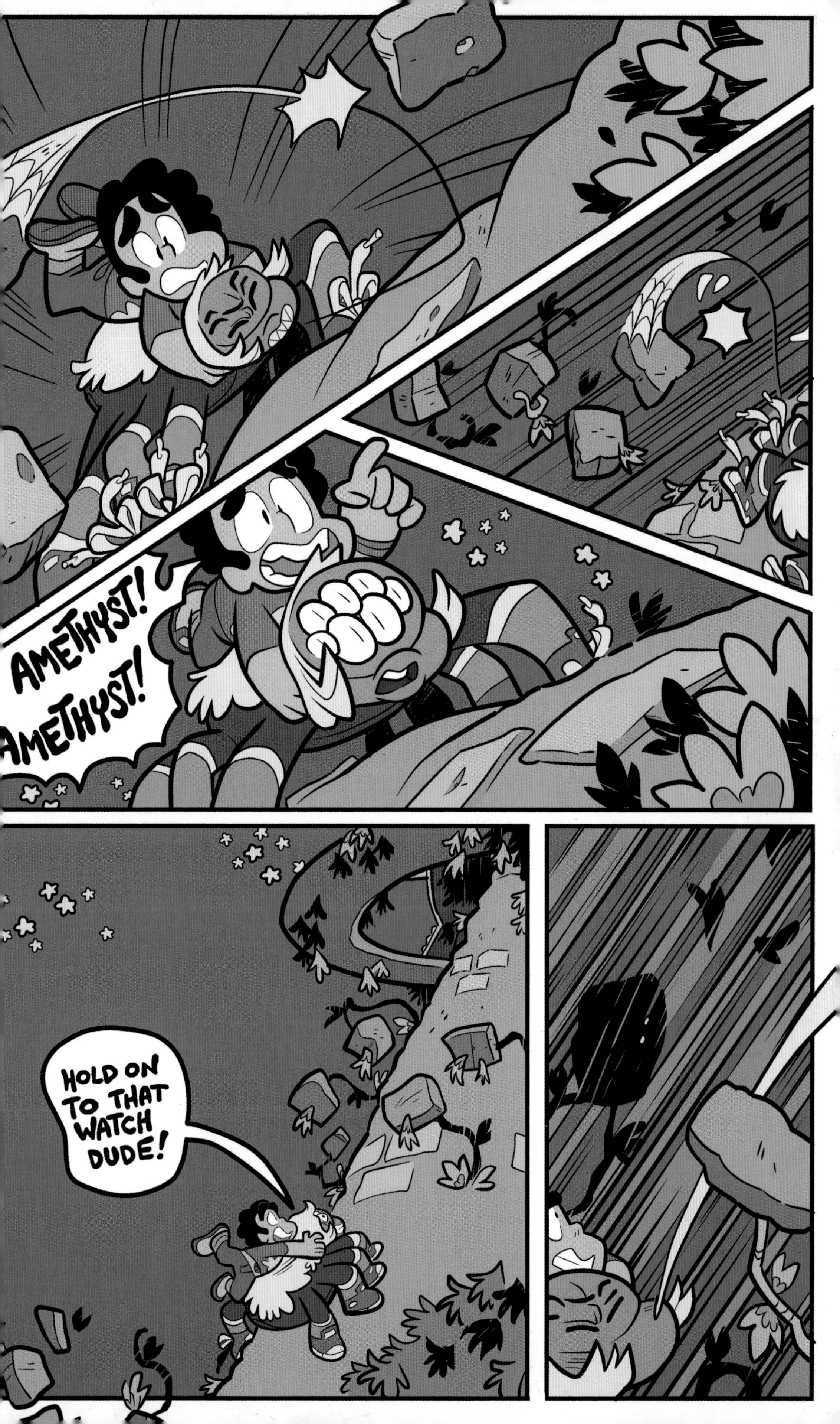
AMETHYST!
AMETHYST!
HOLD ON TO THAT WATCH DUDE!

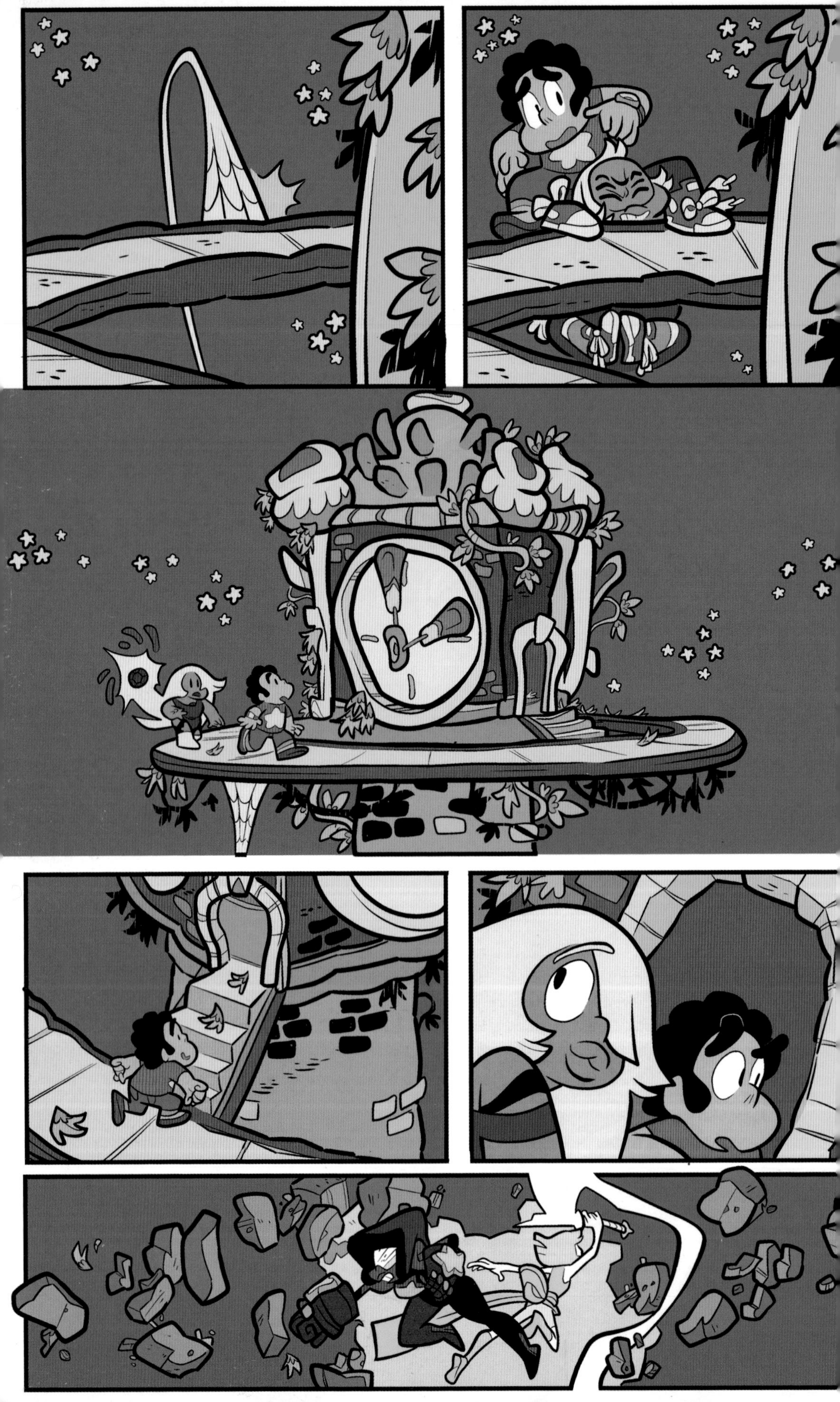

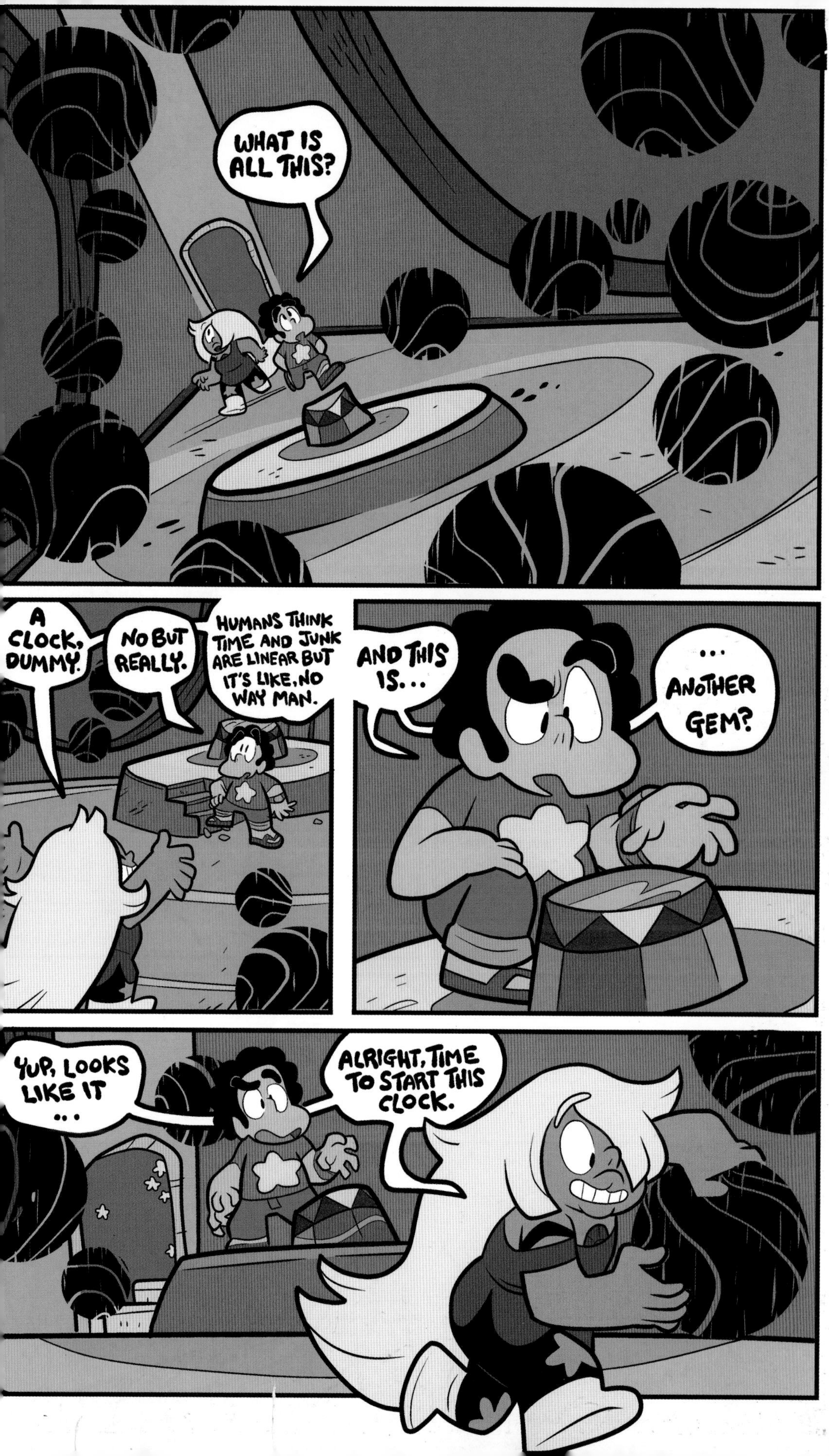
WHAT IS ALL THIS?
A CLOCK, DUMMY.
NO BUT REALLY.
HUMANS THINK TIME AND JUNK ARE LINEAR BUT IT'S LIKE, NO WAY MAN.
AND THIS IS...
... ANOTHER GEM?
YUP, LOOKS LIKE IT ...
ALRIGHT, TIME TO START THIS CLOCK.

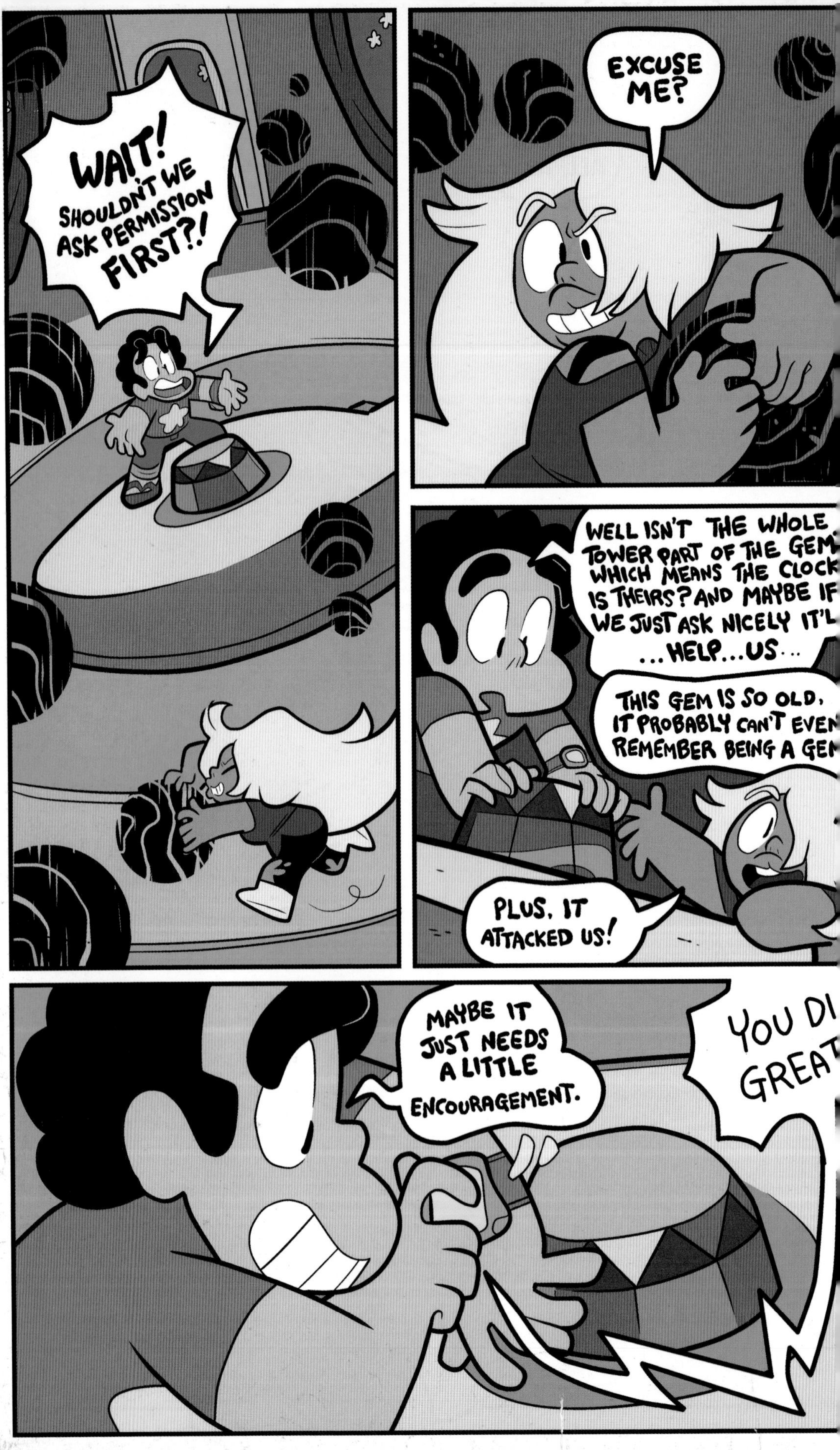
WAIT! SHOULDN'T WE ASK PERMISSION FIRST?!
EXCUSE ME?
WELL ISN'T THE WHOLE TOWER PART OF THE GEM WHICH MEANS THE CLOCK IS THEIRS? AND MAYBE IF WE JUST ASK NICELY IT'L ...HELP...US...
THIS GEM IS SO OLD, IT PROBABLY CAN'T EVEN REMEMBER BEING A GEM
PLUS, IT ATTACKED US!
MAYBE IT JUST NEEDS A LITTLE ENCOURAGEMENT.
YOU DI GREAT

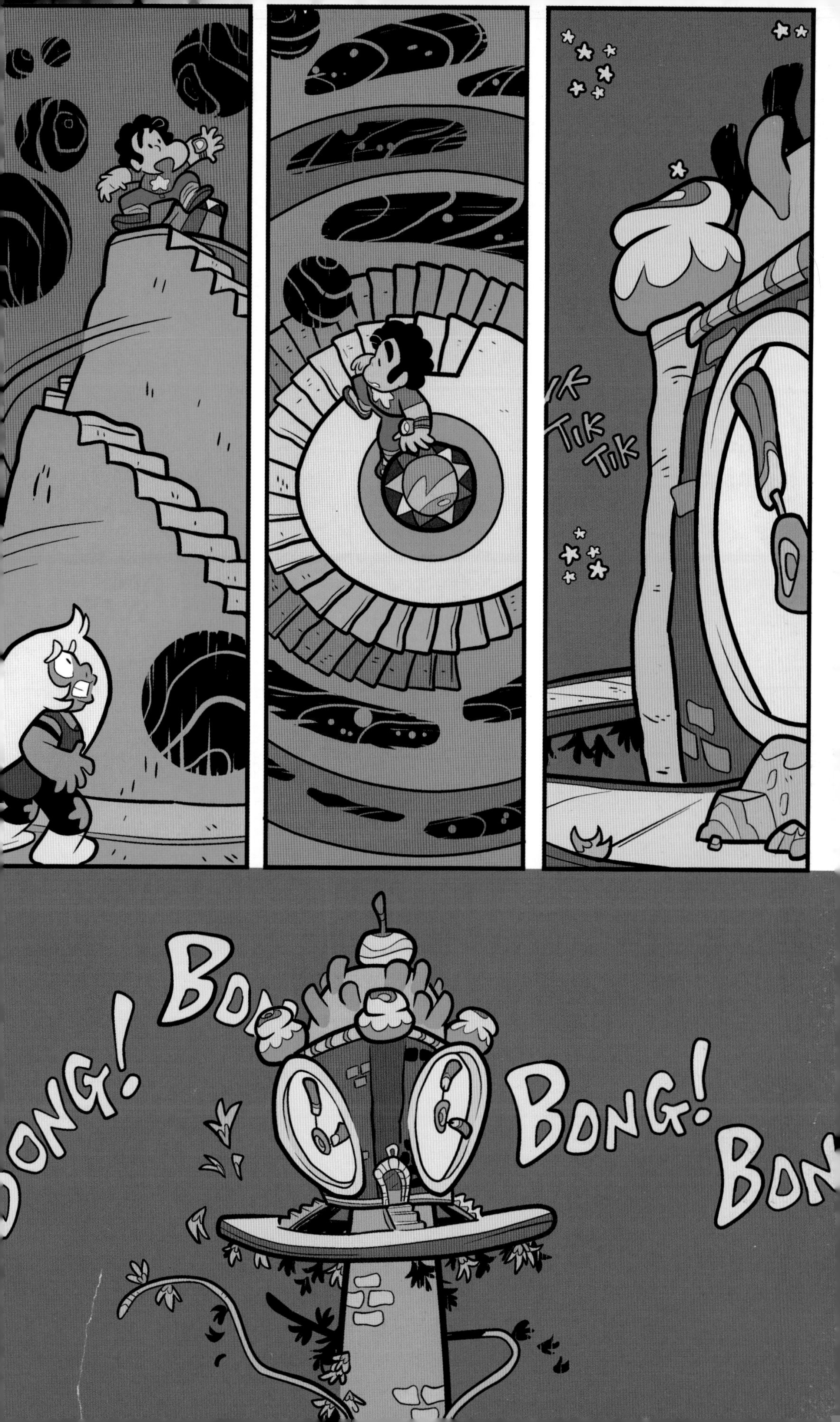

TIK
TIK
TIK
DONG!
BO
BONG!
BON

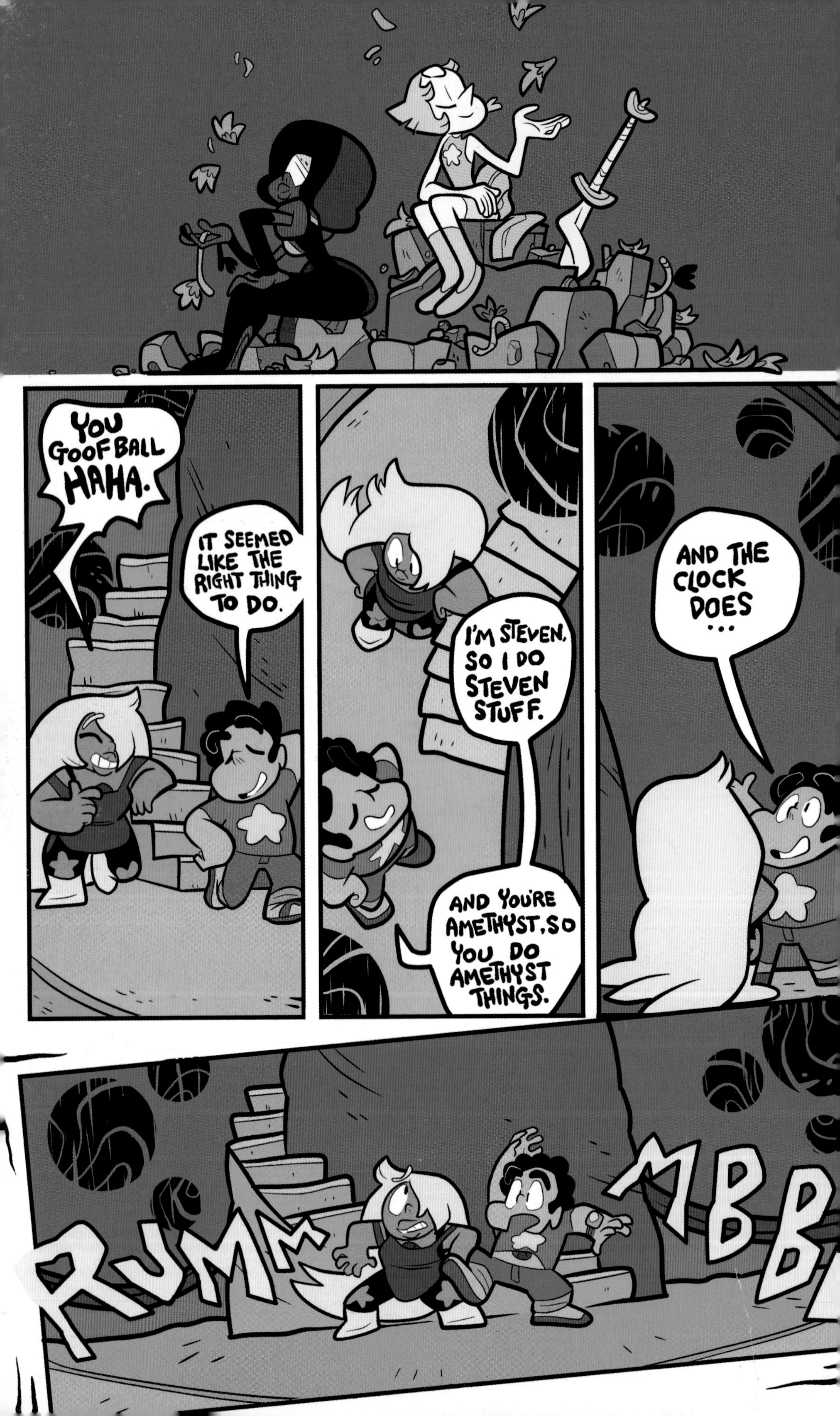
YOU GOOFBALL HAHA.
IT SEEMED LIKE THE RIGHT THING TO DO.
I'M STEVEN, SO I DO STEVEN STUFF.
AND YOU'RE AMETHYST, SO YOU DO AMETHYST THINGS.
AND THE CLOCK DOES ...
RUMMMBB

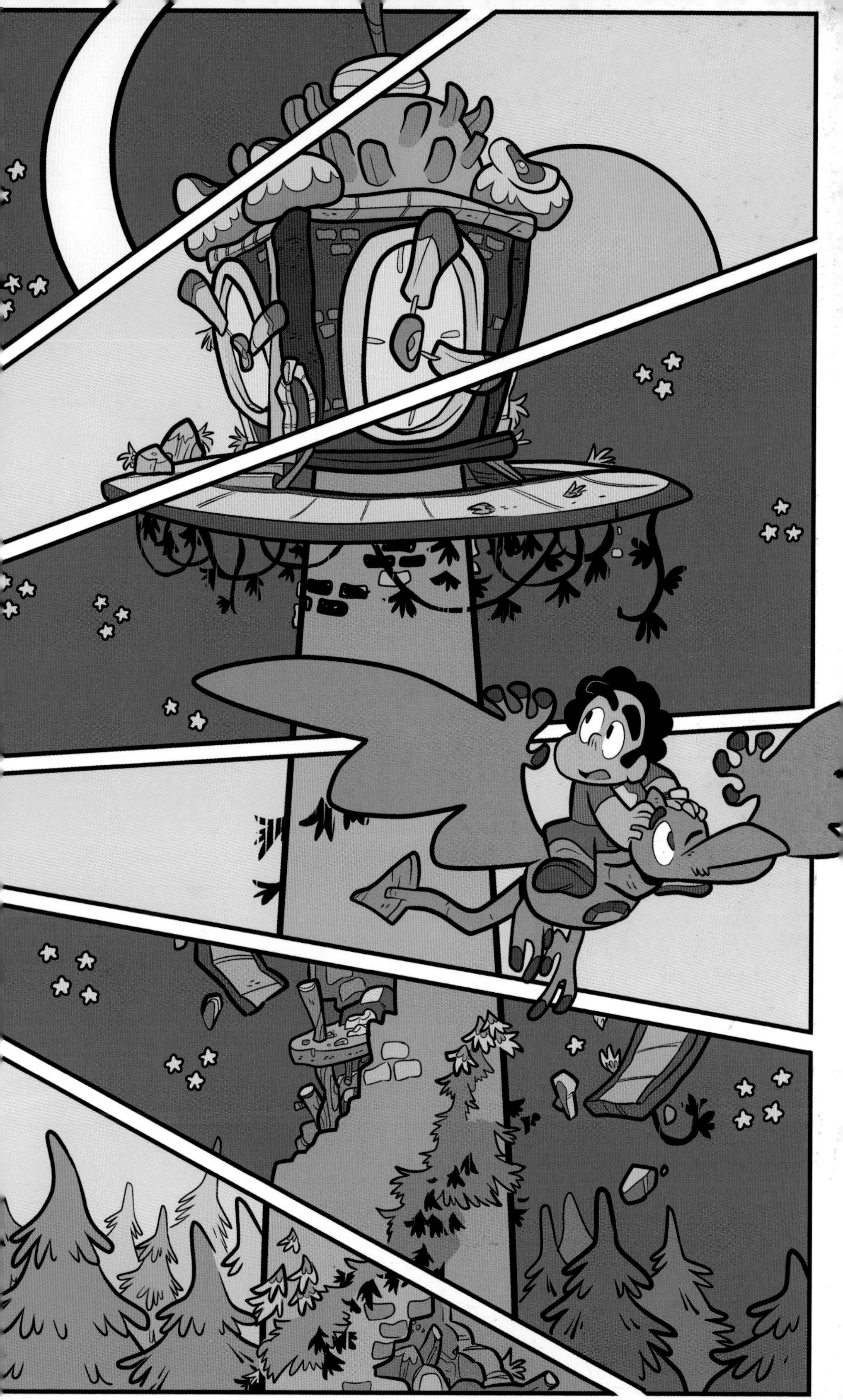

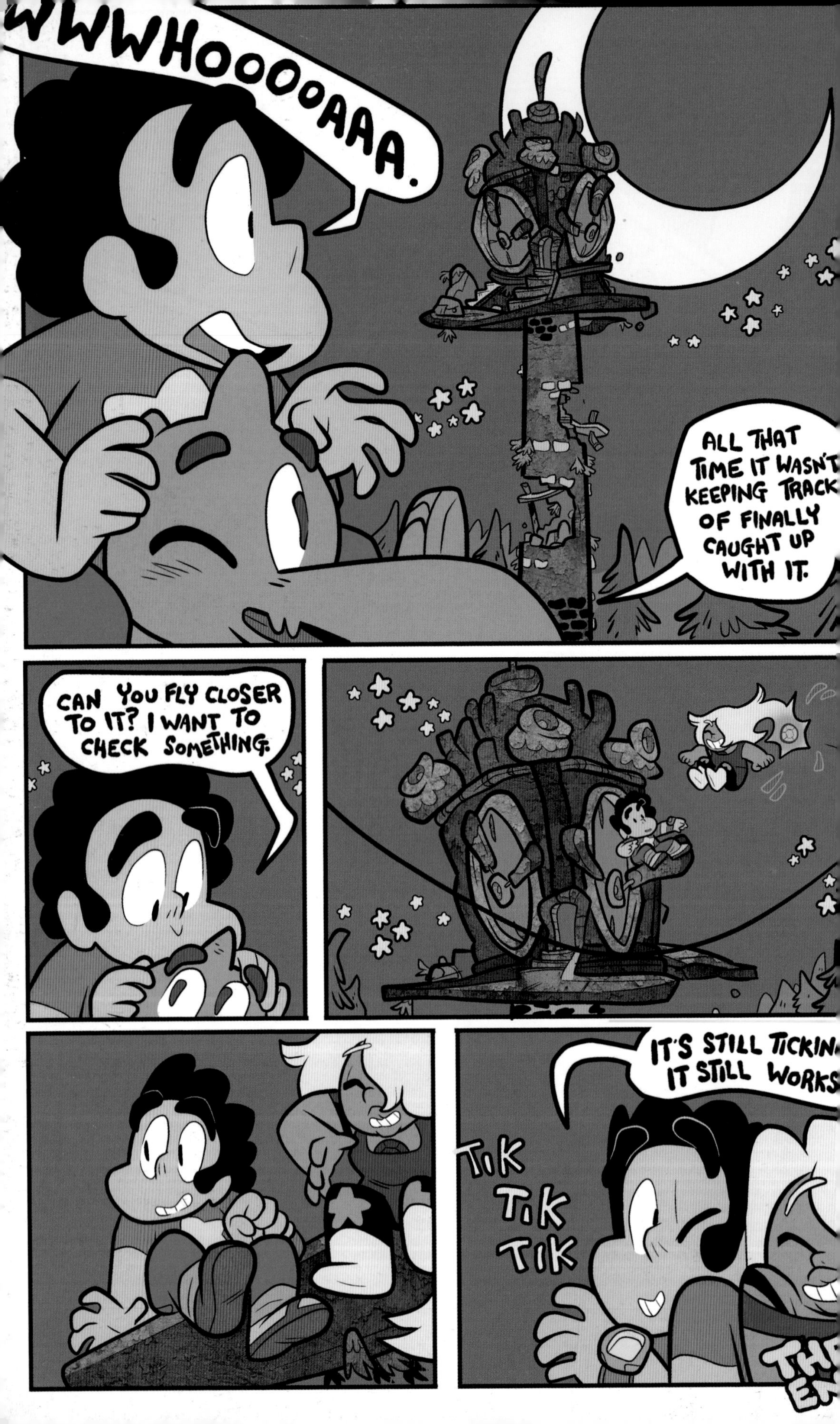
WWWHOOOOoAAA.
ALL THAT TIME IT WASN'T KEEPING TRACK OF FINALLY CAUGHT UP WITH IT.
CAN YOU FLY CLOSER TO IT? I WANT TO CHECK SOMETHING.
IT'S STILL TICKIN
IT STILL WORKS
TIK
TIK
TIK

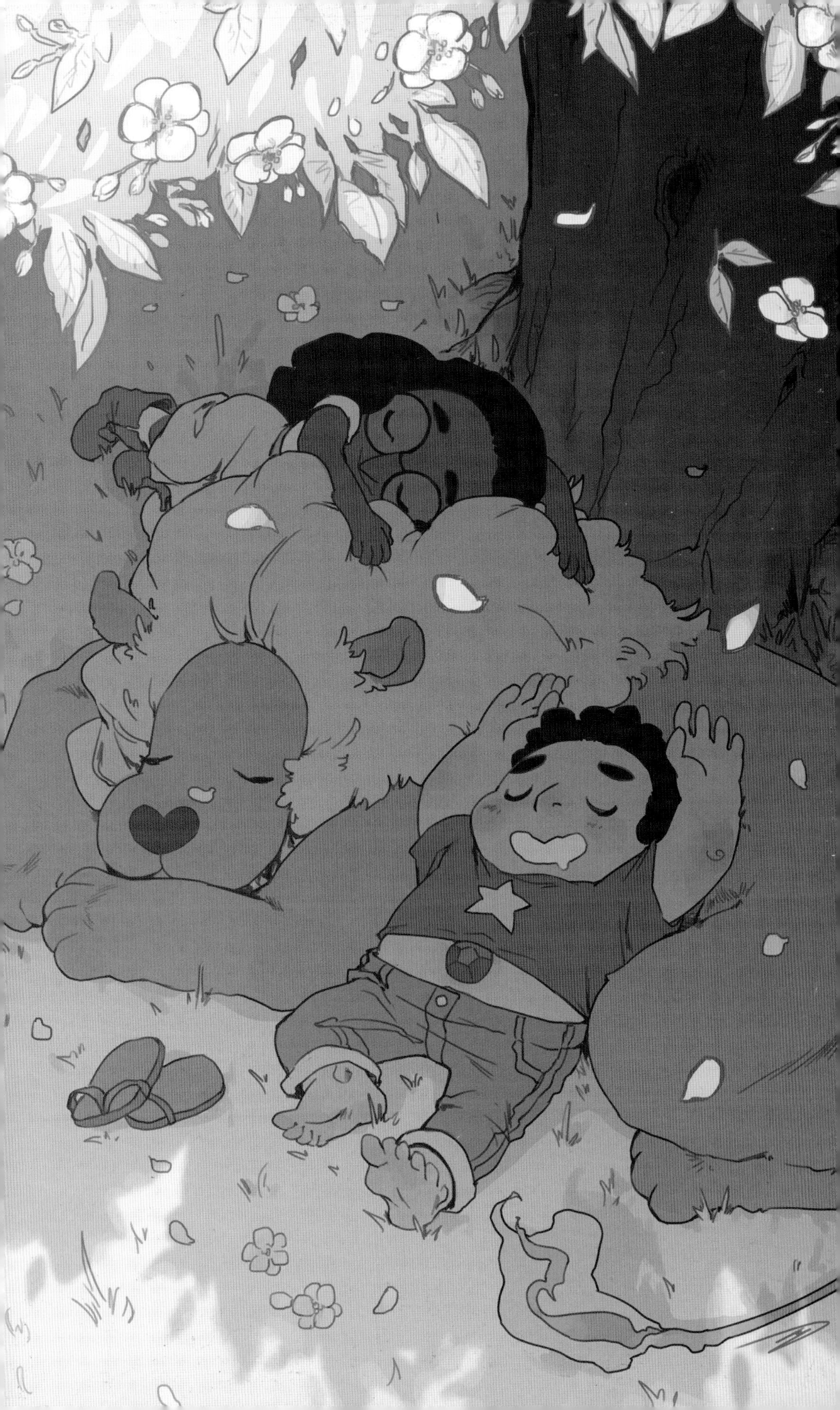

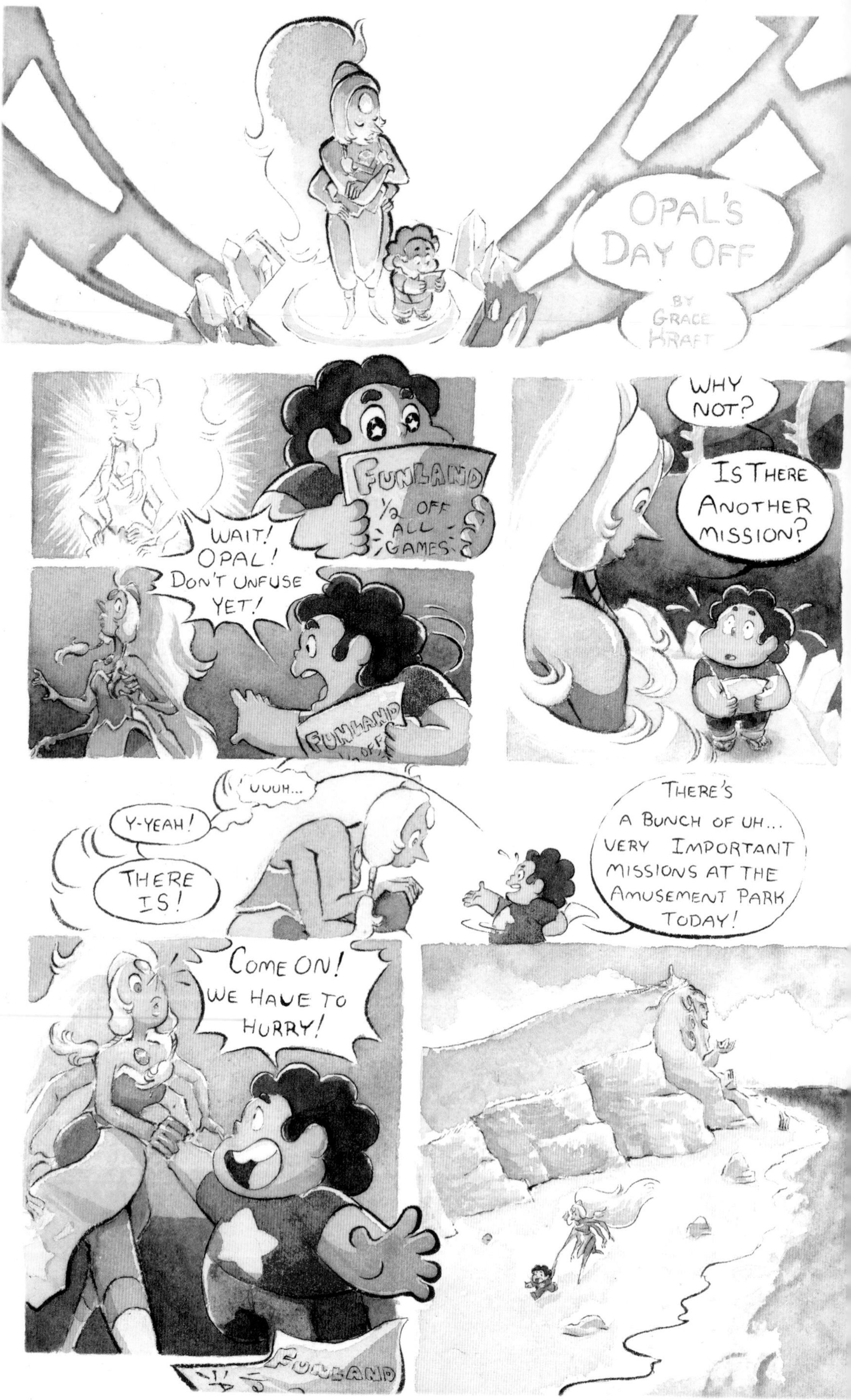

OPAL'S DAY OFF
BY GRACE KRAFT
FUNLAND
½ OFF ALL GAMES
WAIT! OPAL! DON'T UNFUSE YET!
FUNLAND
WHY NOT?
IS THERE ANOTHER MISSION?
UUUH...
Y-YEAH!
THERE IS!
THERE'S A BUNCH OF UH... VERY IMPORTANT MISSIONS AT THE AMUSEMENT PARK TODAY!
COME ON! WE HAVE TO HURRY!
FUNLAND

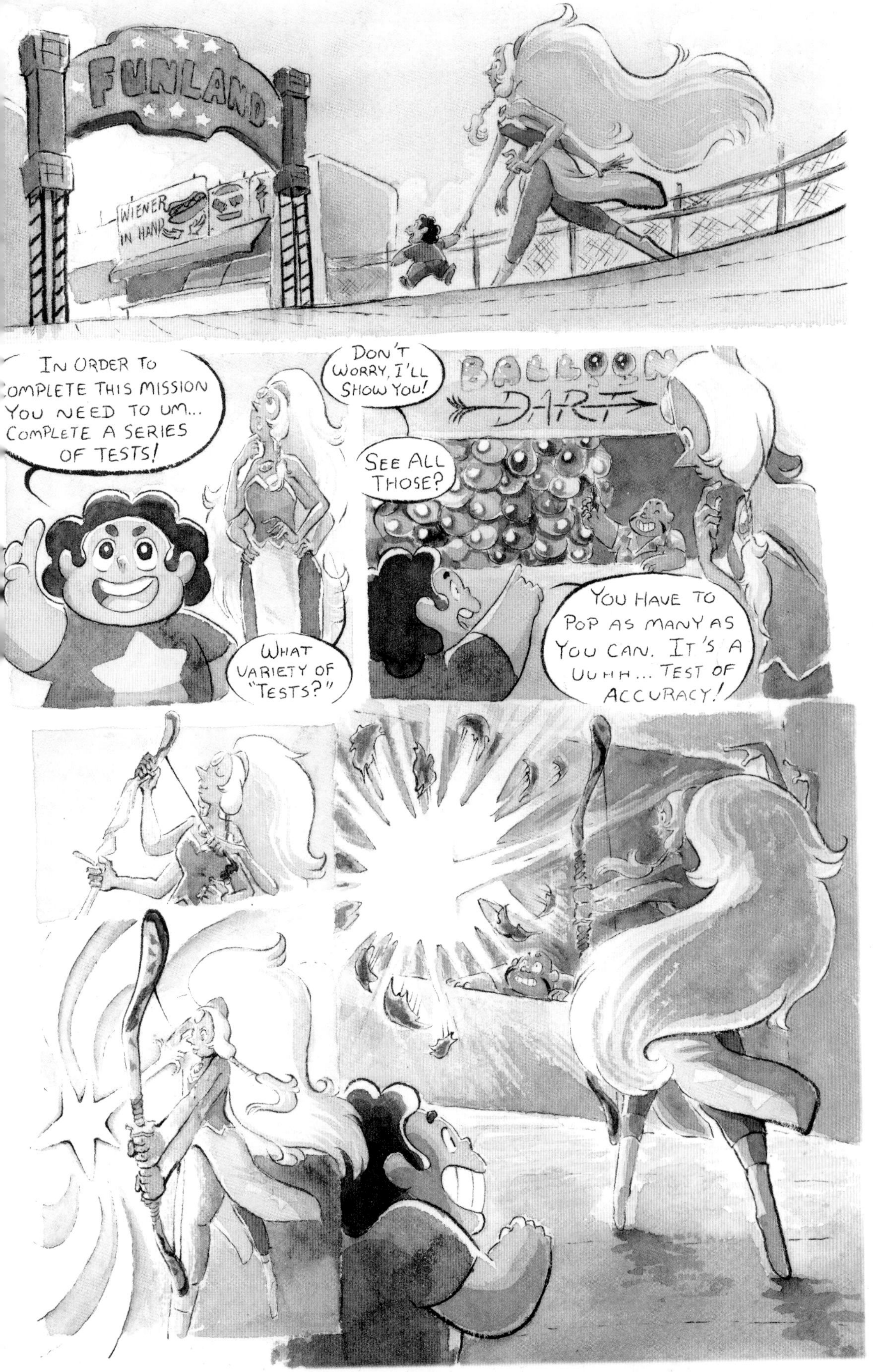
FUNLAND
WIENER IN HAND
IN ORDER TO COMPLETE THIS MISSION YOU NEED TO UM... COMPLETE A SERIES OF TESTS!
WHAT VARIETY OF "TESTS?"
DON'T WORRY, I'LL SHOW YOU!
BALLOON DART
SEE ALL THOSE?
YOU HAVE TO POP AS MANY AS YOU CAN. IT'S A UUHH... TEST OF ACCURACY!

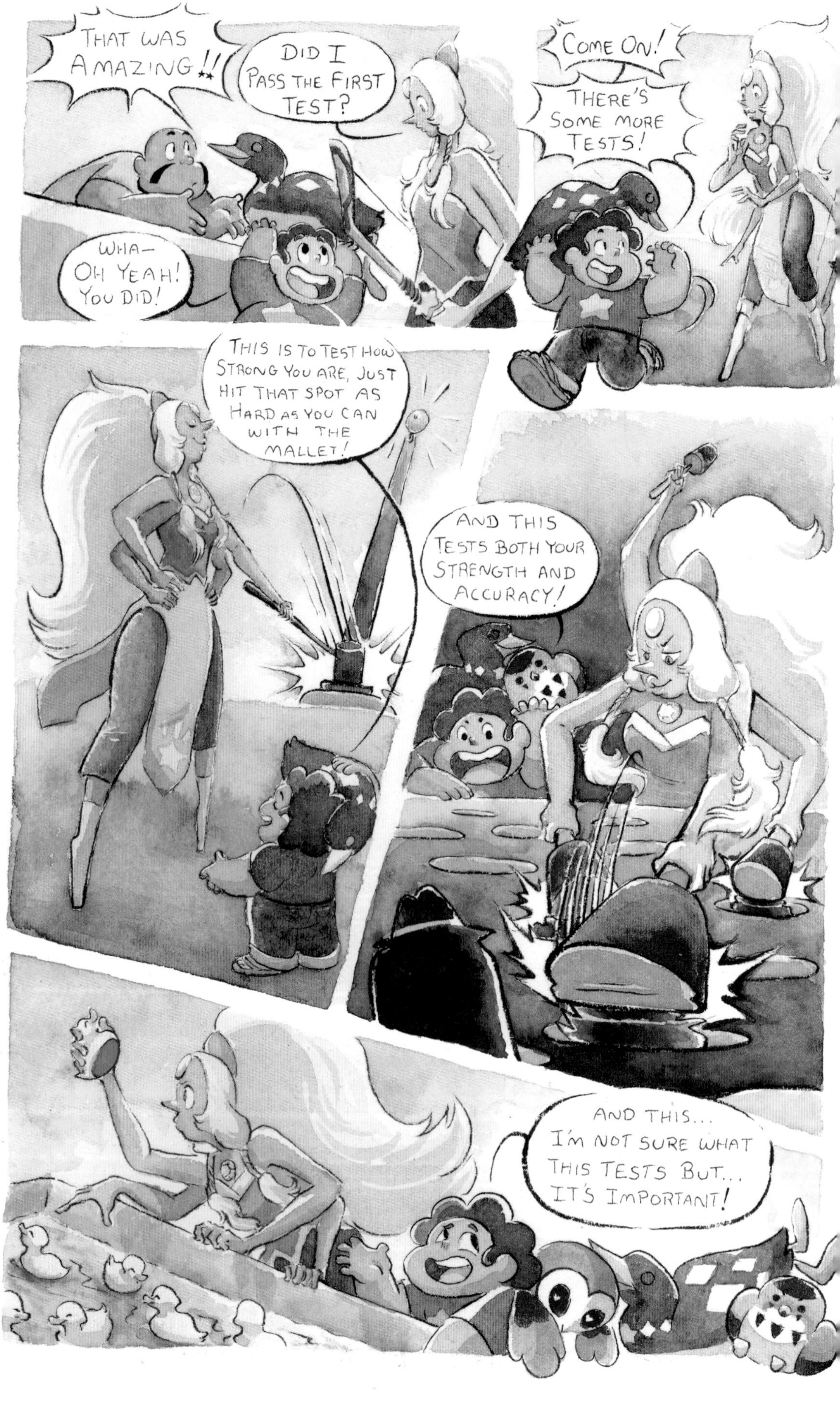
THAT WAS AMAZING!!
DID I PASS THE FIRST TEST?
WHA— OH YEAH! YOU DID!
COME ON!
THERE'S SOME MORE TESTS!
THIS IS TO TEST HOW STRONG YOU ARE, JUST HIT THAT SPOT AS HARD AS YOU CAN WITH THE MALLET!
AND THIS TESTS BOTH YOUR STRENGTH AND ACCURACY!
AND THIS... I'M NOT SURE WHAT THIS TESTS BUT... IT'S IMPORTANT!

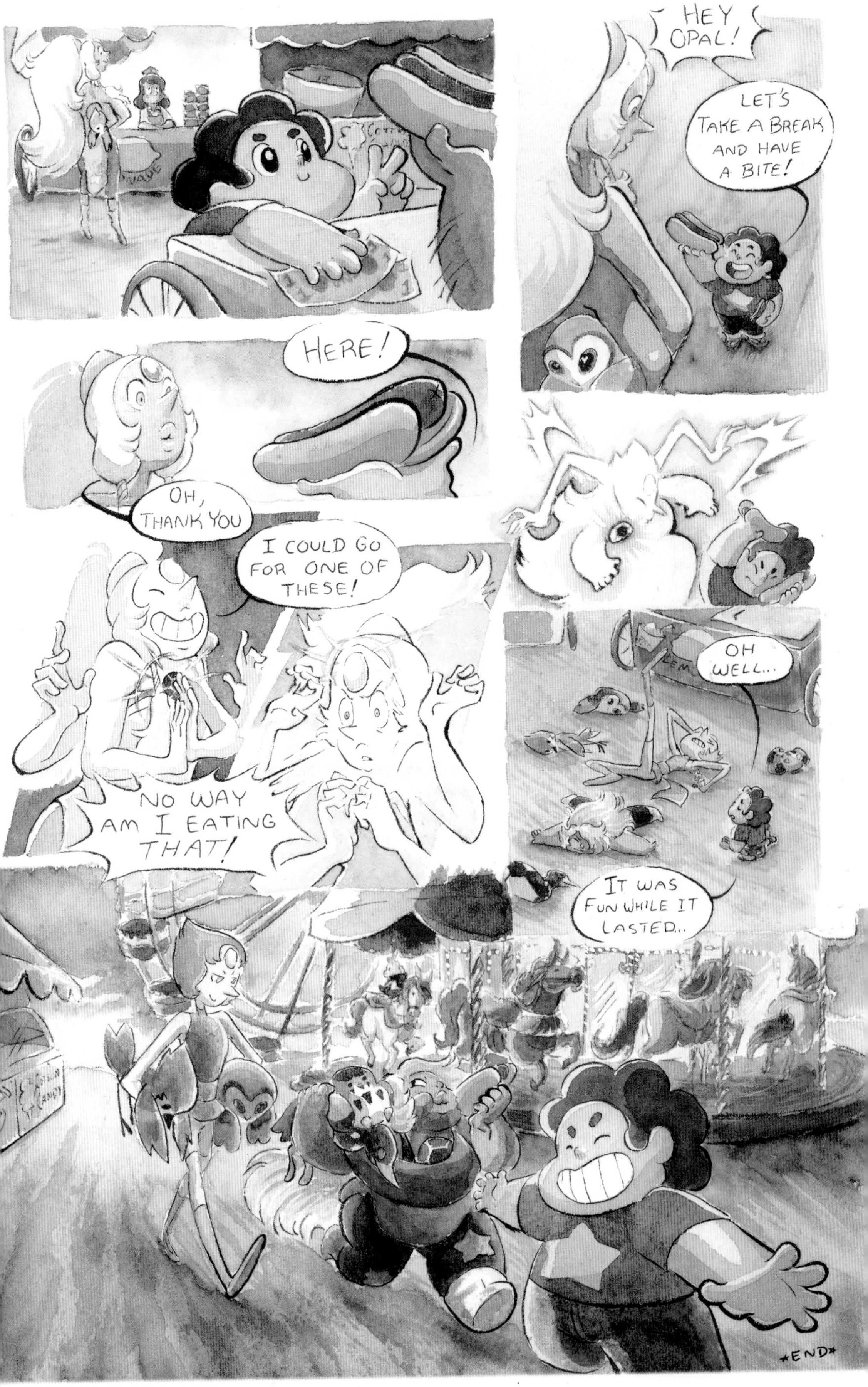
HEY OPAL!
LET'S TAKE A BREAK AND HAVE A BITE!
HERE!
OH, THANK YOU
I COULD GO FOR ONE OF THESE!
NO WAY AM I EATING THAT!
OH WELL...
IT WAS FUN WHILE IT LASTED...
*END*

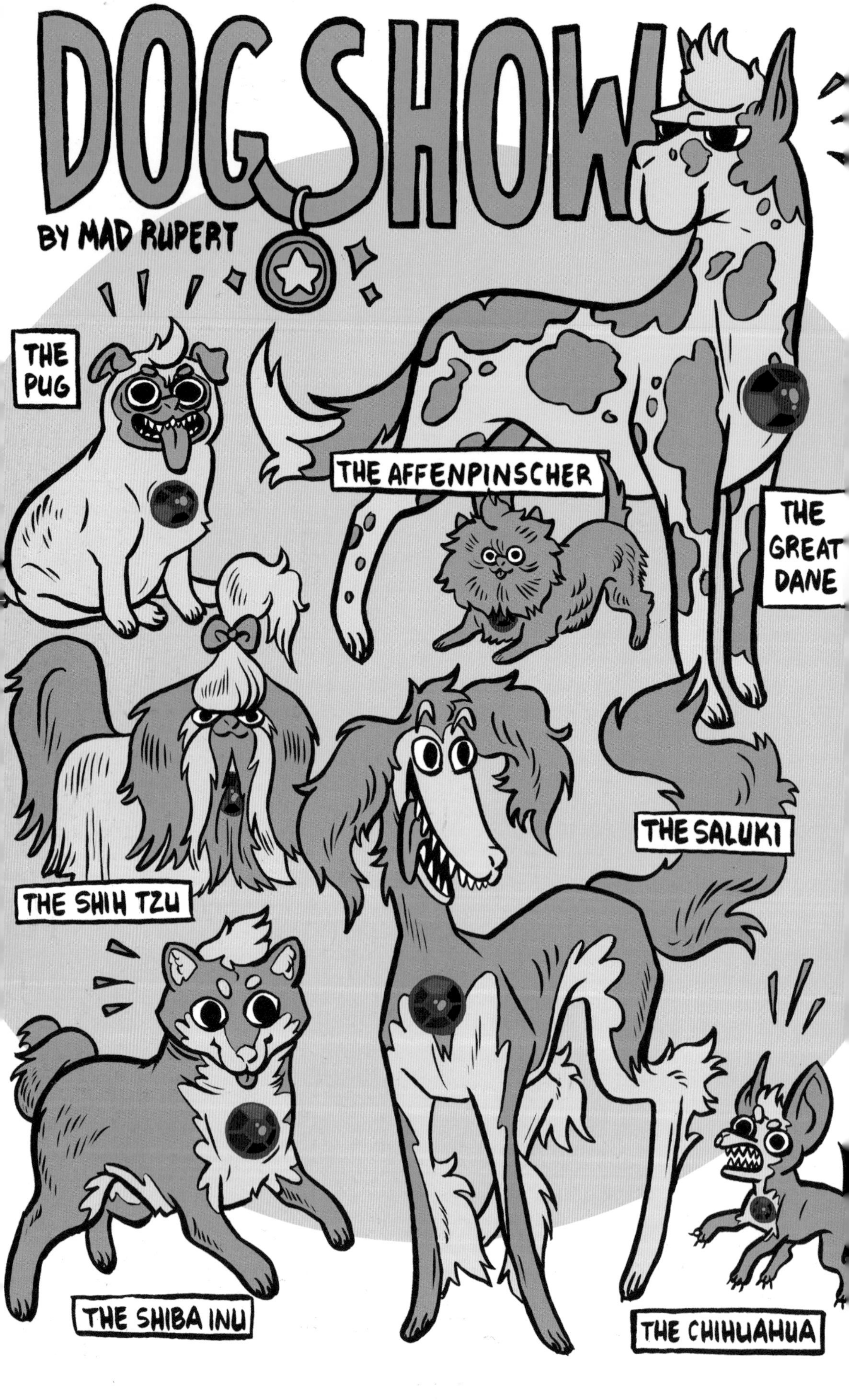
DOG SHOW
BY MAD RUPERT
THE PUG
THE AFFENPINSCHER
THE GREAT DANE
THE SHIH TZU
THE SALUKI
THE SHIBA INU
THE CHIHUAHUA

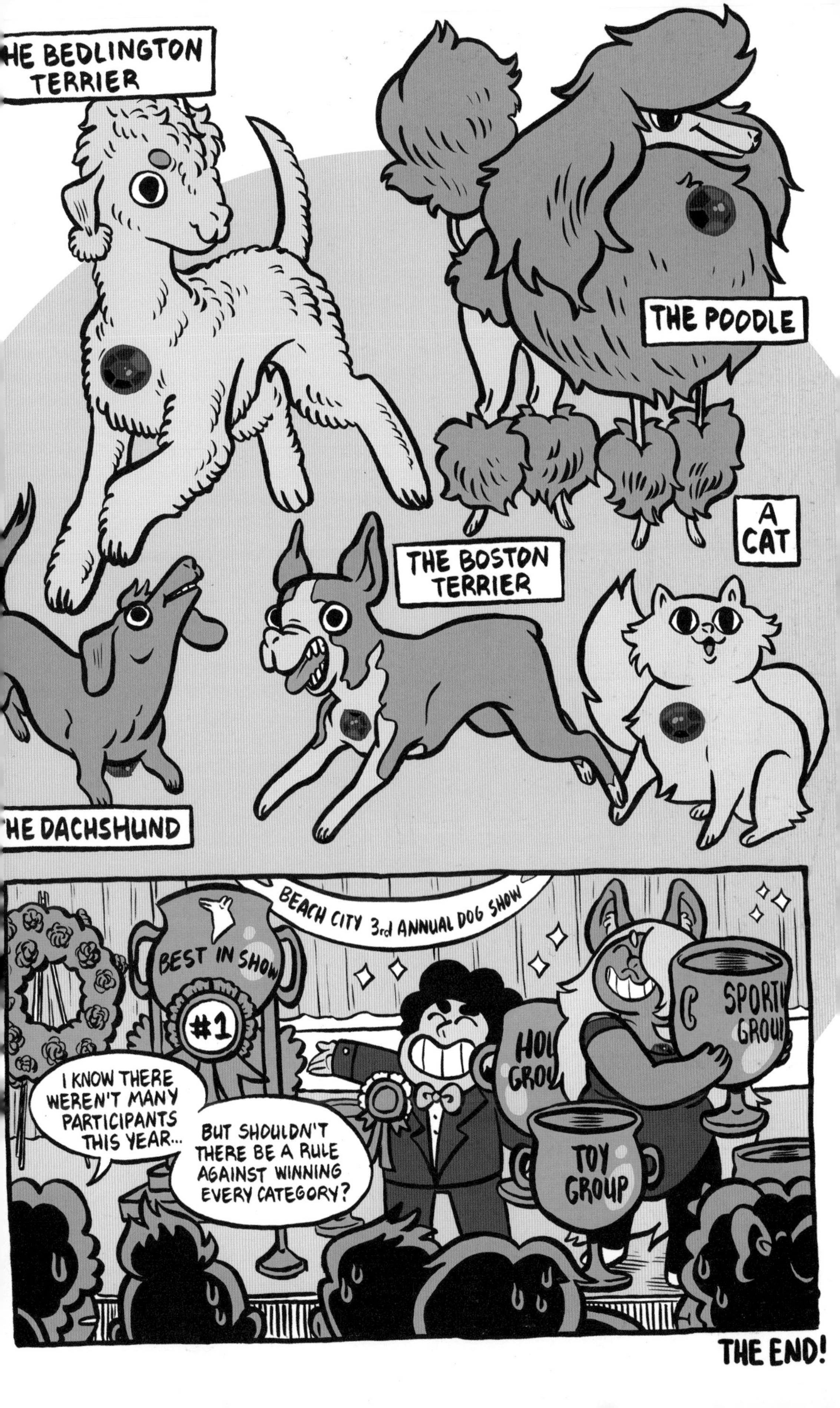
HE BEDLINGTON TERRIER
THE POODLE
A CAT
THE BOSTON TERRIER
HE DACHSHUND
BEACH CITY 3rd ANNUAL DOG SHOW
BEST IN SHOW
#1
SPORTI GROU
HOU GROU
TOY GROUP
I KNOW THERE WEREN'T MANY PARTICIPANTS THIS YEAR...
BUT SHOULDN'T THERE BE A RULE AGAINST WINNING EVERY CATEGORY?
THE END!

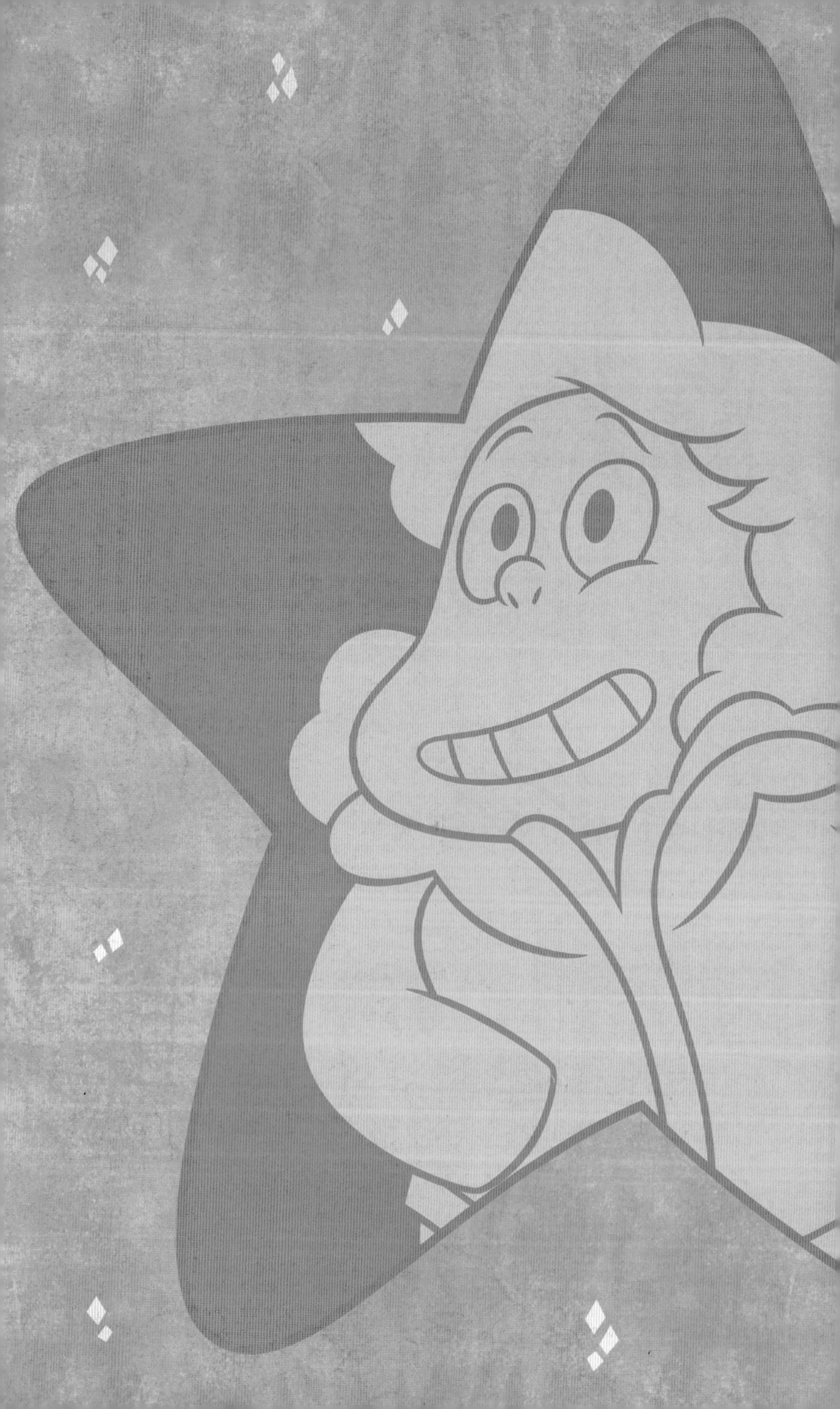

**"TRAFFIC CONES"**
&
**"TENNIS DOUBLES"**

written by
**JEREMY SORESE**

illustrated by
**COLEMAN ENGLE**

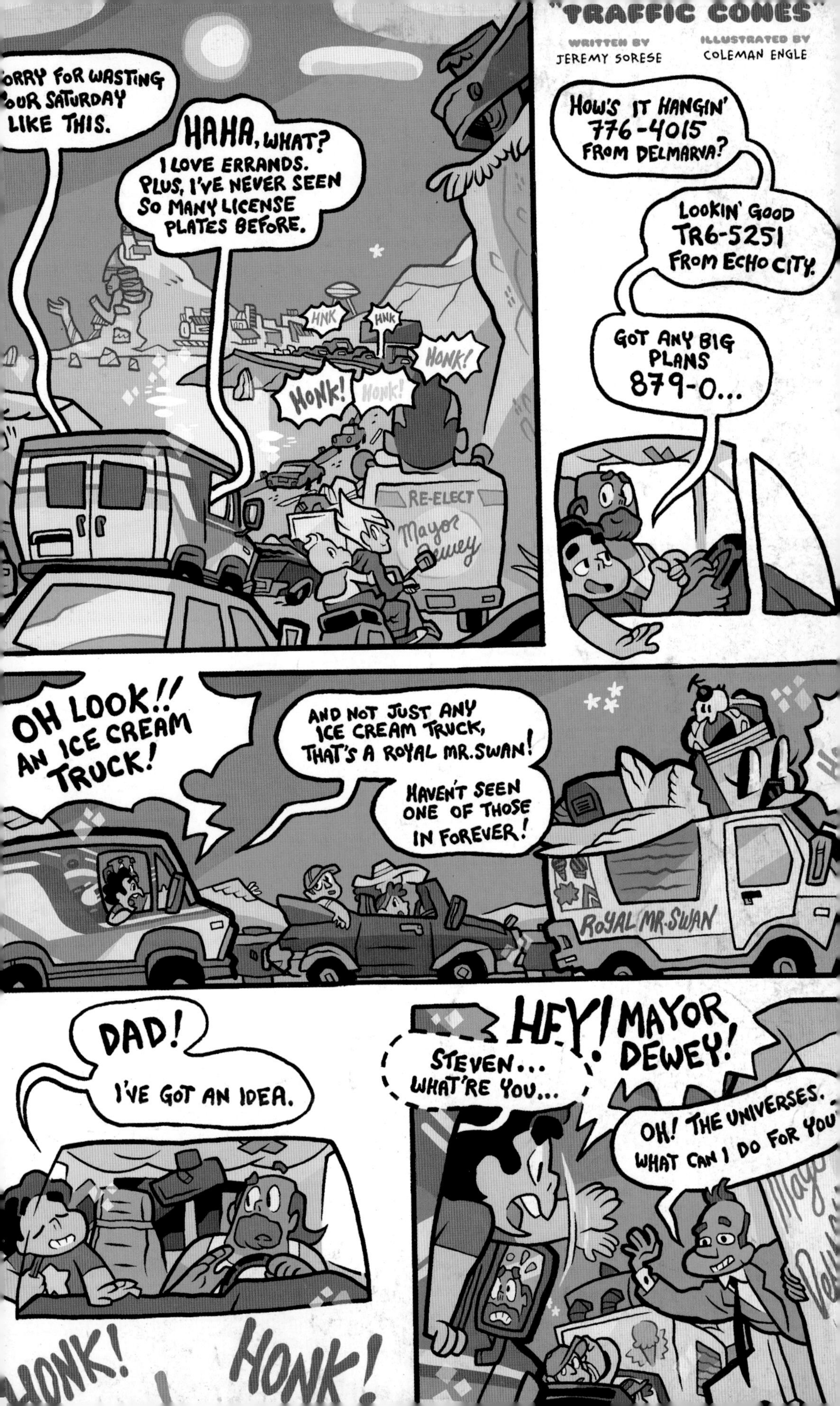

"TRAFFIC CONES"
WRITTEN BY JEREMY SORESE
ILLUSTRATED BY COLEMAN ENGLE
ORRY FOR WASTING OUR SATURDAY LIKE THIS.
HAHA, WHAT? I LOVE ERRANDS. PLUS, I'VE NEVER SEEN SO MANY LICENSE PLATES BEFORE.
HNK
HNK
HONK!
HONK!
HONK!
RE-ELECT Mayor Dewey
HOW'S IT HANGIN' 776-4015 FROM DELMARVA?
LOOKIN' GOOD TR6-5251 FROM ECHO CITY.
GOT ANY BIG PLANS 879-0...
OH LOOK!! AN ICE CREAM TRUCK!
AND NOT JUST ANY ICE CREAM TRUCK, THAT'S A ROYAL MR. SWAN!
HAVEN'T SEEN ONE OF THOSE IN FOREVER!
ROYAL MR. SWAN
DAD!
I'VE GOT AN IDEA.
HONK!
HONK!
HEY! MAYOR DEWEY!
STEVEN... WHAT'RE YOU...
OH! THE UNIVERSES. WHAT CAN I DO FOR YOU

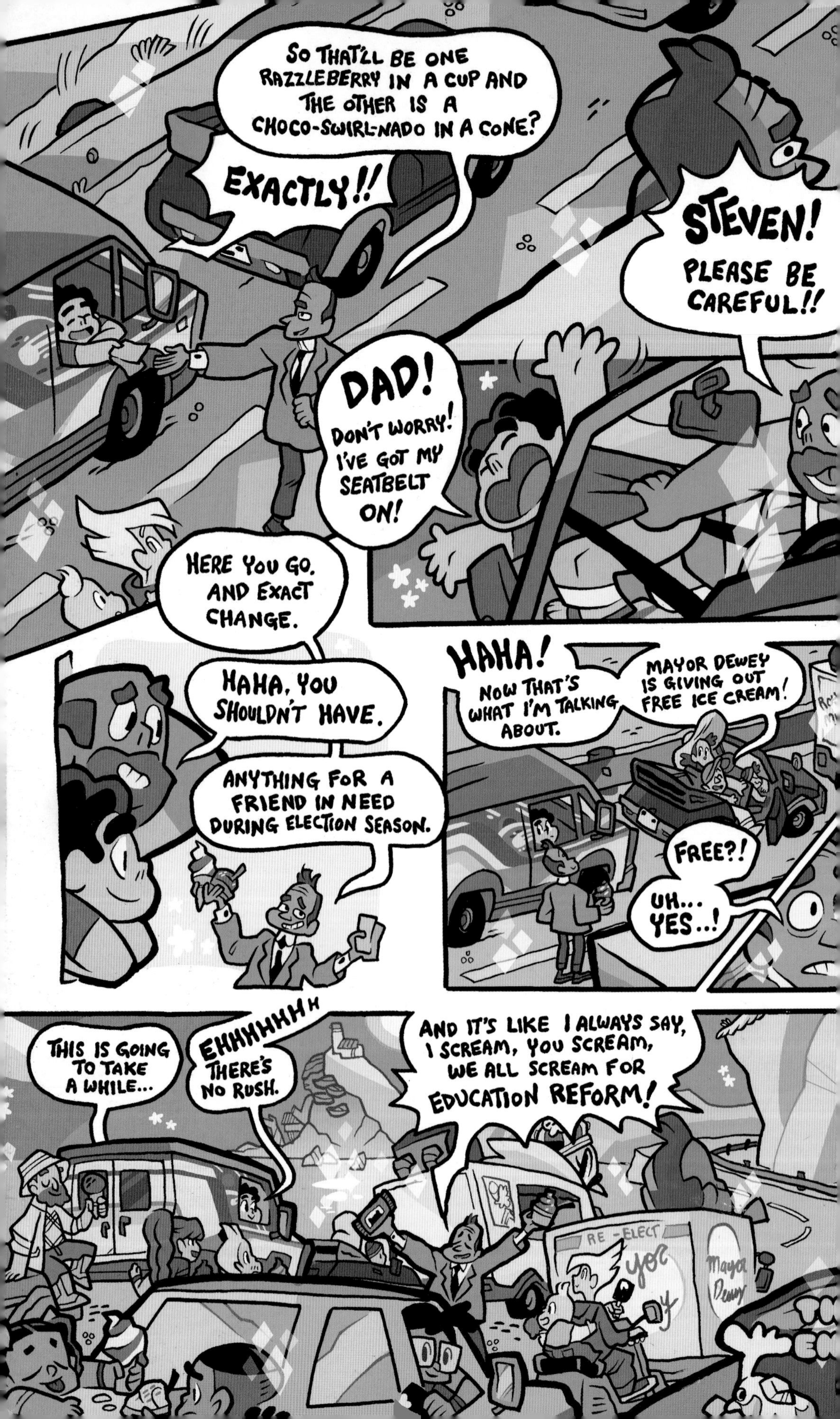
SO THAT'LL BE ONE RAZZLEBERRY IN A CUP AND THE OTHER IS A CHOCO-SWIRL-NADO IN A CONE?
EXACTLY!!
STEVEN! PLEASE BE CAREFUL!!
DAD! DON'T WORRY! I'VE GOT MY SEATBELT ON!
HERE YOU GO. AND EXACT CHANGE.
HAHA, YOU SHOULDN'T HAVE.
ANYTHING FOR A FRIEND IN NEED DURING ELECTION SEASON.
HAHA! NOW THAT'S WHAT I'M TALKING ABOUT.
MAYOR DEWEY IS GIVING OUT FREE ICE CREAM!
FREE?!
UH... YES..!
THIS IS GOING TO TAKE A WHILE...
EHHHHHHH THERE'S NO RUSH.
AND IT'S LIKE I ALWAYS SAY, I SCREAM, YOU SCREAM, WE ALL SCREAM FOR EDUCATION REFORM!
RE-ELECT
Mayor Dewey

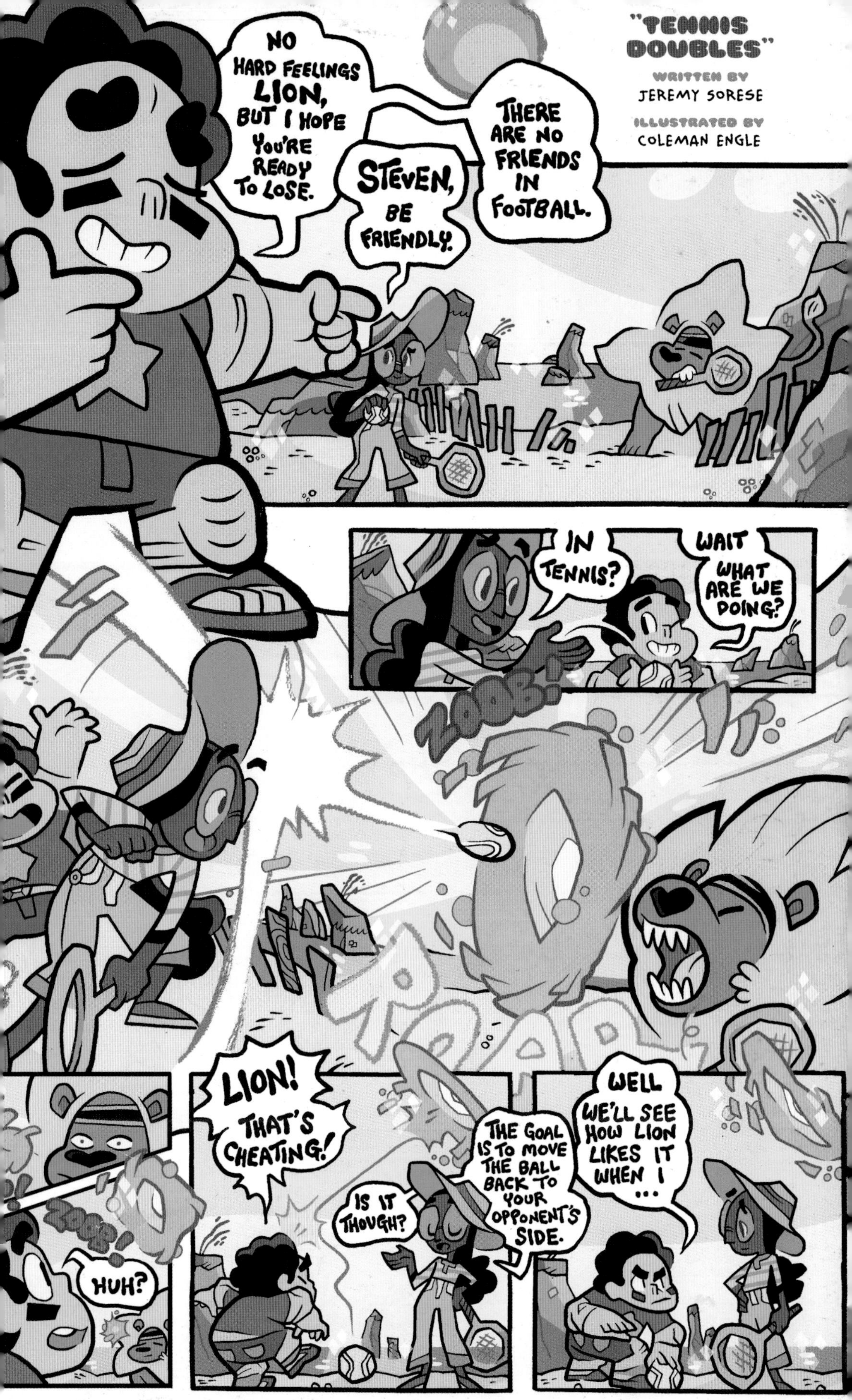

"TENNIS DOUBLES"
WRITTEN BY
JEREMY SORESE
ILLUSTRATED BY
COLEMAN ENGLE
NO HARD FEELINGS LION, BUT I HOPE YOU'RE READY TO LOSE.
STEVEN, BE FRIENDLY.
THERE ARE NO FRIENDS IN FOOTBALL.
IN TENNIS?
WAIT WHAT ARE WE DOING?
ZOOB!!
ROAR!
ZOOB!
HUH?
LION! THAT'S CHEATING!
IS IT THOUGH?
THE GOAL IS TO MOVE THE BALL BACK TO YOUR OPPONENT'S SIDE.
WELL WE'LL SEE HOW LION LIKES IT WHEN I ...

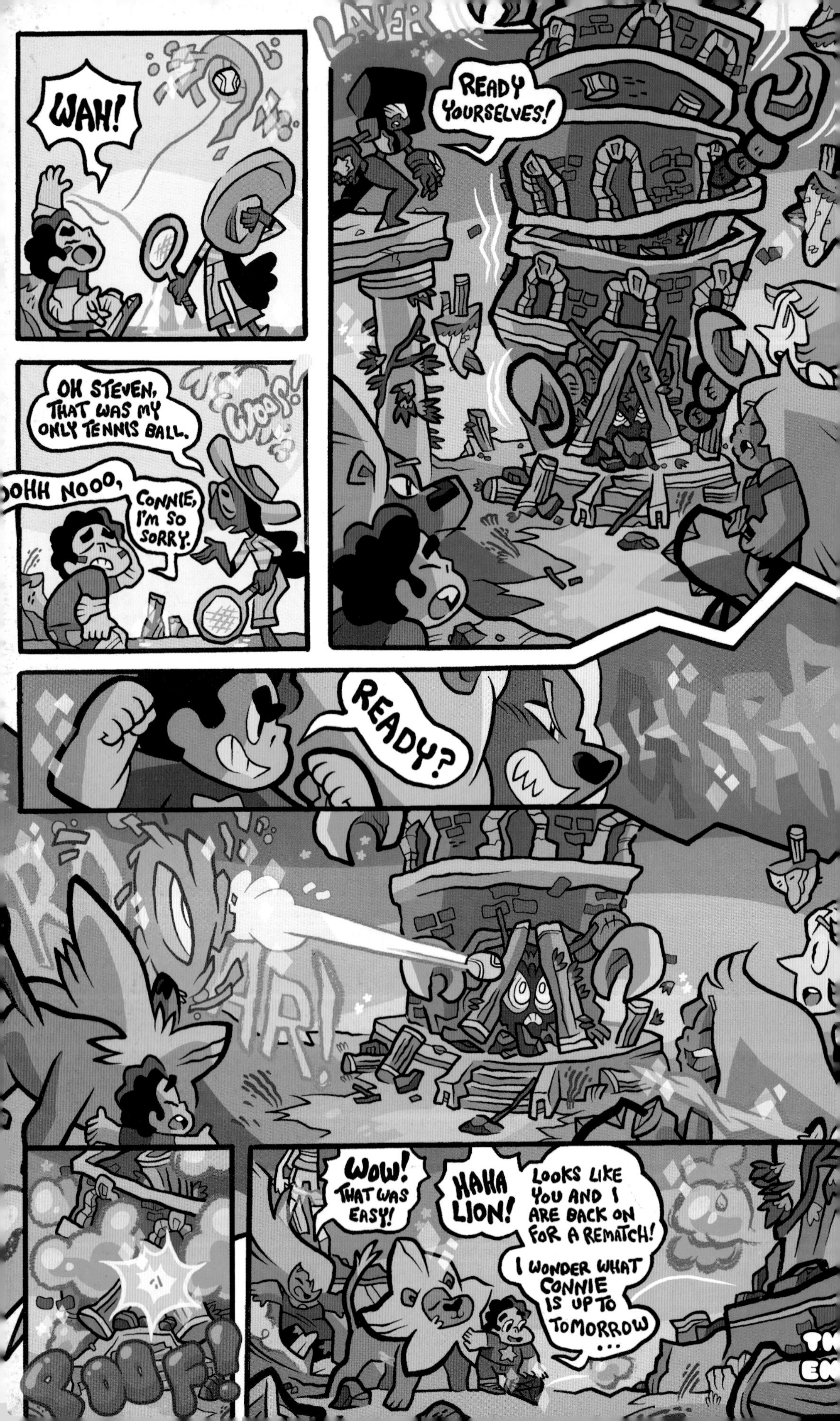

WAH!
OH STEVEN, THAT WAS MY ONLY TENNIS BALL.
WOOF!
OOHH NOOO,
CONNIE, I'M SO SORRY.
LATER...
READY YOURSELVES!
READY?
BOOF!
WOW! THAT WAS EASY!
HAHA LION!
LOOKS LIKE YOU AND I ARE BACK ON FOR A REMATCH!
I WONDER WHAT CONNIE IS UP TO TOMORROW...

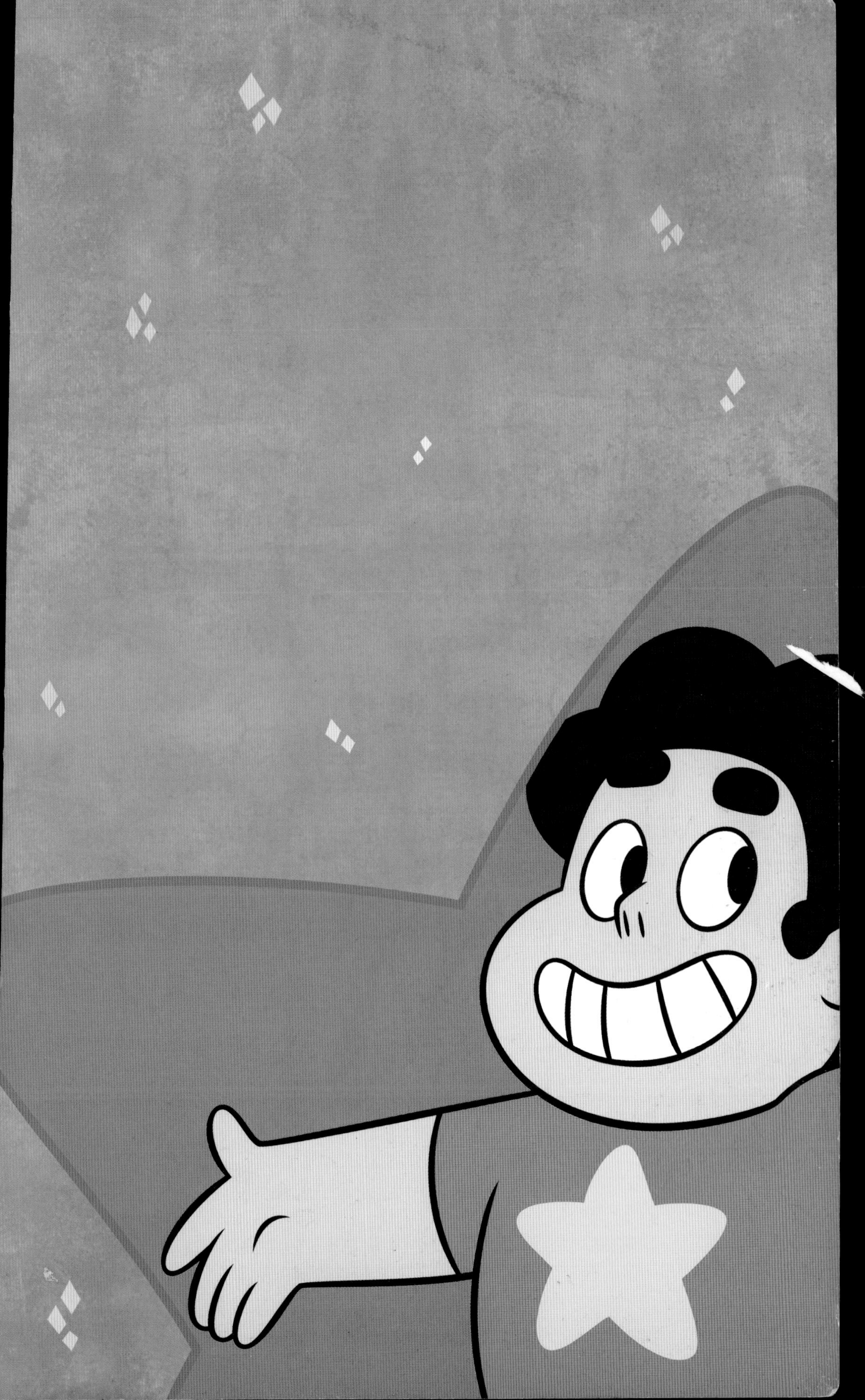

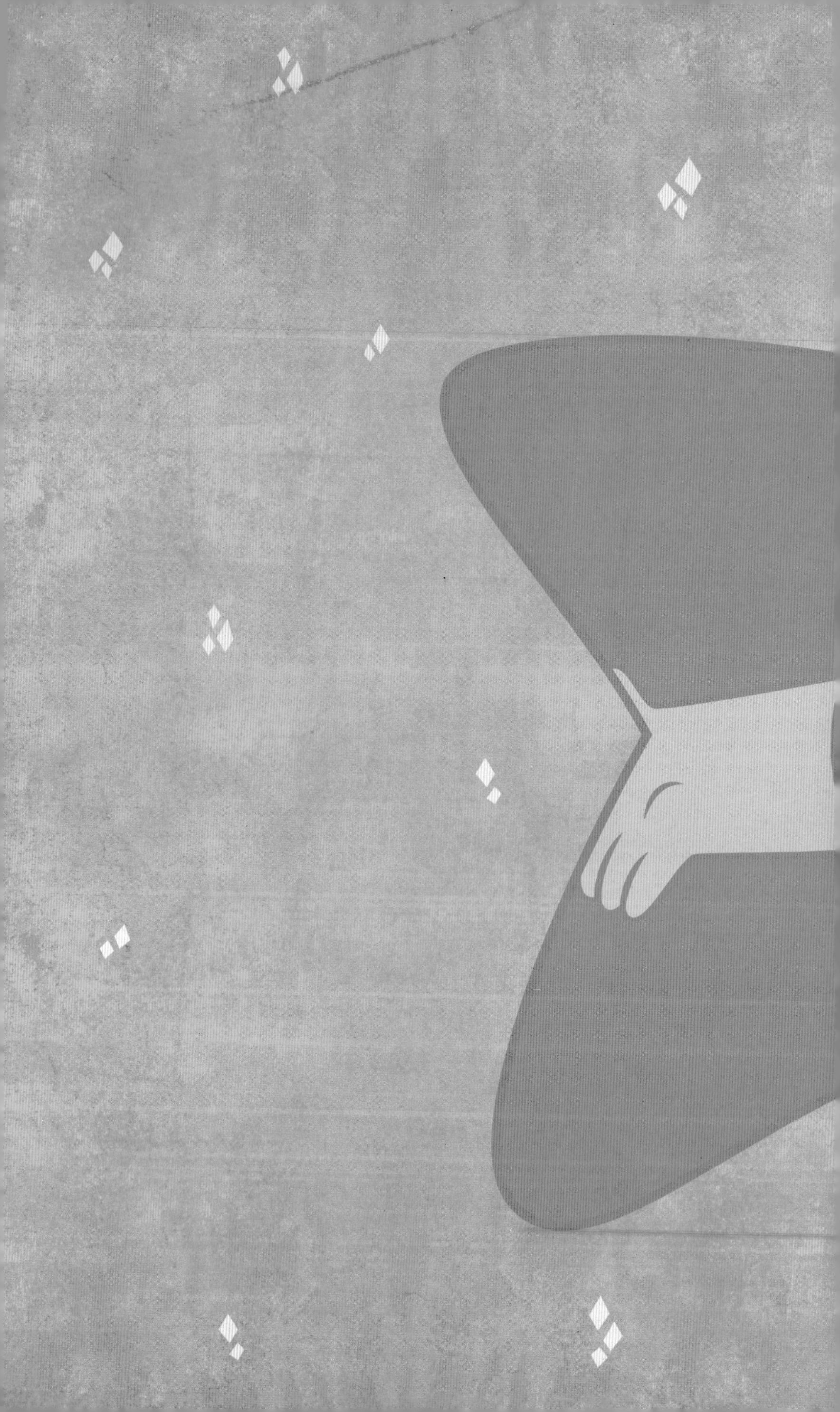

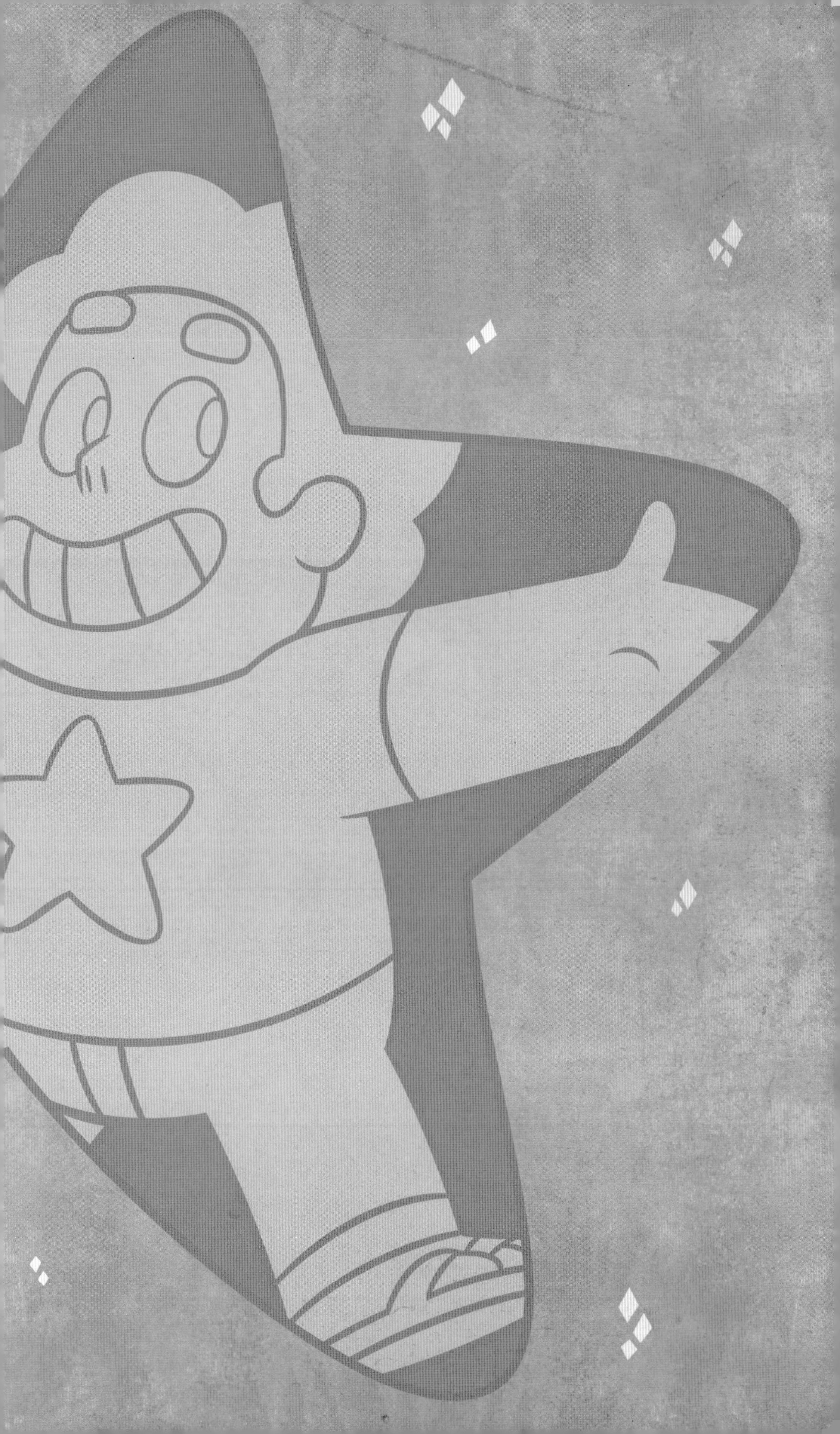

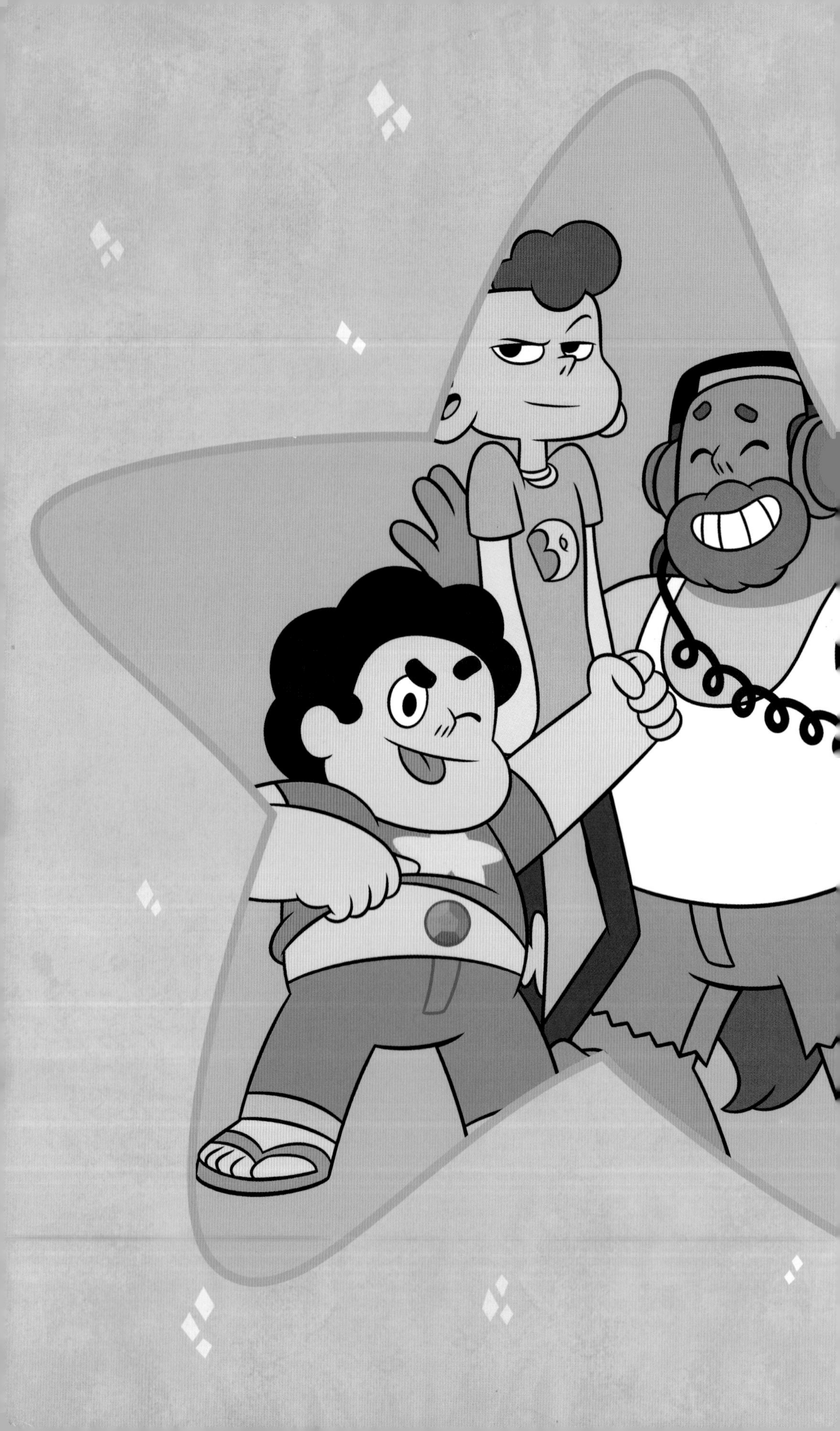

# COVER GALLERY

ISSUE FIVE

**AMBER ROGERS**

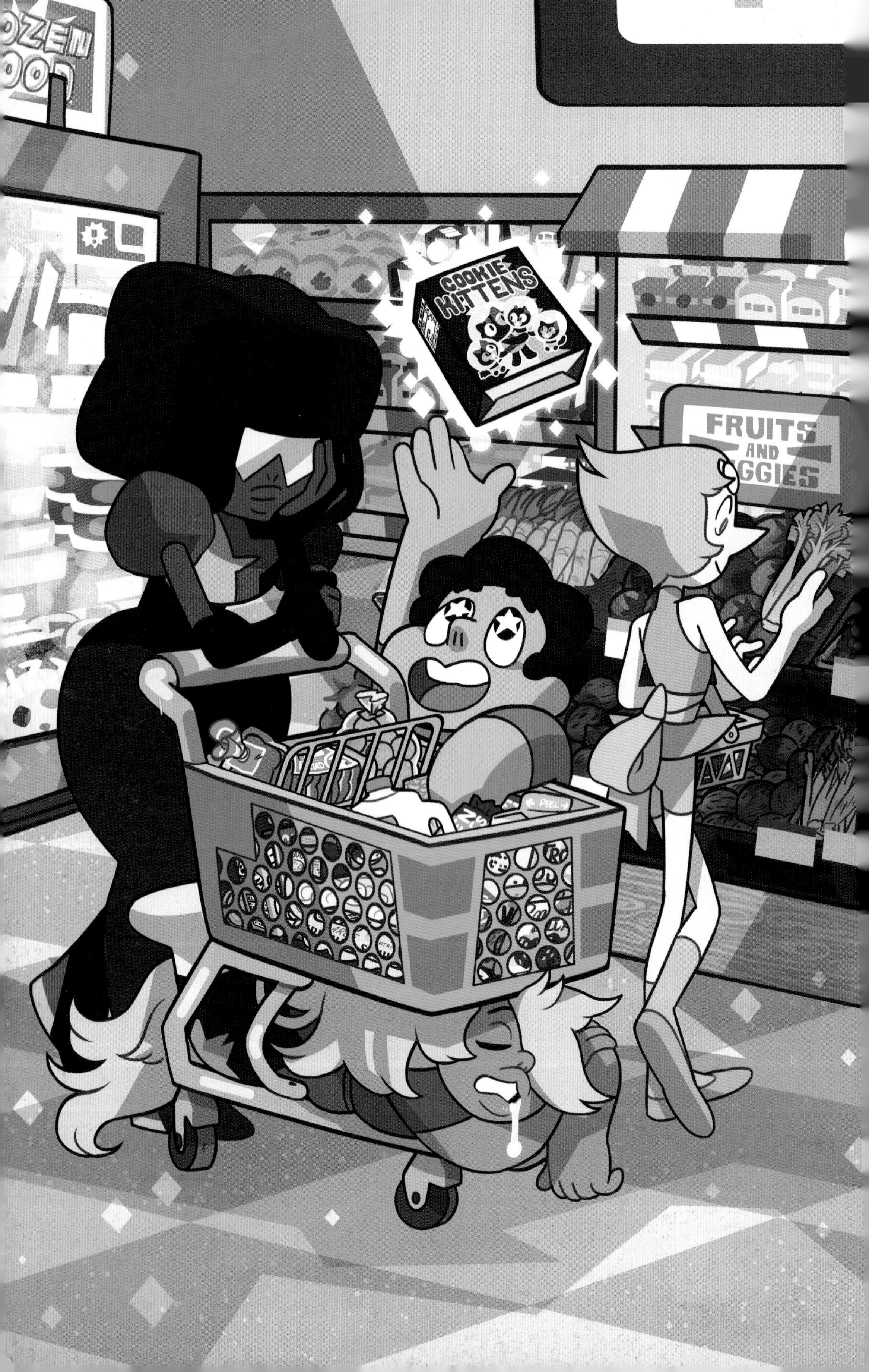
COOKIE KITTENS
FRUITS AND
PEEL

ISSUE FIVE

**GRACE KRAFT**

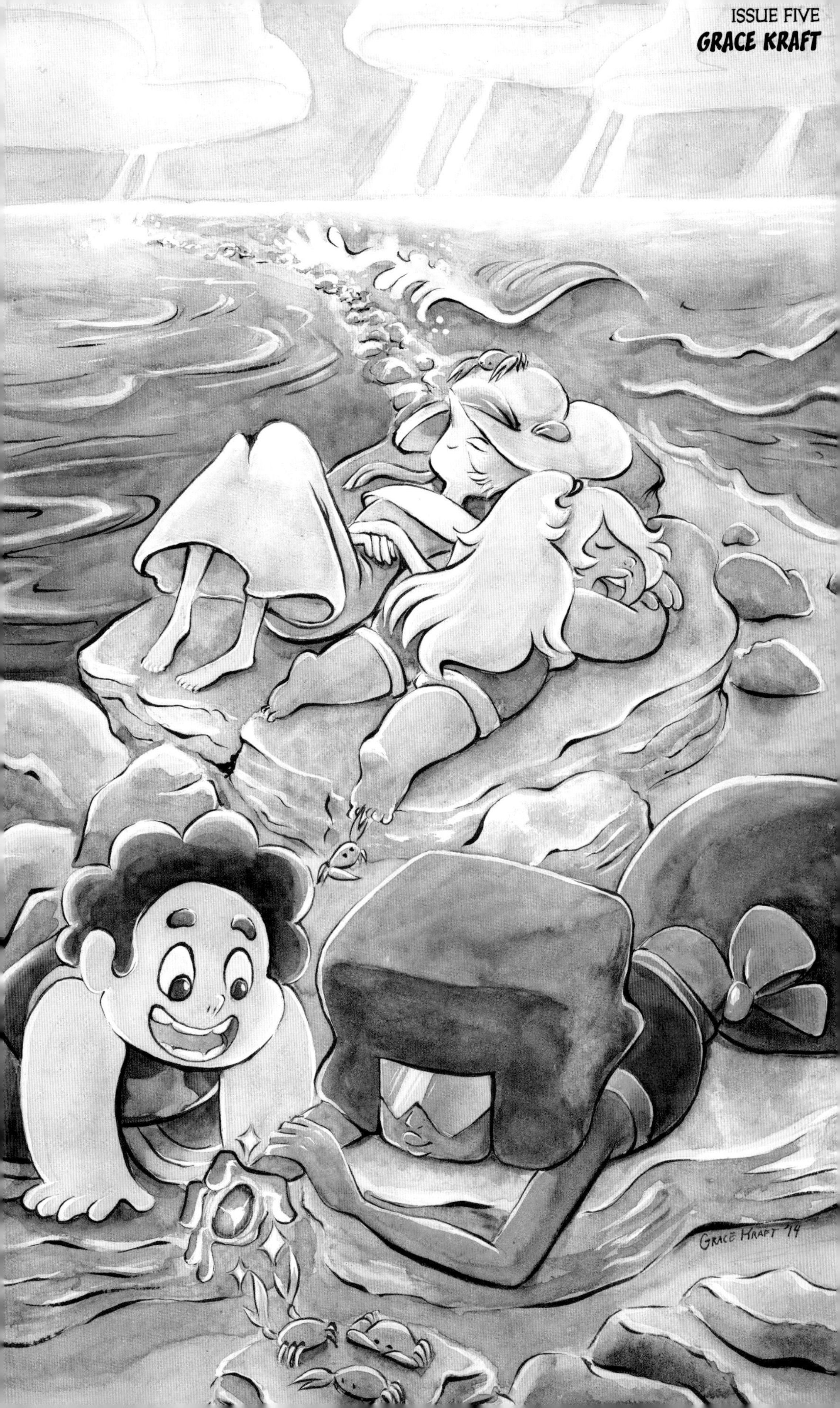
GRACE KRAFT '14

ISSUE FIVE VARIANT
**HELEN YOON**

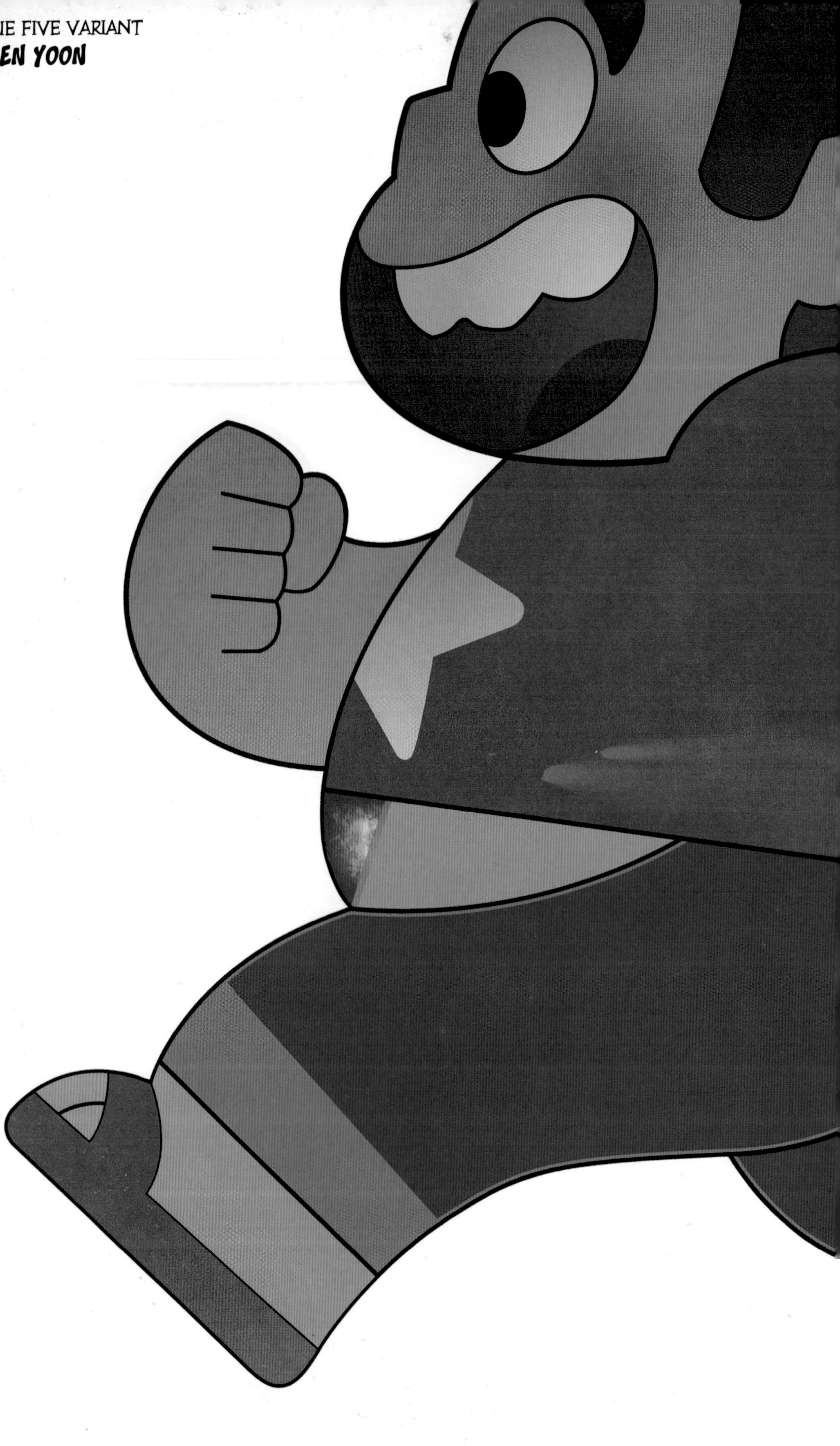

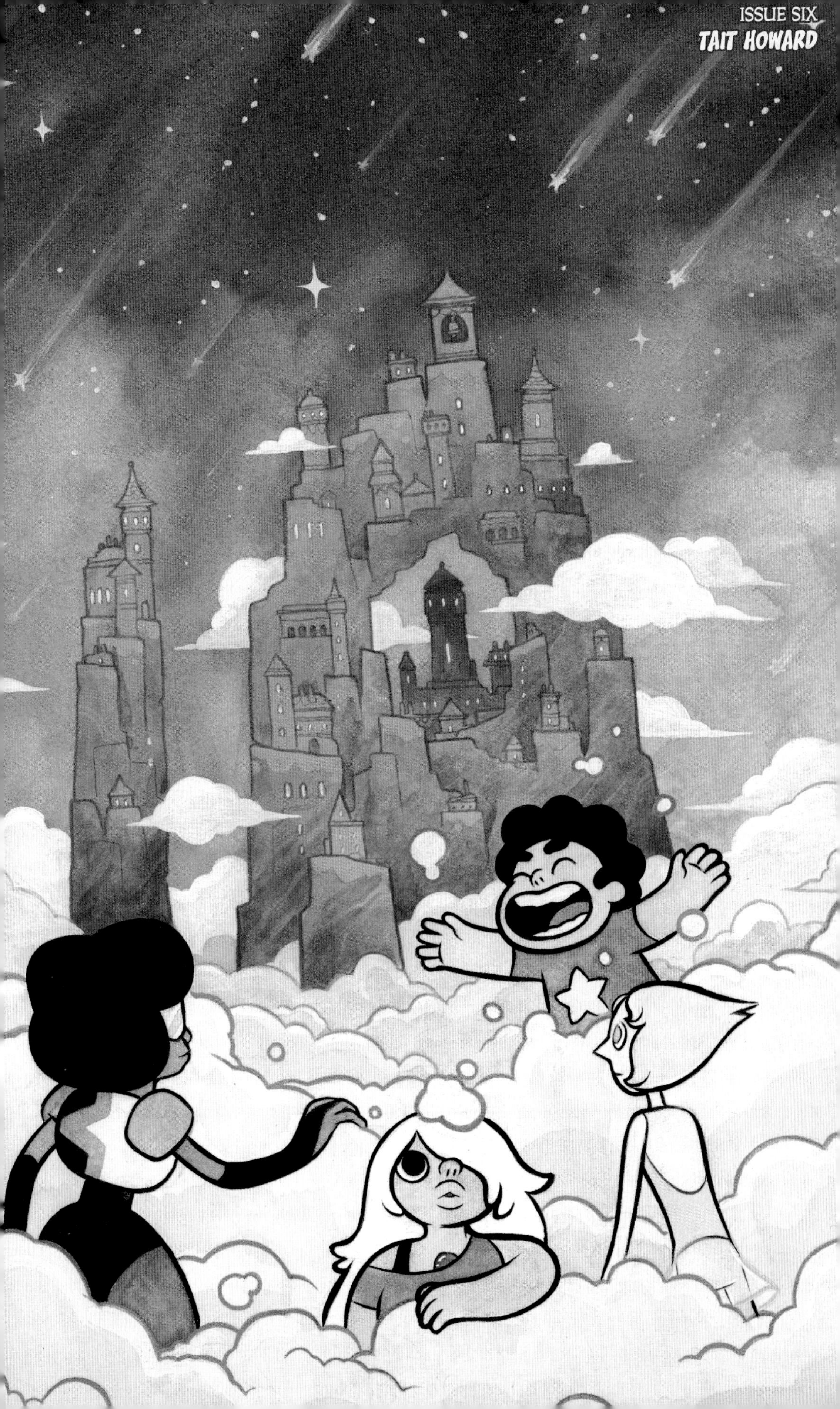
ISSUE SIX
TAIT HOWARD

ISSUE SIX

**MEG GANDY**

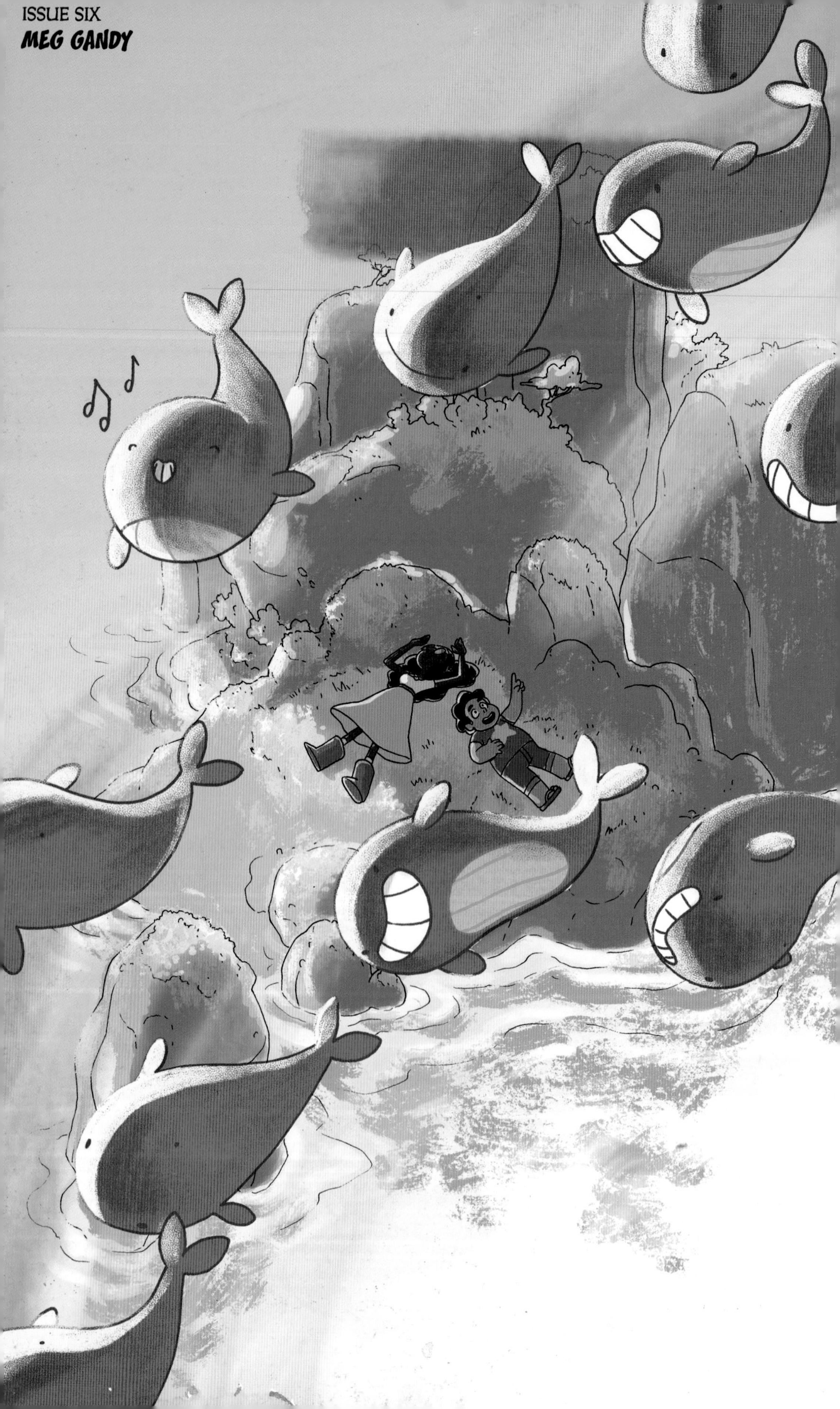

ISSUE SIX VARIANT
**HELEN YOON**

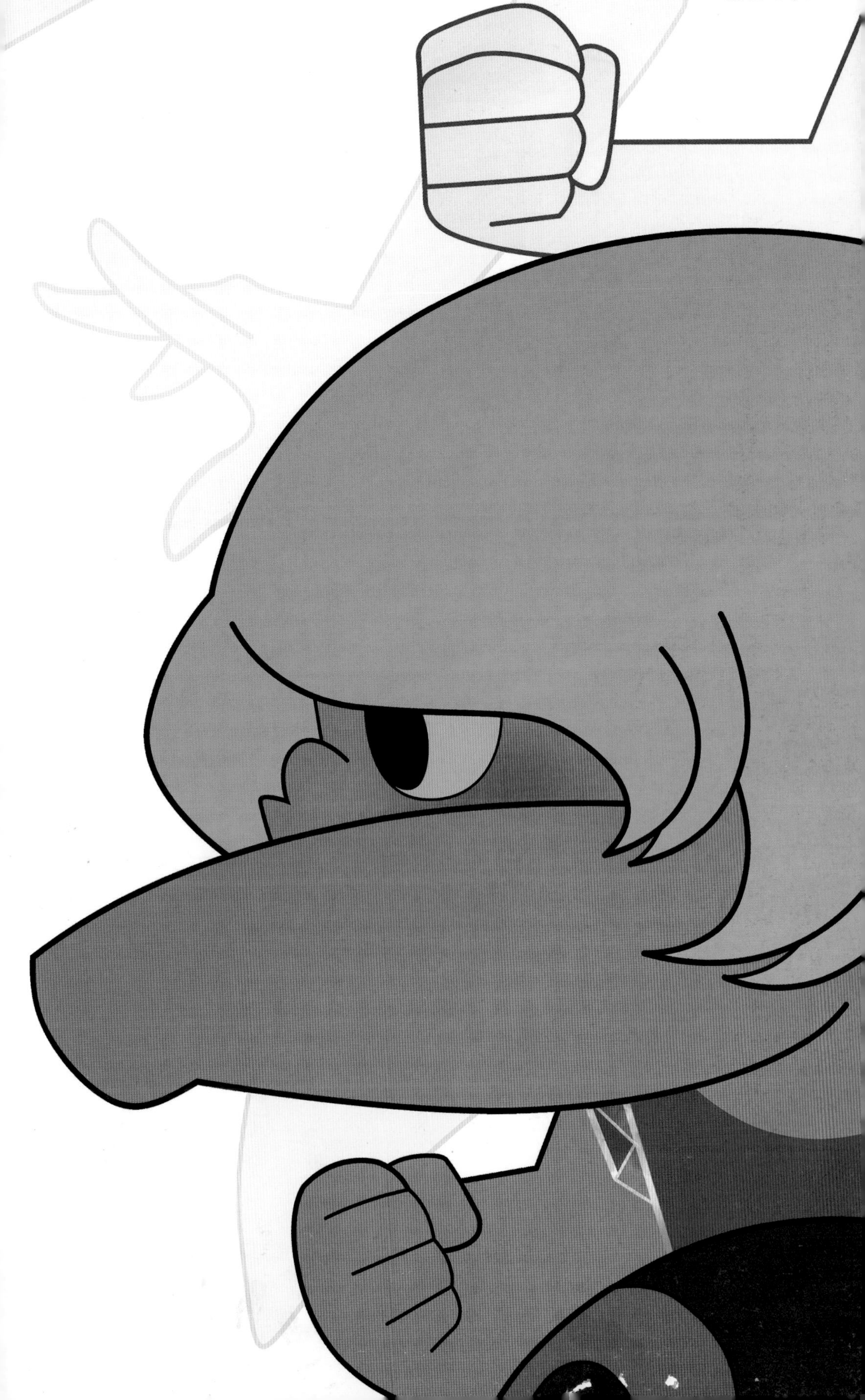

ISSUE SEVEN
**AMBER ROGERS**

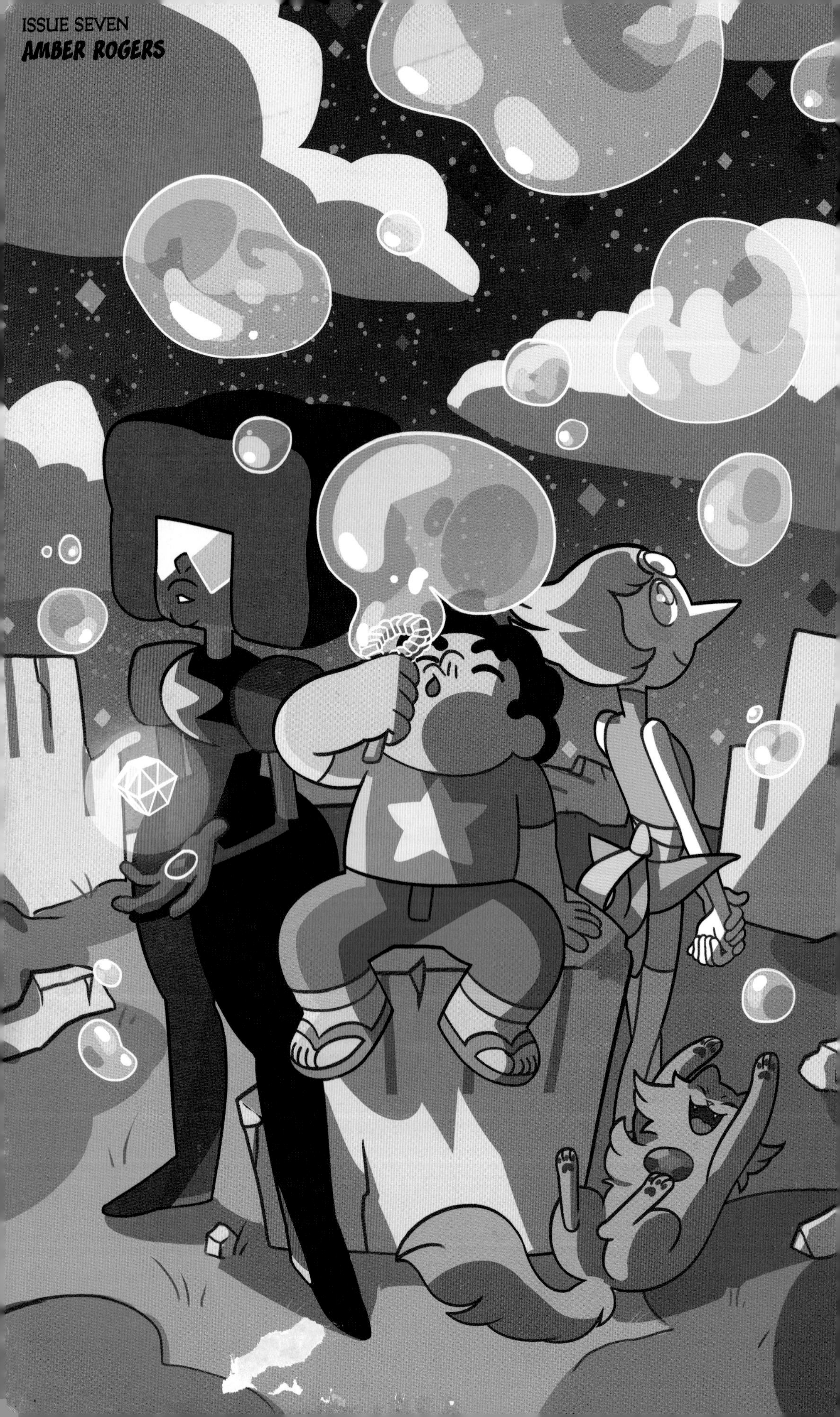

ISSUE SEVEN
**BECKY DREISTADT**

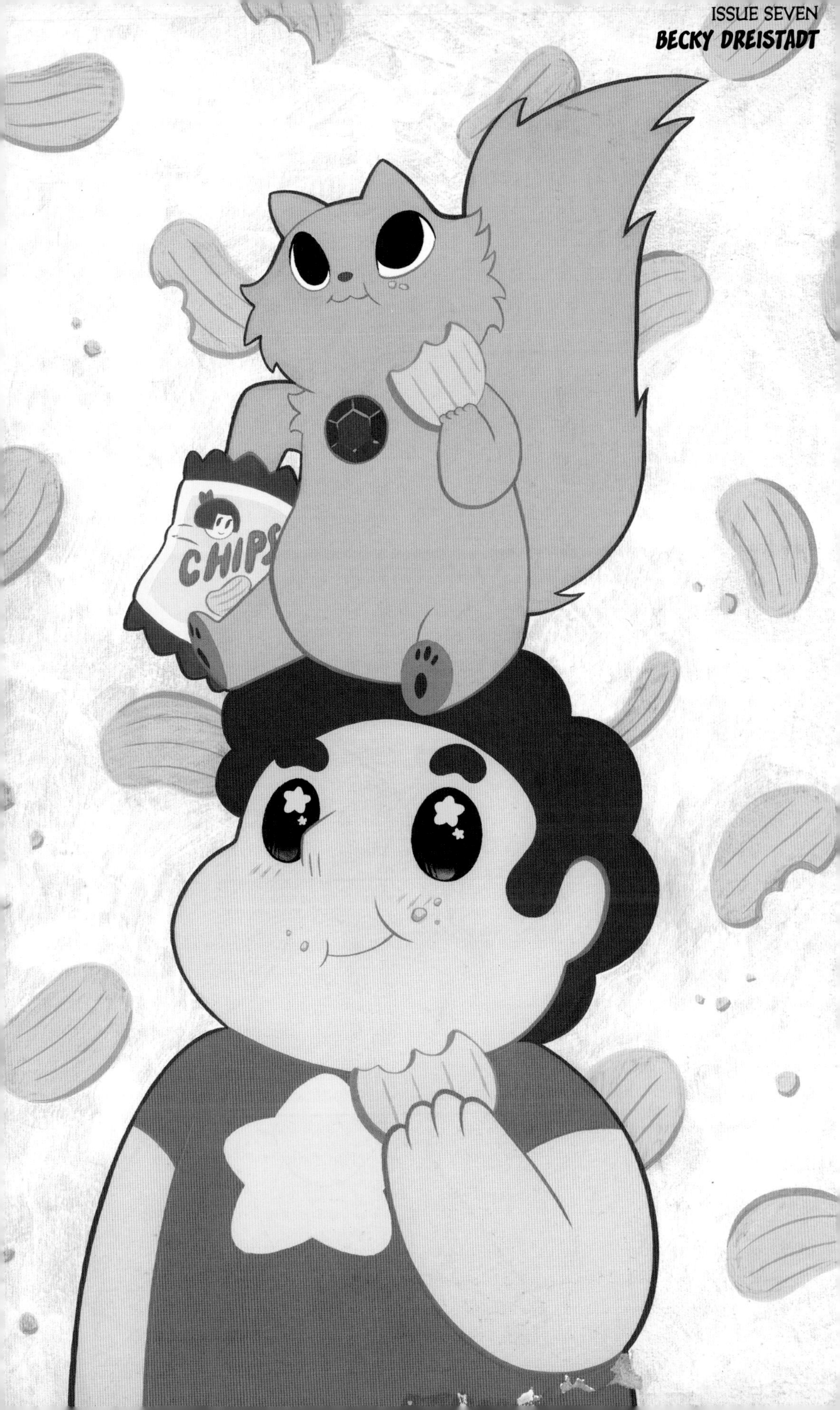
CHIPS

ISSUE SEVEN VARIANT
**HELEN YOON**

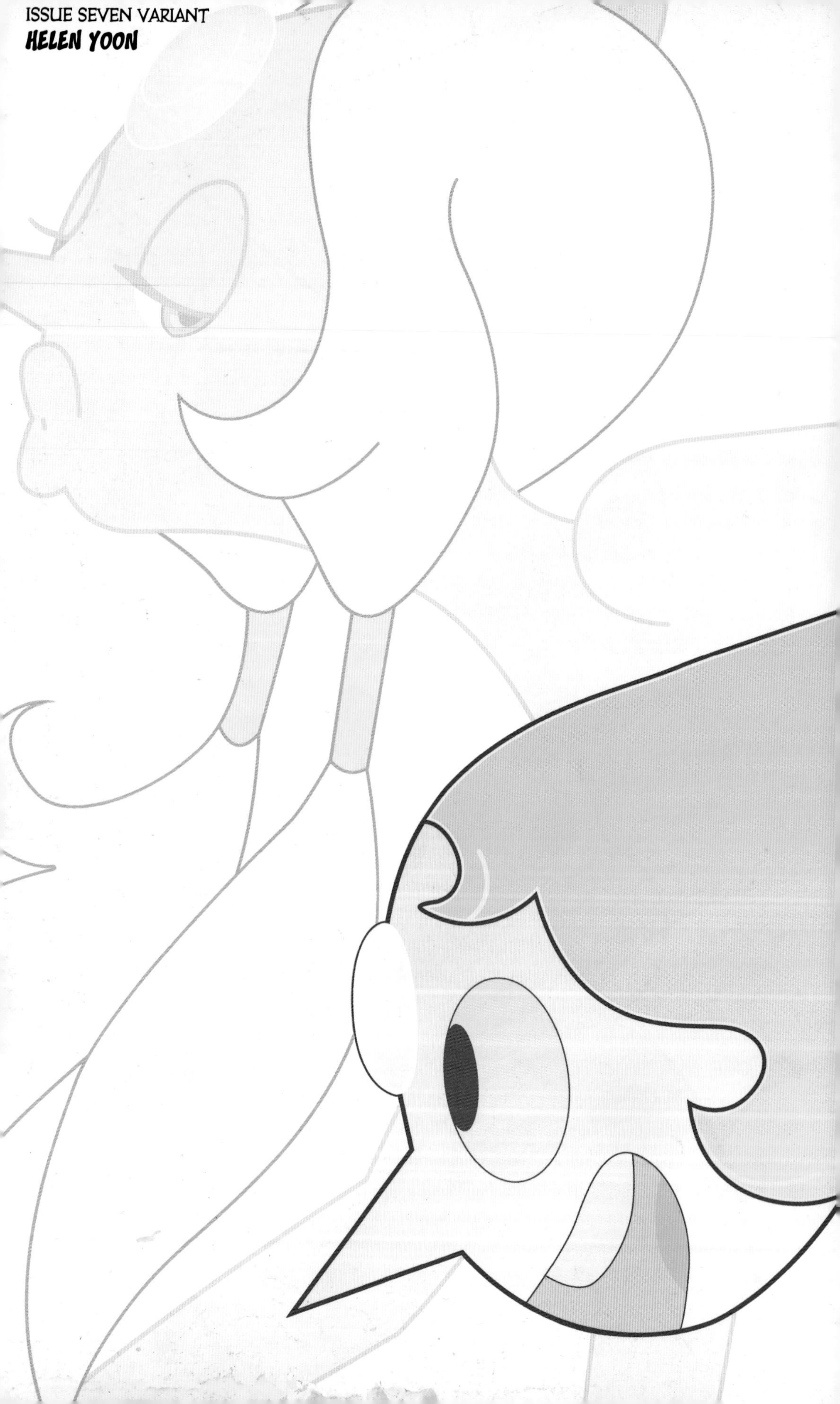

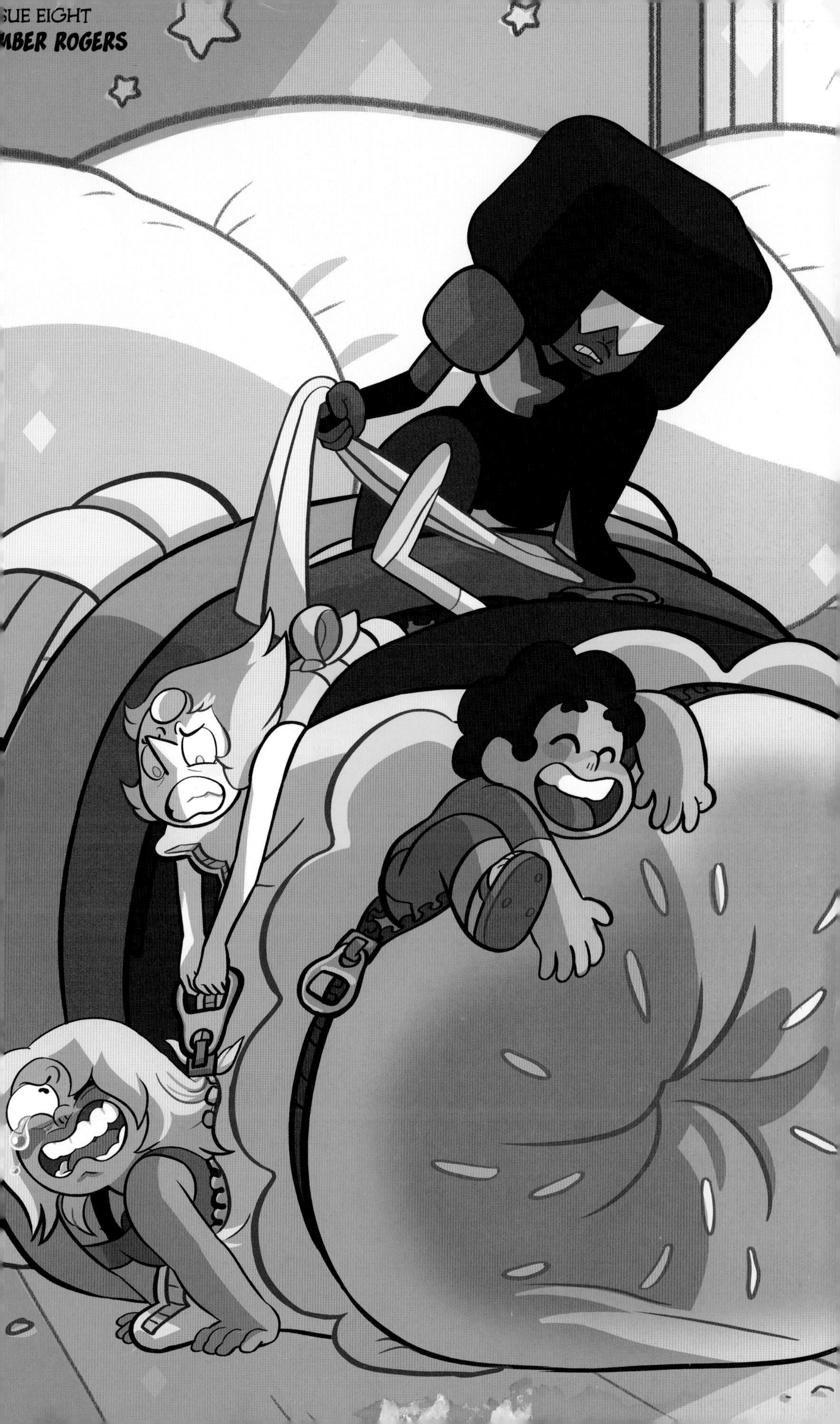

SUE EIGHT
MBER ROGERS

ISSUE EIGHT
**MELANIE HERRING**

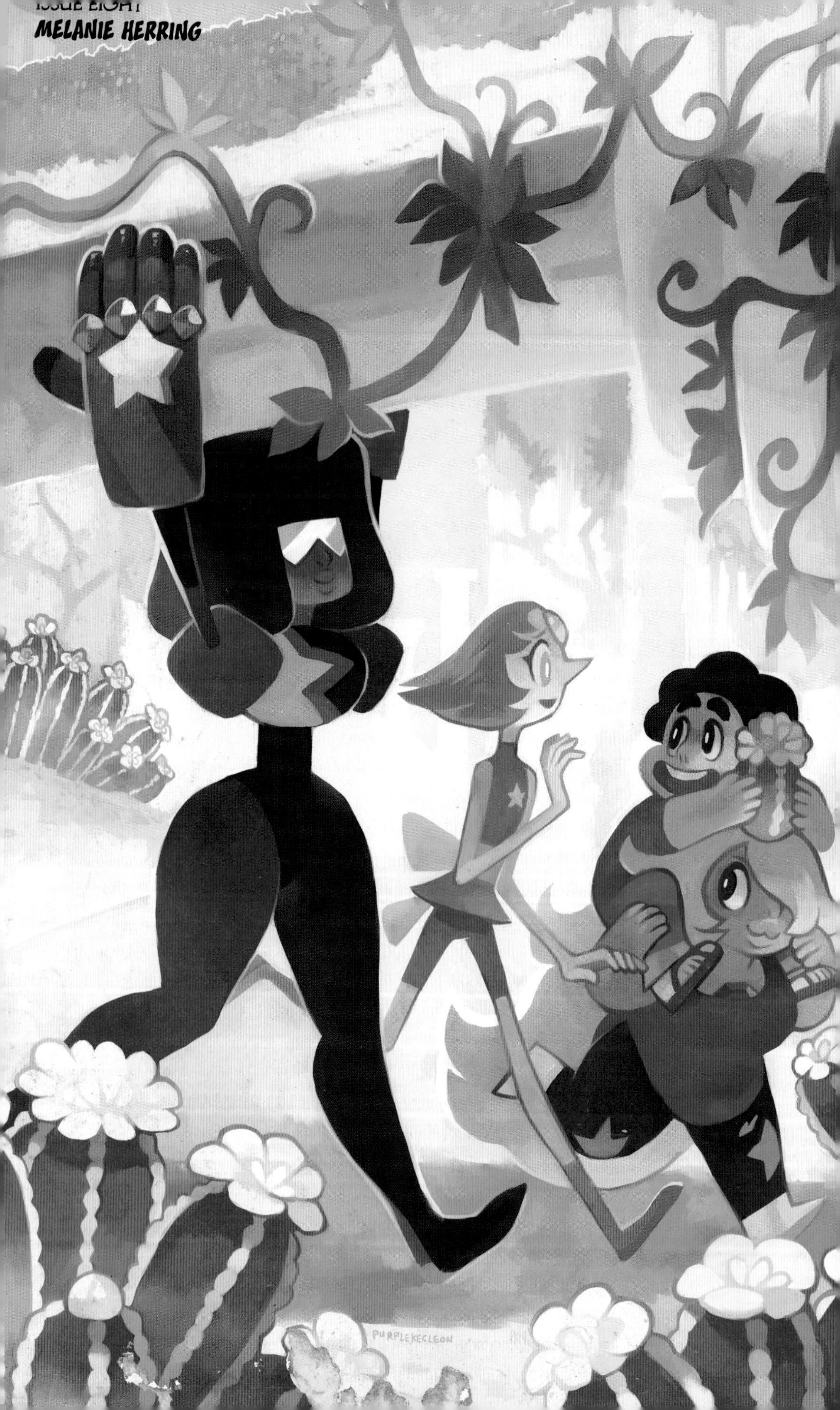
PURPLEKECLEON

ISSUE EIGHT VARIANT
HELEN YOON

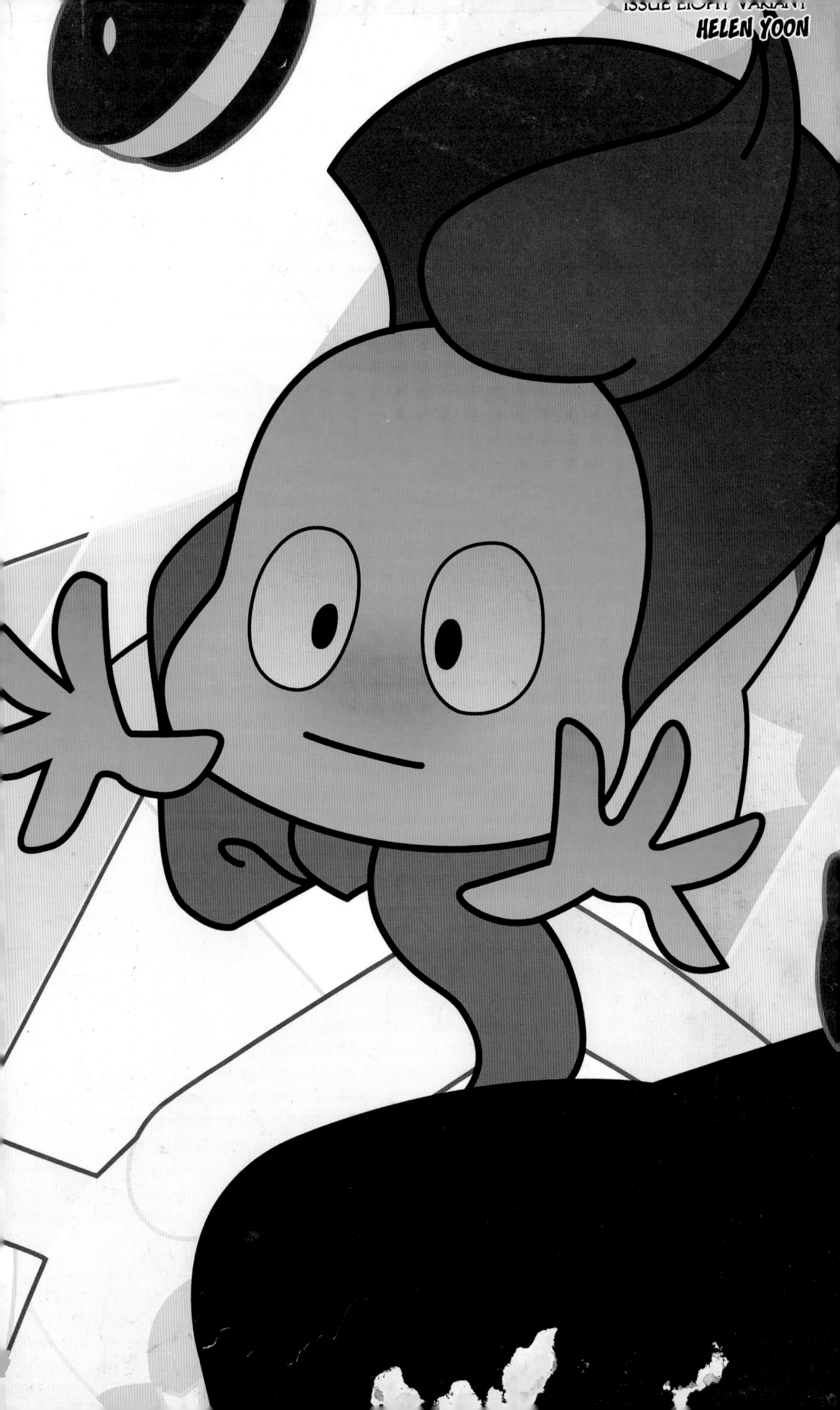